The Darkest
WARRIOR

**Also available from
Gena Showalter
and HQN Books**

Can't Let Go
Can't Hardly Breathe
The Darkest Promise
The Darkest Torment
The Harder You Fall
The Hotter You Burn
The Closer You Come
All For You (anthology featuring
"The One You Want")
The Darkest Touch
Burning Dawn
After Dark (duology featuring
"The Darkest Angel")
The Darkest Craving
Beauty Awakened
After Moonrise (duology with P.C. Cast)
Wicked Nights
The Darkest Seduction
The Darkest Surrender
The Darkest Secret
The Darkest Lie
The Darkest Passion
Into the Dark
The Darkest Whisper
The Darkest Pleasure
The Darkest Kiss

The Darkest Night
The Vampire's Bride
The Nymph King
Jewel of Atlantis
Heart of the Dragon
Twice as Hot
Playing with Fire
Catch a Mate
Animal Instincts
The Pleasure Slave
The Stone Prince

From Harlequin Nonfiction

Dating the Undead
(with Jill Monroe)

From Harlequin TEEN

Everlife
Lifeblood
Firstlife
A Mad Zombie Party
The Queen of Zombie Hearts
Through the Zombie Glass
Alice in Zombieland
Twisted
Unraveled
Intertwined

And look for the first sizzling story
in Gena Showalter's all-new Gods of War series
Shadow and Ice
coming soon from HQN Books!

GENA SHOWALTER

The Darkest
WARRIOR

HQN™

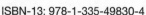

ISBN-13: 978-1-335-49830-4
ISBN-13: 978-1-335-92657-9 (Walmart Exclusive edition)

Recycling programs
for this product may
not exist in your area.

The Darkest Warrior

This edition published by arrangement with Harlequin Books S.A.

For questions and comments about the quality of this book, please contact us
at CustomerService@Harlequin.com.

www.HQNBooks.com

Printed in U.S.A.

For anyone who has ever suffered abuse at the hands of another. For anyone who has ever heard the words "you aren't good enough" and "you have no value." For anyone who has ever been told "you dream too big" and "you can't succeed." You are the only you and the world needs you. I stand with you. I hurt with you. You are priceless. You can do this.

The Darkest
WARRIOR

Prologue

ONCE UPON A TIME IN THE DESERT REALM OF Amaranthia, two immortal princes were born. Púkinn "Puck" Neale Brion Connacht IV and Taliesin "Sin" Anwell Kunsgnos Connacht. Brothers by blood. Friends by choice. Shapeshifters of legend, able to become anyone at any time.

Puck, the elder, grew into a warrior unlike any other, brute force his specialty. No matter the strength or expertise of his opponent, he remained undefeated, his skill on the battlefield rivaled only by his prowess in the bedroom.

Sin, the younger, preferred books to battle and romance to war, though his military triumphs were no less renowned. He could scheme and strategize better than anyone.

The princes loved one another and each vowed to put the other first in all things. But long ago, the Oracles of Amaranthia prophesied one brother would wed a loving queen and slay the other brother, then unite the realm's warring clans at long last.

The Oracles were never wrong.

In the end, no matter the princes' hopes and plans, the prophesy *would* be fulfilled...

Some fairy tales do not have a happily-ever-after.

1

KILL A MAN, ACQUIRE HIS MAGIC. A TALE AS OLD
as time.

With a roar, Puck the Undefeated swung a pair of short
swords at his latest opponent, the king of Clan Walsh. One
blood-soaked blade hacked through the man's metal breast-
plate, sending him to his knees; the other sliced into his throat
from front to back.

No match for a Connacht prince. Who is?

The king gasped with shock and pain, then gurgled as a
crimson tide poured from both sides of his mouth. "Wh-why?"

With only a thought, Puck shapeshifted back to his normal
appearance, letting the dying king see the true countenance
of the one who'd bested him.

"My brother sends his regards." Puck twisted the blades and
said, "May you rest in pieces."

The king gaped, wheezing a final breath before going silent,
his head lolling forward. Puck yanked the swords free, and the
body collapsed on the ground, flinging sand.

In war, there was only one rule: *win, whatever the cost.*

Walsh soldiers retreated in a frenzied rush.

A dark glittering mist rose from the king's corpse and drifted to Puck. Potent magic adhered to the runes branded in his hands—curling gold symbols that stretched from fingertips to wrist. Pure power. *Intoxicating.* Nothing better.

His head buzzed, the blood in his veins heating and fizzing. Because of the magic, aye, but also because he felt triumphant. In a blink-and-you'll-miss-it moment, the newest war in a long string of wars had ended, and the Connachts had won.

Puck maintained his position in the center of the blood-soaked battlefield. Sand dunes stretched as far as the eye could see, broken up by the occasional oasis with towering trees and crystal clear ponds. The realm's twin suns had long since vanished from the skyline. Night ruled, the heavens the same color as mulberries, creating an endless sea of dark purple-red. No stars glittered tonight.

His eyes closed as he savored the victory. The odds had been stacked against him, with an enemy army more than twice the size of his own. So, last night, his brother, Sin, suggested Puck sneak into the enemy camp, kill a Walsh commander, ash the body—and take his place. Not easily done, but done all the same.

In his new guise, Puck had instructed the soldiers to "ambush" the Connachts, and ultimately led the entire army into a trap. From there, reaching the king had been child's play.

Sin could look at any situation—any man—and somehow discern every hidden weakness.

Puck sometimes wondered what weaknesses his brother perceived in *him.* Not that it mattered. Sin only ever sought to protect him, doing anything, everything to ensure he won every battle.

Together, they would defy the prophecy spoken over them as children. One brother kill the other? Never! Puck and Sin would rule the five clans *together,* and nothing would come between them.

A bond as strong as theirs could never be broken.

As a cold wind spit sand, Puck opened his eyes. Despite

the frigid temperature, he radiated heat, adrenaline pumping through his veins. Sweat mixed with the blood of the vanquished splattered on his torso, dripping down every ridge of muscle.

In the distance, someone shouted, "Victory is ours!"

Other cries followed.

"The Walsh magic is ours!"

"We've won, we've won!"

Jubilant cheers rose, a familiar chorus. He'd trained with, suffered with, and bled with—and for—these men. To Puck, loyalty was far more precious than gold, diamonds or even magic.

"Return to camp," he called. "Celebrate."

In unison, the soldiers surged toward the campsite just beyond the dunes—a sub-realm tucked inside a realm, hidden by Sin's magic.

Puck sheathed his swords and picked up the king's blade, the perfect trophy. Pride lifted his head as he followed his men from the battlefield. More dead bodies and a surplus of severed limbs littered the path, the air saturated with the copper tang of blood and the stench of emptied bowels.

Carnage never pleased him. It also never bothered him.

He refused to shy away from violence. Threaten his people, suffer. The day he showed a foe mercy was the day he condemned his clan to bondage or death.

Remaining in the shadows, Puck slipped through an invisible doorway only accessible to people who'd been branded with Connacht magic. For anyone else, the doorway remained closed; oftentimes men, women and children walked past without ever knowing a sub-dimension existed a mere arm's length away.

Suddenly tents, blazing fire pits, soldiers and their females surrounded him. The death-stink evaporated, replaced by the aroma of roasting meat, hard labor and sweet perfume.

A maid spotted Puck and closed the distance, interest glowing in her eyes. "Hello, Your Highness. If you be in need of a companion this evening—"

"Let me stop you there. I never go back for seconds." He never forgot a face, either, and he remembered he'd had this woman in the past year.

Before he'd ever climbed into bed with a female, he'd made sure she understood his one-and-done policy.

Disappointment shadowed her expression. "But—"

Done with the conversation, he sidestepped her and made his way to the fringes of camp, where he and Sin had both erected a tent. A cold move on his part, yes, but necessary.

Puck wasn't like other royals. While most princes kept a "stable," and traveled with their "fillies," even during times of war, Puck refused to bed the same women twice. He could not risk promoting a romantic tie with *anyone*. A romantic tie would kindle hope to marry. No marriage meant no loving queen. No loving queen meant the prophecy remained unfulfilled.

Although, truth be told, Puck adored everything about the "feminine softness" he'd been denied most of his life. He loved kissing, touching and the build of anticipation. Sweaty bodies grinding together, creating friction. Moans and groans and breathy sighs in his ears. The bliss of finally sinking deep inside his lover.

Sometimes, a few hours in a stranger's bed only whetted his appetite...

Deep down, he had a secret, shameful desire to keep a woman all to himself, to learn every little detail about her past, all her hopes and dreams. He dreamed of spending weeks, months, *years* pampering her and her alone, branding himself in and on her. Being branded by her.

He yearned to have a "mine."

Maybe one day he could—

No. Never. *Sin before women, always. Sin before* everything.

Tonight, the brothers would review the battle's successes

and failures. They would drink and laugh, and plan their next move, and all would be right in Puck's world.

A thorny vine surrounded and protected his tent, no one able to enter or leave without his permission. Unleashing a tendril of magic, he forced the vines to part and stepped inside.

When his brother came into view, affection punched Puck dead center in the chest. While they shared the same dark skin, darker eyes, and even darker hair, the same aquiline nose and unforgiving lips, Sin's features were set in a softer frame. On numerous occasions, Puck had been told his face looked "carved from stone."

Sin paced, seemingly oblivious to the world.

"What troubles you?" Puck's fingers tightened around the sword hilt.

His brother had never paced...until recently. A month ago, he'd attended peace talks with a neighboring realm and returned...changed. From calm to paranoid, certain to unsure.

He told Puck he'd woken the final morning to find his army slaughtered. He'd lain among the carnage, the only survivor, with no memory of what had happened. Now he couldn't sleep, startled at sudden movements and noises, and stared at shadows as if someone hid within. He hadn't visited his stable and refused to remove his shirt during training.

Puck suspected new scars littered his brother's chest. Did he think others would consider him weak if they caught a glimpse?

If anyone said a single word against him, "anyone" would die.

Whenever Puck expressed concern, Sin changed the subject.

Sin paused before the crackling fire pit, his gaze finding Puck before darting away.

Gradually Sin relaxed, even grinned a familiar grin only Puck had the privilege to see. "You took your sweet time returning to camp. Old age slowing you down?"

He snorted. "You're only two years younger. Perhaps we should switch places for the next war. I plan, you fight."

"You forget I know you better than you know yourself. Worry for my safety would drive you straight to my side."

Sin wasn't wrong.

His brother could handle himself in a fight, whatever the weapon. He had no equal, except Puck. But if anything were to happen to him…

I will burn this realm to the ground.

Puck stalked to the basin of water perched atop his travel armory. After resting the Walsh sword against the side, he washed away the night's filth.

"When we were children, *you* worried for *me*," he said, drying his face with a towel. "What happened?"

"You learned to use a sword." Sin rubbed his temples, as if he hated the thoughts swirling inside his mind.

He needed a distraction. "Shall we begin our review of the battle?"

"Not yet. I come bearing news." Seconds passed, each one crackling with tension.

Puck stiffened. "Tell me."

Eyes stark, Sin said, "Father announced your betrothal to Princess Alannah of Daingean."

Puck's first reaction: *I will have a wife. She'll be mine!*

Then he scowled. *Must proceed with caution.* From a very early age, he'd seen the world around him through a near blinding filter: *MY brother, MY clan, MY realm.*

He'd seen Alannah only once, and though he'd liked the look of her, he wouldn't deign to bed her, much less wed her. Temptation could not be indulged, even in the slightest sense.

However, he comprehended Sin's concern. King rather than primogeniture decided a successor. Unless the king refused to make a selection, of course, then the strongest warrior *took* the crown. But, with this announcement, King Púkinn III had made his choice.

"Father spoke in haste," Puck said. "I won't be wedding anyone. You have my word."

"This is a political move meant to solidify the alliance between our clans, but...the prophecy..." Sin's voice frayed at the edges. "One will become king with a loving queen at his side, and he will slay the other. The Oracles are never wrong."

"There's a first time for everything." He closed the distance to frame his brother's cheeks with his hands. "Trust me. A wedding will never take place." Neither would wed, and the prophecy would remain unfulfilled. "I choose you, brother. I will *always* choose you."

Sin remained as inflexible as steel. "If you refuse her, you'll insult the Daingeans. Another war will break out."

"Another war is *always* breaking out." Each clan collected magic from the men they slayed, desperate to possess more than the others.

Magic was strength, and strength was magic.

Sin broke away from Puck to worry two fingers against the dark stubble on his jaw. "By wedding Alannah, you *will* unite the clans, as you've dreamed. Connacht, Daingean, Fiáin, Eadrom and Walsh."

How could he make his brother understand? Yes, he dreamed of uniting the clans. War would end at last. Lives would be saved. Peace would reign. Amaranthia would flourish, the lands no longer ravaged by near-constant battles.

But concord without Sin meant less than nothing.

"Nothing matters more than you," he said. Centuries ago, there'd been twelve clans. Now, because of kings and armies greedy for magic, only five remained. If something wasn't done, the entire population would die out. "Not to me."

"You aren't listening," Sin insisted. "Daingean now ally with Fiáin. With your marriage to Alannah, Connacht will ally with Daingean, so Fiáin will be forced to side with Connacht. When that happens, Eadrom, who is currently allied with Fiáin, will have to break their alliance with Walsh in order to keep the peace with us. And they will. They have no familial ties with

Walsh. And now that the current—or rather, former—Walsh king is dead, the new ruler has a clean slate with us."

"I don't care," he said with a shake of his head. "The cost is too high."

Silent, Sin studied him the way he often studied his favorite maps. Sadness darkened his eyes, until it was snuffed out by determination. He nodded, as if making a monumental decision, and motioned to the table in the corner. In the center rested what looked to be a small trinket case.

"It arrived this morning," Sin said. "Just before battle."

"A gift?"

"A weapon."

Weapon? "Worry not. I'll take care of it." Puck would do anything—kill anyone—to fix his brother's problems. Fair was fair. Sin had always fixed *his*.

He crossed the tent to stand before the little case. Mother-of-pearl overlaid some kind of metal. A cluster of diamonds glittered at each corner. As he reached out, a pulse of malevolence brushed his skin. Not magic, but pure unadulterated evil. His blood flashed ice-cold.

"Who sent it?" And what type of weapon was it, exactly?

"A woman named Keeleycael, with the title of Red Queen. She said she hopes we enjoy our downfall."

Keeleycael. He'd never heard of her. "Does she rule a neighboring realm?" To Puck's knowledge, a woman had never led... anything. Not outright, anyway. Females aided their kings.

"I'm unsure," Sin said.

The answer hardly mattered, he supposed. No one threatened his brother and lived. Downfall? Not while Puck lived and breathed.

Sin hadn't just saved his life too many times to count; he'd saved Puck's soul.

Just before Puck's seventh birthday, his cousin died in battle. Needing a new commander from the royal line, the king chose Puck. Meaning, a little prince was ripped from his mother's arms sooner rather than later so that a woman's sweetness would no longer "influence" him.

Ruin a boy, and you ruin the man he will become.

The words his father had shouted at his mother the day Puck was taken.

"I'll go, too," five-year-old Sin had said. "Where you go, I go."

The details of that fateful day were forever branded into Puck's memory. How their mother's sobs could be heard throughout the fortress. *My babies. Please, don't take my babies.* How tears had streamed down Sin's face as he'd taken Puck's hand and willingly walked away from the only home he'd ever known. How comforted Puck had been by the younger boy's unwavering resolution to stay together.

The two boys lived and trained with the clan's most hardened soldiers for years, softer emotion beaten, whipped or cut from them.

At the ages of twelve and ten, they were both given a sword and abandoned by their father in the midst of the most dangerous sand dunes with these parting words: *Return with the heart of our enemy—or stay gone.*

If Puck could flash back in time, he would demand Sin remain cosseted with their mother, safe in her loving arms. Now, guilt was his constant companion. Until he'd learned to fight, and fight well, he'd been unable to protect Sin from daily abuses. Worse, their mother died before they could visit her.

She'd delivered a stillborn babe soon after their departure and, in her grief, purposely burned herself to ash. A warrior could have survived the flames, but not a female without runes and magic.

Massaging the back of his neck, Puck considered the best way to proceed. "Have you opened the case?"

"No. I waited for you," Sin said, with a tremor of fear.

Fear? Impossible. Sin feared nothing while Puck guarded his back.

"I shouldn't have brought the cursed thing to your tent." His brother strode toward the table. "I'll take it and—"

"No." Arm extended, Puck stopped Sin before he could make contact with the case. Yes, Sin had already handled it without consequence. Didn't matter. There was no reason for further risk. "I want to know what's inside." Wanted to know what this unknown queen thought to use against his family.

"I'll fetch one of the commanders. Let him—"

"No. I'll do it myself." A good king did not put his own life ahead of his people. "Leave me. I'll let you know what I find."

"You stay, I stay."

Another log fell into the fire pit of his guilt. He popped his jaw. "I don't want you endangered, brother." Not now, not ever.

For a single heartbeat of time, Sin's eyes glistened with unshed tears. He quickly blinked them back. "And yet," he said, "still I plan to stay."

Why those almost-tears? Suddenly Puck couldn't tolerate the thought of having his brother anywhere but nearby. "Very well. Stand back."

As Sin moved to the other side of the tent, Puck palmed a short sword and braced for the worst. Bomb blast? A magical trap? Then, he did it—he opened the lid.

At first, nothing happened. But between one heartbeat and the next, black smoke rose from the case, the scent of sulfur saturating the air, stinging his nostrils. Glowing red eyes blinked open, focused on him and narrowed.

Puck reared back even as he thrust the sword forward. The metal merely ghosted through the darkness. What the—

A horned creature appeared—the owner of those eyes. With a high-pitched screech, it swooped down. Target: Puck. He tried to leap out of the way. Too late. The creature—

Pain seared him, shoving a roar past his lips. The creature had *entered* his body, and now tore into his organs. It bit and clawed, too, and yet Puck experienced no outward signs of injury.

Frantic, he dropped the sword to rake his nails over his chest, slicing skin and muscle—to no avail. The creature remained inside him, a dark presence, howling with a toxic mix of hate and pleasure.

The blood in Puck's veins might as well have been fuel; every cell in his body seemed to catch fire, melting him from the inside out as he...changed? Two rings of fire erupted on the crown of his skull, as if circles had been burned into the bone. He reached up and felt...horns?

Breath wheezed through clenched teeth as he yanked at hanks of brown fur sprouting on his legs. The fur remained. Next, a hard shell grew over his feet—hooves?—as his leather boots ripped apart at the seams.

Changing shapes wasn't new to him, but this transformation had control of Puck, not the other way around. He couldn't stop it.

Jagged black lines appeared on his chest, small rivers of lava burning as they spread. An image formed. A butterfly with wings as sharp as shattered glass. Different colors shimmered in the firelight, one after the other, altering as various emotions flooded him.

Mostly, panic grabbed Puck by the neck and held firm, choking him. Was this a hallucination, caused by smoke?

Or was he becoming a monster for good?

His knees gave out, unable to support his weight. As he lay on the ground, panting, the panic died. His gaze landed on the Walsh sword, and the pride he'd experienced only moments before faded before disappearing altogether. The devotion he bore for his realm and people...gone. He felt *nothing*. The sword was a scrap of finely honed metal, the realm a meaningless location, its citizens a nonentity.

Puck searched for emotion, *any* emotion, hidden anywhere. There! Love for Sin, a shining beacon.

He would protect the younger male from this...whatever *this* was. But, as he attempted to reach for his brother, muscle locked on bone, holding him immobile, and panic returned.

"Sin!"

Sin wouldn't meet his gaze.

Something's wrong...

A terrible nothingness began to creep through Puck a second time—this one directed at his brother. Precious Sin. *Treasured* Sin. Puck's reason for...everything. But an invisible dagger cut into his heart, affection draining out...draining...

Still he fought. "Love you," he rasped. *Can't lose Sin. Can't...* But even as he spoke, his heart emptied.

One moment his love blazed, a light inextinguishable by war, persecution or travesty, the next it was nothing but a snuffed-out torch.

Puck blinked up at Sin and felt...nothing. He hadn't forgotten their past, or the many ways his brother had aided him throughout the centuries, or everything Sin had given up on his behalf, but he cared not at all.

Sin crouched beside him, sadness once again darkening his eyes. "I'm sorry, Puck. I truly am. I knew what was inside the case... Keeleycael...she knew of our prophecy, claimed we were already on the path to destruction, and one of us *would* kill the other. This way, we can live. I just... I couldn't kill you, and I couldn't let you kill me. You would have hated yourself. I'm sorry," he repeated. "So sorry."

His brother had betrayed him?

Not possible. He would never do such a terrible thing.

"I made a deal with a she-devil," Sin continued. "I'll never forgive myself, but better me than you, aye? Don't you see? You won't concern yourself with the crown, or the clans. You're now possessed by the demon of Indifference." He tapped Puck on the chest, and his voice hardened. "The two of you are joined for the rest of eternity."

Sorrow, determination and fury—so much fury—suddenly

blazed inside Puck. An explosion! His brother *had* betrayed him. Had actively plotted his ruin. But just like everything else, the sorrow, determination and fury faded, until only cold disinterest remained.

Puck the Undefeated had just become Puck the Fucked.

He should leave. He might not have an aspiration to slay his brother, or to stay here, or even to go, but common sense said, *Do not remain with the one who harmed you.*

Muscles unlocking from bone at last, he stood.

"I did this for us." Sin straightened, reached for him. "Tell me you understand. Tell me we'll stay together."

Silent, he backed away from his brother. He would go for a walk, think about what had happened and what he should do next.

"Puck—"

He strode out of the tent, never once glancing back.

2

CENTURIES PASSED. THE EXACT NUMBER ESCAPED
Puck. He didn't care to keep count.

He didn't return to his brother or clan, even when he heard
rumors of Sin's brutality. Apparently his brother had morphed
into the most bloodthirsty tyrant in Amaranthian history. He
destroyed half a forest—one of only two—to build a fortress.
He made slaves of the Connachts and any other clansmen he
captured, and killed anyone who "plotted his downfall."

He believed thousands of people plotted his downfall.

In reality, Puck knew the truth. Sin's black soul had finally
come out to play.

Aimless, Puck wandered from one end of Amaranthia to the
other. Those who got in his way died. If he came across something necessary for his survival, he took it. Food. Weapons.
A night's lodging. Sometimes he accepted a lover. He could
harden, and a female could ride herself to satisfaction, but he
cared nothing about her pleasure—and could not achieve his
own. Though he felt a physiological need for release, no one
had the power to make him come. Not even himself.

He remembered how he'd once secretly dreamed of being

with the same woman over and over again. When he actually did it, he found the experience lacking.

As Puck grew used to Indifference, he realized the demon did not—could not—steal or erase his emotions, only bury and hide them. Which the demon no longer preferred to do; he'd developed a taste for issuing punishment whenever Puck felt too much for too long.

Never indifferent about that, *are you, fiend?*

Even now, the creature prowled through his mind, every step like the swing of a sledgehammer as he waited for Puck to misstep.

He had to learn to bury and hide his emotions all on his own, and cover them with thick layers of mystical ice, summoned by magic he made sure he always had on tap. The kind of magic he could wield anywhere, anytime. With ice came numbness, with numbness, peace.

A necessary process. A well of fury, hate, pain, concern and hope still seethed inside him. He was a powder keg, and one day he would blow.

When that happened...

Would Indifference kill him? Would Puck welcome death, or fight?

At least the demon cautioned him anytime an emotion slipped free. Snarls equaled a slap on the wrist. Roars meant Puck trod upon dangerous ground. When he heard purring, he'd felt too much for too long, and hell was about to be unleashed—upon him.

The demon would deplete him of strength, leaving him immobile for days. Practically comatose.

To circumvent punishment, Puck created rules he followed without fail.

Trust no one, ever. Remember everyone lies.

Kill anyone who threatens my survival, and always retaliate for the minutest slight.

Eat three meals a day, and acquire clothes and weapons whenever possible.

Always follow through.

At some point, Puck came across Princess Alannah of Daingean. She screamed and ran away from him, terrified of the monster he'd become. Oh, well.

Though magic still swirled inside Puck, he'd lost his ability to shapeshift. The horns remained atop his head, two ivory towers of shame. The fur on his legs and the hooves on his feet remained, as well; no matter how many times he hacked them off, thinking maybe, just maybe, he could free his mind of Indifference if he freed his body of its beastly attributes.

As time passed, different males attacked him, determined to kill the disgraced Connacht prince. Puck was stabbed, staked and hung, drawn and quartered, and set on fire. Whenever possible, he fought back. And if he *couldn't* fight back because of the demon, he waited until his body healed, then meted retribution ruthlessly, mercilessly, overcome by a rage he couldn't control.

Of course, Indifference always penalized him afterward.

One morning, as Puck walked the sand dunes he'd once adored, his feet throbbed. Or rather, his hooves. A quick glance down proved he had sustained multiple injuries, leaving a river of blood in his wake. He needed to steal and magically alter a pair of shoes. And clothing. He'd forgotten to dress.

Two golden suns highlighted a small camp in the distance. Perfect. Different garments swung from a rope anchored to the tops of two side-by-side tents. The scent of meat wafted on the breeze as a *coinín* roasted above a fire pit.

No one waited outside, though voices seeped from one of the tents.

"—announced this morning. Prince Taliesin of Connacht killed his father in his sleep."

"Guess that means Taliesin is *king* now," was the grumbled reply. "Prince Neale was to be the successor, but he's dead, I think."

Puck stopped in his tracks. Sin had killed their father?

They'd both despised the male, but cold-blooded murder while the Connacht slept? That was low.

Puck waited for a punch of surprise...disgust...rage...*something*. Not a single hint of emotion seeped past his ice. As he pulled on a pair of too-tight sheepskin pants, he wondered what he *should* feel. All of the above, perhaps? A need to stop his brother, definitely.

"If Prince Neale isn't dead," one of the men said, "he's still a beast."

Neale—Puck.

"Would you rather have Taliesin or a beast ruling over your family?" the other male asked.

"Beast," both men said in unison.

The fact that anyone would want Puck over Sin...the Connachts must be desperate.

Can I really walk away and leave my clan in danger?

And what if Sin married a woman who loved him, killed Puck, and united the clans? Amaranthia would surely collapse.

Sin had to die.

Always follow through.

Well, all right, then. Puck would save the Connachts from a madman and the entire realm from devastation—and finally mete vengeance against his brother. And deep in his heart of hearts, Puck did want vengeance. For the bright future he'd lost, and the love Sin had so coldly destroyed.

Puck deserved to rage against the male. He'd *earned* the right.

Indifference snarled a warning. Puck summoned a tendril of magic to cloak his heart and mind with more ice.

As glacial logic returned, realization set in: if the demon managed to drain him of strength, Sin would best him.

He knows my weaknesses already...

Puck's hands curled into fists. He needed to find *Sin's* weakness.

No one offered better direction than the Oracles.

Puck ate every bite of *coinín*—rules were rules—found, magically altered and donned a pair of boots, then headed east. The Oracles lived in the most dangerous part of Amaranthia, where potent magic thickened the air, creating rifts that led to other realms, endless pits, the center of a volcano and even the bottom of an ocean. Only the most desperate citizens dared to venture here. Those who sought to save themselves or a loved one, kings who needed guidance when choosing an heir, or people like Puck, with nothing to lose.

The three-day journey took a toll on him. No campsites, no food or water. At least he managed to avoid the rifts.

Finally, he reached the realm's tallest sand tower. The Oracles lived up top, with a view of…everything. Too weak to climb, Puck used the last of his magic to create a sand staircase.

He needed to acquire more magic, which meant he would have to kill someone, and soon.

Should he slay one of the Oracles? History claimed the trio created Amaranthia as a safe haven for anyone with magical inclinations. *Their* supply of magic must be limitless, even unending.

At one time, the thought of harming a female would have disgusted him. Now? *Bring it.* A source was a source.

Business first. As he stepped onto the upper level without rails or walls he discovered three females standing together, each draped from breast to thigh in colorful scarfs. A fine, dark mist obscured their faces.

In lieu of a greeting, he said, "You know why I'm here." They must. "How do I regain what's mine? Freedom from the demon. The Connacht crown. Unification for the clans. Protection for my realm. Sin's black heart on a golden platter. Princess Alannah."

He would take her as his due.

As winds grew more violent, the women asked in unison, "What is our credo, Puck the Undefeated?"

All of Amaranthia learned their credo from the crib. *Noth-*

ing given, nothing gained. The more personal the gift, the more detailed the answer.

What was more personal than his blackened heart?

Will be unable to render a kill afterward.

Worth it.

Determined, he withdrew a dagger from a sheath at his waist and thrust the blade into his rib cage. Warm blood poured down his chest. Pain devoured his strength with the same tenacity as Indifference, scorching every nerve ending in his body. Eventually his knees gave out. But even as he fell, he continued to hack through muscle and bone. Finally, success.

As an immortal, he would recover…soonish. Here and now, his mind would remain conscious for a minute, maybe two. Plenty of time to get what he needed. Sin had taught him well: the entire course of your life could change between one breath and another.

With a flick of his wrist, the still-beating heart rolled toward the Oracles. Twitters of acceptance rang out, followed by voices, one Oracle speaking after the other.

"You love our home, our people, despite your…limitations. But what has been spoken cannot be undone. What is to happen, will happen."

"One prophecy can work alongside another, and what was can be made right."

"To save us all, wed the girl who belongs to William of the Dark…she is the key…"

"Bring your wife to our lands and lead the dark one here after. Only the male who will live or die for the girl has the power to dethrone Sin the Demented."

When had Sin earned the moniker "the Demented"?

"Only then shall you have all you desire."

"But do not forget Ananke's shears, for they are necessary…"

Together the Oracles whispered, "There is no other way."

In the ensuing quiet, Puck's thoughts whirled. William of the Dark. He'd never heard of him, or the girl the male would "live or die for." The two needed to be brought to Amaranthia, one after the other. Very well.

As a heavy gloom toyed with the edges of his mind, he ordered and set his tasks.

Find William of the Dark. Wed the girl he loves. War with Sin.

One prophecy would not supersede the other. Instead, the two would work in tandem. Meaning, William would not kill Sin, would only dethrone him. The rest would be up to Puck.

Nothing would stop him from completing each task. William. Wed. War. One day, Puck would wear the Connacht crown, save his people and unite the clans.

Finally the gloom stopped toying and started devouring, swallowing him whole. He knew nothing more.

3

Gillian Shaw, BP (Before Puck)
T minus 4 days and 32 seconds until B-day

I CAN DO THIS. I CAN DO IT.

Sexy lingerie? Check.

Intoxicating perfume? Check.

Teeth brushed once, twice for good measure? Check, check.

Gillian Shaw—also known as Gillian Bradshaw, Gilly Bradshaw and Jill Brads, depending on which ID she used— marched from one side of the bedroom to the other, feeling as if she were a cracked porcelain doll about to shatter. *I'm almost eighteen. I can do this.*

Her stomach said, *Think again, little girl.*

Not wanting to desecrate the Persian rug, she rushed to the bathroom. Just in time. The contents of her stomach spewed into the toilet.

Her boyfriend—who was she kidding? He wasn't her boy- friend. Yet. He was an immortal warrior of incomparable beauty and power, a bazillion years old, and one of nine kings of hell. Or a *former* king. Immortal titles could change as king- doms were won or lost, and she had lost track. What she knew beyond a doubt: William of the Dark was a merciless killer. Both enemies and friends feared him, and yet, when he smiled, panties dropped.

The guy slept around. A lot. He had no sticking power... except with Gillian, whom he *refused* to bed.

Time to teach him otherwise.

Though he'd never made a move on her, he'd always enjoyed being with her. Clearly! He joked and laughed with her in a way he never did with anyone else. This morning, he'd sought her opinion about which T-shirt to wear. The one that read "I Can Make Beer Disappear" or "World's Okayest Friend."

Did he understand what a rarity he was? What a wealth of contradictions? He was uncompromisingly brave while inspiring terror, fierce but honorable, with a skewed moral compass. Willing to commit unspeakable acts of evil, and yet, there were (small) lines he refused to cross.

To Gillian, he was a last hope.

Must win him over. Had she done ample internet research? Picked the right outfit? Brushed her teeth enough? Ugh. Maybe she should go home, before he returned and found her half-dressed in his bedroom, and forever altered the course of their relationship.

Too late. Already altered.

A while back, he'd been bed bound after a particularly gruesome battle. In his weakened condition, he hadn't trusted anyone but Gillian to be near him. As she'd tended his wounds, he'd admitted he sensed her feelings for him, and told her they could only ever be friends, that she was too young to be with a man and understand what it meant.

Thanks to her stepfather, she'd known *what it meant* for years. He'd done sick, twisted things she couldn't contemplate without praying for death. He'd also taught his sons to do sick, twisted things.

But day after day, she kept fighting to live, anyway. She hated her stephorrors too much to let them win.

Feeling rejected by William, she'd tried to avoid him. He'd sought her out, anyway, acting as if nothing had happened. Actually, no. That wasn't one hundred percent accurate. She'd shared the worst of her past, and he'd begun to treat her like spun glass.

Now, there were two Gillians—two wolves at war. One Gillian was afraid of her feelings for William, and the other only wanted to feel more. One looked at him and thought, *He's the scariest man on Earth.* The other looked at him and thought, *He's the* sexiest *man on Earth.*

Talk about mental whiplash! Which mattered more—scary or sexy?

Um, how about *neither*? He was *nice,* the only quality that mattered.

Lately, though, he'd been spending less and less time with her. What if he grew tired of her? What if he ditched her?

There was only one way to keep a man interested in a woman…

Her stomach twisted. *You're proving his point. You aren't ready. This isn't right.*

No. No! Listen to fear? Not anymore. Tonight she took control of her destiny, and proved she could meet all of Liam's needs.

Gillian splashed her face with water and peered at her reflection in the mirror. Dark, haunted eyes stared at her, and she scowled. No one, in this world or any other, had ever hated their eyes more than she hated hers.

You want me to stop touching you? Then tell those beautiful eyes to stop begging for more.

A cold sweat beaded over her forehead, and her stomach threatened to rebel a second time.

Okay. So. Guaranteed, she was going to freak out tonight.

"You are worth the hassle," she muttered. "And so is Liam."

With his kindness and gentleness, he'd earned her trust, loyalty and love. And by some miracle of miracles, she'd earned his, too. He *must* trust and love her, despite his rejection of her. Why else would he throw her a private pre-birthday party yesterday and surprise her with a new car? A Mercedes-Benz S600 Guard, to be exact.

According to her envious classmates, it was the safest vehicle on the market because it could resist sniper fire, rocket-propelled grenades and high-velocity projectiles. Oh, and it had cost six hundred thousand dollars, an absolutely *obscene* amount of money. But William was a savvy businessman on top of everything else and had oodles of cash to spare.

But the thing worth more to her than the Mercedes? The handmade coupon booklet he'd given her. Inside were tickets for all-night video game challenges, dinners anywhere in the world and a shopping extravaganza while he carried her purse.

There were also twenty coupons for "the head or heart of an enemy."

But even better than all of *that*? She'd picked up idle chatter among the group of friends they shared. William considered Gillian his destined mate!

The problem was, he continued seeing other women.

Have to win him now, before he falls in love with someone else.

A little wobbly on her feet, Gillian used the spare toothbrush to scrub her mouth a third and fourth time. *He loves me. He'll always love me.* Surely.

Not too long ago, she'd gone out with some kids from her school. She'd been uncomfortable but determined to have fun. But, when everyone paired up, leaving her alone with one of the boys, she'd panicked. What if he made a move on her? Just when she thought she might snap, William had shown up.

"You do not touch her. Ever," he'd said, his voice pure menace. "You do, you die."

Unlike her stepfather, he protected her. He was a bright light in a life encompassed by darkness.

With him, she almost felt normal.

Gillian *needed* to feel normal. So many girls her age were

excited to discover the "pleasures" of sex. But she already despised the act. The smells, sounds and sensations. The pain, humiliation and helplessness.

What if William could introduce her to those pleasures?

Her phone vibrated. A text from William? Hopeful but also teeming with dread, she checked the screen. Keeley.

Quick question. No wrong answer. If you were a queen—like ME—and someone did something to hurt you in order to save you, would you forgive him or kill him?

Keeley the Red Queen was a Curator tasked with the world's safekeeping, drawing strength from nature. She called her mind a corkboard because she'd lived so long and had so many memories stuck in her brain. Not just of the past, but also the future. Or a future she'd once seen but had forgotten. Now she was remembering, her marriage to Torin helping her achieve mental clarity.

For some reason, she'd decided to take Gillian under her wing and train her to be royalty with lessons posing as a "quick question."

Gillian responded: Those are my only options? Kill him or forgive him? Fine. I'll play along. But before I can render a verdict, I'll need more info. What did this person do to hurt me?

Keeley: Who knows? I wasn't there.

I still need more info.

Keeley: Wrong answer. You must forgive me. I mean him. HIM. Otherwise bitterness will grow like a weed and choke out any joy. Now, then. I hope you enjoyed this lesson in surviving the wonderful world of immortality from Professor Queen KeeKee.

Forgive YOU??? What did you do, K? Or what are you going to do? Tell me!

Keeley: ☺ ☺ ☺ I love you, my sweet little nonhuman you!

Nonhuman? Sometimes there was no understanding the Red Queen.

With a huff, Gillian pocketed her phone and caught sight of her reflection—those eyes. She remembered why she was in William's apartment, and fear annihilated her amusement.

The cons of doing this tonight: (1) she might keep vomiting, (2) if she failed, she might not gather the courage to try again, and (3) doing nothing could mean losing William's friendship.

The pros: (1) she had chosen him of her own free will, (2) she had planned the encounter, and (3) she would control everything that happened. No matter what, sex with him would be different. *Different* meant *better*.

And what if memories of William overshadowed memories of her stepfather? What if William helped rid her of all the guilt, shame and self-loathing that had burrowed inside her heart and taken root?

She wouldn't be a shell of herself any longer. She would regain confidence. The hate inside her would drain. Never again would she feel crushed by life.

Her phone buzzed. A quick screen check had her groaning. Torin.

Where are you?

Torin—another immortal friend—had recently gotten hitched to Keeley. He was a good guy, with a love for sarcasm.

Gillian texted back: Out. Why?

Torin: Why else? Because I like making sure your smart-mouth is safe.

Her fingers flew over the keyboard. Or you promised William you'd check on me while he's out.

Torin: That, too. Now back to business. Out where?

No way she'd lie. "Lie" was the only language her stephorrors spoke. But no way Gillian would tell Torin the full truth, either.

She typed: I'm in my apartment, Dad. Thanks for asking.

She had an apartment of her own right next door to William's. Technically, her apartment belonged to him, too, since he paid for both, but what belonged to him belonged to her—he'd said so! Twice!

Torin: Like I can't track your exact location, sweetheart. Go home. Whatever you're planning, it's a bad idea. Horrible. Terrible. The worst!

What! He knew? Trembling worse than before, she turned off her phone. This was a great idea. Maybe the best she'd ever had.

Breathe. Just breathe. Everything would be fine. William had experience. A *lot* of experience. His friends didn't call him William the Ever Randy and Free Willy for nothing. He would make sure Gillian enjoyed herself to the best of her ability. Right?

Dang it. Where was he? What was he doing?

She remembered the first time they'd met.

Desperate to escape her stephorrors, she'd stolen money and bought a bus ticket from New York to LA. There, she'd gotten a job at the only place willing to hire her. A trashy diner where men like her stephorrors had regularly tried to order a "happy ending meal."

Then Danika Ford had come along, a street-smart scrapper who had the supernatural ability to see into heaven and hell. Danika had been on the run from a group of demon-possessed immortals known as the Lords of the Underworld, each one more terrifying than the last. There was Paris, host to the demon of Promiscuity. Sabin, host to Doubt. Amun, Secrets. Aeron, Wrath. Reyes, Pain. Cameo, Misery. Strider, Defeat. Kane, Disaster. Torin, Disease. Maddox, Violence. Lucien, Death. Gideon, Lies.

Against all odds, Danika had fallen in love with Mr. Pain. The happy couple invited Gillian to move to Budapest with them, and because she'd been dealing with a creepy super, spending every night pressed against her front door, a baseball bat at the ready, she'd thought, *Why the heck not?* Her stephorrors would never be able to find her overseas.

Except, the second she'd arrived, she'd felt as if she'd gone from bad to worse. She'd been too afraid of her new roommates to sleep, and had camped out in the entertainment room—a central location with multiple exits.

One day, William plopped onto the couch and said, "Tell me you're skilled at video games. Everyone else sucks, and I need a challenge."

For months, they'd played video games at all hours of the day, and she'd felt like a kid for the first time in forever. She went from hating all men to loving one as an unlikely friendship bloomed. He quickly became the most important, treasured and wonderful thing in her life. The person she counted on above all others.

Hinges squeaked as the front door opened and closed.

William had returned!

Heart thudding against her ribs, she raced into the bedroom. Footsteps echoed from the foyer. Though her legs felt like jelly, air wheezed between her teeth, and she teetered in high heels, she struck a pose, placing one hand on a bedpost and the other on her hip.

William strode into the bedroom—holding another woman's hand.

Humiliation flash-froze Gillian's blood, tremors nearly toppling her. The woman was breathtakingly lovely, as dark as Gillian was fair, and probably immortal to boot.

When William spotted Gillian, he stopped short. As his gaze roved over her and narrowed, she had to fight the urge to look down, and hide her eyes.

"You shouldn't be here," he said, his voice cold and hard and terrifyingly calm. The kind of tone she suspected murderers used. "I gave you the spare key for emergencies, poppet. Not...this."

"I didn't agree to a three-way, Will." The other woman smiled brightly. "But I'm totally into it. Let's do this!"

Someone kill me. Please.

William pointed at Gillian and barked, "Don't you dare move." Then he dragged the beauty out of the bedroom, despite her sputtering protests.

Gillian pressed her hands over her galloping heart. Should she run?

No. Absolutely not. Girls ran away, and women fought for what they wanted.

A loud slam echoed. Footsteps sounded again. By the time William reappeared in the doorway, alone, Gillian had given up trying to stand and plopped onto the edge of the bed.

Silent, he strode to his closet. When he emerged, he draped a pink silk robe over her shoulders and forced her arms through the holes.

Definitely wasn't *his* robe. Did it belong to one of his many women?

Vulnerable to the max, Gillian watched him through the thick shield of her lashes. He was so beautiful, with jet-black hair, bronzed skin and eyes the color of a morning sky. He was the tallest man she knew, as well as the strongest.

"What's this about, poppet?" He remained in front of her, his muscular arms crossed. At least he didn't sound murdery anymore. "Why here? Why now?"

"Because...just because!"

"Not good enough."

"Because..." *Just do it. Tell him.* "Because guys need sex, and there's no better way to keep one interested. And also because I want you." Maybe. Surely. "Do you want me, too?"

He traced his tongue over his teeth. "You aren't ready for the truth."

"I *am* ready." She jumped up to clutch the collar of his shirt. "Please."

"Your family took something precious from you," he said, prying her fingers loose, his grip firm without bruising. "I won't do the same."

"You won't. By being with me, you'll help me forget." *Begging now?* A new stain of humiliation spread over her cheeks. "We're destined mates. Aren't we?"

The look he gave her...so gentle, so tender it *devastated* her. "I don't want a destined mate. I'm cursed, remember."

Yes. The moment he fell in love, a switch would supposedly flip in his ladylove, and she would do everything in her power to murder him.

He owned a book with a detailed depiction of the curse, and possibly a key to breaking it. Problem was, those deets were written in some kind of code, with strange symbols and odd riddles. So far, no one had been able to decipher *anything*. But they would.

"You have the book. You have hope." *We have a future.*

"I'll take no chances with my heart, emotionally or physically." Gaze locked with hers, he toyed with a lock of her hair. "One day, though, we will be together." One day soon. Four days, in fact. Then I'll make sure you're ready.

Realization: he planned to sleep with her, just like he'd slept with so many others. When their relationship fizzled out—and he clearly expected it to fizzle out—they would, what? Return to their friendship as if nothing had happened?

At least I'll have him in my life.

I'm pathetic. "I...you...never mind. I'm going home."

His big hands framed her face, keeping her locked in place. Fear crawled up her spine. The kind she'd lived with 24/7 in New York.

You'll leave your hands where I put them, pretty girl, or I'll break them.

Her lungs constricted, making it impossible to breathe.

"All right, poppet. Calm down." William combed his fingers through her hair. "Take a deep breath for me."

Open your mouth for me.

Gillian erupted, beating at William. "Let me go. You have to let me go." As her fists bloodied his nose and cut his lip, she had no pride. No ambition but escape. "Don't touch me! You have to stop touching me!"

"Shh. Shh. I've got you." He yanked her against the hard line of his body and wrapped his arms around her, holding her captive. "I won't let anything bad happen to you, I swear it."

Still she fought. He only held her tighter.

Ultimately, her strength drained, and she sagged against him. Sobs racked her.

"I'll help you overcome this," he said, "but not tonight. With us, sex won't be a bandage meant to hide a wound."

She stiffened, opened her mouth, snapped it closed. Why couldn't he see? She *needed* a bandage. Her wound seeped poison. One day soon, it would kill her.

But he was right about one thing. She wasn't ready for sex.

Scratch that. She might not *ever* be ready. Her stephorrors had ruined her. Because, if she couldn't remain calm with William, the man she trusted above all others, she couldn't remain calm with anyone.

Gillian did the only thing she could, and put sex on her never-never list. Never acknowledge, never consider.

No hope. A ragged, broken sound left her. The kind injured animals made just before dying.

"One day, my silly Gilly Gumdrop, we'll look back on this night and laugh," William said, still so gentle, so tender. "You'll see."

"Maybe you're right." She prayed he was right.

"I'm the wisest man ever to walk the Earth," he said with a wink. "I know all."

No, not all. Not the key to breaking his curse.

"One day isn't now," she croaked. This time, as she fought to disentangle from his embrace, he let her go. "I'd like to go home."

"Don't be embarrassed," he said. "Not with me. We'll pretend this never happened. In fact, it's already wiped from my memory. We'll continue on as before." He took her hand, the same way he'd taken the other woman's hand, and another piece of Gillian's heart withered. "Let's fire up some video games and do a little zombie slaying."

"No." She shook her head, locks of hair slapping her cheeks. "Don't worry about me, okay? We're friends. We'll always be friends. I just… I need to be alone right now."

"Poppet—"

"Please, Liam."

The look he gave her broke her already broken heart.

Tomorrow, they'd go back to business as usual, and she'd go on living half a life, afraid of men and sex and maybe even happiness. Tonight she would cry.

4

Three days later

SO. THIS IS THE WOMAN WILLIAM OF THE DARK *will live or die for.*

Puck crouched on the railing of an eighteenth-story balcony, gargoyle-style, and peered into a spacious apartment with only two occupants. William of the Dark and Gillian Shaw.

Soon she would be Gillian Connacht.

William. Wed. War.

Now that Puck had found William, his tasks shifted: *wed the girl, cart her to Amaranthia, return for the male.* Wed. Cart. Return.

Perhaps he should stop staring at the female first?

Impossible.

While the demon growled with displeasure, Puck drank in Gillian's dark fall of silken waves and eyes the color of whiskey. Seductive eyes filled with kindling. One day, a male would light her match, and she would burn for him, and him alone.

Flawless golden skin and blood-red lips only added to her appeal, making her the embodiment of a fairy-tale princess.

My princess.

Puck bit his tongue—he should have tasted blood, but because of Indifference, he tasted nothing. There was no denying the truth. Being near the female he planned to wed came with an unexpected complication. Indifferent? Hardly. She roused his most possessive instincts.

Soon she would belong to him. She would be his first and only "mine," *without* actually being his.

Must police my thoughts about her, or I'll ruin everything.

He felt as if he'd been watching Gillian for days, even weeks, as if he knew her, and yet he marveled over every new detail he learned. She was shockingly human, with a gentle spirit and an aura of kindness. Her beguiling smile was infectious, the rare times she revealed it.

Mostly she studied the people and world around her, somehow both present and detached, all while radiating bone-deep sadness.

Too many centuries had passed since Puck had experienced such heartfelt emotion. Before his possession, he might have sympathized with her—whatever her troubles happened to be—and sought to make things better. Now? He would use her without hesitation. He must.

War before a woman.

"I'm needed elsewhere," William said, and kissed her cheek.

Puck scrutinized his competition for the female's affections: six-five, solidly built, black hair, blue eyes, handsome if you liked perfection, and soon to be sporting a broken nose if he kissed Puck's future bride again.

Inner slap. To achieve his goals, Puck needed both Gillian *and* William to cooperate.

"Hades requires my expertise to obliterate Lucifer's newest palace," William continued.

Lucifer. The male's older brother.

Gillian scowled. Soon she would smile. Around William, her moods tended to change lightning fast, as if she wanted to feel one way, but he made her feel another.

"No, you're staying here." Her voice, even laced with a thread of anger, had the power to seduce.

No wonder William had fallen hard for her, and no other.

Puck had actually found the male hundreds of years ago, not long after the Oracles spoke their prophecy. Back then, William had loved no one but himself, forcing Puck to turn his efforts to obtaining the shears of Ananke.

She was the goddess of Bonds, and rumors claimed her shears could sever any spiritual, emotional or physical tie without consequence. Of course, rumors also claimed the artifact severed more than the user bargained for.

What was truth? What was lie?

At first, Puck had contemplated using the shears to sever his bond with the demon. The creature had become a part of him, another heartbeat he needed to survive. Ditching him without penalty...could anything be better?

Why else would the Oracles instruct him to find the shears?

But, if using the shears on Indifference had been the answer to Puck's dilemma, why instruct him to marry Gillian, and recruit William?

What if the shears severed Puck's connection to Indifference, but also his emotions? He would be in worse shape than before. What if he used the shears and died? The artifact might consider death a blessing rather than a consequence.

Too many risks.

In the end, Puck had opted to stick with his original plan, and work with William.

Help me defeat my brother. In return, I'll divorce your female and give her back to you.

Puck returned his gaze to the dark-haired Gillian. She had such lush breasts. A flat stomach, and rounded hips. Long legs meant to wrap around a man's waist—*my waist*.

His heart beat with renewed determination, as if the organ had come back to life, even though it had never died. As if it said, *I've been waiting for her.*

His ears rang as his blood turned to fuel. He sizzled, hungered and craved, and shot as hard as a rock, his erection straining against his fly.

Want to touch her skin. Would she burn him alive? What a way to go.

Want to kiss those plump red lips. Would she taste as sweet as sugar, as he suspected? *Must know.*

Did she have the power to make him come? Really *must know.*

He gnashed his teeth. The answers didn't matter. He needed to utilize his famous control.

Too late. Indifference already clawed through his mind, making him feel as if he were hemorrhaging internally.

Time for ice. Puck hesitated...then issued the summons.

Nowadays he almost always hesitated to use magic to put his thoughts and feelings in a literal deep freeze. Not because using magic outside of Amaranthia required an extra boost of energy—it did—but because he became a savage killer without mercy or regret.

Like you weren't a savage killer before?

He wouldn't soften until the ice cracked or thawed, a process he couldn't control. Instead, he had to wait for something or someone to prick an emotion strong enough to shatter—or hot enough to burn.

If the ice remained, he could lose interest in his goals.

Worth the risk. He couldn't meet his goals if Indifference weakened him.

The deep freeze numbed him out, as expected, but not as quickly or densely as usual. The layers were too thin, his emotions too fervent to be denied, all on their own.

Fervent enough that he experienced an emotional hangover that left him with a headache and churning stomach.

He summoned more ice. More, still.

There. Better. Even the hangover vanished.

He might find the girl fascinating, but so what? She was a means to an end, nothing more.

Once Sin had been dethroned, Puck would wed someone else and, with his loving queen at his side, he would finally kill his brother, thus fulfilling both prophecies.

Gillian anchored her hands on her hips, breasts straining against her shirt. With the ice in place, Puck had no reaction. Excellent. "Whatever brand-new, shiny war you're hoping to start can wait," she told William.

The male offered her a mock growl. "You're not the boss of me."

"I beg to differ." Head high, she dug a crumpled piece of paper from the pocket of her jeans. "I'm redeeming one of my coupons. The right to—what? Boss you around for twenty-four consecutive hours."

William hunched his shoulders and heaved a defeated sigh. "Give her a coupon book, they said. It's fun and creative, they said."

She laughed an enchanting laugh, proving Puck's suspicions—and cracking his hard-won ice, just like that.

She might be human, but she is also an enchantress, and more dangerous than any foe I've ever faced.

Usually he eschewed distractions, but he needed one now and allowed his mind to wander...

What would his friends think of Gillian?

During his search for the shears, he'd met demon-possessed siblings. Cameron, keeper of Obsession, and Winter, keeper of Selfishness. They'd understood his plight and offered to help. Meaning, Cameron had obsessed over Puck's mission, and Winter had decided she could work the situation to her favor.

Every hardship they'd endured would soon pay off.

The doorbell rang, drawing Puck back to the present.

With a heady aura of innocence and wickedness, Gillian batted her long, black lashes at William. "Be a lamb and welcome our guests inside."

Mumbling under his breath, the Ever Randy strode to the door, opened up. Different immortals poured into the apartment. Among them, Harpies, a Sent One, a goddess and twelve demon-possessed warriors like Puck. Hugs were exchanged and gifts given to Gillian.

A birthday celebration?

"No, no, no," a petite blonde said as she breezed into the foyer. "Not yet. This is only a pre-celebration. Or is it post-pre-celebration since William already threw a pre-celebration? Anyway! The real party is tomorrow. Maybe. But probably definitely not."

"Keeleycael," William said with a nod of greeting. "Can you do me a solid and stow away the crazy today?"

She blew him a kiss. "But I'm speaking with your competition. Spoiler alert. He wins!"

"I'd be mad at you for daring to lie to me," William replied with an easy tone, "if I had competition."

Puck frowned. Keeleycael, the Red Queen? Suspicions danced inside his head, tension tightening each of his muscles—the ice cracking once again.

As Indifference snarled, Puck ignored his usual reluctance and summoned another layer of cold disinterest. So what if she was the same Keeleycael who'd given the small, bejeweled case to Sin. What did Puck care?

Keeleycael nipped at a warrior's ear—Torin, the keeper of Disease—before whispering something to William.

Puck picked up only a handful of words. "Danger...waiting... plan to eliminate..."

William frowned, his body going rigid. "You're sure?"

The blonde nodded, adamant. "Your enemies plan to kill her."

Her—Gillian?

Fury pulsed from William as he stalked to the girl's side and led her into a private corner. "Something dire has come up. I need to leave for an hour, maybe two. Let me go without protest or demanding details, despite the coupon, and I'll make it up to you. I swear it."

Disappointment flashed in her dark eyes, but she nodded. "Of course. Do what you need to do."

"Thank you." He tweaked her nose before flashing away— moving from one location to another with only a thought. Where had he gone?

Puck stayed put, observing Gillian. The allotted hours passed, but William never showed. Eventually, the others said their goodbyes and trickled out of the apartment, until only Keeleycael remained.

Should Puck approach? He might not get another chance to speak to Gillian without William nearby. But what would he say?

Centuries ago, I was told you are the key to dethroning my brother. Marry me?

"Quick question," Keeleycael said to Gillian.

"Keeley," the girl replied with a moan. "Must we do this now?"

Keeley. A nickname.

"We must," the pale-haired woman said. "What is your greatest wish?"

"Besides a female-ruled society where men are pets?"

"Obviously." Thoughtful, the blonde tapped a razor-sharp nail against her chin. "I'm going to save that particular wish for your eight-century birthday."

Gillian snorted. "Eight centuries? Please. But you know what I really want? To be more like you. So strong. So brave. So...free."

Puck stored every "wish" in a mental file labeled *Wife*. Ways to win her? Make her feel strong, brave and free.

"Ding, ding, ding. Absolute right answer, so go ahead and consider me your fairy godmother." Keeley yanked a small vial of liquid from a leather cord hanging from her neck. "Here. Drink this, and thank me later."

Gillian's brows knit together. "What is it?"

"Less talking, more drinking. Bottoms up. And happy eighteenth birthday, little one. This is going to make all your dreams come true…dreams you don't even know you have. You're so welcome." Keeley urged Gillian's hand to her mouth, even helped her tilt the vial, pouring the contents down the girl's throat. "You didn't refuse to drink, so you won't die, driving William to *his* death. Or did he already die? Wait. I'm confused."

"William's going to die?" Gillian croaked.

"Weren't you listening? He's not. *Now.* I might change my tune in another five hundred years or so."

Puck sniffed the air and frowned. He scented a powerful potion meant to turn a human into an immortal. A *rare* potion, thought to be extinct.

As Keeley continued to babble nonsense, Gillian grew still. The color drained from her cheeks. Sweat beaded on her brow, and she clutched her stomach. "Keeley, what did you give—" Her eyes widened as she gasped.

Whimpering now, she rushed out of the living room. Puck vaulted to the next window ledge, unwilling to let her out of his sight, even for a second. She stopped in the bathroom, where she vomited.

Too weak to stand, she collapsed to the floor. Groaning, she closed her eyes and curled into herself.

Keeley followed her, saying, "I'm one hundred percent certain that I'm ninety-three percent certain that I gave you the correct dose. Hmmm. Your symptoms are…well, I'm not pleased. Maybe we'll have to go with Plan B?"

The urge to crash through the window bombarded Puck. He would gather the girl in his arms and…what? What could he do to help? How did one care for a sick mortal-almost-immortal?

Soldiers in Amaranthia were forced to tend to their own ailments and injuries with magic. If you weren't strong enough to recover without aid, you didn't deserve to live.

Never mind. No need to help her. Keeley flashed away just as William burst inside the bathroom.

Seeing Gillian, his concern was palpable. "What's wrong?"

Puck ran his tongue over his teeth as his butterfly tattoo *moved*, like a snake slithering to a new hiding place. From his chest, to his back, to his thigh. Just as he had wandered across Amaranthia, aimless, the demon wandered across the contours of his body anytime Puck experienced some kind of life-changing emotion.

What life-changing emotion did he experience now?

A quick peek beneath the surface of the ice revealed…compassion and envy?

Want nothing, need nothing.

Besides, William didn't measure up to Puck in any way. Despite Puck's handicap, he was stronger, faster and far more capable.

Truth was truth.

"S-sick," Gillian whispered in a broken voice. "Hurt."

"Don't worry," William said. "I'll take care of you. I'll take care of everything." He stretched out a hand suddenly glowing with power.

Puck did a double take. William had runes. Golden scrolls twined from his fingertips to his wrist, a conduit for whatever magic he possessed.

With a single wave, he cut a rift in the air, opening a doorway between two different realms. Through the doorway, Puck saw…a wall of stone?

"I will fix this, you have my word." Gentle, so gentle, the warrior scooped the dark-haired beauty into his arms and carried her through the doorway.

Just before it closed, Puck burst through the window, shattering glass, raced through the room and dove.

5

PUCK ROLLED TO A STOP. AS HE STRAIGHTENED, HE studied his new surroundings. A cave heavily guarded by wards—a type of protective magic derived from symbols. These particular wards were set to react to an invader's intentions. Purposely sneak into the realm? Lose your eyes. Have rape on your mind? Lose your shaft. Ready to commit murder? Say goodbye to your head.

There was also a ward set to alert William of a newcomer's arrival. For the first time, Indifference served Puck well; the wards treated him as they would a wild animal, ignoring him.

Outside the confines of the cave, he discovered a tropical paradise. Yellow palm trees, heavy with fruit. A white sky. Miles of pink water. Waves lapped at glistening white and purple sand, the scent of salt and coconut coating a gentle breeze.

He tracked William to a sprawling home, where large birds with metal beaks and claws guarded the perimeter. Once again, Puck was considered a nonthreat and ignored.

The preoccupied William had no idea he'd been followed. *See, Gillian? I'm the better warrior.*

Finding a shadowed alcove on a balcony, Puck watched

through a window as William placed the brunette atop a massive bed and tenderly wiped her brow with a rag.

"This isn't how I thought to spend your birthday week, poppet. You need to get better." Regret layered the male's voice. "Tomorrow is supposed to be the beginning...well, it doesn't matter right now." He brushed his knuckles along her jaw and said, "I'll be back."

The barest protest escaped her before he flashed away.

One minute passed, two. Ravaged by fever, Gillian tossed and turned. Puck hung back, awash in longing...sympathy?

With a curse, he focused inward to fortify the ice around his heart. He'd had enough of emotion, enough of Indifference.

How did the girl affect him so strongly, so quickly, anyway? And why was she sick? The potion should have strengthened her as she made the transition—

The answer slapped him upside the head, and his lungs constricted. *Morte ad vitam.* She *couldn't* make the transition. Her little body wanted to evolve, and continued to try, but it wasn't strong enough to finish the deed; with every hour that passed, she would weaken further.

She would weaken until she died.

A surge of fury and fear caused the ice to crack. As Puck's claws cut into his palms, a shout of denial brewing in the back of his throat, Indifference protested with a growl.

Careful. More ice. Now!

Puck calmed, even as he acknowledged the unacceptability of this development. Gillian wasn't permitted to die. They had to wed, and he had to use her to gain William's allegiance.

He would just have to proceed as if she would live—because she would! If William failed to save her, Puck would do so.

He considered his options. Approach her now and initiate a conversation? But how would he begin?

You know what they say—once you go beast, you'll always feast.

No. All wrong. He had to make her feel strong, brave and free.

Be mine, and you'll never again know weakness.

She might take one look at him and die from fright.

The outcome of a "meet cute" had never been so important. He needed to put his best foot—hoof—forward, needed to charm and seduce.

He thought back to his predemon days. Females had feared him, the Undefeated, but many had encouraged him, anyway. But whatever charisma he'd had, he'd lost. And his appearance...

Well, it hadn't always been the hindrance he'd expected. A certain type of woman *liked* his beastly form. Horns were in, and incredibly popular in romance novels.

He knew this, because he sometimes read books to Winter, at her request. Apparently phrases like "her succulent nipples" and "quivering desire" sounded amusing in his monotone voice. Whatever. In every story, Puck had identified most with the villain, but he could certainly role-play the part of hero. He could act like a knight in shining armor, at least for a little while, and offer to rescue his damsel in distress.

She wouldn't know the truth until far too late.

With a plan in mind, he stepped forward.

William materialized in the room with another immortal at his side, and Puck went still.

"This man is a doctor," William said. "He's going to examine you."

Her only response was a moan of pain.

The doctor spent the better part of an hour examining Gillian. When he whispered the diagnosis to William and proclaimed there was nothing he could do, William punched him so hard he flew into the far wall.

"Wh-what did he say?" Gillian asked.

"Doesn't matter. He's a quack," the warrior announced. "I'll find you another doctor. A better one."

He vanished, but still Puck hung back, expecting the male to return any—

William appeared with a second doctor...then a third and a

fourth. Each one checked the girl's vitals as she slipped in and out of consciousness, trembling as William barked orders and issued threats. Blood was taken, tests run, but the diagnosis remained the same.

She would die sooner rather than later.

"Go to the living room," William commanded the plethora of physicians. "Set up a lab. Do more tests. Find a way to save her or die yourselves. And if you think to sneak away, know that I will find you, and I will hurt you. You'll *pray* for the day I kill you."

As they rushed to obey, he sat at the side of Gillian's bed, his expression gentling. "There, there, poppet." Once again, he wiped her brow with a rag. "You'll heal. That's an order."

"What's wrong with me?" she managed to rasp. "What did Keeley give me?"

"Something supernatural, but don't worry, I've got the best immortal doctors searching for a cure."

Puck pursed his lips. Why keep the full truth from her?

As Gillian fell into a fitful doze, the other male held her hand, perhaps attempting to will his strength into her fragile body.

Puck wanted to hate the male. He was ready to get off the bench and in the game.

At some point, William's father appeared. Hades, one of nine kings of the underworld. He was urbane but uncivilized. A tall, muscular man like William, with bronzed skin, jet-black hair and eyes so black they had no beginning or end. He had a silver hoop in his nose and stars tattooed on each of his knuckles.

How many other tattoos were hidden beneath his pin-striped suit?

"What's so special about her?" Hades asked.

"I'm not discussing her with you," William snapped.

"I'm discussing her with you, then. You can't be with her. You can't be with anyone. You know as well as I that your happiness walks hand in hand with your doom."

"I'm searching for a way to break my curse and—"

"You've *been* searching," Hades interjected. "For centuries."

"My book—"

"Is nonsense. A trick to make you hope for what can never be so that your demise will be sweeter—for your enemies. If the book could be decoded, it would have been decoded by now."

Puck didn't agree with Hades. In all his research, he'd heard much about the book of codes meant to save William from death at a lover's hand. Multiple sources had confirmed the book's validity.

"Did you come here to piss me off?" William grumbled.

"Pissing you off is a bonus," Hades said. "I came to warn you."

"Well, you've done both."

"No, son, I haven't." The king's voice hardened, sharp enough to cut steel. "The warning is this—if I think you're falling in love with this girl, I'll kill her myself."

William stiffened.

In a deep freeze one second and boiling with rage the next, Puck bowed up.

Kill Gillian, my key? Try, and see what happens.

With a war cry, William launched himself at Hades. A fierce, bloody battle ensued, nothing held back. Punches to the nose and teeth. Elbows to the chest and gut. Knees to the groin. And yet, one opponent never actually tried to kill the other.

They must have affection for each other, the way Puck and Sin—

No. Not Sin. No matter the provocation, an adoring brother would not curse another to a hellish eternity, forcing him to exist rather than live.

I would have rather died than hurt him. Now I'm willing to die in order to hurt him.

As Puck waited for the fight to end, he did his best to calm. But a weird buzz soon began to vibrate in the back of his mind, and if not for Indifference, he would have blamed the sensation on impatience.

Finally, Hades left. William petted the top of Gillian's head, muttered something about finding a better doctor and dematerialized.

Showtime.

Puck eased into the room, silent, and padded forward. Wait. Had he remembered to dress today? A quick glance down revealed his sheepskin pants had been torn so much they resembled a loincloth.

No matter. Barbarian chic really made his horns pop, and fit the whole romance-novel-hero mystique he'd hoped to convey. He might even pass for Prince Charming—well, a prince in need of true love's kiss.

Puck's pulse points spun into a wild rhythm when he reached the side of the bed and spied his future bride. He wasn't the only fairy-tale character in the room. *Sleeping beauty lies before me.*

Dark ribbons of hair spilled over the pale pink of the pillow. Her eyes were closed, long black lashes throwing shadows over her cheeks. A rosy flush spread over her delicate features as she parted her lips.

Practically begging *for my kiss.*

Focus! Keep this short and sweet. No telling when William would return.

"Gillian," he rasped, surprised by the husky tone of his voice.

A sweet fragrance wafted from her. Breathing in, he detected a note of poppiberries, and his head fogged. His blood heated. The butterfly tattoo *sizzled* on his torso, surely melting his skin.

Indifference snarled with more force and slashed at his mind. Trouble brewed.

Fortify ice. Regain control.

Gillian turned her head toward him and blinked rapidly before focusing on him. Panic filled her whiskey-colored eyes before she looked away—anywhere but Puck. Her mouth opened wide, as if she was trying to scream. Only a squeak escaped.

"There'll be none of that now." To prove himself harmless, he tucked the covers around her, as he'd seen William do. "I'm not here to hurt you." *Truth.*

The movement caused the razors woven into his hair to clink together, drawing her attention. Her gaze darted to him, and darkened with shock and dismay. He swallowed a curse. Romance novel heroes didn't usually smuggle weapons in their hair.

Must proceed anyway. Puck wouldn't part with his razors; they were his saving grace. Anytime he was challenged, and had no sword or dagger, he plucked a razor free and started slashing.

Tears rained down Gillian's cheeks, and her chin trembled. So vulnerable. So broken. A pang of…something lanced his chest.

As gently as possible, he wiped her tears away. *Skin as soft as silk and hotter than the sun.*

The action helped relax her, even as it hardened muscle after muscle inside *him*. Her panic began to fade—until her gaze snagged on the loincloth. Or rather, the erection underneath the loincloth. With a whimper, she began to thrash atop the bed in a desperate bid to escape.

Thought he would take what she had not offered? Never. "Eyes up here, lass."

Her gaze lifted up, up…she gasped, as if she'd noticed his face for the very first time. Confusion contorted her features before a deeper shade of rose spilled over her cheeks.

Did she like what she saw?

"I was told I could aid you." Again truth—he'd told *himself.* "That we can aid each other."

Her brow furrowed, her confusion intensifying.

"I *wasn't* told you belonged to William of the Dark." A necessary lie, and something the old Puck would have protested. Demon-possessed Puck had few scruples. Like everything else, means had ceased to matter. Only the end result. "I also wasn't told you were sick. Or human," he added. *Look at me, female.*

So innocent. I know nothing about you, but my curiosity is great. Be flattered rather than frightened. "What are you doing with a male of William's…reputation?" There. Sowing dissent. A tactic he'd learned from Sin.

"Wh-who are you?" she asked, reciprocating his curiosity.

A good sign, aye? He sifted a lock of her hair between his fingers, savoring the sleek texture.

Savoring? Puck?

What is she doing to me?

Indifference snarled.

He purposely fixated on her question, and how best to answer—until she cringed, as if disgusted by his touch. Another pang, this one sharper, as he dropped his arm to his side.

He *wasn't* upset by her reaction. He wasn't! "I'm Púkinn. You may call me Puck. I'm the keeper of Indifference." He forced himself to pause, as if he needed time to consider his next words. "I'm not sure you can aid me, but I think I'll allow you to try." Another lie. *You* will *help me, female. One way or another.*

Was she intrigued?

She remained silent, simply peering up at him, as if he were a puzzle she couldn't solve.

Aye. Intrigued.

Another pang razed his chest, creating fractures in his ice, allowing emotions he'd buried to rise to the surface of his mind. Arousal. Hunger. Impatience. Longing. Fury. More arousal. His body seemed to expand to accommodate the influx, the butterfly tattoo moving again. Muscles plumped and knotted. Skin stretched taut. Beads of sweat popped up on his brow and between his shoulder blades.

Indifference geared up to deliver a lethal strike.

No, no, no. Not here, not now.

Concentrating on his breathing, Puck shifted from one booted foot to the other, never allowing his body to assume a warrior's stance…even though warriors took what they desired, when they desired.

Reach out. Touch her. Satiate your hunger...

No! He shouldn't hunger at all.

Go. Leave her wanting more. "I'll return after you've gotten used to the idea." *And after I've calmed.*

He opened his mouth to tell her he would find a way to save her—to plant seeds about the possibility, but Gillian's eyes had already closed. She'd fallen asleep. She must feel safe with him, at least on some level. Otherwise, adrenaline would have kept her conscious.

Victory, within my grasp...

Though every step away from her proved a special kind of hell, considering his lust for her, he returned to the balcony, intending to watch over her the rest of the night.

"Well, well, well," a familiar voice said from behind him. "Who do we have here?"

6

BEFORE PUCK COULD TURN AROUND, HARD FIN-
gers tangled in his hair and yanked, flinging him from the
balcony. One of his razors slashed his cheek when he crashed
into a bank of trees. Bark and sand sprayed in every direction.

For a moment, as he lay upon the ground, a memory wafted
through his mind.

After a particularly gruesome day of training, he and Sin
had huddled together, eating the rodents they'd managed to
catch, because soldiers were responsible for their own food. If
you didn't hunt, you didn't eat.

*I wish you'd stayed with Momma, Sin, but I'm so glad you're with
me.*

*You're my favorite person in all the realms, Puck. I'll stay with
you always.*

But "always" hadn't lasted long, had it?

Puck swallowed the bitter lump in his throat and forced the
past from his mind. Fighting for breath, he sprang to his feet.

In a whirlwind of black smoke, Hades appeared directly in
front of him. "So. You're the one possessed by Indifference.
I've wondered about the unlucky twit she'd given him to, all
those centuries ago."

Puck unsheathed a dagger, the metal glinting in the sunlight. "If you mean Keeleycael—Keeley—she gave Indifference to my brother, and *he* gave the demon to me."

Gave. Such a pretty word for such a terrible betrayal.

Then realization struck. Hades knew the truth of Puck's possession. Others assumed he was given Indifference while locked in Tartarus, a prison for immortals. Which was an understandable mistake.

Long ago, when Zeus ruled Mount Olympus, twelve members of his elite army stole and opened Pandora's box—a container much like the one holding Indifference. Only, this one unleashed countless demons on an unsuspecting world, the worst of the worst. The soldiers were punished for their senseless act, and forced to play host to a demon, just like Puck. With more demons than soldiers, however, the leftovers needed a host. Select prisoners were chosen.

Hades grinned a cold grin. "Keeley does nothing without understanding the grand finale."

Keeleycael... Keeley... Gillian's friend *was* the infamous Red Queen.

"Why would she meddle in my life? Why would she want me possessed?" Puck had done nothing to hurt her. Hadn't even known of her existence until she'd struck at him.

"To save my son. Keeley and I were engaged at the time, and she knew I would do anything—and I do mean *anything*—to ensure his safety."

Forcing Puck to play host to Indifference had somehow saved William's life? Ridiculous! He suspected Hades saw the past through the lens of his pride.

But either way, Hades had made it clear he planned to destroy those who got in his son's way.

Kill anyone who threatens my survival, and always retaliate for a slight.

Indifference snarled as fury spiked.

Inhale, exhale. Puck summoned the ice...to no avail, as if

the king had negated his only defense. Or his emotions were too far gone already.

"Would you like your freedom?" Hades asked. "Once, I ruled the demons. I could remove Indifference, no problem... but I would damage you in the process. A perk for me, since I enjoy damaging others."

Fury, intensifying. "I'll pass."

"Then listen up, little princeling, because it's story time." Hades stalked around him, menace in every step. "The Red Queen also told me that my life would change the day I flashed upon a warrior of unequaled strength and ferocity, who would help me fix my beloved son's problem. *If* I was a good boy and stopped myself from killing him. Now, here you are, sniffing around the very son and problem in question."

Unequaled strength and ferocity—*sounds like me.* "Does this problem have a name?"

"She does."

She. Gillian, then. "She might be a problem for William, but she is a solution to me. I won't leave this realm without her."

"Will you not, then?" Hades arched a dark brow. "Already possessive of her, despite only just meeting her. Despite Indifference. Well, consider my curiosity mildly piqued. Actually, a notch below mild. Slightly."

If Hades thought to keep Puck from his future wife—from his future, period—Hades would die.

"*Is* your strength and ferocity greater than mine?" Hades asked.

No need to ponder. "Yes."

"Let's find out for sure, shall we?"

One second Hades stood out of striking distance, the next his breath fanned Puck's face.

In swift succession, Puck blocked the first, second and third punch, saving his nose from being shattered. But Hades was touted as a master of strategy for a reason, and clearly expected the resistance; by forcing Puck to play defense, he was able to use his free hand to steal the other dagger sheathed at Puck's waist. Jab, jab, jab. Hades stabbed his kidney, liver and intestines.

Any one of those blows could have killed a human. All three? Certain death. Though agonizing pains shot through Puck, warm blood flowing in crimson rivers down his legs, weakening him, he remained unfazed.

Unhampered by a need to fight fair, he slammed his knee between Hades's legs. *Testicles, enjoy your meet and greet with your master's throat.* As the king hunched over, gasping for breath he couldn't catch, Puck coldcocked him in the jaw.

Hades stumbled back, his infuriated bellow echoing through the realm. When he straightened, his gaze landed on Puck and narrowed.

As Puck's stab wounds healed, he checked his cuticles. Huh. They could use a trim.

Now Hades laughed a sound of genuine amusement. "You think you've got me beat, do you? Hate to break it to you— who am I kidding? I *love* to break it to you, just as I'll love breaking *you*. I was winning battles when you were soiling your diapers. You cannot defeat me. Especially when I know Indifference better than you ever will."

A taunt meant to elicit fear, and knock Puck off his game? Too bad.

Utilizing the preternatural speed he'd been born with, he closed the distance and punted Hades in the stomach. The king stumbled, and Puck dived at him, knocking him down.

They toppled. Midair, Hades attempted to claim the superior position—and failed. *Boom!* Impact. Air gushed from the other man's lungs, momentarily rendering him immobile.

Puck suffered no such impairment and took full advantage, yanking a razor from his hair and slicing through his opponent's eyes, temporarily blinding him.

With a roar, Hades whaled on Puck, shattering his cheekbone, jaw and trachea. He'd experienced worse a thousand times over and fought through fresh waves of searing pain, repeatedly swiping at the king's face. Blood poured from multiple lacerations.

At the same time, Puck used his free hand to steal back the dagger Hades had stolen. But the king expected that action, too, and angled the blade to slash through Puck's palm. Flesh and muscle tore. Bone cracked.

Hades power-drilled a fist into his jaw. Newly healed joints dislocated. Stars winked through his vision and more waves of searing pain joined the party. But not by word or deed did Puck reveal it. He simply maneuvered to his feet and slammed a boot into Hades's nose, shattering cartilage. A reprieve. He forced his jaw into place. Better.

When he raised his foot to deliver a second stomp, Hades caught his ankle and flipped him over. Upon landing, Puck flipped backward and glided to his feet a good distance away.

"I can do this all day," he said. "Come. Give me your worst." He gave an exaggerated wince, a taunt. "Or did you give me your worst already?"

Standing with far more grace than anyone should exhibit after taking a foot to the face, Hades offered him another amused laugh. "You want the girl, fine, she's yours. Because, no matter what my son thinks, she isn't the one for him. According to Keeleycael, he'll die if he weds Gillian. So. Tomorrow, I'll keep him busy, allowing you to do a little romancing. Or a lot of romancing. Have you looked in the mirror lately? You're going to have to work a lot for a little tail. Bond to her—it's the only way to save her—and take her far away from here."

Marriage to Gillian would cause William's death? Interesting. Maybe that was why Puck had to wed the one the underworld prince would live or die for, so that William survived long enough to dethrone Sin.

Maybe Gillian would cause William's death *after* Puck returned her.

Not my problem. Once William fulfilled the prophecy, Puck

didn't care what happened to him. But he kept his lips zipped. No way would he admit he planned to take Gillian away from William only temporarily.

Let Hades think what he wanted to think. He—

Bond to her, he'd said. Not marry. The only way to save her.

Realization and shock hit Puck with enough force to topple an elephant. Bonding would unite their souls, allowing Gillian to draw on his strength and finish her transition into immortality. She would be more than his wife. She would become his other half.

Mine!

Slight problem. As weak as she was, she might act as a siphon and drain him completely, killing them both. An outcome William must fear. Otherwise he would have bonded to his ladylove already, aye?

Worth the risk.

He would propose, and she would agree, if only to save William heartbreak and guilt—or stop him from taking the same risk. She wouldn't want to jeopardize the life of her precious.

Advantage Puck.

Her unrelenting loyalty to the male should have pleased Puck—it would ensure his victory. So why was he grinding his teeth and squeezing his fists so tightly his knuckles attempted to tear through his skin?

Didn't matter. Potential dilemma: divorce would no longer be possible. Separation would mean death.

William would never agree to—

Puck sucked in a breath. The shears. Of course. He could use Ananke's shears to free Gillian from their bond, allowing her to return to William alive, free of her husband's claim.

Every action dictated by the Oracles had a reason, and finally those reasons made sense.

Puck readjusted his tasks. *Bond to Gillian. Escort her to Amaranthia. Return for William.*

Bond. Escort. Return.

Cold grin back in place, Hades saluted him. "Excellent. I see the wheels turning in your head. I'll leave you to your schemes. Good luck, Pucker. You're going to need it." After blowing him a kiss, the underworld king vanished.

Alone, Puck stared up at Gillian's balcony, waves of determination spilling over him, antagonizing Indifference all over again.

Inhale, exhale. Hades had promised to distract William tomorrow. Puck didn't trust him. Or anyone. Sin had taught him better. But doubt and worry were currently beyond him. He would continue on, as planned, and whatever happened, happened. He would deal.

What he wouldn't do? Give up.

Lass, you're as good as mine.

7

PUCK SPENT THE NIGHT APPEASING INDIFFERENCE
by refortifying every layer of ice around his heart and mind.
Feel nothing, want nothing. War before women, always.

When next he faced Gillian, he would be ready. Her beauty
would not affect him, nor would possessive instincts lead him.

So it was decided, so it would be.

As the sun rose, Puck positioned himself in a bank of shadows, watching as Hades tried—and failed—to convince William to leave the realm. Hours passed, the sense of impatience
returning.

Time wasn't his friend. Time was not *Gillian's* friend.

Finally, Hades told William he had a lead on a cure for Gillian, and William happily abandoned ship, granting Puck an
opportunity to meet with Gillian unencumbered. Unless the
king of the underworld intended to ambush him?

No matter. I'll be ready.

Puck prowled through an oasis of palm trees, his gaze locked
on his target. She lounged on the beach in a cushioned chair, a
wispy white canopy providing shade. Already she'd lost weight
she couldn't afford to lose. The shine in her hair had dulled,
and the lovely tint of rose in her cheeks had abated.

How much time did she have left?

Protective instincts surged. Ice cracked as his butterfly tat traveled from his shoulder to his thigh.

Breathing deeply, searching for calm, he closed in on Gillian. A golden sun set in the horizon, painting the sky with a rainbow of different colors and reflecting off the water—and her eyes. Such a beautiful, tranquil setting, perfect for seduction. He almost smiled. William had set the stage for his own downfall.

Around her, eight armed guards.

Only eight?

My future wife—rephrase. The girl *deserves better. Must teach William the error of his ways.*

"Do you need anything, Miss Bradshaw?" one of the guards called.

Bradshaw—one of her aliases. Did William not want anyone to know her true identity?

"No, thank you," Gillian rasped, her voice little more than a whisper.

So weak. So close to the end. *Crack, crack.* If the demon were to take out Puck before he'd secured a bond with her... *Must act faster.*

Moving at a speed neither mortal nor immortal could track, he felled the first four guards. As the others realized an enemy lurked nearby, weapons were cocked. Too late. Puck defeated them just as easily and swiftly.

Brushing his hands together in a job well done, he stalked to Gillian's side. The scent of poppiberries filled his nose, deliciously intoxicating and as magical as home, urging him closer, closer still, and—

Snarl.

Puck nearly lost his footing. *And I considered myself prepared?* The girl wielded some sort of strange enchantment over him, able to do in seconds what most people couldn't do in months: affect him.

Spotting him, she gasped. Then she looked down, as if she couldn't bear the sight of him. Panic radiated from her, the very emotion he hadn't wanted her to feel—and he hadn't yet spoken a word!

Why would she fear his presence when he hadn't hurt her last time? Why would—

Her gaze darted to him, lingering on his loincloth, before she once again looked away.

The material was damaged, frayed, and revealed more than it concealed. Easily remedied.

Should he remedy the situation, though? Perhaps she feared her reaction to his body. Perhaps she liked the sight of him *too much*.

A man could dream.

In a blink, Puck returned to a fallen soldier, stole a shirt and fit his arms through the holes. The man's pants were too small. *Every* pair of pants proved too small. Very well. At least the shirt was long enough to cover his shaft as it grew…and grew.

As he returned to Gillian, he buttoned the lapels, not realizing until too late that he'd aligned the two sides incorrectly.

"Better?" he asked.

"Did you kill them?" she demanded in her broken voice, ignoring his question.

He settled next to her chair and peered out at the water, giving her a moment to adjust to his presence, doing his best to convince her—and Indifference—that he wasn't aware of her every move. "I merely put them down for a nap. But I can slit their throats, no problem. Just say the word."

Her wish, his command.

"N-no. Please. No." She gave an almost imperceptible shake of her head.

Upset by the thought of a few murders? Adorable. "Very well, then." *See how accommodating I can be, female? I'm perfect for you.*

As she studied him more intently, taking his measure, her

panic receded. Excellent. He stole a quick glance at her face to judge how long it might take to get her from calm to intrigued— the way he'd left her during their last visit—and frowned.

She wasn't just calmed. She was *grateful*. Poor lass. How low were her standards for male decency?

Not that Puck cared. Of course he didn't care.

"Why are you here? Truly?" she asked, her brow furrowing.

He needed an excuse, something believable yet interesting, perhaps even steeped in truth rather than lies. "I told you I am the keeper of Indifference, and that you can help me. You can help me *feel*." Or rather, feel without consequence. Once Puck had claimed the Connacht crown, killed Sin and united the realms, he would risk using the shears on Indifference.

"I promise you," she said, utterly earnest, "I can't make you feel anything."

You already have. More than anyone else ever had.

As necessary for my goals as she is dangerous... One day, he might be better served to kill her.

This! This was the danger of the ice.

Unaware of his thoughts, she shifted to be closer to him, reminding him of a kitten seeking more warmth. How he longed to reach out, comb his fingers through her hair, trace his knuckles along her jawbone and bask in her softness.

Bask? Me? Resist her allure. "You can. You will," he said, dismayed by the huskiness of his tone. He should have no problem remaining detached.

Time to lie. "I was told your situation is so sad, I'll come to care. And I so want to care..."

The fairer sex liked bad boys—or rather, projects—who melted for only one special woman. *Don't you see, lass? You are the only one with the power to save me...*

"Who told you this?" she asked. Her gaze took on a faraway cast, as if her mind had wandered even as she next spoke. "And why would you *want* to care? Take it from me. Caring for someone else is highly overrated." She fretted her bottom lip. "*Do* you care...about anything?"

He pretended to mull over his thoughts, and sighed. "Not even a little." Though she appeared lost in her thoughts again, he added, "The Oracles in my home-realm are the ones who told me about you. And I want to care because it is my right." More truth, harder tone, the words escaping unbidden. Caring without punishment was a right for everyone, human and immortal alike.

If she heard the last part of his speech, she gave no notice. "Do you *ever* feel?" she asked, something akin to envy pulsing from her, and confusing him.

"Only very rarely, and then..." He pursed his lips. There was no good reason to tell her about the weakness the demon inflicted upon him, and *every* reason to keep the info secret. Knowledge was power, and Puck would never willingly grant someone else power over him.

"Lucky," she muttered. She *was* envious of him. What a strange creature.

But then, she didn't know the price of an apathetic existence. How she would lose loved ones and friends, hearth and home. How her favorite foods would become tasteless. How living would equate to surviving. How beloved hobbies would no longer spark joy. How sex would leave her empty and hollow.

"Lucky? Lass, I could set you on fire. As you screamed in agony, I could watch you burn, only interested in the warmth of the flames on a chilly night."

"Okay," she said, her calm acceptance of his unintentional admission surprising him, "maybe *lucky* was too strong a word." Once, twice, she stole a glance at him through the thick fan of her lashes. "Are you going to set *me* on fire?"

"No." In an effort to tease her as heroes often teased their heroines, he added, "I left my matches at home."

Success! The hint of a smile curled the corners of her Cupid's bow mouth, as if *she* found *him* adorable.

Desire heated his blood and hardened every muscle in his body, earning a snarl from Indifference. Puck's hands curled into fists.

For his plan to work, he had to stop responding to her every word and action, and fast.

A cool, salty breeze tumbled across the sands, and Gillian shivered. Still feverish?

Want nothing, need—

Screw it. Then. That exact moment. Puck became indifferent to *the demon*, to punishment, to any consequence he might have to face. Trembling with the need to care for his future wife, he removed his shirt and draped the material over her dainty shoulders. As she curled into the garment's warmth, a shocking jolt of satisfaction nearly unmanned him. He savored it, his mind robbed of any defense.

Satisfaction…how he'd missed it. Not just sexually, but in a job well done. A war well fought. *Give me more. I need more.*

SNARL.

Puck stiffened. Perhaps he should leave, take time to regroup and return when he'd successfully rearranged his priorities. Yes, yes. That was exactly what he should do. As he made to stand, however, Gillian's gaze dropped to his chest and lingered, and Puck wanted to roar with pleasure. Without conscious thought, he found himself switching gears…and settling more firmly in place. Perhaps he'd stay a bit longer.

"Thank you," she muttered.

For the shirt? "You're welcome." *Anything for you, lass. Trust me…*

Guilt pricked him—*I want her trust, but do not deserve it.* Still, he ruthlessly slashed the emotion to ribbons.

"So, uh, how did you go invisible?" she asked. "When you fought the guards, I mean."

"I didn't. I moved too quickly for you—or them—to track."

"That's nice."

Merely *nice*? "My skills are legendary." Bragging now? Hoping to impress her?

She licked her lips, as if gearing up for an argument. "To acquire such skill, you must have lived a long time. You probably know all kinds of facts about, say, a supernatural disease... like *morte ad vitam*."

Ah. She'd overheard the term and now searched for answers. To tell or not to tell?

"What is *morte ad vitam*?" she asked when he remained silent.

He stroked his jaw, thick stubble greeting him. "Is that what's wrong with you, then?"

"Yes. Every doctor agrees." She gulped. "What does it mean?"

Tell, he decided. "You were given a potion. Your body is trying to evolve, trying to become immortal, but it isn't strong enough. Now there's only one possible chance for survival." He paused for dramatic effect. "You must marry...*bond* with an immortal and link your soul to his."

Hope lit her eyes. *Blink.* The hope was gone.

"But even that isn't a guarantee," he continued. "You could drain his strength and kill him. Or worse, make him human."

First she displayed shock. Then horror, acceptance and fear. Finally disgust. His confusion returned, redoubled. Why disgust? Didn't females dream of wedding a strong man who would offer lifelong security?

The fear he understood and expected, even as a part of him resented it. She recoiled at the thought of endangering William's life.

Lucky William, to have a woman so concerned with his well-being that she would do anything, even die, to save him.

Die...to save another man... For a moment, Puck saw red. Literally. *My wife will be loyal to me, and no other!*

Indifference roared with displeasure.

Inhale, exhale. *Proceed with caution. So close to crossing the finish line.* Inhale. Good, that was good. Exhale. The crimson haze faded from Puck's gaze.

"Well, that sucks," Gillian muttered, oblivious to the turmoil she'd caused. Gaze faraway again, she began to babble. "I had no idea…thought immortals were created fully formed or born from other immortals."

"Immortals are born in more ways than one."

She blinked rapidly, attention returning to him. "How much time do I have before…"

"Considering your current condition, I'd say another week, maybe two." At most.

"Bummer." Her nose scrunched up, creating adorable little crinkles on the sides. "I'll never get to do the things on my bucket list. If I had a bucket list, I mean."

"Perhaps you should make one. I can help." His first suggestion: *bond to a beast.*

Her head canted to the side, her whiskey eyes once again admiring. "Why would you want to help me with that, of all things?"

Somehow, her scrutiny made him feel less like a monster and more like a man, as if she didn't see what he was, but what he could be.

An illusion, nothing more. "You could use a distraction, and I could use a new goal." A kernel of truth meant to garner pity. Others might disdain a blow to their pride, but not Puck. Not any longer. "The woman I wanted didn't want me back, so we parted ways." Truth. *No one wants me, boohoohoo. Poor me.* "Now…" He shrugged. *Comfort me?*

The woman in question—Winter. He'd hungered for her as much as he was able; he'd never met a woman like her. Strong enough to topple an army all on her own. But, when she'd rebuffed him, he hadn't cared enough to try to change her mind.

Sorry, beasty boy, but I'm in love with someone else. Me! You understand, right? No hard feelings. Other than the hard feelings in your pants.

He'd walked away without a single twinge of regret.

"Women are goals to you?" Gillian asked, sounding a little offended but a lot curious by the prospect.

Continued curiosity was a very good sign. "Why not? My goals, as well as my rules, keep me from sitting on a couch, watching soap operas all day, every day, while eating old pizza."

Bond. Escort. Return.

Hesitant, she said, "But, if you're unable to feel, how do you want a woman?"

"I rarely feel emotion, but I often feel desire." *In particular, I desire a certain little dark-haired beauty.* "The two aren't mutually exclusive, lass."

If Gillian wanted him, he would bed her. The things she made him crave...

Once again he wondered if she would have the power to make him come, and how Indifference would react.

There was only one way to find out...

If he had to lie and tell William he wouldn't ever touch her, he would. Anything to achieve his goals. Or maybe he would be better served refusing to keep his hands to himself. Jealous men did foolish things, like agree to help a total stranger murder another total stranger.

Of course, everything hinged on Puck's ability to save Gillian from certain death.

"You make a good point, I suppose." She offered him a small smile, and yet, never had a female looked sadder. "I feel all kinds of emotion, but never ever desire."

So she didn't yearn to bed her precious William? A lie, surely. "You've never desired a man?" *Tell me the truth. Tell me now.* For some reason, Puck had to know.

Indifference dug his claws in deeper while issuing another warning roar.

Gillian shifted away from him, her little body even more tense than before, her dark eyes haunted. Haloed by the setting sun, she radiated more pain than any one person could possibly endure. Or survive. Especially a fragile human on the verge of death.

Whatever ice he'd managed to maintain—toast.

"I don't want to talk about it." Reminding him of a wounded animal cornered by a hungry predator, she lashed out, saying, "Change the subject or leave."

8

PUCK DIDN'T CHANGE THE SUBJECT, AND HE DIDN'T leave. *I'll take door number three, lass.*

"Ah. I understand," he said. "Someone hurt you." He uttered the words matter-of-factly, but deep, deep inside, he seethed. Who had dared to brutalize his wife?

Thinking of her as wife *now, rather than* future *wife?*

The butterfly tattoo sizzled on its return to his shoulder.

Because of the punishments meted by his demon, Puck was intimately acquainted with the helplessness that accompanied the inability to stop an attack. While incapacitated and unable to fight back, he, too, had been brutalized in the worst of ways. Only, when his strength had returned, repaying violence with worse violence had been easy. He doubted this fragile flower had ever gathered the power to do the same.

"I'll kill the man responsible, whoever he is." Gladly. Bloodily. "Just tell me his name."

"Names. Plural," she snapped, then pressed her lips together.

"One man or one hundred, it makes no difference to me." He would kill them all. Blood would flow in great, sweeping rivers.

"Thanks for the offer," she mumbled, deflating, "but I think they're already dead."

She thought, or knew?

Considering her relationship with the dark one... "William must have meted punishment." And kept the details from her?

From everything Puck had observed about the secretive male—yes, absolutely.

One of her delicate shoulders hiked in a shrug, her only response to his question. "Are you on friendly terms with William?"

"I know of him, and I'm sure he knows of me—" who didn't? "—but we've never officially met." Truth.

"If you want to be his friend, sneaking around his property isn't—"

"Oh, I don't want to be his friend." Another truth emerged unbidden. "He can hate me." Hatred was a guarantee. "I don't care one way or the other."

"That's unwise. If you aren't his friend, you're his enemy. His enemies die painfully."

"Do *you* care?" If she could accept William's dark side, she could accept Puck's. A point in his favor. "My enemies die gratefully, glad to finally escape me."

Now she rolled her eyes. "You immortals and your blood feuds."

"Don't you mean *us* immortals?" Best she accepted her fate as soon as possible. An eternity awaited her, ready or not.

Longing pulsed from her. "No, I don't. I'm going to die, remember? *Before* the transformation is complete. Which means a bucket list is stupid."

Because she would be forced to pick things she could do from her sickbed? How...sad.

"You will die, yes." He found a pebble, tossed it into the water, giving her words a moment to sink in. The time to play the hero had come. "Or I could bond with you." Too eager?

"I suppose," he added. Not good enough. He needed to spell out his role. "I could save you by joining our souls."

She gaped at him...with interest? "Um, the only way to save me is bonding to me? So, are you actually *proposing* to me?"

"Yes." Verging on too eager again? "No," he said then. Too disinterested? A frustrated sound brewed in his chest, and he pursed his lips. "I don't want to bond with you, but I don't *not* want to bond with you." If he could have kicked his own ass, he would have. *Blowing this big-time.* "It's just something to do. Something mutually beneficial." Better.

Her hands flattened against her stomach, as if to ward off a terrible ache. "Aren't you worried I'll make you mortal?"

Not anymore. Not even a little. "I'm the dominant between us. My life-force will overpower yours, I'm sure of it." *Then you will be mine, and mine alone...for a time.*

She opened her mouth, snapped it closed. Opened it, snapped it closed.

Inside Puck, anticipation and nervousness vied for supremacy, inciting Indifference to slash and riot.

Come on, lass. Hurry! Tell me what I need to hear.

Finally Gillian sighed and said, "Thank you for the kind offer/non-offer, but I think I'm going to pass."

A new surge of frustration joined the deluge, causing the demon's tantrum to intensify another degree. *Careful.*

No! Not careful. Not here, not now. Puck needed to know where he'd gone wrong.

Trying for a reasonable tone, he said, "Is it because of my horns?" The fur? Hooves? If only he could shapeshift, as he'd done before his possession.

Seeming lost again, she crossed her arms over her middle. Rousing sympathies...

"I can hack them off," he said, proceeding. "They'll stay gone, for a time."

No response.

"I haven't always looked this way."

"No," she replied, and he had to backtrack to figure out what she denied.

His horns, he realized.

"Appearance has nothing to do with it." When she peered at him again, her breathing was labored, her skin dotted by perspiration. "You would want to have...you know."

You know? "Sex?"

A glorious flush appearing in her cheeks, momentarily giving the illusion of health, she nodded.

Often and thoroughly, lass.

If he could come without punishment. Hell, if he could come at all. Though the girl had made him feel more in the past twenty-four hours than anyone else had managed in...he couldn't remember how long...she might not be able to overcome his constant need to cater to Indifference.

"Correct," he said, his voice harsher than he'd intended, all force and no seduction. Considering the tragedy of her past, she would require gentling. A skill Puck wasn't sure he employed. Before his possession, he'd taken his women for a hard ride. "I would, yes."

"Well, I wouldn't. Ever."

"You think that now, but I would change your mind." Or die trying.

No, absolutely not. *War before women.*

If he had to take sex off the table, he would. And he would tell her so...would reassure her...any second now...

He pressed his tongue to the roof of his mouth, and remained silent. No way would he limit himself to such a degree. Because, when it came to sex, he would not lie. In this, he would always be truthful with her.

As he carefully considered his next statement, he found and threw another pebble. "I would never force you," he said. "I would wait for you to want it...to want me."

"I'm telling you, no matter how skilled you think you are, you'd have to wait forever."

"I'd have you in bed within the month, guaranteed."

She softened, regret radiating from her, as if she feared she'd hurt his feelings. At the same time, goose bumps graced her flesh, as if she *liked* the idea.

So expressive…so beautiful.

More ice cracked, heat blooming in the center of his chest. He shot hard and aching, his body desperate for release.

Oh, yes. With her, he would be able to come.

Arousal smoldered deep inside him. Silently, he told her, *Trust me, female. Let me set you free from your fears.*

ROAR.

Puck jolted, the heat cooling.

In the distance, a twig snapped. Ears twitching, he stiffened and searched the oasis…soon catching William's murder-and-mayhem scent on the breeze.

"William has returned." Dismal timing. "He'll be here in five…four…three…"

"You should go." Gillian made a shooing motion with her hands. "Please."

Did she worry for Puck's welfare? How sweet, and adorable. And utterly unexpected.

"One," he said, finishing the countdown. He darted to a palm tree a hundred yards away, the thick trunk hiding him while also allowing him to maintain a vigil over Gillian.

William exited the house, his legs taking him straight to the girl. When he noticed the unconscious guards, malice blazed in his eyes, momentarily turning crystalline irises neon red. "Are you all right, poppet? The guards—"

"I'm fine," she said, scanning the area. Finding no sign of Puck, she breathed a sigh…of relief? Happiness that he'd gotten away safely? Or happiness that Puck wouldn't fight—and hurt—her precious William?

He curled his hands into hard fists.

"What happened to my soldiers?" William demanded as he crouched beside her.

Would she tell him the truth? Would she attempt to protect Puck? Did he *want* her to try—to care?

"*Someone* happened to them," she said, then hesitated. "A man. Puck."

A flicker of disappointment. Would she mention his proposal? If William managed to bond-block him, all hope would be lost.

"He came here and moved so quickly I couldn't track him," she added. "The guards were no match for his speed and strength."

She praises me. A tingle of pride sent another fissure racing through the ice.

Indifference clawed at Puck's mind, sending tendrils of weakness to his bones. He cursed, because he knew. This was it, the final warning.

Next, the demon would purr, and Puck would be screwed, unable to move or protect himself. Unable to help Gillian as the disease drained her.

He doused the pride with a splash of cold hard truth: if he failed to achieve his goals, Sin would remain on the Connacht throne. Citizens would suffer. *Amaranthia* would suffer.

Anger flickered to life, and he issued another curse. No help for it. He had to summon more ice. There. Better.

"Puck. Keeper of Indifference." William stood, a dagger clutched in both of his hands. It seemed Puck's reputation had preceded him. "He's sworn vengeance on Torin for trapping him in another realm."

Wrong. Cameron and Winter had sworn vengeance on Torin. Puck hadn't cared enough.

"But how did Puck escape?" William asked, as if thinking aloud.

Easily. Cameron, being Cameron, had been obsessed with finding an exit.

Gillian frowned. "How do you know what he's sworn if you've never met him?"

"My spies are everywhere, poppet." Neon red returned to William's eyes. "Did Puck say anything to you? Did the bastard *do* anything to you? Hades mentioned him, said he might be nearby and I should leave him alone, but that just makes me want to hurt him *worse*."

She huffed and puffed like the big bad wolf she absolutely wasn't, and the corners of Puck's mouth twitched. "He told me what *morte ad vitam* is." As William lamented loose tongues and unwanted visitors, she added, "You won't hurt him for it. And you won't kill him. Or pay someone else to kill him. I should have heard the truth from you, but I didn't, so he kindly offered to help."

She *was* trying to protect Puck.

Ice, cracking all over again. Body, going molten.

"Offered. To. Help. How?" William demanded.

"Promise me first," she insisted, and if she hadn't looked like death, she might have pulled off fierce-ish. "Please."

Silent now, the warrior reached out to rip the shirt Puck had given her. She gasped, startled. Then she whimpered. William showed no mercy, pulling the material from her shoulders. Once the garment was free, he tossed it into the water.

Interesting, and revealing—in more ways than one. Though William knew nothing about the proposal, he was already eaten up with jealousy.

The exact reaction Puck wanted, *needed*. So why was he eyeing the other man's chest, imagining sinking a blade through his heart?

Gillian's second whimper had Puck marching forward, eager to make fantasy a reality, with no thought or concern about Indifference, ice completely melted. William would *suffer*.

Another tendril of weakness settled in his bones, and he tripped. Puck caught himself on a tree, ducked behind the trunk.

Muttering an apology, William scooped Gillian into his arms, infinitely tender now, and carried her inside the house.

Though Puck knew he should leave and seek shelter, he drew closer…closer still. Floor-to-ceiling glass walls welcomed nature inside—as well as his gaze. There was nowhere in the house he couldn't watch.

"—just so you know," Gillian was saying as William carted her upstairs, "I'm not going to bond with you."

Puck's heart nearly stopped. Had the other male issued a proposal of his own, then?

William placed her atop the bed, perched at her side and offered a stiff smile. "I don't remember asking, poppet."

A heavy sigh of relief escaped Puck. No, no proposal had been issued.

"I know you haven't asked, just as I know you *won't* ask," she said. "This way, when I'm gone, you won't waste time feeling guilty, wondering if you *should have* asked."

"You're not going to die." Despite William's soft tone, unmistakable malice laced every word. "I won't let you."

Wrong. I won't let her.

Trembling, she reached out to clasp William's hand. "I love you, Liam. When I had nothing and no one, you gave me friendship and joy, and I will be forever grateful to you."

Puck sucked in a breath. She was saying goodbye, preparing for death, wasn't she?

Fight, Gillian. Fight to live.

Aggression pulsed from William. "Stop talking as if this is the end for you."

She offered him the same sad smile she'd offered Puck. "You have faults. A *lot* of faults. But you're a wonderful man."

"This wonderful man will find a way to save you," William said, his tone hard as granite. "I'm working every day, every hour, every minute to ensure bonding won't be necessary. Now get some rest." Head high, he stood and stomped from the room. The door slammed behind him.

Rather than watching that door for William's return, Gillian

peered at the balcony, her expression unreadable. Was she waiting for Puck? His chest puffed, and there was no stopping it.

When her eyes closed, Puck snuck into the room and stalked
to her beside, as if drawn by a waft of magic. He breathed in
her poppiberry scent.

"Sleep, lass. I'll make sure you're safe." Another lie. Because,
even as he spoke, Indifference began to purr.

9

LIKE A PLUG HAD BEEN PULLED INSIDE A BATHTUB, might and vigor drained from Puck, until his knees could barely hold his weight.

Time to go.

He wasn't able to leave the room as quietly as he'd entered, but Gillian never roused. He would go somewhere safe, endure Indifference's punishment, then rebuild his strength and return. If the girl died in the meantime…

She had better not die.

Puck stumbled through the trees, the injustice of his predicament seething inside him. Experience told him he would soon be too weak to move. At times he would be completely unaware of his surroundings. At others, he would know what happened around him, but remain unable to act.

For days, anyone could stumble upon him, attack him—do anything they desired to him. Abduction. Imprisonment. Rape. Even chop him into little pieces.

But he wasn't concerned for himself. Considering Gillian's swiftly deteriorating condition, time was her greatest enemy—and his.

Must ensure my survival. He couldn't help her if he died.

First order of business: securing a hideout.

Never approach an enemy until you've scouted your location and secured a safe haven.

Sin's voice rose from the mire of Puck's memory, as welcome as it was despised. He'd been so wrapped up in Gillian, and the strange things she made him feel, he hadn't given his surroundings a second thought. He probably wouldn't have cared, anyway. And not just because of Indifference. Sin used to do all the scouting and securing, leaving Puck to do the fighting. Now, at his weakest, he had to find shelter *and* craft an indestructible defense.

Unless Hades intervened, William would come searching for him.

At times like this, Puck missed Cameron and Winter. In their own special way, they'd loved him when no one else would, or could. Anytime Indifference had overtaken him, they'd guarded him. For centuries, they'd ensured his battle skills remained well honed, forcing him to practice. And when he'd lost sight of his goals, they'd reminded him.

The relationship hadn't been one-sided, either. Whenever Obsession had overtaken Cameron, the warrior had spent days—weeks—locked inside a room, talking only to the demon, refusing to eat or sleep. He'd needed a champion willing to fight, and fight hard, to distract him with a brand-new obsession. Winter had never been the best candidate. For her, a single selfless act came with devastating consequences.

Demons *always* came with a price.

Anytime Winter had defied Selfishness and acted altruistically, she'd descended into a week-long odyssey of madness. Just long enough to rip an entire realm apart, leaving zero survivors…and Winter with violent memories she could never shake.

Puck had helped the siblings in ways no one else could, and shared his ice.

Had the siblings suffered without him?

Maybe, probably, but at least they had each other, the way Puck had once had Sin.

Puck! Puck! Another memory surfaced, eleven-year-old Sin sobbing at Puck's bedside. *You had better heal from this injury, or I'll be forced to kill...everyone. I can't do life without you.*

Oh, how Puck missed the boy Sin had been. The friend he'd become.

Indifference purred louder while slithering through his body and siphoning more and more of his strength. Tremors cascaded through his limbs. One by one, his bones seemed to morph into noodles, and his muscles into soup. Every step forward became a lesson in anguish.

When his foot met a rock, he tripped forward. Though he tried to steady himself, his knees gave out. He toppled, grains of sand clinging to his sweaty skin. Darkness teased the edge of his mind, quickly gaining new ground.

No. Fight! Out in the open like this, he was a target. An *easy* target. But even as he struggled to stand, the demon drained the rest of his energy, turning breathing into a chore.

"There you are. Finally!" Feminine laughter filtered into his awareness. "I was starting to think I'd gotten the days mixed up, but then I remembered the only time I've ever been wrong was when I thought I was wrong."

He recognized her voice. Keeley, the Red Queen. Gillian and William's friend. The one who'd given Indifference to Sin, with instructions to possess Puck, then commissioned Hades to offer aid to him.

What fresh horror did she have in store for him today?

"Torin, a boost, if you please," she said.

Torin, keeper of Disease. The one who expected Puck to attack at the first opportunity.

He was too weak to protest as rock-solid arms wrapped around him and swept him up, up, against a muscular chest. Inside, though, he fought like the beast he'd become—to no avail.

"Where do you want him?" Torin asked. "And don't you dare say *in my pants*. Not again."

"Whose pants? Yours or mine?"

"Either," the keeper of Disease replied.

Keeley *humphed*. "I like him right where you've got him. Look at you, darling. Your biceps are bulging!"

A soft *pff* left Torin, as if he battled a mighty urge to laugh and curse at the same time. "Concentrate, princess, and tell me where we're going."

"To our secret love shack, of course."

The patter of footsteps blended with the snap of twigs, creating an ominous chorus. Puck loathed this with every fiber of his being. The helplessness. The uncertainty. The way the darkness around his mind taunted him, threatening to send him into oblivion at any moment.

"My sexy beast is magnificent, isn't he?" Keeley said. Warm, soft fingers traced his brow.

A growl reverberated in Torin's chest, no hint of amusement. "Hearing you wax poetic about another man tends to put me in a murderous mood."

Sexy—Puck? *Her* beast? Did the couple know about his plan to bond with Gillian, blackmail William and slay Sin? Had Keeley truly known what would happen all those centuries ago when she'd given the box to Sin? Hades seemed to think so.

"Aw, my baby's self-esteem is smarting." Her voice was low, raspy. "Here, let me help make you all better."

Whoosh. The sound of a palm slapping skin.

"Ow." Torin's entire body jerked. "That hurt."

"And there's more where that came from," Keeley said, and Puck imagined her wagging a finger at her husband. "You're the most incredible male in the history of ever, and I'm the most faithful woman. Act like it."

"Yes, ma'am." Torin chuckled, only to sober. "William will be *tee-icked* if he finds out we're helping Gilly's future husband."

Helping the girl's future husband—*me?* The Red Queen had predicted even this?

Of course me! I've got this in the bag.

She heaved a weighty sigh. "I'll deal with William when the time comes. You know, when he realizes I saved Gillian's life, and his eternity, and his true mate, and he begs for my forgiveness. Oh! So, check it. Earlier this morning I spoke with Hades's magic mirror."

"The one containing the goddess of Many Futures?"

"Exactly. Now I have a pretty good lead on Willy's best path and oh, wow, is that boy in for a world of hurt. His mate is going to lead him on a merry chase. Which reminds me. I'm supposed to tell Gideon and Scarlet about their baby."

"Is something wrong?" Torin asked, his concern evident. "Or are you trying to tell me Gideon and Scarlet will give birth to William's mate?"

"No, nothing like that. But they need to know illusion isn't just illusion but also vision, and William needs to know… what? I've forgotten. Something about the code breaker…an illusion…"

"I have no idea what you're talking about, princess."

Nor did Puck, and he didn't care enough to expend energy to fit the puzzle pieces together.

Torin sprang over a rock, the abrupt motion ramming Puck's brain into his skull. The darkness stopped playing and started cloaking his mind. He slipped in and out of awareness, only coming to when his rescuer placed him on a hard, flat surface, cold rocks digging into his back.

"—doing this?" Torin was saying.

"He was almost my stepson," Keeley replied. "I want to see him happy, which means he has to be shoved onto the right path. But I love Gillian, too, and I want *her* happy. I also love Puck, and want him happy. Or I will love Puck, one day. This is the only way to achieve the perfect end for all three players, a plan I put into motion a long time ago."

She loved Puck—or would love him—even though she didn't know him? She'd thought forcing him to host Indifference would help him achieve the perfect end?

Crazy female. She'd ruined *everything*.

"You were wrong before, you know. He won't thank us," Torin muttered. "Ever."

"Have I taught you nothing?" Keeley said. "We have to do what's right, no matter the reaction we'll receive from others. Besides, people can surprise you."

"You're right. People can surprise you—with a knife in the back."

Darkness closed in once again...

As Torin unleashed a string of profanity, Puck's eyelids popped open. Through a haze, he thought he spied rocky walls, the shadow of a warrior and the profile of a busty blonde.

"She's not going to thank you for this, either," Torin said.

"She will," Keeley replied, then sighed. "Well, maybe not at first but one day. If the payout wasn't worth the pain..." Soft fingers *tap, tap, tapped* against Puck's cheek. "You had better be worth it, Plucky. Time is running out. She's dying. You're almost too late. Or maybe you're *already* too late. Life and death are *so* confusing for the psychically inclined."

Though he fought to rise—*must get to Gillian!*—darkness descended once again.

Gillian fell in and out of consciousness. In her feverish daze, she thought she maybe/maybe not, probably was/probably wasn't having a conversation with Keeley.

She couldn't decide what was real and what wasn't because, for once she had no idea if she was dreaming or awake, or if she was confusing present with past and past with future, just like the Red Queen, who had lived for thousands of years, memories and predictions stacking on top of each other, details getting lost in the mire.

Was this a taste of immortality? Could Gillian live this way forever?

Would she even remember this odd interaction, or would she forget, as the Red Queen often did?

"You forgive me, right?" her friend asked, sounding nervous and unsure. "I'm not just a stranger, remember. I'm your best friend. And I did save your life."

"Forgive..." Why? Oh, wait. Keeley had tricked her into drinking an eternal curse. "Should have...let die..." To be saddled with her fears and phobias forever? No, thanks.

"Nonsense! Now be a good girl, and say yes to Puck, okay? You're going to be *such* a lovely bride."

Okay. This *had* to be a hallucination. None of the Lords or their mates would ever encourage her to wed Puck.

"You've got some growing up to do, of course," her friend continued. "Let's face it, baby girl, you're immature and rash. You do foolish things. You're confused. You change your mind in a snap. See if this rings a bell." In a falsetto, she said, *"Oh, William. You're so perfect for me. No, no, William, I'm determined to remain alone all the days of my life. William, I want you. William, I'm not interested in any kind of romantic relationship with you."*

Fire spread over Gillian's cheeks, and she doubted it had anything to do with her sickness.

"You don't know what you want, or what you need," Keeley continued. "You just know you need change, right? Well, ta-da! Today is your pucky lucky day. You just have to fight for better. Fight, Gillian. *Fight!*"

Her fragmented thoughts struggled to keep up. Pucky lucky... Puck. The most beautiful man she'd ever seen. Yes, he overshadowed William, reminding her of an Egyptian prince she'd once seen in a history book, but with a lot more bulk. Seriously, the guy looked like he'd taught Jason Momoa how to work out. And when he spoke...goodbye sanity. He had a slight Irish accent that had sent shivers down her spine.

His eyes were the color of frosted coal and rimmed by the

longest, thickest lashes of all time. At first glance, she'd thought he wore eyeliner, and a thousand layers of jet-black mascara. Nope. On him, the smoky look was all natural.

He had cheekbones as sharp as glass, an imperial nose, and lips as soft and dewy as a dark pink rose, the bottom one plumper than the top one.

Also at first glance, the sight of his horns had frightened her. She'd flinched, the urge to fight or take flight rising up strong. *Fight? Me?* Please! Had she been strong enough, she would have run as if her feet were on fire.

At second glance, those horns had intrigued her. She wasn't sure why.

The man never smiled. Actually, his expression never betrayed a hint of emotion. He appeared detached from the world around him, unaffected by...absolutely everything. *Except maybe...me.* Once or twice he'd seemed to burn for her.

A mistake on her part?

However, despite his beastly attributes and cold demeanor, he'd been nothing but honorable. He'd asked for her help, and in return, he'd wanted her to help him feel some kind of emotion. Could she?

Shouldn't she try? On one hand, Puck was her last hope. Her *only* hope. Possibly her salvation. On the other hand, if she died, there'd be no more misery or fear. No more weakness. The past would be wiped away.

Fight at long last, Gillian. Please. Fight!

Fight to live? Fight evil? Could she? she wondered again.

This time, the answer crashed into her mind with the force of a Mack truck. Yes! She could fight evil. *Needed* to fight evil. There were too many young girls and boys being abused by people in positions of power, and they deserved a champion.

I want to be a champion.

Hello, bucket list.

For too long, she'd had no purpose. Fear had owned her, robbing her of joy, hope and pleasure. But no longer! Today was a new day. The girl she used to be was gone, a new one rising in her place.

For the first time in her life, she had a reason to live. So, yes, she would fight.

"That's right," Keeley said, as if reading her thoughts. "This is your destiny. The reason you were born. The first step is always the hardest, but don't worry, soon you'll be running." She cleaned Gillian from top to bottom with a wet rag, then combed her hair and brushed her teeth. "Bonus: William won't spiral and blame himself for your death, yesterday, today or tomorrow."

William, sweet William. "Maybe one day someone will make a movie about your life," Keeley said. "*Eighteen and Married to an Immortal—and a Demon! But truth is stranger than fiction, eh? Who would believe it?*"

Gillian was *living* it and *she* could hardly believe it. Puck had said a bond to him would do the trick. She might have agreed, if he hadn't wanted to have sex with her.

Sex remained on her never-never list.

"There will come a time when you eagerly, happily put sex on your always-always list," Keeley whispered, again seeming to read Gillian's thoughts and more certainly proving herself to be a hallucination. "Admit it. You ache for Puck."

Her? Ache? When the beautiful warrior with muscles galore had looked at her with ice-cold eyes—the eyes of a predator. Eyes that said he would hunt his prey for hours, days, waiting for the perfect time to strike. No. But when he'd maybe/maybe not looked at her with smoldering heat, her body had seemed to wake from a deep sleep, her heart rate speeding up, different parts of her throbbing, desperate to learn the meaning of bliss.

Could he teach her?

Of course, an all-too-familiar fear had engulfed her each time. Almost as much guilt, too. How dare her body betray William?

Such a foolish thought. William was a friend, nothing more.

Did she still want more? If not, fine. She could bond to Puck and save her life. If yes…she had to proceed with caution. If she bonded to Puck, she'd have zero chance of being with William, ever.

Keeley pressed her lips against Gillian's forehead. "Marriage to Puck will give you a clean slate. You'll reset, have a fresh start. Just…survive now, and figure out the rest later, okay?"

Clean slate. Fresh start. From frightened mouse to fearless champion.

As sleep beckoned, Gillian got trapped on a single thought: William or Puck?

10

EYES SPRINGING OPEN, PUCK JOLTED UPRIGHT. PANT-
ing, he scanned his surroundings. An empty, wardless cave,
with a doorway to another realm in the far corner. But…it
wasn't the same doorway he'd used to enter the realm. Where
would this one lead?

On the far wall, he spotted a message written in blood. Some
of the letters had dripped together.

ASK AGAIN. SHE'S READY TO SAY YES TO THE DRESS.

The dress? What dress?

Facts rolled through his mind, an avalanche picking up debris along a downward slide. Torin and Keeley, carrying him
to safety… Gillian, dying…too late.

Too late? No!

An unfamiliar tide of urgency propelled Puck to his feet.
His strength had returned, and he needed to keep it. *Allow no
emotion. React to nothing.*

How much time had passed since last he'd been with Gillian? A few days? A week?

He did a quick survey of his attire. Clean T-shirt, new loincloth. He thought he remembered Keeley saying, *Barbarian works for you. Let's maintain the look.*

As he rushed out of the cave, instinct demanded he grab the nylon bag in his path. Without slowing his pace, he checked the contents. Toothbrush, toothpaste, mouthwash, hairbrush. Courtesy of Torin and Keeley? Wanting him to look and smell his best for Gillian?

Puck used each item, refusing to be grateful.

The closer he came to the beach house, the more Gillian's pained moans assaulted his ears. He fought a pang of sympathy, and summoned a new layer of ice—more than ever before—until only his goals mattered.

He pumped his arms and legs faster. "You had best hold on, lass. I'm almost there."

Finally! He reached his destination. As he scaled the second floor, a warm tide of relief swept through him only to freeze when it encountered the ice. Excellent.

The balcony doors were already open, making things easy for him. He leaped onto the railing and flew inside the bedroom, where he found Gillian on the bed, as still as a statue.

As she inhaled a breath, death rattled in her lungs. Blue tinged her lips. She wasn't getting enough oxygen. She was nothing but skin and bones, wasting away.

Will not react.

William knew what was wrong with her, knew there was only one way to save her; the bastard could have bonded to her and saved her from this. Instead, he let her suffer while he searched for nonexistent, unproven ways to *maybe perhaps hopefully* keep her around a little longer.

He didn't deserve her. But he would learn better. Sometimes you had to lose a treasure in order to understand its value. Today, Puck would begin William's lessons.

Determined, he slid his arms under Gillian's body. Afraid of breaking her fragile bones, he lifted her against his chest as gently as possible. She was too light, frighteningly so.

Seeking warmth, she curled against him. *WILL NOT REACT.*

When her beautiful lips formed the name *William*, Puck went stiff. So. She thought the other male carried her. Didn't matter. The mistake worked in Puck's favor. He had no desire to terrify her.

"Gillian!" William's voice reverberated through the entire house. His tone was strained, as if he spoke while struggling against an opponent.

Had Torin, Keeley or Hades come to offer Puck more aid?

Puck expected Gillian to turn rigid when she realized her beloved wasn't the one absconding with her, but she softened further, relief seeming to overtake her. She'd *wanted* Puck to come for her?

Ask again. She's ready to Say Yes to the Dress.

Just in case he'd read her body language wrong, he rushed to reassure her of his good intentions. "I'm not going to let you die. The last time I was with you, I felt—I *felt.*" True, in every way, and a reason to avoid her, but also the reason she believed he continued to seek her out. He couldn't forget he had a part to play. "I regretted leaving you—" *regretted my tangle with Indifference* "—and I'm not going to do it again."

Incoherent words spilled from her, and he tried to decipher them. Something about making him feel, after all?

Because he'd admitted to feeling regret, she thought her job was done?

Think again, lass.

Stride long and sure, he stalked to the balcony, climbed the railing, and leaped. When he landed, he managed to remain upright through sheer grit. Impact proved jarring, however, and Gillian moaned.

"I'm sorry," he muttered, and wondered if he meant it, despite the ice. As he raced forward, twigs and rocks cutting his feet, he decided to return to Torin and Keeley's cave and use their doorway. Wherever it led, he would deal. "I want to bond with you, Gillian. Do not say no."

"Won't. Yes," she whispered. "Will...bond. What...need...do?"

She'd agreed? A momentary blast of shock tripped him up, but he said, "Just repeat after me." He raced through the realm, faster and faster, heading for the exit, putting as much distance between Gillian and William as possible. "Yes?"

A murmur of agreement.

Good enough. "I give you my heart, soul and body." He waited until she'd echoed his words. Every time she paused to catch her breath, his nerve endings buzzed. "I tie my life to yours, and when you die, I die with you. This I say, this I do."

The significance of the moment wasn't lost on him. They were tying their souls together. Until he used the shears, they would be two halves of a whole.

Had his life unfolded according to his original plan, he would never have considered bonding. He would have remained single, never sleeping with the same woman twice, never knowing true satisfaction in bed.

After Gillian—after Indifference—his life would be his own once again. *I'll share with no one, ever.*

He would *trust* no one, not even the next wife he would take. The loving queen.

"Repeat the rest," he commanded.

Tears welled in Gillian's eyes, making all that whiskey-colored gold appear liquid. Did she regret her decision already? Too bad. She'd run out of time, and had no other options. Her life was fading right before Puck's eyes.

If he had to force her to finish, he would.

Then, a miracle happened. She echoed his statement, willingly accepting his claim. "This I say, this I do."

So close to victory!

Indifference snarled, and Puck ground his teeth.

"I don't think...it worked." Gillian's brows drew together.

"Are you sure...bonding is what...saves me? I feel...same. Weak as ever."

"Don't worry, lass. We aren't done yet."

Finally they reached the exit. Puck zoomed through the mystical doorway, entering a new realm. One he'd never before encountered. There was no beach, or people, only an endless expanse of jungle.

Possible threats: poison foliage, wildlife, man-made traps and the males who'd constructed them.

In a rare act of protection, he pressed Gillian's face into the hollow of his neck before shouldering through a sea of branches and leaves. He would claim the first shelter he found, by fair means or foul, and finish the ceremony.

There. A tree house came into view, large and luxurious.

Puck draped Gillian over his shoulder as gently as possible and climbed up, up. At the top, he found a beautiful bedroom furnished in white. Who lived here?

Hardly mattered. He placed Gillian in the center of the bed and withdrew a dagger. After slicing his wrist, he placed the wound directly over her lips. Blood dripped into her mouth, and she gagged.

"Swallow." He barked the command, showing no mercy.

Feverish and frantic, she shook her head, and precious drops dribbled down her cheek.

"You will do this." She must. Her life—and their bond—depended on it.

He fit the heel of his uninjured hand against her forehead to hold her in place and pinched her nose closed. Cruel on his part, but also necessary. *She will die otherwise.*

She would forgive him. Or not. He placed his wound over her mouth a second time. Because she had to open up in order to breathe, his blood trickled down her throat.

She gagged again but ultimately swallowed, and he heaved with relief. There. It was done.

He lifted her arm and picked up the dagger. He knew what

he had to do—slice her beautiful skin—but still he hesitated. Take blood she couldn't afford to give? How could he dare?

No other way. Her pain would be fleeting. Once it was done, she could siphon his strength and finally, blessedly complete her transition into immortality. All would be well. She might even thank him.

Puck inhaled sharply—and slashed Gillian's wrist. She cringed as he placed the wound at his mouth and drank.

"Blood of my blood, breath of my breath," he rasped, his heart thudding against his ribs. "Until the end of time." Or until the shears were used. "Repeat the words, lass."

Her eyes widened, and straight white teeth chewed on a bottom lip still coated with Puck's blood. "No," she said, and shuddered. "Need to think. No longer sure…"

Refusal? Now? *Running out of time.* "If you don't do this, you will die, and I will war with William for nothing." Without a bargaining chip, William would have no reason to become Puck's ally and every reason to become his enemy.

A thousand different emotions swam in her eyes, despair at the forefront.

Puck thought he understood. A bond saved her life, but also destroyed any chance of being with William. In her mind, at least. She had no idea Puck planned to use the shears, and he wasn't going to tell her. Yet. For all he knew, William had tagged her with some kind of ward after finding out Puck had come sniffing around, allowing the other man to listen through her ears. The warrior would learn the truth when Puck decided to share, and no sooner.

"You understand William would have let you die?" he said, the words lashing from him. "I'm here. I'm willing to risk everything—for you."

A whimper opened the floodgates, heralding a sob. Had she even heard him?

Frustration and rage battered his ice. Snarls echoed inside his head.

Inhale, exhale. "Gillian." He cupped her jaw, keeping his hold as soft as possible. "Give me a chance. Let me save you."

Again, he wasn't sure if she'd heard him or not, but she closed her eyes and leaned into his touch. One second passed, two, a seemingly endless agony. When finally her eyelids parted, he met a golden gaze more haunted than ever before—windows to the wounds festering deep inside her.

Tears streamed down her cheeks and tremors rocked her delicate body, but at long last, she repeated the words. "Blood of my blood, breath of my breath. Until the end of time."

11

BETWEEN ONE HEARTBEAT AND THE NEXT, GILLIAN'S life forever changed.

As strength and warmth sped through her body, darkness and ice sped through her soul. The dual sensations battled for supremacy, leaving her reeling. So badly she wanted to cry out for William. He would make everything better.

But he wasn't here, and what could have been would never be.

A sob lodged against a lump in her throat, and a choking sound escaped. She'd aligned her life with someone else. A stranger.

And that was a good thing, right? She'd reset. Today marked Day One of her fresh start. She had a new path to walk—without William. What if he decided to cut her from his life altogether, because she was no longer Gillian, but Gillian plus one?

How could she say goodbye to the greatest man she'd ever met? Tears distorted her vision.

William would have let you die. I'm here. I'm willing to risk everything.

Old Gillian would have lamented. New Gillian would rejoice. For the first time, she had a plan for her life. The rescue of abused kids. Every time she succeeded, she would be kicking evil in the nuts.

Finally the dark fog that had plagued her since she'd fallen ill lifted, the past few days—weeks?—becoming a blur as the present cleared.

An open, airy bedroom greeted her, pure rustic glamor. Sunlight flowed through cracks in wooden walls. She filled her lungs to capacity, the scent of lavender and peat smoke teasing her, rich and decadent, even soothing—Puck's scent. *Delicious.*

Gillian lay on a large bed with a soft mattress. Her husband perched at her side, watching her with a strained expression. Because he'd shared so much of his strength with her?

When his gaze collided with hers, a sensual haze clouded her thoughts. Puck was…he was…

More beautiful than I ever realized.

The ivory horns gave him an otherworldly mystique. Silky black hair beckoned her fingers…kohl-rimmed eyes burned with possessiveness, melting the frost from his coal-colored irises. Today, his irises reminded her of a midnight sky scattered with stars. His lips were a darker shade of rose than before and begged to be kissed—demanded to own the mouth pressed against his.

No man had ever looked so hard and gentle at the same time, as if he could kill you or seduce you just as soon as he made up his mind.

An odd sensation prickled the crests of Gillian's breasts and between her legs. *Unimportant. Ignore.* What mattered? She was alive! Thanks to Puck, she had hope, and a future.

Laughing, she threw her arms around him. She owed him big-time. But all he wanted in return? To feel an emotion, *any* emotion.

Sounded easy enough. In theory, at least.

How was she supposed to make the keeper of Indifference laugh? Tell him jokes? How was she supposed to make him cry? Share stories about her childhood?

And where were they gonna go, huh? Back to Budapest with the Lords? She doubted Puck would be welcome, and knew he wouldn't blend in with modern society.

Actually, he didn't have to blend in. People would assume he wore a costume, and probably post reviews online.

Did you see the "monster" in the castle district? So fake!

His makeup artist should be fired.

He wouldn't fool my blind uncle. Grade: D-

Gillian released him, eager to discuss her thoughts, plans and hopes, but he wrapped his arms around her and held her firmly in place. Her heart kicked into a staccato rhythm, and her blood ran cold.

Panic surged, and she wrenched back, gaining her freedom. Relief bloomed...until she heard a quiet, sinister roar in the back of her mind.

Puck battled the fiercest erection of his life. Poppiberries—Gillian's scent—filled his nose. Except, her sweet fragrance now had added depth, because it blended with *his* scent, becoming *their* scent.

They were well and truly bonded.

Her fragile body had demanded its due, taking what it needed from *his* body. He'd only just recovered from Indifference's punishment; now, a good portion of his newfound strength had already deserted him. But...he was glad. Or almost glad.

Such a small price to pay for Gillian's stunning transformation.

Color had returned to her skin, the beautiful golden tones now flushed with rose. The weight she'd lost had reappeared in a blink, her eyes no longer sunken, her cheeks rounded once again. Dull, lifeless hair had new luster and gleamed as if dusted with diamond powder.

Purely feminine. Lusciously carnal.

More radiant than ever. Because of him. Because of Púkinn

Neale Brion Connacht IV. Because his power flowed through her, ensuring her heart continued to beat.

Pride puffed his chest. No man had a lovelier wife.

No man had a more *frightened* wife, he realized, his chest constricting. Her gaze darted to the left, then to the right. Searching for a way out? Just then, she reminded him of injured prey cornered by a hungry predator.

"Be at ease, lass," he rasped. He thought…no, surely not. But…maybe? Emotion seemed to flow between their bond. Fear, sadness. Hope, happiness. Rage, concern.

Had to be a mistake. And yet, Indifference remained silent.

Gillian drew a heavy breath through her mouth and closed her eyes. For several seconds, she sat as still as a statue. When she exhaled, she focused on Puck, the wildness fading from her eyes. Eyes that shifted down to avoid his gaze.

"I'm sorry," she said, and rubbed at her temples.

He pressed two fingers beneath her jaw and lifted her chin. Her gaze lifted, as well, and held his own, unwavering.

"Better," he said. "I like your eyes—want to see them."

She blinked, as if surprised.

When he smoothed a lock of hair behind her ear, his fingertips tingled, and white-hot desire speared him. And yet, still Indifference remained silent. Even more shocking, Gillian softened and leaned into his touch.

"You are exquisite," he said, and no truer words had ever been spoken.

Darker pink circles spread over her cheeks, lending an air of innocence to her carnal sensuality. "Thank you. And you—"

"Are not. I know."

"Hey. Don't put words—"

"Gillian!" William's hard voice echoed off the walls, shaking the planks.

Finish your sentence, Puck wanted to roar. What did she think he was?

"William," she mouthed. Excitement lit her eyes, drawing a ragged growl from Puck.

Ragged growl? *I'm using her. Her feelings for another man do not affect me.*

Dagger in hand, he jumped up. Perfect timing. William burst through a wall, wood shards flying in every direction. Rage crackled in his electric blues—no, his neon reds. Arcs of lightning zipped under the surface of his skin, while smoke and shadows stretched above his shoulders, like wings. Raven locks billowed around his face, lifted by a wind Puck couldn't feel.

What kind of immortal *was* this man?

He was Hades's son through some sort of immortal adoption; the two shared no blood ties.

Whatever he was, William had lost his chance to make a move against Puck. Now, what happened to husband also happened to wife. Cut Puck, and Gillian would bleed. Break his bones, and hers would shatter.

Those neon red eyes narrowed on him, crackling with the kind of rage Puck longed to feel. "You're going to die, but not until you've begged for mercy you'll never receive. She's mine, and I protect what's mine."

And so it begins.

The first rule of negotiation: establish a solid foundation on which to stand. The second: rip your opponent apart in every way possible. The more off-kilter William felt, the less confidence he would have. The less confidence he had, the easier Puck could work the situation in his favor.

"No," Gillian croaked, rising from the bed to move beside Puck. "No killing."

Thinks to protect the man who could have saved her days of agony?

Forget a solid foundation. Puck went straight to ripping. "She's yours?" He sneered. "I did what you were too afraid to do. I fought for the prize—and I won."

A bomb detonated in William's eyes, literal sparks crackling at the corners. "You have sealed your fate, demon."

If Gillian heard the exchange, she gave no notice, her gaze pleading with William. Hoping he would save her from Puck?

The rage he'd longed to feel only moments ago now filled him, his butterfly tattoo blazing and dancing over his skin. Muscles bulged and bones vibrated. His claws sharpened.

His mind—remained quiet. Even still, he summoned ice. He'd never needed his strength more, couldn't risk a punishment.

Cold and calculated, he stepped closer to Gillian, and said to William, "She's mine. I would never harm my female."

William lifted a dagger, ready to strike.

"No, William. I mean it." She stepped in front of Puck and stretched out her arms, as if to...shield him? "You can't hurt him."

Oh, yes. She thought to shield him. Something his brother had not done, there at the end.

A part of Puck longed to investigate the source of her protectiveness—desire? Something he could do. Just for a day. Maybe two. Perhaps a week. However long it took to reach Amaranthia. According to the Oracles, he had to tuck Gillian away before dealing with the other key.

Besides, the more time that passed between the bonding ceremony and Puck's negotiations with William, the more the warrior would understand the brevity of his circumstances.

My logic is sound.

"Oh, poppet." William directed a smile full of malevolence at the girl. "I assure you I *can* hurt him."

"You don't understand. He saved me. He's...he's my husband now. We bonded." She licked her lips as she shifted from one bare foot to the other. "Hurting him hurts me. I think." Looking over her shoulder, she met Puck's gaze. "Am I right?"

He nodded.

A mix of shock and fury played over William's features. "The bond. You agreed. Performed the ceremony."

Tears refilled her eyes. "I didn't want to die."

"You have no idea what you've done." The other man stumbled back, as if he'd been kicked. "He's using you for something."

"I know," she replied, and she sounded a little sad, a lot worried.

No, she knew only the lies Puck had fed her.

"You know?" Menace pulsed from William. "Do you also know you belong to him, spirit, soul and body? That the ties can never be broken?"

"I belong to myself," she said. Then her bravado evaporated. "I'm sorry. I just...there's so much I want to do. So much I want to accomplish."

Puck placed a hand on her shoulder, careful not to scratch her with claws ready to rip William to pieces. Just as before, she leaned into his touch; only for a moment, a beautiful stolen moment, before she realized what she'd done and straightened.

A moment was enough.

William noticed.

With a dagger flattened against his heart, he took another step backward. Fury and civility had been stripped from him, revealing hopelessness and blatant desire. Once, Gillian had been a lifeline to him. Did the male now consider her an anchor?

"I can lock him up. I can keep him safe while keeping him away from you," William said. "It's a win-win."

A whimper left her.

"Go ahead. Try," Puck said, before she had a chance to agree. If she turned on him...

Would she?

"Gillian." William used the dagger to point at Puck. "Do you want me to lock him up?"

Her eyes welled with tears once again, the droplets streaming down her cheeks. "No," she said. "I'm sorry. I don't."

Puck released a breath he hadn't known he'd been holding.

"Very well. We'll do this your way." Expression stony, William turned and exited the tree house.

Another whimper left Gillian, her whole body shaking. "What have I done?" With a gut-wrenching sob, she threw herself onto the bed.

The ice split down the middle, but he clung to both sides. He'd met the first part of his objective, saving and bonding to Gillian; the state of her mind should be the least of his worries.

So why did he sit at her side and comb his fingers through the softness of her hair?

When finally she quieted, he found himself asking, "Do you love William?"

"Yes," she admitted with a sniffle. "He's my best friend. Or was. What if he never forgives me?"

He will. The way William had looked at her...proof the male would forgive her for anything. He only required time. But a dark side of Puck didn't want Gillian pinning her hopes on a reconciliation.

Need me. *Want* me. "I will be your best friend now," he said.

"If that's an order..."

Yes! "Merely a suggestion."

Her body went lax, the tension draining from her at last. Because Puck had calmed her...or because Indifference had access to her through the bond?

The thought jolted him. *Could* the demon affect her now?

"Am I immortal?" she asked, rubbing her temples again, as if to ward off an ache. "Or did I make you human?"

"Immortal. I told you, I'm the dominant."

He continued to finger-comb her hair, soon becoming mesmerized by the feel of silk against his flesh. The contrast of dark tresses against the bronze of his skin. The way the strands fluttered over the elegant line of her back.

My wife is sprawled across a bed...

Desire swung through his mind, a wrecking ball to what remained of his frigid resolve. Hunger clawed at him. Between his legs, his erection throbbed.

His mind shouted, *Must brand my woman. Show her—show William. She belongs to me, and only me.*

Yes, yes. Puck would give her great pleasure. He would teach her to love his touch. Soon, she would crave it.

And when I must give her back to the other male?

William would *thank* him for preparing the way.

William will die if he dares to touch what—

A low rumble escaped Puck. When the time came, he would do what needed doing. "We will cement our bond now," he said, his tone thick, almost drugged. *And I will come. Finally!*

Gillian whipped around, her eyes wide with fear. "No. No sex. Not ever. I give you permission to sleep with others. As many others as you want, but never me."

An invisible knife twisted inside his gut. "We are husband and wife. Let me ease your fears."

"I know we're husband and wife, okay," she said, "but I told you I'd never experienced desire, that I never *wanted* to experience desire, and I meant it."

Her willingness to share him...irritated.

"Very well. It shall be as you wish."

She sobbed on, so he continued on, even if she'd stopped listening. "There are things I must do before we leave. You will stay here, and I will ensure your safety." He stepped away from her then, never looking back, and jumped from the tree.

He would take a little time, ice up, reclaiming the reins of control, and figure out what had happened to Indifference.

Afterward, he would meet his next goal. All would be well—or he would make it so.

12

WHAT THE HECK IS WRONG WITH ME?

The moment Puck had left, Gillian had burst into tears? Now different emotions continued to bombard her, making her feel as if she was tripping on a deluge of estrogen, adrenaline and acid. Basically, hysteria played Russian roulette with mania while sadness and happiness engaged in a game of chicken. She was up, she was down, she was round, round, round, and all while strange growls and roars sounded inside her head.

The bond had to be responsible. But how did bonds work, exactly? Puck felt nothing, so it wasn't like she'd inherited his sorrow, rage, guilt, grief and…desire. Had she? The odd prickle had returned, her nipples hardening and the apex of her thighs aching—stronger than before, and this time there was no mis-taking the reason.

Some part of her hungered in a way she'd never before known, not even with William.

When Puck had stood, ready to get down and dirty, a small part of her had *welcomed* the idea of being with him. But of course, fear had swiftly overshadowed everything else.

If he had tried to force the issue…

But he hadn't. He'd saved her life and walked away. Now, she owed him.

He claimed he wanted to feel something—anything. As Gillian thought back over their interactions, her mind no longer clouded by sickness, she began to suspect he'd maybe, possibly… lied to her, that he really didn't want to feel. Because, anytime he'd softened the minutest bit, he'd quickly retreated behind a frigid exterior.

Why would he lie? He had no other reason to marry her. Also, as a teenage runaway, she'd gotten a crash course in deception; her lie-dar would have pinged.

But she thought she might remember him feeling regret at some point? Yes, maybe. If he'd felt it before bonding to her, though, why go through with the ceremony and risk his life? Unless he just wanted to feel *more*?

And, okay, maybe he wasn't to blame for her current predicament. Maybe all brand-new immortals went through this— or her freshly broken heart was unleashing years of turmoil.

Broken, because William demanded she choose between him and the man who'd saved her. But how could she betray Puck, after everything he'd done?

How could she hurt William like that? Would she ever see him again?

What kind of life could she and Puck actually have?

When Puck returned to the tree house, he found Gillian on the bed, exactly where he'd left her.

"Are you still crying?" he demanded as he stuffed her feet into a pair of boots he'd confiscated for her.

"I'm not crying. *You're* crying," she replied, petulant. Red splotches littered her face, and her eyes were swollen.

She mourned the loss of her precious William.

Puck waited for a pang of outrage. Felt nothing but a slight tightening in his chest. Good. Ice surrounded his heart in impenetrable layers.

Surely they were impenetrable.

"Let's go." He yanked her to an upright position.

"Where are we going?"

Ignoring her question, he maneuvered her outside the tree house. Then, using his daggers, he fought through the thick foliage that cluttered their path. He'd already scouted the realm, but had found only two doorways. One led to a fiery realm where certain death awaited while the other led straight back to William's tropical paradise, neither of which put Puck in the direction of Amaranthia.

They returned to the tropical paradise. Though he expected an ambush, William never appeared.

"Where are we going?" Gillian asked again. "Because I'd like to put in a request for Budapest. I have friends there."

"No."

"William mentioned you're having trouble with Torin. I could run interference and—"

"I'm not having trouble with Torin."

"Okay, great. We can—"

"No."

"Hold up." With a huff, she anchored her hands on her hips. "Let's get a few things straight before we continue on."

"Yes. Let's." He turned to meet her gaze—and got pummeled by a sudden and intense tempest of desire.

How? How did she do this to him?

"Well," she prompted, as if *he* were the ringleader of this conversation. She held her head high, even as a blush stole over her cheeks.

Such a sexy blush...how far did it travel?

Control! No need to be nice, he decided. He'd wooed, and he'd won. Now he could be himself.

"Our relationship isn't a democracy, but a Puckocracy. I saved your life, lass. From now on, I speak and you listen. I command, and you obey. Understand?"

She began to draw back, only to catch herself and square her shoulders. "By your logic, you must listen when I speak and obey when I command. I saved your life, too."

Oh, really? "Explain."

"In his wrath, William would have imprisoned you."

"Wrong. At worst, he would have yelled at me." The barest glint of pride compelled him to add, "Besides, I've defeated stronger opponents than William of the Dark."

She ran her tongue over her teeth, the picture of female stubbornness, and beautiful beyond imagining. "No one is stronger than William."

Chest tightening again. "What has the male done to earn your loyalty?"

"For starters, he's never lied to me, never taken advantage of me, even when I tried to force the issue," she said.

Interesting. "How did you try to force the issue?"

The blush intensified. "Never mind that. He spent time with me, making no demands, simply enjoying my company. He protected me when I wouldn't protect myself. He—"

"Enough! He's perfect. I get it." The tightening ebbed, replaced by aching; something dark and barbed razed all that so-called impenetrable ice.

Still Indifference remained quiet.

The bond to Gillian *had* affected the demon. There was no other explanation. But, no matter how Puck had sliced and diced the situation, the answer remained at bay.

What did this mean for him? What did this mean for his wife?

"If you were bonded to William," he found himself saying, "would you be in his bed right now?"

A shudder racked her, the color draining from her cheeks. "No."

That was something, at least.

They resumed their journey and reached the cavern. The next glittery doorway loomed straight ahead.

"I'll go first. Stay directly behind me. And wife? If a fight breaks out, you will run to safety. I will find you."

"I...okay. Yes."

Puck tightened his grip on his daggers before stepping through...

Bitter winds pelted him, like knives against his bare skin. He scanned, spotting ice mountains studded with trees, a gray sky peppered with black clouds heavy with rain. Practically a metaphor for his heart.

So. William's doorway was mobile. Meaning, it opened into a new realm every time someone other than its owner passed through.

Gillian gasped, her little body instantly struck by shivers. As his blood thickened, turning to sludge in his veins, he wrapped an arm around her, offering warmth.

In the distance, an animal howled. Other animals answered in kind. Wildlife. Excellent. Puck could feed his—Gillian.

Time to stop referring to her as *wife*. Soon, he would let her go. Nothing would change his mind.

Her teeth chattered as she said, "Oh, my, ice hell."

As an immortal, she would survive the bleak temperature. But...urgency beleaguered him. *Must get her warm.*

"This way." He ushered her into a nearby thicket of trees, blocking the worst of the wind, then moved toward a pile of furs—

Well. The furs came with bodies. At some point, humans had stumbled through the doorway and died. They were perfectly preserved, and at first glance, uninjured. No bloodstains.

Puck freed the smallest coat and draped the material around Gillian's shoulders. "This should help."

Clutching the lapels tight, she stared up at him, gratitude glinting in those intoxicating eyes. "Thank you."

Will not soften. He offered a stiff nod in acknowledgment.

Between breaths, whenever the mist in front of his face evaporated, he scanned the area to find the yawning mouth of a cave, hidden by sheets of falling snow. Did predators nest within?

After gathering wood and starting a fire, he urged Gillian to sit before the flames and said, "Do not move from this spot."

"Wait. You're leaving me?"

"If I shout, you run."

"But—"

Weapon at the ready, he entered the cave, ending the conversation. A spacious entryway led to a narrow hallway with twists and turns—a hallway that exited into a large room with a bubbling hot spring. Steam curled through the air, carrying the scent of—he sniffed. Cleanliness, no hint of blood or rot.

A pile of bones littered one corner, each bearing fang and claw marks. A predatory animal *had* made its home here, but hadn't returned in ages. No fresh blood.

Puck marched outside but avoided nearing Gillian. If he caught a whiff of poppiberries, he might not gather the will to leave her, and he had to leave her to see to her wants and needs.

"Back with thirty-three seconds to spare," she told him with a relieved smile.

That smile...

His shaft pulsated with desire, and Indifference—there! The demon scrambled through his mind, clawing and slashing, but with far less force than usual.

Where have you been, fiend?

Of course, no answer was forthcoming, only a muted snarl.

"Stay out here," Puck told Gillian. "Do not go inside the cave without me, just in case its owner comes back." If she were cornered... If the rocky walls kept him from hearing her cry for help... "I'll catch our lunch," he ended a little too harshly.

"What? No." She lumbered upright, the cold making her clumsy, and reached for him. Just before contact, she frowned at her hand, as if the cursed thing had dared to act against her will. Dropping her arms to her side, she said, "I don't want to be alone. Please. Stay here with me."

Remain unconcerned. "I'll only be a scream away."

As she stared up at him with wide eyes—gifting him with a view of all the kindling still waiting inside her, ready to catch fire and burn—he began to understand William's dilemma. How the warrior had left her behind in an attempt to better provide for her.

"A scream away," she echoed. "Wow. That is *sooo* comforting. Thank you very much."

"Don't worry. If you're attacked and injured, you'll heal. You're immortal now, remember? And we're bonded, your life tied to mine. If you die, I die. Do you know what that means?"

"No," she whispered.

"That I wouldn't leave you if I thought something catastrophic would happen."

His words—meant to comfort her—only antagonized her. All piss and vinegar, she said, "Is there anything else I should know? Like, am I going to grow a penis now that we're sharing a life?"

He didn't want to admire her spirit, or enjoy how she could be both soft and forceful. No, he didn't. "The only penis you'll have to deal with is mine." And the current conversation had it agonized, razing the demon further. "I'm unsure what other ramifications we'll face."

Her cheeks pinkened, and she opened her mouth to respond.

Unwilling to hear any other arguments on the subject, he left her then, heading into the thickest part of the forest.

Her curses followed him, rousing instincts he'd never before encountered, and he almost turned around. Something inside him demanded he pamper his new wi—Gillian. Demanded he do everything in his power to make her happy every minute of every day.

Foolish! "Why aren't you more upset?" he snapped at Indifference. "Where is my newest punishment?"

Snarl, snarl.

Had the bond weakened the demon? Perhaps even *subdued*

his ability to affect Puck? Possibly. How? He wasn't sure. Could Indifference still weaken him? Maybe.

Truth was, Puck didn't *want* to feel right now. For the first time since his possession, he actually craved the cold nothingness offered by the ice. No desire for Gillian. No longing to ease her fears. No problem letting her go.

He threw himself into the hunt, scouring the land for tracks. There! As he followed a secluded path, he pocketed petals of every winter orchid he came across, intending to use them in the hot spring because—just because.

Finally he reached the source of the tracks. A pack of wild… something. Some kind of oversize rabbit-pig hybrid, with wiry fur and a snout.

The moment they scented him, they erupted into a chorus of screeches and rushed him, as fast as jaguars, their long, sharp teeth glinting in the moonlight.

No time to prepare. Puck dodged the first wave of attack, spun and just started slashing. His daggers cut through throats and bellies, blood spraying, viscera plopping to the ground. The second wave knocked him down, but never had a chance to bite. He fought too diligently.

His injuries would become Gillian's injuries, and the thought of her cut and bleeding…

With a roar to rival those Indifference used to unleash, Puck slashed with more force. His supernatural speed prevented the creatures from ever locking on him. One by one, they succumbed to his blades.

By the time the battle ended, he was drenched in blood and panting, dead bodies piled around him. Darkness had fallen— how long had he left Gillian alone?

He selected two creatures before hurrying back to camp, following the fragrance of poppiberries. No doubt he could be blindfolded and dropped in the middle of nowhere, and still find Gillian without difficulty.

She sat before the fire, alive and well, and relief skittered through him. Relief and awareness, both antagonizing the demon. Moonlight paid her skin glorious tribute, causing her rich brown mane to glisten like silk.

"Lunch and dinner." After dropping the bounty in front of her, he said, "Clean and cook them while I bathe."

Anger contorted her exquisite features. "You were gone *forever*. And oh, yeah, I'm not cleaning and cooking those."

"You aren't hungry?" No matter. She would eat. This, he would force. Physical weakness would not be permitted.

"I'm starved, but—"

He cut her off, saying, "Then clean, cook and eat. Problem solved."

"I don't want to touch a dead animal, and I certainly don't want to eat an animal. I'm a vegetarian."

In Amaranthia, females rarely naysayed their males. Though Puck wouldn't be keeping Gillian, he wouldn't tolerate disobedience, either.

"You'll do what I command," he said, his tone pure menace. "Nothing else is acceptable."

Walking away had served him well last time, so he did it again. In the cave, warm, damp air enveloped him. Water *drip, drip, dripped* from the walls, growing louder the deeper he traveled.

When he reached the spring, he tossed the orchid petals into the water. His new husbandly instinct demanded he go outside, gather Gillian against him and get her settled, keep her safe. Instead, he stripped down to skin and fur and stepped into the liquid. He could use a few minutes away from his tormentor.

He dunked once, twice, rinsing off the blood. Footsteps sounded behind him, followed by a soft feminine whimper, and every muscle in his body tensed.

She'd come to *him*.

Ignoring a new chorus from Indifference, Puck kept his back to her, unsure what he would see on her features. Disgust? Approval? What did he *want* to see?

Nothing!

She stomped her foot, saying, "You are my...my husband. You'll feed me fruits and vegetables. It's your duty."

Face her. Get it over with. See.

Slowly he turned. As his gaze found Gillian, the air in his lungs evaporated and his butterfly tattoo trekked to his lower back. Indignation had flushed her cheeks, and soulful eyes beseeched him—*save me from my troubles.*

No! There would be no saving. From now on, he would keep her at a distance. "I may not care about much of anything, lass, but I live by certain rules. I have to. Rules keep me alive despite my affliction. Keep the people around me alive."

She licked her lips, and though he commanded himself to look away—to look anywhere else—he followed the motion of her tongue, earning more protests from Indifference.

Enough! "The rule you need to memorize?" he continued, his tone harsher. "Eat three meals a day." Lest she think he would cater to her every whim, he added, "Also, you will work or you will starve." Conflicting statements. Or maybe not. Three meals a day—three meals she would work for.

"I told you, I'm a vegetarian. I don't mind working for my food, as long as it's food I can eat."

He narrowed his eyes. "You *can* eat the food I provide, you simply prefer not to. What you don't understand is this. You don't have to like the tasks I give you, but you still have to do them. You don't have to like the food I give you, but you still have to eat it."

Up went her chin. "I'd rather starve to death."

He offered his cruelest smile, a mere twisting of his lips. "That is no longer an option for you."

"But—"

"You'll do as you're told, or you'll suffer."

Fear pulsed from her, and her teeth began to chatter. "You would hurt me?"

"Yes." He would always do what he must to gain what he needed.

She stumbled back, as if she'd been pushed. "I'll hate you."

As Indifference grew louder, the invisible knife returned, twisting in Puck's gut once again. "As you've probably figured out, I won't be bothered in the least."

Different emotions played in her eyes, fear giving way to anger, anger giving way to incredulity. She lifted her chin another notch. "Okay, we're done. I want to go home."

Denial screamed inside his head. "*I'm* your home." For now.

"I want to go to my *old* home."

"No. You'll live in my realm."

As white as morning fog, she grated, "Fine. Tonight I'll gather twigs and search for berries—"

"Twigs are for fire, and there are no berries in this realm."

"What do the rabbits eat, then?"

"They aren't rabbits, lass."

After absorbing his words, she pressed her hands against her midsection, as if she feared losing her last meal, whatever it had been. "Your situation has changed. Shouldn't you change your rules, too?"

Her point...had merit. Also, forcing her to eat meat—and earning her hatred—could slow their journey home. She might fight him every step of the way. But lack of nourishment could slow them down, too.

A compromise could save him a whole lot of trouble.

Very well. Puck waved his fingers, beckoning her. Though she dragged her feet, she obeyed the summons without protest. And, when he patted the stone ledge, she sat without hesitation and crossed her legs.

Silent, motions slow and careful, he removed her boots and socks. The sight of her delicate toes, with her nails painted baby blue, sent his heart thudding against his ribs. Temptation beckoned...and he caved, tracing a fingertip over the sweet little digits. Indifference roared.

At the first brush of skin against skin, Gillian flinched.

Cursing the males who had brought her to this point, he dipped her bare feet into the hot, bubbling water, and she gasped, surprised, before closing her eyes in delight.

One day, he would see that look on her face for another reason entirely...

Puck gnashed his teeth. "Why do you not eat meat? Meat makes you strong."

Her eyelids fluttered apart, her gaze finding his. "When I was younger, my stepbrothers would whisper to me at the dinner table. If we had hamburgers, they asked how long I thought the cow had screamed before it died. If we had chicken, they asked if I imagined baby chicks crying for their momma."

His poor, sweet Gillian. Abused physically, mentally and emotionally.

Remain objective! Refuse to sympathize. "You are far more damaged than I realized." A statement of fact, without any hint of emotion. Good.

"I know," she said, and heaved a full body sigh. "Maybe we could bargain? If you'll find me something to eat...besides animals...I'll do my best to make you feel an emotion, like happiness, or even sadness. That's why you bonded to me, after all. So I would help you feel something, anything."

His lies were coming back to haunt him. He'd wanted to be a project for her, so she would have a reason to spend time with him. If she constantly tried to make him happy...

He would weaken. Maybe. Maybe not.

Why do I not feel you as strongly, fiend?

There was no need to continue the deception. Besides, she'd already made him feel plenty. Pretending he'd felt nothing, so she would continue to try, would make him a liar.

So? He'd been much worse.

He should tell her the truth, and promise to punish her if she attempted to make him feel *anything*. Except...

Despite the danger, he *liked* the idea of Gillian doing everything in her power to make him feel...satisfied. Yes. That.

He would give anything—except his mission—to be "seduced" by his wife. First, he would have to edge her in that direction.

"You'll do your best to make me feel, anyway," he said. *This villain-pretending-to-be-a-romance-novel-hero will make his heroine work for it.* "Bargain or no."

Smug now, she flicked water droplets at him. "Is that something you can force me to do?"

"No," he said, and plastered on a frown meant to intimidate her. She thought she had him by the balls.

Soon, little wife. Soon.

"Then a deal is the only way to guarantee my cooperation. So, if you want me to make you feel something, you'll feed me something other than meat. Oh! And you'll agree to take me home after I succeed. And you won't hurt William. Or Torin. Ever."

He almost snapped, *Do not speak the names of other males.*

Stiff now, he spread her legs and stepped between them. Quick as lightning, she placed her hands on his chest to push him away. He merely flattened his own atop hers and stayed put.

He yearned to ease her fears of intimacy—soon, he reminded himself.

"How will you make me feel an emotion?" he asked. An emotion he would never admit to feeling, forcing her to continue trying.

"I—I'll tell you jokes," she said. "Or sad stories."

Gaze hot on her, he said, "Others have tried to amuse me or make me sad and failed." Truth. Once, Cameron had been determined to force some kind of reaction from him. The attempt hadn't ended well for the keeper of Obsession, who suffered punishment whenever he failed to complete a "mission."

"Were the others able to make you feel anything previously? Anything at all?"

"No."

Smug again, she said, "Then I have an advantage."

"But I want to feel something other than amused, or sad."

She gulped. "I don't... I can't..."

"How else will you do it?" he asked. "Try to make me feel, I mean."

Her breath turned ragged, every inhalation labored. "You'll just have to wait and see, I guess."

"If you fail to amuse me or make me sad by the time we reach my homeland, will you try what *I* suggest?"

As she shifted underneath his hands, debating her response, anticipation held him in a savage vise grip. She knew what he would request—desire.

"Yes, I will." A croak. "*If* you'll feed me fruits and vegetables while we're together and return me to Budapest once I've made you feel...something."

A bright but brief flare of triumph teased him, and he almost grinned. Though he wanted to linger near Gillian, he forced himself to release her and moved to the other side of the spring.

"Very well, lass. You have a deal."

13

Day 3 of Marriage

"IT WAS A TRUTH UNIVERSALLY ACKNOWLEDGED that a married girl in possession of a dagger would eventually stab her husband," Gillian muttered, hurrying to keep up with Puck.

Not too long ago, they'd entered a new realm. A dew-drenched rain forest with waterlogged swamplands and a dense undergrowth of vegetation, all tied together by a thick canopy of foliage overhead. Though pretty, the terrain proved unfriendly. Fire erupted along every body of water, spikes popped from tree trunks whenever she approached and leaves snapped at her with actual fangs.

Each creature she encountered turned out to be a mix of two types of wildlife: a gorilla with the bottom half of a spider; a snake with hind legs; palm-size flies with scorpion stingers.

Not once had Gillian screeched with shock or fear. A true miracle. She'd even managed to keep up with Puck without complaint, huffing and puffing. The only advantage? The scent of peat smoke and lavender remained strong in her nose.

Oh, and she wasn't hungry anymore. At some point, he'd

fed her a delicious meal of berries and plants. Good man...bad man... The jury was still out.

Any time thoughts of William arose, she beat them back with an icy determination she'd never before possessed. Sadness would only slow her down. And if ever the sadness proved stronger than her determination, she focused on Puck; wariness mixed with fascination, overshadowing everything else.

He was shirtless, his strength on spectacular display. A butterfly tattoo would appear on his back only to vanish, then reappear somewhere else. Once, when he'd pivoted to avoid a limb to the face, she'd caught sight of the butterfly on his chest. Sometimes, it even changed colors.

Every Lord of the Underworld bore a similar mark. Or rather, all demon-possessed immortals did. Gillian had never found it sexy.

I still don't. No way, no how. Except...

Can't stop staring, my mouth watering.

At least that odd roaring had stopped blasting through her head.

Another image adorned Puck's chest: a cluster of flowers twined around an azure peacock with a long beak and two circles for feet. One of those circles snaked around his nipple while the other rested in the center of his sternum. Exquisite detailing made the bird look ready to fly out of his skin.

He'd replaced his tattered loincloth with a pair of pants he'd made using the inside lining from the coats they'd found in ice hell. Quite resourceful, her Puck. And somehow more beautiful with every hour that passed.

How hard were those horns? Was his dark skin as cold as his attitude, or as hot as fire? How soft was the fur on his legs?

What would he look like if ever he cared about something, anything? If he ever cared about *her*?

She shivered and shuddered at the same time, simultaneously intrigued and dismayed.

All right. Enough mooning. Time to make him laugh. As

soon as she succeeded, he had to take her home. They had a deal. And she had, what? A few days to get this done? Maybe a week? If they reached his home-realm first, she would fail. If she failed…

He expected Gillian to "try" to seduce him.

The moisture in her mouth dried. *Could* she try? Sex still topped her never-never list. Never acknowledge, never consider. Face it, she wore an imaginary chastity belt with no key.

So why had she dreamed of Puck last night? Dreamed of his lips on hers, his hands roaming over the curves of her body. Why had she *liked* it?

Upon awakening, she'd found her nipples hard, and her core hot, wet and aching.

The bond *must* be responsible. And okay, okay, maybe even Puck himself. He'd slept behind her, his strong arm wrapped around her, offering warmth. The fur on his legs had been soft, so soft; he hadn't complained when she'd rubbed against him. Even better, he hadn't made a pass at her.

But come on! One bizarre night couldn't overcome a lifetime of fear. She *had* to make the man laugh or cry. Something!

"Are these other-realms we're visiting attached to Earth or, like, part of another galaxy?" she asked.

"Both." He offered nothing more.

The ensuing silence scraped her nerves raw. How could he be so cold now? During his bath, he'd smoldered, giving her a look that said *I will do wicked things to you and you'll beg me for more.*

At the time, she'd been unprepared and had freaked out. Now, she kinda wanted to see that look again. He'd just…he'd been so *distant* with her.

He moved a branch out of their path. When a leaf attempted to bite his wrist, he crunched the foliage in his powerful fist.

Gillian watched, her fascination with Puck deepening. He was more confident and commanding than…anyone. Nothing frightened him. No challenge proved too difficult.

For too long, she'd had zero self-esteem and just as many

skills. She'd survived the mean streets of LA and New York with only her wits and bravado.

I think he's becoming my role model.

In many ways, he reminded her of William. He was fearless, headstrong and fierce. In other ways, the two were as different as night and day. William teased. Puck hadn't yet mastered the skill. William loved women of every size, shape and color. Puck seemed to notice no one but Gillian. William treated her like glass. Puck threatened her as easily as breathing.

This morning he'd said, "New rule. You'll do what I say, when I say, without hesitation, or I'll put my hands on you and *make* you do it."

She'd wanted to run away, but had forced herself to stay and snap, "My new rule? Stab you in the gut every time you put your hands on me." Brave words. Meaningless warning.

Lost in thought, she failed to see the rock in her path. Her boot snagged on the protuberance, and she tripped. Puck never tried to help steady her.

"All right. It's time to slow down," she grumbled as she climbed to her feet. "I'm beginning to lag."

"Beginning to? Your perception of time is adorable."

Jerk. He could travel for hours without taking a break. He never seemed to need food and water, a bathroom, or rest. "At this rate, my heart is going to explode."

He decelerated at last, muttering, "Wives require more care and feeding than I realized."

Ouch. "All wives or just me?" she muttered.

"Considering you are my first wife, I can only reference you, now, can't I?"

See! He had no idea how to tease or be teased. The man took everything she said as gospel. And what did he mean, *first* wife? They were bonded. Divorce couldn't be added to the menu—but maybe separation? Either way, he would never have a *second* wife, right?

Okay. Time to get this conversation on the right track.

"What made you laugh before your demon possession?" she asked.

"Sin."

"Sin. As in...wickedness?"

"As in my younger brother."

He had a brother? "Tell me about him."

"No."

Oookay. Short, non-sweet answers were Puck's specialty. Got it. Maybe she wouldn't go with amusement, happiness or even sadness. Maybe she'd go with anger.

Yeah. Anger worked.

"Random gravity check," she said, just before hooking her foot around his ankle.

He stumbled, but managed to avoid a major face-plant. Besides casting her a frown over his shoulder, he gave no outward reaction. "What are you doing, lass?"

"Making you furious. Obviously."

"Why?"

"You want to feel, remember? And, according to Professor Puck before he tried to change his tune, one emotion is as good as any other."

Another glance over his shoulder revealed a deeper-set frown.

Mental note: *subject does not respond to slapstick or subtext.*

Back to sadness. "This isn't the life I envisioned for myself, you know." She pretended to sniffle. "I'm despised by my best friend—" Okay, she didn't have to force the next sniffle. Was William still angry with her? Or had he come to his senses? "—and I'm being rushed to a new home. A new world I know nothing about! The only person I'm familiar with is a man I know nothing about."

"This life is better. Think of it. You are now Gillian Shaw, adventurer."

Yes. Yes, she was. And she—

Wait. Back up just a little. When the Lords of the Underworld married their girlfriends, said girlfriends immediately acquired a new last name: Lord. So, having said "I do"—or whatever Gillian had parroted during their impromptu ceremony—she was now… Gillian Lord? Puck was possessed, so, in theory, he was also a Lord of the Underworld.

Crap! Who was she?

"Don't be offended but—who am I kidding? You're never offended. What's your full name?" she asked.

"Púkinn Neale Brion Connacht the Fourth." His accent, slight though it was, made each syllable sound like a song lyric.

"I guess that makes me Gillian Elizabeth Shaw-Connacht. First of her house. Daughter without parents. Immortal. Wife to Puck. Friend to the Lords of the Underworld. Soon to be defender of the innocent. Bringer of smiles. Former world champion worrier."

Again, no reaction from him.

"My sparkling wit is wasted on you." Wonderful.

"Púkinn is a family name," he continued, as if she hadn't spoken. "The name of every firstborn since the crowning of the first Connacht king."

Well, well. He'd offered information without prompting. Sweet progress.

And he wasn't done. "My brother called me Puck. It means *mischievous spirit*. My people called me Neale, which means *champion*. My army called me Brion, which means *he ascends*. My friends call me Irish, because of the Púca. Well, the Púca and a thousand other reasons. The name Connacht is, apparently, a province in Ireland."

"Púca?" So, in his homeland every name meant something?

"The Púca are shapeshifters in Irish lore. Usually the creatures take the appearance of an animal, and are considered bringers of both good and bad fortune."

"You've *goat* to be *kidding* me," she said, wiggling her brows. "Huh, huh? Come on! That's funny!"

"No," he said. "I'm not kidding. And no, it's not funny.

Are you even trying, lass? Perhaps you want to fail so you'll be forced to do what we both know I'll request."

She gulped. Was he right? Even now, he drew her gaze like a magnet. She drank in all that flawless dark skin, those muscles, the wide breadth of shoulders that led to strong arms and claw-tipped hands.

Turned on by those monstrous qualities? No! *The bond, only the bond.*

"So, your family was named after the Irish?" she asked.

He flicked a glance over his shoulder, his expression blank. "The Irish were named after *us*, a group of Amaranthians who moved to the mortal world. But I'm not a Púca. I'm more like a satyr or faun, I suppose."

"What does *Gillian* mean?"

"Youthful."

"Ugh."

When he flicked her a second glance, as if *she* were a magnet for *him*, her heart rate sped up and warm tingles ignited low in her belly. Her legs went weak, tremors of desire sweeping through her.

She reeled. How had he elicited a response even William had not?

"I answered your questions," Puck said. "Now you will answer mine."

Despite a spike of foreboding, she nodded. "All right."

"In the ice realm, you rubbed against me as you slept."

Groan. Gonna go there, was he? "I don't hear a question."

"What did you dream about?"

A hissing sound registered. A second later, a reptile-thing launched from the trees. Target: Gillian's face. Puck reached out without a hitch in his step, caught the little bugger and tossed it like a baseball.

After swallowing a scream of shock, she scrambled to put her thoughts together. She owed Puck an answer. Lying wasn't an option. She despised lies—the language of her stephorrors.

But there was no way she'd admit the truth, either. He might consider it an invitation.

"I dreamed of...an impossibility," she said. Before he had a chance to respond, she placed the focus on him. "You used past tense with your family, people and army. What happened?"

"I haven't been home in a while." The muscles in his shoulders bunched as he pointed to the distance. "Another doorway is up ahead. This one leads to Amaranthia, the realm of all realms, and the greatest home in the history of homes. Or it will be, soon."

"Wait. We're already at the end of our journey?" Her gaze skipped past him, searching, searching but finding no hint of a doorway. "But... I thought it would take us days or weeks." As soon as they stepped past the doorway, the terms of their bargain changed.

And no, she *wasn't* excited.

"Some things you should know," he said. "Amaranthia has long stretches of desert sand, the occasional oasis, only three major bodies of water, magic and endless wars."

"Magic?" As in, hocus-pocus?

"Time uses a different clock there," he continued, ignoring her question. "A hundred years in Amaranthia can be minutes, hours, days or weeks in the mortal realm. The clock speeds up or slows down depending on the season."

Was he kidding? He had to be kidding.

Tension crackled over every inch of her body. "When I turn one hundred and eighteen years old, my friends might have only lived another couple of hours or days?"

"Exactly," he said with a nod. "I have lived thousands of years moving between realms. You won't know the difference."

"But *they* will." She dug in her heels, saying, "I'm not going to your realm. Take me to Budapest. Or anywhere, as long as I stay on Earth."

He pulled her along, increasing his pace. "Be thankful Amaranthia is not a realm where time flows *backward*. And you already agreed to go. There will be no take backs."

"No, I—"

"My friends are there. Cameron, keeper of Obsession, and Winter, keeper of Selfishness." He tilted his head to the side, and pursed his lips. "She could inadvertently learn the truth, perhaps cause problems."

Was he talking to himself—about Gillian? "What truth?" she demanded. "Cause problems? Why?"

"Very well, I'll do it," he said, still speaking to himself. Then, "I have a confession to make, lass. And when you learn the truth, you will not cause me problems. Understand?"

"What truth?" she repeated. "Tell me."

"Before we married, I told you that I didn't know you belonged to William of the Dark, but I lied."

"Wait. What?" Lied? But her lie-dar had never pinged! And despite her earlier suspicions of this very thing, shock managed to punch her in the gut, stealing her breath. "Lying is the language of my stephorrors."

"I'm nothing like those men. I never harmed you. I ensured you were made healthy...while also putting myself on the right path to achieve my goals." As if he were reading from a script, he said, "Bond. Escort. Return. The bonding is done, the escorting close to an end. Then I'll return. William. War."

"War?" Gillian ears began to ring. "You acted as if you were doing me a favor, you rotten piece of garbage, but you were only helping your *goals*! One of which includes war."

As calm as ever, her insult of no consequence, he said, "I misled you for three reasons. One, I needed to convince you to bond with me. Two, you would have resisted our travels. And three, I need William's help, and you are my bargaining chip."

Even worse! He'd used her against William, a man who'd only ever protected her. Dang it, she should have protected him right back.

"Our deal is off, Puck! Off! Do *you* understand?"

"I understand you are being irrational."

Irrational? "I'm not going to make you laugh or cry, you miserable piece of crap. I'm going to make you *dead*."

A bomb of fury discharged inside her, leaving a trail of devastation in its wake. Her heart melted against her ribs, warping the beat, and the sides of her lungs fused together.

Red dots flickered through her sight line, giving her tunnel vision. *Must destroy Puck!*

Launching onto his back, she hammered her fists into his chest. With each blow, sharp pains consumed *her* chest. Who cared? What was pain?

"Coward! Liar!" The worst insult of them all. "You disgust me." Not good enough. "You *repulse* me." Better.

"You are alive because of me."

"I'm miserable because of you!"

Regret seemed to pulse from him, there and gone in a flash.

An illusion? Too late to tell. With a screech, she switched her aim to his face, and battered his nose. More pain, blood pouring down her mouth and chin. Still she didn't care.

Puck caught her wrists in a bruising grip, effectively ending her tirade. "My news should thrill you. After I drop you off with my friends, I'll return to the mortal realm to recruit William. He'll help me win back my crown, and I'll sever my bond to you."

Deep breath in, deep breath out. *Tamp down your fury. Act as if all is well. When the time comes, strike.*

First, she had to gather information. "What do you mean, you'll sever our bond?" she asked through clenched teeth. "We can officially divorce without dying?"

"That is the plan, aye." He offered no more, just resumed marching forward.

Um, did he not realize plans could be derailed? "Explain," she insisted, trying to hop off his back.

Silent, he readjusted her position and tightened his grip, ensuring every step rubbed her breasts against him. Lance after lance of pleasure tore through her, and she hissed.

"Let me down. Now. I won't fight you anymore." Not yet, anyway.

Perhaps the fear in her voice spurred him on. He wrapped an arm around her waist and swung her around. For a split second, she hung upside down. Then he righted her and placed her on her feet, directly in front of him.

"I will do *anything* to win my crown," he told her. "No deed is too dark. No task too gruesome."

The fire in her veins cooled. "Why?"

"Long ago, my brother betrayed me. He turned a champion into a monster and later killed our father, all to keep the Connacht crown for himself. He is destroying my home, hurting my people, and he must be stopped. I will save the lands and the clans, and I will avenge the wrongs done to me. According to the Oracles, my only hope of success was finding William of the Dark and wedding his woman."

Oracles? And oh, how casually he spoke of Gillian's doom.

"I *deserve* to wear the crown," he added. "I deserve vengeance. And I will be good to my people. I just need William's help."

"You're despicable," she spat.

"I know. But at least you're still alive. I saved you from certain death, something your precious William *wasn't* willing to do."

"Thanks for the reminder, goat man. But to what end?" she snapped. "Sometimes death is preferable to life." Her stephorrors had taught her that lesson very well. "William is smart. He'll know better than to trust you."

Puck hiked his wide shoulders in a shrug—a *shrug*!—and offered no assurances to the contrary.

She had to escape him, had to warn William.

Gillian faked left and darted right, but only made it four steps away before Puck caught her.

"Brace yourself," he said. "We enter Amaranthia in five, four, three, two..."

She attempted to wrench free, but he tightened his hold.

Between one blink and the next, everything changed. The humid heat of the rain forest morphed into cold desert winds, grains of sand pelting her skin. The drop in temperature shocked her system and momentarily rendered her immobile.

Two golden suns shone from a purple-red sky. There were no homes that she could see. No animals, bodies of water or people.

Escape. Now! She spun, shoved Puck out of the way and soared through the invisible doorway they'd just exited—

Nope. She ate sand.

"Where is the doorway?" she screeched. Where had it gone?

Puck peered up at the odd-colored sky, his arms spread, his legs braced apart. Before her eyes, he transformed, the horns vanishing, and the fur on his legs quickly following suit. His cheekbones, once sharp enough to cut glass, softened somewhat. His claws retracted, and the boots and hooves turned to mist, revealing human feet.

Not just beautiful. Utterly exquisite... But also a stranger to her. She'd rather deal with the devil she knew.

He closed his eyes, inhaled...exhaled...as if savoring the moment. Another deception, surely. This horrible male savored nothing.

"How is this possible?" she demanded.

"A right of birth and magic. But it hasn't happened in so long... I thought the ability gone forever."

No way, no how magic controlled his appearance. Absolutely impossible! Except, he'd just gone from beast to chic in less than a blink. Denial was silly. Magic truly existed, and not just the hocus-pocus variety.

One day, too many fantastical things would happen and her mind would break.

A right of birth, he'd said. "So you didn't have horns and hooves as a child?" she asked.

"Not until my possession."

"Can you use magic to morph into other forms, as well?" she asked, wanting—needing—to know the depths of his power.

"Once, but no longer." Just as quickly as Puck had transformed into a normal man, he returned to his beastly form.

"Why don't you stay normal, then?"

A muscle jumped underneath his eye. "You think I don't want to?" He took her hand and—

She gasped. His skin—calloused and warm—*glowed*. Beautiful, sweeping symbols stretched from the tips of his fingers to his wrists. Reminded her of henna markings, except actual jewels seemed to glitter beneath the surface of his skin.

As he kicked onward, dragging her along, she asked, "How are your hands lit up like a Christmas tree?"

"How else? Magic," he repeated.

Magic he could use against her?

Gillian pondered her options. She could try to run—again—but how could she hope to evade him? She had no idea where she was, or what dangers awaited her. Or how many other warriors wielded magic. She could stay with Puck and bide her time, but the clock had officially started. Hours or days for William now equaled one hundred years for her.

Her friend was lost to her forever, wasn't he, despite what Puck had claimed?

Tears spilled from her eyes, leaving hot tracks as they streamed down her cheeks. "If you're gone for even a few days, hundreds of years could pass for me. I'll change, but you won't. *William* won't," she croaked. Time always left some sort of mark. "He might not want me anymore." Who was she kidding? He didn't want her now. He'd washed his hands of her.

The muscles in Puck's hand clenched and unclenched. "Changed or not, he'll want you. No man can look at you and *not* want you."

"*You* don't. You plan to happily, eagerly let me go." *Am I complaining?*

"I will let you go, aye. One day, I'll even remarry. My father announced my betrothal to Princess Alannah of Daingean the same day my brother betrayed me. I'll claim her and open a stable."

Breath wheezed through her nose. "What if she's already married by then? And what's a *stable*?"

"I'll murder her husband." His tone remained casual, unconcerned. "You would call a *stable* a *harem*."

No, she would call it a nightmare. This *is the man I pledged my eternity to?* "I'm sure the two of you and your harem will live happily-ever-after," she snapped.

Two men sprang up from hiding places in the sand, and Gillian reared back, startled. Puck had no reaction whatsoever. Of course.

As daggers glinted in the hands of each assailant, fear crept up her spine. "Run!"

Silent, Puck yanked her to his side.

With a war cry, the men rushed forward. To Puck's credit, he didn't throw her in their path to slow them down. Instead, he shoved her to the ground and spun, his long hair flinging out, razor blades cutting through the eyes of their would-be attackers. As the pair screamed, he unsheathed a dagger and slit their throats.

Both men collapsed in front of her, blood pouring from gaping wounds. A strange black mist rose from the bodies and enveloped Puck. He closed his eyes, inhaling sharply, and the mist disappeared—inside him.

Horrified, Gillian watched as he casually cleaned his razor blades on a dead man's shirt.

What have I done?

14

ANOTHER GOAL MET. PUCK HAD FOUND WILLIAM, bonded to Gillian, and now had her tucked inside Amaranthia.

Next up? Bargaining with William, warring with Sin. *William. War. Divorce.* So close.

Then his goals would shift again. *Remarry. Murder. Unite.*

Puck should celebrate, but he was too busy fighting Gillian's magnetic appeal, calling on centuries of emotional disconnect to keep from pouncing. Why had he insisted she continue to try to make him feel? Foolish!

Indifference kicked up a fuss, only to go quiet between one heartbeat and the next.

Gillian groaned and rubbed her temples. "Ugh! The roaring is back."

He jolted. "Roaring?"

"After we bonded, I heard an animal-like roar in the back of my mind. Then it stopped, but now it's back. I don't know why."

"I do," he grated. So that's what had happened. Indifference now moved between them. Like an unwanted child shuffled between divorced parents. *I'll take Diff on Christmas, if you'll take him on New Year's.*

The fiend must be weakened, though, because he'd had plenty of opportunities to impair both Puck and Gillian, but hadn't. Between them, they'd experienced guilt, envy, sadness, hope. Desire. So much desire. Fury.

Oh, had Gillian indulged in fury. She'd come alive. A warrior ready to be trained for battle. Savagely fearless.

Puck had seen *potential*...and had only wanted her more.

Whenever he'd scented poppiberries—a fragrance innate to her—he'd wanted to taste her. Whenever she'd spoken, he'd longed to whisk her away and keep her forever.

Can't keep her. Must let her go.

But right now, she's mine.

No, no. Enough of that. Better to maintain as much distance as possible, before she burrowed any deeper under his skin. And she *had* burrowed under his skin.

But through it all, he'd remained strong and fierce, never weakening.

He wondered if he'd shared his hidden emotions with Gillian, too. He felt more in control of everything but desire, and her moods kept shifting...

Maybe, maybe not. But either way, her dislike of him was all her own.

He could win her over. And what if he *could* keep her? What had the Oracles said about William, exactly?

Wed the girl who belongs to William of the Dark...she is the key...

Bring your wife to our lands and lead the dark one here after. Only the male who will live or die for the girl has the power to dethrone Sin the Demented.

Only then shall you have all you desire.

But do not forget Ananke's shears, for they are necessary...

There's no other way.

Puck wouldn't live or die for her. *My kingdom for my wife? No!* But William wouldn't live or die for her, either; he would have let *morte ad vitam* kill her. And in the end, he *had* let her go without a fight. But Puck's actions had most likely caused a change…right? By now, William had to understand the treasure he'd lost. He *would* live or die for Gillian. He *would* fight for her.

Puck's hands curled into fists. If William happened to be slain immediately after Sin lost the Connacht crown, well, Puck could have his clan, his realm, and keep the woman… and launch all of Amaranthia into a war with Hades. And the Red Queen. And the Lords of the Underworld. And Gillian herself. She would never forgive him.

"Well?" she asked, and he realized he'd gotten lost in his head. "Why am I hearing roars?"

The truth would frighten her. But shouldn't he warn her?

"Indifference has invaded your mind," he said.

"Indifference…the demon?"

He nodded in confirmation, and she went rigid.

"There's a demon inside me?" she gasped out.

"He's still tied to me, but he's using our bond to hide inside you."

"Get him out! Get him out right now."

He tried, he did, willing the fiend to return but…nothing happened.

Gillian tugged at her hair. "He's not leaving!"

"I don't think you'll weaken with emotion, as I do. Or did," Puck said. "I think our bond weakened *him*."

Ashen, she wrapped her arms around her middle. "Before our bond, you weakened when you felt emotion?"

"Yes." Something he'd never admitted to another, not even his friends, after they'd witnessed an episode. The information could have been used against him. "That's why I stayed away from you so many days after our first meeting. I didn't have the strength to return."

The panic leached from her, leaving her lax. "That's awful. I'm so sorry, Puck."

Sympathy? For him? "Enough talk." What was done was done, and he would not feel guilty. Nope, he wouldn't. "Come." Determined, he pulled her upright and, maintaining hold of her hand, kicked into motion. "The longer I'm here, the longer you'll be parted from William." The words lashed from him, more vehement than a whip.

"You've placed too much importance on my relationship with him. He has hundreds of lovers. Maybe thousands. I'm just a friend. Or rather, I *was*."

"Friends are better than lovers. His desperation to save you from my sinister clutches will only increase. He'll happily bargain for your freedom."

"Okay. Let's say you're right, and I'm special," she said. "Do you really think he'll help you after everything you've done?"

"Yes. Because to him—" *to me?* "—your safety means more than your pride."

"Just…let me go." She sounded deadened now. "This isn't going to end well for you."

Puck stopped, turned and locked gazes with her, only to have his thoughts derail.

Breathtaking. Stunning. Exquisite.

Tantalizing. Titillating.

Mine.

Never mine.

She wore her immortality well.

Earlier, he'd stolen clean clothes for her. As wind gusted, a gauzy white dress clung to one side of her curvaceous body. Around her delicate face danced long locks of hair; as beams of sunlight caressed her, the strands gleamed with different shades of brown: maple, umber and cinnamon.

One touch, and he would—

Must focus. "William might be able to best Sin, but your male will never best me. I am second to none." Puck leaned down, letting the tip of his nose brush against hers. "Perhaps you think little of my worst because, so far, you've only seen my best. Would you like a taste of the terrible things I can do?"

She paled but found the strength to hold her ground. "Go ahead. Show me your worst, then. Make me hate you."

He arched a brow. "You don't already?"

"Not yet, but I'm close."

If she hated him, parting with her would be easier.

Very well. Puck faltered a split second before summoning a new layer of ice, different emotions fading from his awareness. First hope, then any semblance of tenderness. Finally, desire.

Merciless, he lifted his arm and extended his index finger. Best Gillian learned how things would be between them. Threaten his victory in any way and suffer the consequences.

"Oh no. Not the finger," she said, her tone as dry as the sand dunes.

With his free hand, he made a fist around the finger—and snapped the bone like a twig.

Gillian screamed and clutched her injured hand to her chest. Her knees buckled, and she fell, agony twisting her features, every breath now labored.

After a few minutes of pain, however, the wound healed, thanks to Puck's age and experience.

She glared up at him. "Congratulations," she said, her tone flat once again. "You exceeded my expectations. You have my hate, and bonus, you have my mistrust. You're a sociopath willing to break a girl's bone to make a point."

"You're right. I am a sociopath. I feel nothing, want nothing."

"Ice, baby, ice," she muttered.

Could she feel the ice through the bond? "I see we understand each other," he said.

"Want to know what makes this whole thing even more awful? Sometimes you're actually kind of warm."

Him? *Warm?*

Shockingly—yes. Deep inside, a tendril of heat stirred, an instinct to protect her, never hurt her.

But still he said, "If you delay me, I'll break another bone. If you run from me, I'll cut out one of my organs every minute until you return. Because of our bond, you will lose the organs, too. And just so you know, I never make threats. I make promises. I always follow through."

She sputtered for a response.

Wasting time. When he marched forward, she had a choice: pursue him or delay him and suffer the consequences.

Though reluctant, she pursued.

The warmth continued to stir, until relief and guilt seeped through the ice. He found himself saying, "You'll be well occupied while I'm gone. You'll cook, clean and sew, like all the other females in Amaranthia."

"Are we rich?" she demanded.

"Very much so. Why?"

"Then I'll be *paying* someone to cook, clean and sew for me. And when we get that divorce—because we will—I'll be taking half of your belongings with me."

Now he wanted to smile with genuine amusement? Impossible. "In Amaranthia, the doorways between realms constantly move. I told my men to wait with our transportation at a fixed location, every day, until my return, no matter how much time passed."

"How wonderful for you."

"You should rejoice. As soon as we reach camp, you'll be rid of me. For a little while, at least."

The barest hint of eagerness vibrated along their bond, and he jolted. Her eagerness? His impatience?

Irritation sparked. For centuries, he'd had no problem ignoring, burying and erasing emotions. Now he had to battle his own—and hers?

"Well. What are you waiting for?" Gillian jutted her chin. "Put a little pep in your step, Pucky, and try to keep up."

Marching around Puck, doing her best to ignore the demonic snarls in the back of her mind, Gillian struggled to maintain her composure. Within the hour, her husband—*loathe that word!*—would exit the realm and leave her behind. He would find William and strike some kind of bargain. Maybe. *If* William felt like bargaining.

If not, Puck would try to *make* William feel like bargaining. Ruthless man!

He expected William to go to war with his brother, Sin. If Puck couldn't defeat him, how could William? Her friend would get hurt.

Somehow, she had to follow Puck out of Amaranthia, without getting caught, and warn William.

"Tell me more about the realm," she said. The more she knew, the better. "And about magic."

To her surprise, Puck complied. "Our ancestors claim three Oracles created Amaranthia as a safe haven for magic-wielders."

"Even safe havens can become a war zone, eh?"

He shrugged. "Kill a man, acquire his magic. For centuries, clans have been slaughtered, just so their magic could be stolen. Greed rules too many hearts."

To acquire magic of her own, she'd have to commit murder? Ugh.

They crested another sand dune, two men and three camels coming into view. Had to be their ride to camp! She picked up the pace. Except, when she stood before the animals, she gasped.

The animals were some kind of cross between camel, rhinoceros and something beyond hideous and utterly frightening, with a row of horns that went from its forehead, along the back of its skull, to its nape. It also had a mouthful of saber teeth and a blend of fur and scales, layered in shades of black and white, like a zebra.

One of the creatures disliked her on sight—the one she was supposed to ride. It bucked her off the first time Puck seated her. Spitting sand, Gillian stood.

"Stop playing around," he commanded. All liquid grace and masculine assurance, he settled atop the creature's back and held out his hand.

Close proximity to Puck the Liar while sitting on a monster-dinosaur-thing? *Welcome to my nightmare*. But even though she would rather run away screaming, she accepted his help without protest. Why fight the inevitable?

He lifted her with ease, his bicep barely flexing, and she refused, absolutely refused, to be impressed. She expected to ride behind him. The women of A-man-ranneth-thine-life-ia who cooked, cleaned and sewed clearly had their place, after all. But Puck placed her in front of him, surprising her.

"What is this thing, anyway?" she grumbled.

"A chimera." One muscular, bronzed arm wrapped around her waist to prevent another spill, and she tensed. If he copped a feel...

She might melt. Her body was already tingling, warming. But then she would erupt in fury! Absolutely. Probably.

She could not, would not, desire this man. No way, no how.

As his other arm stretched forward, she prepared for battle... but his fingers bypassed her entirely to tangle in the creature's mane, sending the chimera into a gallop.

A screech of shock split her lips as her surroundings blurred. She clung to Puck's arm, pretty sure her nails were slicing and dicing skin and muscle. A necessity as well as a sadistic pleasure, despite the sting in her own arm.

They traveled at warp speed, reaching camp only a few minutes later. Puck hopped down, lifted her and set her on her feet. Nausea churned in her stomach. Light-headed, she swayed...fell.

Her jerk of a temporary husband watched, once again not even trying to help her.

Buck up. He's leaving, and you're following. You'll beat him at his own game.

The chimera trotted off, purposely stomping on Gillian's hand. As bones snapped, she screamed. Sharp pains shot up her arm and pooled in her shoulder.

Puck's hand broke, too, but his emotionless expression never wavered.

When the worst of the pain subsided, she whimpered and clutched the new injury against her chest. But she didn't cry. She would shed no more tears for her treatment here.

You can break my bones, but you won't break my spirit.

"You're already healing. Shake off the pain and stand. Seeing you on the ground makes me—" His eyes narrowed, and he bared his teeth. "Stand. Now."

Seeing her like this made him…what? Feel guilty for his poor treatment of her?

Not so icy after all, huh. "I'm fine, thanks. And oh yeah. Screw you," she muttered, remaining in place as she looked around a thriving village.

Tents abounded, intermixed with mud huts. Multiple fire pits added a waft of heat to the wind, the flames licking the skinned animals currently anchored to spits. Children played in every direction. Males were shirtless, wearing only sheepskin breeches. Females wore drab scarves from head to knee.

Everyone had one thing in common. They were staring at her.

"This clan is made of outcasts," Puck explained, offering no further rebuke for her disobedience. A small mercy. "They value strength above all else and despise weakness."

So, basically, Gillian was the most despised girl in town already? *Go me.*

"Irish!" a female voice announced. "About time you returned. I'd started to think you'd died."

The growing crowd parted, revealing a twenty-something man and woman. And good gracious, they were gorgeous. Both had the most amazing lavender eyes rimmed with silver, hair the color of melted pennies and skin a few shades lighter. They had to be siblings.

Unlike the other males in the camp, this one wore a black T-shirt that read Winter Is Coming and a pair of jeans. Unlike the other women, this one wore a leather crop top connected by metal mesh to a matching miniskirt with pleats. The outfit was both sexy and protective.

Both the male and female had short swords strapped to their backs, the hilts rising over their shoulders.

They are magnificent, and I'm cowering on the ground.

Fast as she could, Gillian lumbered to her feet.

"This is Cameron, keeper of Obsession, and his sister, Winter, keeper of Selfishness," Puck said. "The friends I told you about. My *only* friends. Cameron, Winter, this is my…wife."

Gillian gulped. Obsession and Selfishness *on top of* Indifference—who was now expressing his displeasure with growls. Just peachy.

"Hello," she said, pushing the word past the barbed lump in her throat. Meeting new people had always been tough for her, and her association with Puck hadn't helped. Now she would forever wonder who plotted ways to take advantage of her.

Cameron looked her up and down and smiled a wicked smile. "Hello, beauty."

Winter looked her up and down as well, and promptly decided she wasn't worthy of a greeting. Her gaze returned to Puck. "Words cannot describe how much I missed you. But numbers can. Three out of ten. You promised me gold and jewels. *I want my gold and jewels.* And magic. Yeah, I'd like a little magic. Or a lot. Definitely a lot."

Ignoring her, Puck gave Gillian a gentle push in Cameron's direction. *At least I'm not the only one to receive the silent treatment.*

"I'm off to recruit William," he said to the other male. "I trust you're obsessed with Gillian's protection, now that you've met her? She is weak and fragile, aye, but she is also the key to my victory, and your sister's gold and jewels."

"Obsessed and impressed," Cameron said, his smile spreading.

Puck stiffened and ran his tongue over his teeth. "Gillian isn't to be touched. By anyone. Ever."

Well, well. The man had some scruples. Another small mercy.

Too little, too late.

And what did he mean, weak and fragile? Since she'd met him, she'd done her best to cope, adjust and thrive, despite the many obstacles.

"If, at any time, she desires a male," Puck added, his tone sharpening, "kill him. Do not hesitate."

"You can't be serious," she said, gaping at him.

Cameron rubbed his hands together, as if excited by the prospect. "Consider it done."

"What about me? Does no one want to kill the men I desire? Also," Winter added, deigning to focus on Gillian, "you're immortal now, which means your time here is your origin story. Every story needs a villain." She raised her hand. "I volunteer."

"Accepted," she replied, because she wouldn't be here long. She'd be right on Puck's heels. "Spoiler alert. Villains always die in the end."

Puck took her by the shoulders, ensuring she faced him, and stared down at her, his expression blank. When she refused to glance away first, he moved his hand into her hair and fisted the strands at her nape.

Just like that. Breath hitched in her lungs—and heated. She blamed their marriage bond. Oh, how she detested it!

"I'm going to tell you something my father told me when I was young," he said, his grip tightening. "If anyone harms you, kill first and ask questions later."

"*You* harmed me."

"You are an extension of me, which means I simply hurt myself." Leaning down, he brushed the tip of his nose against hers. "Try not to miss me, lass. I'll only be gone a hundred years, maybe two. Hardly a blip."

Jerk. "Yes, but only a few minutes, days or weeks will pass for you."

"You can use the time to strengthen. Train, learn how to fight."

He expected her to spend hundreds years without friends

or family, living in unfamiliar terrain, training? He wasn't just indifferent; he was also insane.

"What if I'm killed while you're gone?" The words rushed from her. "You'll die, too. Just…take me with you and oversee my protection yourself." That way, she wouldn't have to risk following him on her own.

"You won't be killed, I promise. And I will be…annoyed if you are harmed."

Though his voice remained monotone, he somehow made the word *annoyed* sound like a threat to destroy the entire realm. "Annoyed? How terrible for you."

"You'll be well-guarded here," he continued, tilting his head to the side. "I promise."

"First of all, your promises mean nothing to me."

He shrugged. "That doesn't sound like a *me* problem."

Do not lash out. Do not dare lash out. "Second," she continued, "well-guarded things get boosted all the time and—"

"Enough." The lights in his irises brightened as he cupped her jaw and traced his thumbs over her cheeks. "I'm going to kiss you goodbye, wife. The barest tasting."

What! Her heartbeat stuttered against her ribs, her blood flashing white-hot in an instant. Tingles tantalized her breasts, and the now aching place between her legs. After everything he'd done, he expected a make-out session in front of other people?

"Why?" *Really? I ask him why? I don't tell him to get bent?*

Indifference tap-danced across her mind, sharp claws slicing through gray matter. She cringed, even whimpered.

"Focus on me, not the fiend," Puck said, perhaps recognizing the signs of the demon's interference.

She obeyed, peering up at him, this man who'd become her husband, who'd been at times unnecessarily cruel and at others surprisingly kind. How could she even consider kissing him? She didn't know him, not really, and definitely didn't trust him.

Despite those moments of kindness, he was a liar. He had

ice for a heart. Or maybe that was why she *should* kiss him.
He wouldn't get overly excited. He might not even get turned
on. Which was what she wanted, kind of. But kind of…not.

Great! There were two Gillians again.

"You will remember me—*think of me*—while I'm gone," he
said, and he wasn't asking a question but issuing a command.

Protest. Now. Before you start to panic, and the demon reacts worse.
But…the part of her who wanted him turned on also wanted
him to think of *her* while he was gone. Wanted him know what
he'd lost the moment he'd used her.

Oh, really? What did he lose? Tell me.

Shut up.

Spiteful Gillian won. She rose to her tiptoes, saying, "Kiss
me, then. I dare you."

He met her halfway, and slanted his lips over hers. Erotic
flicks of his tongue coaxed more tingles to the surface and
fanned the flames of desire. Hot, so wonderfully hot. The aches
magnified as he thrust with more force, his divine taste and
ever-increasing frenzied pace dragging a moan of surrender
from deep inside her. A sound he utterly devoured, as if he'd
never been so starved—or enjoyed a tastier meal.

His skill, expert. His ruthlessness, on full display.

Puck didn't bother to learn her, or explore her nuances; he
took, gave and demanded…everything, his tongue dominating
hers with a promise of untold riches. She was helpless to resist.

The demon quieted, her mind suddenly her own, different
thoughts rabbling into her awareness, one after the other. This
kiss was a horrible idea. This kiss was a wonderful idea. She'd
had enough. She'd never have enough. This might help her.
This would probably hurt her. Enslave her. Free her at last.
This was nothing and everything.

This was…delicious.

Then her thoughts quieted as well, her body taking charge.
Her nipples puckered against her dress, as if seeking Puck's attention, and her belly quivered. Liquid heat soaked her pant-

ies, and her limbs trembled, hunger gnawing at her. Hunger that only intensified as his flavor registered: the most potent champagne.

More!

Just as she leaned into him, softening, flattening her hands on his pecs, he clasped her wrists, stopping her from making contact, and lifted his head.

"Do not touch my peacock tattoo, lass." The roughness of his tone thrilled her. "Not now, not ever. It's off-limits."

Gillian blinked back into focus, her mind forced to play catch up. Off-limits? Why?

Who cared? *Breathe.* She'd just experienced her very first kiss. No, she'd just experienced her very first kiss, *and she hadn't panicked.* Even better, she'd wanted—and given—pleasure.

I kissed a monster, and I liked it.

She should be beyond disgusted with herself. And Puck... he should be indifferent. Was he?

Did she want him to be?

"The demon returned to you?" she asked, embarrassed by the huskiness of her voice.

He nodded, his gaze hot on her, his pupils enlarged. "You were right before. Our deal is off. But we will make a new one. When I return—I will make *you* want *me.*"

Before she could respond, he chucked her on the chin, turned and walked away.

What are you doing, just standing here mooning? Follow him! Right. Jolting into motion, Gillian took a step forward, but Winter and Cameron moved into her path, stopping her. Oh... crap. She was going to be stuck here, wasn't she?

While her plans crashed around her, Puck continued onward like a prisoner finally released from prison, never once glancing back.

Winter twirled a dagger. "You ready to have fun, little girl? Because I am."

15

A PRICKLE OF URGENCY BESET PUCK. TO SHAKE IT, he would have to summon a fresh layer of ice, something he wasn't currently willing to do. There was no need. Except for a handful of hour-long silences, Indifference remained in his head, emitting a constant stream of noise, but never weakening him—and considering all the other things he was feeling, he should have weakened. The demon *had* lost the ability to act against him.

So why wasn't he overjoyed?

Because...just because! After weeks of traveling outside of Amaranthia—weeks away from Gillian and days in Budapest—he'd made no progress unearthing William's location.

How much time had passed for Gillian, Cameron and Winter? And Sin, who continued to rule the Connachts unchallenged? About three hundred years would be his guess.

Had Gillian forgiven Puck for breaking her wee finger?

The memory of his actions sickened him. How could he have done such a thing?

Despite the few weeks—for him—their bond had strengthened as if they'd been together for centuries. Which they had, according to *her* timetable. He felt as if he'd known her forever. As if he'd missed her forever. As if he'd craved her forever.

He wanted her back. *Now.*

How had Gillian changed? What was she like? Still sweet… or hardened? What trials had she faced without his aid and protection?

Raw instinct burned inside him, birthing a need to commit violence against anyone who had harmed her.

During the first few hours outside of Amaranthia, many years had passed for Gillian. During that time, she had suffered terrible injuries. He knew, because he'd suffered the injuries with her. One second he'd been fine, the next multiple bones had snapped for no apparent reason. Bruises had formed and vanished. Twice his hands had fallen off his wrists. Talk about awkward. Once, he'd lost a foot. However, between one heartbeat and the next, his body had grown new appendages.

What had happened to her? Why hadn't Cameron or Winter saved her from pain?

Along with the biggies, he also worried about the small things. Had Gillian gotten enough rest? Had she eaten properly? Did she laugh anymore? Had the kindling been wiped from her eyes? Or had she finally caught fire and burned?

Rage rose up strong, a battering ram to his calm. Why had he not made a clean break with her, with no promises lingering between them? Why had he insisted on a new deal? Why had he kissed her?

The woman had him twisted up, that kiss playing on constant repeat inside his head. The taste of her as decadent as her scent, all poppiberries and seduction. The feel of her, all softness and heat.

Did she hate him still, or had the kiss won her over?

Guilt pricked him. *Of course* she still hated him. He'd tricked, tortured, abandoned and lied to her.

One side of him said: *Will make it up to her as soon as I return.*

The other replied: *Oh, really? I'll make it up to her, with William at my side?*

Every muscle in Puck's body knotted, the rage gaining new ground. The thought of Gillian and William together again…

I think I'd rather pardon Sin for his crime against me.

Common sense balked. *Would you? Because that is your only other option. Allowing your treacherous brother to destroy your clan, and your realm.*

SNARL.

Inhale, exhale. Puck scoured a hand down his face. *You are nothing but a nuisance, fiend.*

And Puck had better things to do than listen to a tantrum. Or debate the wisdom of his plan. A short while ago, he'd uncovered a lead to William's whereabouts.

Rumors stated the male had been spending quality time in downtown Oklahoma City. Gossip meant to send Puck straight into an ambush? Possibly. Going to stop him? No.

He stole a cell phone and, just as Cameron and Winter had taught him, posted an ad on Immortal Wanted, a site on the dark *dark* web.

Needed: one flash from Budapest to Oklahoma City.

Payment: Amaranthian gold.

He added his exact coordinates and waited.

Posting the ad cost just as much as the ride itself, but the benefits far outweighed the expense. If someone accepted a job and harmed the person who'd hired him, that someone would be hunted down and executed by the site's owner—Rathbone the Only, one of nine kings of the underworld.

Puck had never met Rathbone, but had only ever heard others speak of him in hushed tones.

On the opposite end of the spectrum, if someone posted a job and harmed the person he'd hired, or even failed to pay, *that* someone would be hunted down and executed.

Only minutes later, his ride appeared. A tall, muscular male with long black hair, eyes like diamonds and skin as dark and red as blood. Power radiated from him. He was shirtless, his bottom half covered by black leather pants. From the neck down, he had hundreds of tattoos, every image the same. A closed eye.

"You the one looking for a ride?" the newcomer asked. He had a deep, raspy voice.

"I am."

Those diamond eyes glittered with wicked amusement as he held out a hand. "I'm nothing if not cooperative…when I'm not killing in cold blood."

A threat? Good luck with that.

Puck placed a gold coin in the center of the male's palm, expecting the male to wrap an arm around him; most immortals needed to touch the one they transported. Not this one. Budapest vanished, an abandoned alleyway, with multiple Dumpsters, taking its place.

The other man was gone.

A small cat with matted fur and scars approached Puck and twined between his feet, rubbing against his legs.

"Nice doing business with you," he muttered.

Intense heat enveloped him, the air humid, oppressive. Sweat beaded on his skin as he checked his weapons, just in case his escort had decided to disappear with them. Two daggers, two semiautomatics. Excellent.

Remaining in the shadows, Puck studied the milieu. Old buildings with red brick interspersed with the occasional brownstone. Multiple alleyways branching off the one he'd been transported to. A few pedestrians meandering along the sidewalks.

Left with no other recourse, Puck stalked forward, revealing his presence to the humans. Something he'd never done in the past—without killing everyone who'd spotted him. Today, there was no reason to hide his identity and every reason to reveal it.

People stared. Some even whipped out their phones to take

his picture. No one screamed, or ran away. Interesting. Perhaps they assumed he played dress up?

Let word of his presence spread. Let William come to him.

A sudden crackle of energy charged the air, stopping him. A split second later, the entire sky blackened, as if the sun had flashed to another realm. Humans gasped and shouted for help, only to be drowned out as anguished cries spilled from the sky: wails of pain and grief.

What the hell?

Before he had a chance to reason out what had happened, the sun shone from a baby blue sky once again. The chorus quieted, even as fearful humans hurried from the area.

The answer came to Puck in an instant, as he'd witnessed this type of event before. Sent Ones—winged demon assassins—lived in the third level of the heavens, the level closest to the human realm. One of their leaders had died.

Not my problem.

Focus. Puck entered the first hotel he encountered, leaving his cat-shadow outside. He would hole up in a room, and wait for William's arrival.

Would the male show up?

The employees gave Puck twice-overs, and guests gave him the side-eye, but no one asked any questions. After acquiring a key, he dismissed the bellhop and took the stairs, stopping on every floor to ensure no exits were blocked.

In his room, he found a king-size bed with a white comforter, a desk, dresser, television and coffee table. He moved everything to a single corner and—

Boom!

Hinges on the front door shattered. Wood split. In the center of the chaos stood William of the Dark. At his feet, the cat—the smiling cat. Had the feline led William to Puck? Possibly. Even probably. How else would William have arrived so quickly?

Puck did a quick visual survey. William held a small gold

torc but had no discernible weapons. Of course, if he was anything like Puck, his body was weapon enough.

Silence stretched between them as they took each other's
measure. During their last meeting, William had sported red
eyes. Not so today. The blue had returned.

Did eye color matter to Gillian? Did she prefer—

Fool! Her preferences had no bearing on the situation.

"You may go," William said.

"Go?" Puck popped his knuckles. "Why would I—"

"Not you."

The cat began to grow, and grow. Shapeshifter, Puck realized. Fur disappeared, replaced by red skin, revealing the immortal who'd flashed him to Oklahoma.

Red took a bow. "My pleasure doing business with you,
Puck. And you as well, William. Though I'd love to stay and
witness the carnage that comes next, I'm needed in the heavens. Where there's turmoil, there's me." He tipped an invisible
hat before flashing away.

Turmoil in the heavens. Knew it. "The Sent Ones," Puck said.
"Something happened."

"You shouldn't concern yourself with them. Only yourself."
William spoke at a normal volume, but menace laced every
word. "Tell me where Gillian is, or I'll turn your testicles into
tiny disco balls."

Resentment flared, spurring Indifference into a frenzied
pace across his mind. Back and forth, back and forth. "She is
safe. Right now, that's all you need to know."

Ding, ding, ding. With a maddened war cry, William launched
at Puck.

As they plummeted to the floor, the other male grabbed
hold of his wrist and anchored the gold band around it. An
unexpected action, and odd development. The metal pulsed
with magic.

Impact. Air gusted from his lungs, the floor underneath
him, his opponent on top of him. William rose to his knees

and whaled, his fists raining down furious blows. Puck's brain rattled against skull. Pain. Dizziness.

The rage sharpened, Indifference clawing at his mind harder, faster. *Steady. Do not give in.* Though the demon no longer had the power to weaken him, emotion would drive him to kill the male he needed.

Puck blocked the next crushing blow. Of course, unwilling to give up, William threw a punch with his free hand.

Blocking it, too, Puck said, "Think. You can't hurt me without hurting Gillian."

"Wrong." The male smiled a cold, calculating smile, all pearly whites and malice. "Did you think I'd twiddle my thumbs after you bonded to *my* woman? I learned everything I could about you, *as well as* marriage bonds. You were betrayed by your brother, your kingdom stolen. Ring any bells? Oh, and I made you a gift." He motioned to the gold wrist cuff with a tilt of his chin.

Symbols had been carved into the metal. "What kind of magic is it?" Puck asked.

"What you call magic, I call power. As the son of Hades, I have power—in spades. Now, your pain will remain your own. And I know what you're thinking. *Wow, that Willy sure is the total package.* Beauty, brawn and brains. You are right, but you are also a dead man walking." Punch, punch. "I cannot be beaten."

Puck caught his fists once again and offered a cold smile of his own. "Despite your power, you cannot sever my bond to Gillian. It's alive and well, tying my life to hers, and there's nothing you can do about it."

Fury glittered in those ocean-water blues. "Don't worry. I'm not going to kill you, Pucker. Oh, no. You're going to suffer for *centuries.*" He punctuated every word with a new punch.

Puck endured the newest round of hammering fists without fighting back, all the while working his legs between their bodies. Success. He grabbed the male by the arms and yanked, at the same time kicking him overhead. William soared across the room and slammed into the wall, cracking the plaster from ceiling to floor.

Dust plumed the air. Muscles rippled with raw power as Puck stood, and warm blood dripped from his mouth. He would unsheathe a dagger and hack through William's—

No! *Must not kill.*

"Here's what is going to happen," he said, his harsh voice barely recognizable. "You're going to raise an army to help me dethrone my brother and reclaim my kingdom. Afterward, I will use the shears of Ananke to sever my bond to Gillian. She will be free of me, once and for all."

And I will not miss her, even for a second.

"I don't need an army. I *am* an army." Teeth bared, William straightened and rotated the bones in his neck. "Where is she? Did you bed her?"

"I have not." He told himself to shut up. But his lips parted, allowing a single word to escape. "Yet."

Growling, William took a step forward.

"Only after we've dethroned my brother," Puck continued, "will I use the shears." The promise tasted foul, but he refused to negate it. "Agree to my terms. Now."

"Instead, I think I'll steal the shears and sever the bond myself. Then I'll sever your twig and berries, and stuff the little trio down your throat. As an appetizer. After all those centuries of suffering I mentioned, I might grow sick and tired of hearing you beg for mercy, so finally I'll consider killing you. *Then* I'll conquer your kingdom, just for grins and giggles."

Yawn. "Trust me when I say you won't find the shears without me." He'd taken extreme precautions to hide them. "So. Either you agree to help me within the next five seconds, or I return to Gillian and bed her for the first time. And second... third." Anticipation consumed him, setting him on edge. "Do you like the idea of her splayed across my bed, naked, her dark hair spilling over my pillow, her legs spread wide for me, and me alone?" *Because I do.*

He expected another explosion from William.

Instead, the male arched a dark brow and raked his gaze over Puck. "Are you sure she'll welcome you? Nice legs. Shave much?"

"Why would I shave, when my wife loves to rub against me and use me for warmth? Four seconds."

Nostrils flared, William circled him. "Do you have a pedigree? Nah. You're a mutt, guaranteed. Do you keep your hooves off the bed or do you not care about dirtying the sheets?"

Head high. Shoulders back. "Sheets can be cleaned. My mind cannot. Oh, the things I long to do to my wife… Three."

Rigid, William said, "Shall I turn around and let you sniff my ass?" He *tsked-tsked.* "If the bed is a rockin', don't come a-knockin'—because you're probably under it, chewing on a shoe, *amirite.*"

"Or giving my wife her next dozen orgasms. Two."

Nostrils flared. "Be honest. Is that a furbaby in your pants, or are you just happy to see me?"

"That is all me, and I can hardly wait to gift every throbbing inch to my wife. One."

William huffed and puffed, but offered no agreement.

"Very well. I'll mark plan A as unsuccessful." He would return to Amaranthia and proceed without his other key. What else could he do?

Cameron and Winter would aid him. They'd killed some of the biggest baddies in "mythology."

First problem: Cameron was too easily distracted by trivial obsessions.

Second: Winter would betray *anyone* to appease her selfish nature.

Outcome: the siblings might cause more harm than good.

And these are the ones you left in charge of Gillian's care?

Pressing his tongue to the roof of his mouth, Puck ignored the demon's newest round of roars and stalked toward the door.

"What? No goodbye?" William stepped in his path. "Perhaps I'll help your *brother* defeat *you*."

One second Puck intended to leave, the next he had the other male pressed against the wall, his fingers wrapped around his neck. The remaining plaster crumbled.

"Perhaps I'll kill you," he stated. Gillian would cry, but tears could be dried. Broken hearts could be mended.

William kicked his outside leg up, up and hooked his ankle over Puck's wrist. Then he brought his leg down, hard. It happened in less than a blink, but Puck's thoughts were *faster*. He knew he had a choice. Release his opponent and emerge unscathed, or hold on and deal with a broken arm.

Finally, an easy decision to make. *I'll take option B.*

The bone in his forearm snapped, pain searing him. He welcomed it, and maintained his iron grip. At the same time, he dropped into a crouch, forcing William to do the same, and used his free hand to press multiple razors against the immortal's throat.

William laughed, the sound half wild, half insane. "You want her for your own, don't you, and think she wants you back? Well, too bad. You'll never have her. Bonds make couples think they desire each other, meaning any desire she has for you is false. After all, what woman in her right mind would ever willingly choose someone like you? Those horns..." He shuddered.

"Your mother *loved* my horns last night. Polished them up real nice."

Another wild, insane laugh from William before he sobered. "During my search for information, I learned I am somehow the key to your success. You can't dethrone Sin without me. So, if you want your brother out of the way, you will swear an unbreakable blood oath to cut your tie to Gillian the moment I present you with the Connacht crown."

He'd...won? This was it. The moment Puck had schemed and fought for. He opened his mouth to agree but, with a surprising amount of bite, said, "I'll accept your terms if you'll accept mine. While we're in my home-realm, you will not touch Gillian."

The statement registered in his mind, and he jolted. What he didn't do? Negate it.

"I'll touch her when and where I please," William snapped.

Puck unveiled another cold smile—a promise of pain. "Then we do not have a deal."

"You won't walk away from vengeance against Sin. You won't abandon your people to a life of fear and torment."

"I can. I will. You forget who I am." He turned on his heel with every intention of jumping out the window. Sometimes he despised Indifference for shaping him this way; other times, he reveled in his ability to compartmentalize.

Today, he reveled. *Ice, baby, ice.*

"Fine," William snarled. "I've waited this long, I can wait a little longer. I won't attempt to seduce her. If she attempts to seduce me, however..."

Teeth, grinding. Hands, fisting. Puck turned and faced his second key.

Feel nothing, want nothing.

Sirens sounded in the distance. Someone had heard the commotion and called the cops.

If he stuck around much longer, he would face arrest.

He raised his chin. "I accept your terms."

"I'll have your blood oath about the shears." William reached out, yanked a razor from Puck's hair and made an incision in his own wrist.

As soon their blood mixed, as soon as the oath left his mouth, Puck would be forever bound, physically unable to renege.

No other way.

Using the same razor, Puck mimicked the warrior. Blood welled inside the wound as he clasped the other male's hand. "The day we defeat Sin…the day you give the Connacht crown to me and leave my home, never to return, never to strike out at me or my realm or my people in retaliation for deeds I committed…that is the day I will use the shears of Ananke to sever my bond with Gillian Connacht. This I vow."

There. It was done. His course had been set, his future decided.

Any other man would have experienced triumph. Puck nodded, confused by the hollow sensation in his chest.

William stared at him, silent, before returning the nod. "Now we dethrone Sin and win back your kingdom. Let's go."

16

Day 41, AB (After Bond)

GILLIAN FLEW ACROSS THE SAND AND LANDED with a grunt. As she climbed to her feet, knowing she would be kicked in the face if she stayed down, she tried to catch her breath. A nearly impossible task. She spit out a mouthful of blood and maybe even a tooth.

She ran her tongue over her aching gums. Yep. Definitely a tooth. Thanks to her immortality, she'd grow a new one by morning. She knew this beyond a doubt, because she'd already had to regrow four others.

"Rush me again," Winter said. "And be faster, stronger and three hundred percent better at it this time."

Sure, let me get right on that.

"Give me a sec." Gillian cracked the bones in her neck and rotated her shoulders, praying the dizziness in her head would clear.

"In battle, there are no *secs*."

Didn't she know it!

After a failed attempt to follow Puck out of Amaranthia, Gillian had agreed to train for combat. Why not put her hatred for her absentee husband to good use? And really, she couldn't live her dream and fulfill her purpose—helping abused women and children—if she remained weak.

Winter would teach her how to use every weapon available in this primitive sand hell *after* she learned how to fight hand-to-hand. Only one problem. Colonel Winter believed pain was the best motivator.

Every night, Gillian went to bed with fresh breaks and bruises. At least she'd stopped crying herself to sleep.

One day she would be strong and skilled enough to repay the favor.

It was nice to have goals.

"Well?" Winter prompted.

Trying not to broadcast her intentions, Gillian rushed forward, and drew back her elbow. Before she could deliver a punch, Winter swooped around her and kicked her so hard she feared her spine had been snapped. She fell to her hands and knees. No time to rise. Winter straddled her, grabbed her by the hair and wrenched up her chin.

Cool metal pressed against the racing pulse at the base of her neck.

"How can you protect yourself if you can't, you know, protect yourself?" Winter demanded. "I love Puck. Well, not love. He's not me. I like him. He calms me. If you die, he dies. So you can't die. Is your feeble brain beginning to comprehend?"

Gillian didn't enjoy hearing that another woman liked her husband. Because Puck didn't deserve such devotion, of course, and no other reason.

"Do something." Winter pushed the blade deeper, drawing blood. "Don't just passively accept my—"

Gillian erupted, throwing back her head to nail the other woman in the chin. A grunt of pain sounded. Without pause, she spun and punched. Her fist made contact with Winter's nose for the first time ever. Cartilage snapped, and blood poured from her nostrils.

A glorious tide of satisfaction made all of Gillian's aches and pains fade.

She expected Winter to explode into a fit of rage, but finally, shockingly, her trainer looked at her with something akin to pride. "All right. Now we're getting somewhere."

"Bring it," Gillian said between panting breaths. Her sternum burned with every inhalation, and she wondered absently if she'd broken another rib.

And oh, wow, they *were* getting somewhere. The idea of a broken rib wasn't sending her into a tailspin of panic. The thought of more pain wasn't engaging her fight or flight response.

"Um, no. Not today," Winter said. "You look ridiculous with your missing tooth. We'll reconvene tomorrow when the sight of you doesn't make me want to weep for all of womankind." She strode away without striking back, leaving Gillian alone on the crest of the sand dune.

Camp was below, at least fifty eyes on her, all glittering with mirth. Puck's clan of outlaws found her determination to develop combat skills hilarious.

"Suck it," she shouted. Something she'd learned: the men of Amaranthia treated the women deplorably.

Sorry, boys, but one day soon your world is going to change.

Abusers would be punished. Stables would be abolished.

For most of Gillian's life, she'd lived in a cage, held prisoner by fear and misery. While actual walls and locked doors kept women trapped in stables, she imagined the "fillies" felt a similar helplessness and dreamed of freedom.

Must train faster. "Winter," she shouted. "Get your sweet butt back here." From now on, Gillian gave this her all. Nothing held back.

When Puck returned, he would find a much different wife, and a much different realm.

22 years AB

Dear Puck,

Cameron let it slip that you commissioned him to keep a detailed history of everything that happens during your absence. I decided to help him out because (apparently) I need an outlet for my rage. I've started Hulking-out.

See, one second I'm calm. The next I feel as if I'm experiencing the rage of a thousand men combined. I'm able to toss 250-pound losers like they're pebbles.

Weak and fragile, Pucky? I don't think so! Not anymore.

I blame you and your demon. What did you guys do to me?!

During a Hulk-out, only two things are able to stop me. I eventually tire and pass out, or I'm force-fed syrup from a *cuisle mo chroidhe* tree.

As you probably know, harvesting the syrup takes massive amounts of time and energy. The trees are hard to find, and their poisonous bark is a major bummer.

I'm ready for your return. If you're thinking *she wants to show me one of those rages up close and personal*, you're correct. You deserve it. You know you do.

If you're thinking *she's the same girl I left behind, and I can easily intimidate her*, you're wrong. Over the years I've been punched, kicked, jabbed, stabbed and hacked. And let's not forget the few times Indifference has returned to drive me crazy. Now? I'm tough as nails, baby.

Anyway. You'll be happy to know—wait. Rephrase. You won't care to know I've grown to *like* Winter. Yes, she's selfish to the max. Yes, she looks out for #1, always and forever. But those she considers her "personal property," she protects with her life. Through famine, plague and war with other clans, her fierce spirit has helped keep us going.

To combat her demon, she turns *everything* into a game. Her way of inviting someone into her world, I suppose, since overtly giving anything to anyone causes Selfishness to make my girl flat-out lose her mind.

What does Indifference do to you?

By the way, I haven't thought about our kiss at all. Nope. Not once. I don't miss you, and never wonder where you are and what you're doing. Thought you'd want to know.

Gillian Connacht

PS: Puck sucks.

106 years AB

Dear Puck,

I'm too excited, and have to share with someone—even you. Check it. I acquired magic!

Wait. Maybe I should backtrack a little, since you're so big on history and all. About sixtyish years ago, Cameron branded runes into my hands at my request. Fastforward a few weeks. A man ambushed me, thinking to take something I wasn't offering. (FYI. Your little bride hasn't taken a lover yet. And not because she's devoted to you. She's waiting for William. Boom. Mic drop.)

Anyway. Cameron noticed the commotion and rushed over, but he was too late. I'd already started slashing.

After my attacker-victim expelled his final breath, dark mist rose from his motionless body. The same mist I saw my first day in Amaranthia, after you killed our ambushers. Remember? Only this time, the mist absorbed into ME. Oh, the warmth! The tingles!

Drunk on power, I decided to leave Amaranthia, visit the Lords and their Ladies in Budapest, do the whole reunion thing with William, and find out if he'd locked you up somewhere, just liked he promised. I mean, it wasn't

like anyone could stop me. The student had already sur-
passed her teachers.

And no, I wasn't *wishing* you'd gotten yourself locked
up. I no longer hate you, okay? I only mildly dislike you
now. Time has softened me, I guess. Also, I finally understand why you did what you did.

I had a light bulb moment after one of my recruits fed
me bad intel in order to lead me into a trap. Crap move,
right? She planned to present me to a stable master as a
gift. Like I'm some filly who needs to be broken and rid-
den. I barely knew her, and yet her deception hurt. In
more ways than one! How much worse was it for you,
when your own brother betrayed you?

More than that, you believe the Connachts will thrive
under your rule. Whether they will or not, *I* believe
they'll perish without you. So, yeah. I get it, I really do.
I want a better future for my squad, too, and the children
we save. I'd do *anything* to ensure their well-being, even
gut you where you stand. But here's the thing. If you ever
purposely injure me again, or lie to me, I'll make a kabob
with your favorite man parts and host a weenie roast.

Won't be my first, or my last.

Now, what was I saying? Oh, yeah. My exit. As soon
as I reached another realm, my magic vanished. Maybe
because I'm not Amaranthian born? Maybe because I'm
not yet strong enough. Whatever the reason(s), I backtracked in a hurry.

I keep what's mine.

Now I spend my time targeting bad guys: rapists, mo-
lesters, and abusers of any kind. Anyone who hurts women
and children, really. I'm a killing machine, and I'm living my dream. In fact, I relish the kill almost as much as
the magic.

Is that bad? That's probably bad. What has two thumbs
and doesn't give a crap? This girl. (I mean, who will

have two thumbs after she regrows the one she just lost? This girl!) If anyone could appreciate my sentiment about villain-like tendencies, it's you, right?

We're changing Amaranthia bit by bit. We've built an orphanage, as well as a shelter for women. Though many men have tried to stop us, no one has managed to *slow* us.

Once, I wanted to be normal. Foolish! Why settle for normal when you can be extraordinary? Pucky, this girl loves her life! Except for—well, it's none of your business.

Oh, and the squad I mentioned? We started an all-star clan of our own. We're the Shawazons, and we rock the house. Cameron is our studly mascot, and he's obsessed with making us the greatest clan in history. Winter is my second in command. The darling girl has only tried to overthrow me six times, but I outwitted her each and every one, and we later had a good laugh about 'em. I know Selfishness is responsible. Demons are the worst!

The Shawazons are made up of freed stable members, former prostitutes, survivors of abuse—basically anyone other clans have deemed "unworthy." These people are my family.

Recently I promoted two of my best soldiers to general. Wait till you meet them. Johanna and Rosaleen got our backs, and we've got theirs. Girl power!

Uh-oh. I better go. Winter is shouting for me, and that only happens when disaster is about to strike. Or she wants me to clean her tent. Or brush her hair. Or find her shoes. Commander Gillian Connacht

PS: I've renamed you Pucky the Lucky because you're married to me. Face it. I'm AMAZING!

201 years AB

Dear Puck,

Dang it, where are you? You said you'd be back by now.

I'm not missing you or anything—definitely not dreaming about our kiss every night—so don't go getting a big head. But come on! I'm ready to divorce you and start dating again. Or for the first time. Whatever! Gotta have experience before William gets here, right???

Here's the deal. I've never trusted men. I've always freaked out when things got intimate, except for—it doesn't matter. I'm finally at a place where I want... *I want.*

Winter says she'll help me pick a man because she's Selfishness, and she selfishly wants me happy. (Yes, she loves me more than she loves you.) She even wrote up a single's ad: *Magic warrioress on the battlefield looking for Magic Mike in the bedroom. A total catch! Prone to murderous fits of rage. Gorgeous, sometimes plays nice. House-trained. Comes with an even better best friend.*

If only Amaranthia had a daily paper!

Okay, okay. I'm not a cheater, so I won't be going on any dates until we get that divorce. I really, really want a divorce, Puck. Please hurry home.

It's not you, I promise; it's me realizing I'm better off without you. I'm sure there are plenty of single ladies out there, just waiting to stare into your blank eyes and never receive a compliment or any kind of encouragement. And okay, yes, I know only a few hours, days or weeks have passed for you, but two centuries have passed for me. My Hulk-outs are getting worse, and I could use an outlet for excess energy.

Besides, you're better off with me. I recently learned the down and dirty about your prophecy, how your loving queen is supposed to help you unite the clans and all. Loving queen? Nope. Not me. And I've managed to cause irreparable friction between every clan.

Nowadays the only thing they have in common is their abhorrence for me. I've killed their men, stolen their magic and helped their women escape gilded cages. The Shawazons have even taught other clanswomen to demand respect from their men—or else.

You're welcome, genitalmen.

BTW. Everyone calls me Gillian the Dune Raider now. How awesome is that?!

Gillian ~~Connacht~~ Shaw, Dune Raider

PS: Puck is getting chucked.

300 years AB

Dear Puck,

Where are you??? You said you'd be back by now.

Whatever. Doesn't matter. Your delay is going to cost you regardless. Consider yourself officially separated. FYI I won your friends and all of your possessions in the settlement.

But dang it, I still can't date other men. Stupid bond! Maybe I despise you again. I'm more than ready to cross sex off my never-never list, but because of you, I can't. I can't move on with my life *in any way.*

So I'll ask again. Where are you? What happened to you? I know you were injured earlier, because pain exploded through my head for no apparent reason, and a cold sensation wrapped around my wrist. Then…nothing.

Look, I'm worried about you, okay, and I do not like to worry. Worry distracts and drains.

Note to self: find a way to break the bond without Puck's shears.

Wait a sec. The shears. You plan to use them after William helps you murder Sin…which means you must have already found the shears…which means you've *hidden* them somewhere in Amaranthia.

Well, well. If you have 1 pair of shears, and your wife has 0 pairs of shears, your wife now has 1 pair of shears and you have 0.

New goal: Find the shears, even if I have to flash into a volcano to retrieve them.

Oh, did I forget to mention I can flash? It happened accidentally the first, oh, bazillion times, and I vomited whenever I reached my destination, but I've since mastered the skill.

Winter tells me not to get too attached to the ability because magic comes and goes so quickly—and she plans to steal mine—but I'm enjoying the ride.

Gillian the Dune Raider

PS: Puck's gonna get his shears plucked.

343 years AB

Dear Puck,

Winter was right. I lost my ability to flash when my supply of magic got low.

I visited the Oracles, hoping to discover *eternal* magic. Before the three even deigned to speak to me, I had to offer a token of my appreciation. (You might have noticed that I cut off my hand with my middle finger extended. I'm sweet like that. What do they do with all the body parts people give them, anyway? I'm imagining steaming caldrons with eye of newt or something.)

The Oracles told me three things, and none of them about magic.

(1) The man I love has a dream, and I will kill it.

(2) I must choose between what could be and what will be.

(3) A happy ending is not in my future.

I'm not gonna worry about #1, because you're never coming back with William, and he's the only one who could ever tempt me to fall in love. (That's right. I went there.) As for #2, I have no idea what it means, so I've decided to consider it absolute hogwash. And #3? Screw the Oracles. I'm going to prove them wrong.

And when I do, you'll know you can prove them wrong about YOU. You don't need William's help to overthrow Taliesin Connacht. You can do it on your own. Or I can do it for you, if the price is right. So come home and set me free already.

Gillian the Dune Raider

PS: Puck sucks <—classics never get old.

405 years AB

Dear Puck,

You STILL haven't returned, and I still haven't found the shears, which makes me wonder if the Oracles were right, and I'm destined to have an unhappy ending after all. What if I'm forever stuck with an absentee husband, a visiting demon, Hulk-rages, and no love life?

I'm being wooed, Puck. Wooed! By soldiers, princes, even kings. Yep, you read that right. Mating season has hit Amaranthia, and I'm the novelty at the top of everyone's Hit It list.

At first, everyone wanted to capture or kill me. I even received Trojan horse–type gifts: poisonous flowers, notes with evil spells, and assassins. You know, the usual. When the whole capture-kill thing failed, guys started sending me all kinds of romantic crap. Gold, jewels, fruit from their private orchards, tents, cattle and magic. Well, not magic, exactly, but men for me to slay so I can tap into their magic like a beer keg. In that regard, I'm always happy to oblige.

The only leader who hasn't shown any interest in me is your brother.

I haven't purposely avoided Sin or anything, but I've only come across him twice. He built a massive compound on Connacht land and created some sort of maze around it. His people are forbidden to leave. Other clans must survive the maze to get inside. I've heard horror stories about monsters, tests of strength and endurance, puzzles, and total mind-screws.

The first time I saw Sin, I knew he was your brother without being told. He looks a lot like you. Same long, dark hair—sans razors—same dark eyes.

I'm sure most women consider him the beauty of the family—because Winter has mentioned it about a thousand times. To me, he's not as striking. (Tell the truth. My compliment made you jizz your pants.) Plus, he doesn't have horns. Or furry legs. Or hooves. Not that I'm digging on those or anything. It's just, winter has come— the season, not the woman—and I remember how toasty warm you are.

Not that I want to cuddle with you or anything.

Though I admit I've thought about our interactions a lot. Most of the time, you were Ice Man. Other times you were nice, despite the demon. What gives?

Anyway. I'm tempted to sneak into the Connacht compound and do a little spying. I mean, how would you feel if you returned, and I'd already taken care of your brother? Would you thank me with a little bond severing? Or resent me?

Gillian the Dune Raider

PS: Did you know Sin is engaged to your former fiancée?

422 years AB

Dear Puck,

I've decided you're never coming back, I do indeed hate you again and I'm destined to die without ever having an orgasm. At least I've made a new friend. Remember the chimera-POS who broke my hand the day you abandoned me in Amaranthia? (Soon after YOU broke my finger??) Well, about two-and-a-half years ago, her great-great-granddaughter gave birth to a baby boy. A little runt who has come close to death more times than I like to admit. Momma wanted nothing to do with baby—the POS gene is strong in this bloodline, I suppose—so I took over his care.

His name is Peanut, and he looks at me as if I'm the Amaranthian version of Santa Claus, and every day is Christmas. He's jealous of Winter, Cameron, Johanna and Rosaleen, and any other chimera I attempt to ride.

Tomorrow, his training begins. He's going to be my warhorse.

I guess I owe you a debt of gratitude, Puck. If you hadn't brought me here, I wouldn't have met him. I wouldn't have trained, and strengthened, and grown. I wouldn't be this happy, or have a family of my own.

Okay, okay. I don't actually hate you. And I know chimeras only live for about two hundred years, and I'll lose my Peanut at some point—unless I find a way to make him immortal, of course.

WHERE ARE YOU??? Where's William? I kinda sorta miss you both. I regret how things ended. I want to talk to you guys. Please, Puck. Hurry home.

Gillian the Dune Raider

PS: Keep me waiting much longer, and Pucky gonna get stucky—with a sword.

17

501 years AB

PUCK STEPPED THROUGH A FINAL DOORWAY, EN-tering Amaranthia. Just as before, magic brushed against his skin and filled his veins, thrilling him. Unlike before, he didn't use magic to transform into his natural form; he had no desire to impress William.

Reveling in his beloved homeland, Puck breathed in deeply. Tepid sunbeams shone upon the sea of sand. He glanced up. A storm brewed, the sky redder than usual. As Gillian must have learned, Amaranthian storms were extremely dangerous.

Gillian…

He wouldn't think about her…or how he would see her, breathe her in, *touch* her. Those thoughts would make him harden—well, hard*er*—and Indifference would…what? Puck waited, his ears twitching, but the demon had gone quiet.

Anger coursed through him at the thought of Gillian being bothered by the dark presence. Anger he ignored as he forced his mind on the weather. In winter, hoarfrost covered every-thing, becoming a metaphor for his life. Spring brought warm days and rampant rains that produced daggerlike hail. In summer, lakes and ponds gradually dried out, and acid occasionally poured from the sky. During fall, the days fluctuated between too hot, too cold and perfect.

He'd returned in the middle of spring.

There was no campsite within sight, and no bodies of water nearby. No one waited nearby with transportation, either.

No matter. He could run.

"You brought my little Gilly Gumdrop to a dump like this?" William demanded.

My Gilly Gumdrop! Mine!

No one had ever tried his legendary patience like this male. How could Gillian stand him? The irreverent bastard complained about everything, took nothing seriously and never under any circumstances missed an opportunity to taunt Puck.

"There is no better realm. And when Gillian is no longer mine, you can take her wherever you'd like." He wouldn't be bothered by it, either. Not in the slightest degree. "*If* she decides to go with you, of course. Did I forget to tell you? Time passes differently here. I'm guessing five hundred years have passed for *my wife*. She might have forgotten all about you."

With a hiss, William palmed a dagger and pressed the tip into the pulse at the base of Puck's throat. "You did *not* just say five—hundred—years."

"I did." He blinked at the male, unfazed by the weapon. "Gillian is now half a millennium old."

Flickers of red in those blue, blue eyes, like rivers of lava cracking the surface of a volcano. "The girl I left better be the girl I find. She was perfect, just the way she was. If the centuries have changed her…"

"You mean you want her to be the girl who chose me over you?" Two could taunt. "In that regard, I'm certain she's the same." A lie. He was certain of nothing.

Another hiss, the blade digging deeper. A bead of blood dribbled down his torso.

"Either strike or back off," Puck said. "Gillian awaits."

A tense pause. Then, with a great show of reluctance, William lifted the dagger.

"This way." Eager, Puck jetted forward.

The other male remained close on his heels. Having a vengeful immortal at his back was foolish, lethally so, but at the moment he didn't exactly care. *So close to seeing my wife…*

This time, he couldn't push thoughts of her from his mind. How would she react when she spotted him? How would she react when she spotted *William*?

A sudden and soul-deep ache threatened to rend Puck's chest in two.

"You're wrong, you know," he said. "She wasn't perfect back then. She was afraid of males and intimacy." Although, there at the end, she'd kissed him as if she wanted—needed—more.

Will kiss her again. Will—

William snarled, reminding him of Indifference. "How do you know she was afraid of intimacy?"

He hiked a shoulder in a shrug. "The subject came up."

"As long as it was the only thing that *came up*," William snapped.

No, William of the Dark. I hardened for her every day we were together. Now I harden for her even when we're apart.

"The abuse she suffered as a child…worse than you can imagine," William said. "And she suffered for years! With no one to help her, she ran away and lived on the streets—because the streets were safer. *That* is the girl you use against me."

Puck's butterfly tattoo scorched his skin on a downward slide to his leg as he grappled with remorse, with self-loathing so strong he wasn't sure he'd ever be free of it.

"Enough chatter," he croaked. He increased his speed, arms pumping and legs eating up the distance.

William never lagged, a feat few had managed when up against Puck.

When they came upon his camp, he had to do a double take. Tents had been replaced by homes made of stone and wood.

Men meandered about, each dressed in a tunic and sheepskin pants. Fashion hadn't changed, at least. There were no women in sight. No sign of Gillian, or even Winter. The females must be inside the homes, cooking and cleaning.

"How quaint. A sausage fest. My least favorite of all the fests," William said with a dry tone. "If any of these bastards touched my girl—"

"*My* girl." Puck closed his eyes for a moment and breathed, doing everything in his power to stop the erosion of his control. *Not mine. Never mine.* He'd chosen vengeance. War over a woman. He would not stray from his path.

Better off alone. No family, no chance of betrayal.

He scanned every face, but found no sign of Cameron, either.

"Where is she?" William demanded.

"I will find out." Puck approached a man who sat in front of a roasting *coinín*. Cooking? A duty usually performed by females. Except when those females were vegetarian, and made bargains with their husbands, of course. "You."

The man glanced over at him, and darted to his feet, eyes going wide. "My lord. You're back."

"Where is my wife? For that matter, where are Cameron and Winter?" He was—not impatient, but close to it; he was *ready* to read the detailed history Cameron had written, and find out everything that had happened in his absence.

The color drained from the other male's cheeks. "She… they…they all moved, my lord. Took all our women with them."

A fresh surge of fury radiated from William as he sidled next to Puck. "He didn't ask you what they'd done. He asked you where they were. Answer!"

"Do not intimidate my subjects," Puck snapped. To the man, he said, "I didn't ask you what they'd done. I asked you where they were."

The man gulped and pulled at the collar of his tunic. "To the east, my lord. They're part of a new clan. One that raids other camps, kills soldiers and steals magic. They've caused a war between...everyone."

Things had gotten worse since his departure, not better?

"My good mood is deteriorating at a rapid rate," William said, his tone nothing but menace. "Either someone produces Gillian, or I—"

"Will throw a tantrum," Puck interjected. "Yes, I know. Instead, why don't you do what you do best and screw anything with a pulse. I'll hunt for my wife and figure out what's going on."

"Have I told you how badly you suck?" Winter asked with genuine cheer.

"Many times." Gillian blew her friend a kiss—with her middle finger. "You should try thanking me. I'm fixing your mistake, aren't I?"

"No, you're saving Johanna. There's a difference. I just wish we could go in guns blazing."

"Me, too." Unfortunately, guns didn't work in Amaranthia. Something about the magic being incompatible, blah, blah.

Two days ago, Clan Walsh had captured one of Gillian's generals. Considering the Walshes were douchebags—men who believed women were less important than cattle—she would make the sands run red with their blood tonight.

Steal from me and suffer.

When roars and snarls suddenly sounded in her mind, *she* snarled. Indifference had returned. He liked to pop in every couple decades, drive her insane and take off.

Ignore him or go insane. No other choices.

"Just so you know," Winter said, "I never made mistakes before I met you."

Snort. "You made them, all right. People were too afraid to tell you."

Gillian pressed her body deeper into the crest of the sand dune, and tightened the camo scarf wrapped around the lower half of her face. The thin material protected her from biting winds and sprays of sand. Since waking up this morning, she'd been inundated with impatience. For Johanna's situation, of course, but could there be more?

Here she was, about to save her friend. But rather than anticipation, she felt dread, her nerve endings wrecked.

Indifference only made it worse.

"Why aren't *you* too afraid to point out my flaws? Not that I have any flaws. Is it because you've seen me in my Wonder Woman Underoos? That's it, isn't it?" The lovely keeper of Selfishness was stretched out beside her. "And why are we doing this, anyway? We have a no-rescue policy for a reason. I remember all those pesky traps, tricks and ambushes. Do you?"

She waited, knowing her friend was far from done.

"If other clans find out we're willing to go to war to save a general nowhere near as beloved or powerful as the Dune Raider's second in command—me," Winter added, as if clarification was needed, "they're more likely to abduct our clanswomen."

Gillian sighed. The crux of the matter? Selfishness felt slighted, because no one had tried to capture her. "On the other hand, other clans will be more likely to abduct our women if we do nothing. They need to know there are consequences if they mess with us." Severe consequences.

"And if we're walking into an ambush today?"

"It's not an ambush if we *know* it's an ambush. It's an opportunity." Resisting an opportunity wasn't part of Winter's skillset.

Bingo. The beauty now *seethed* with eagerness.

Walshes gonna die bloody.

Though both Shawazons were loaded with weapons, the deadliest one pulsed in their hands. Gillian extended an arm, moonlight glinting off the runes branded from fingertip to wrist. *So pretty.* The twisting, twining lines had become a portal, allowing magic to enter her body whenever she made a kill.

Magic was power, and power was *everything.*

Never again would she be a helpless little girl, pretending to sleep while the scum of the earth violated her in the worst ways, or, when she couldn't pretend, doing everything commanded of her, hoping her abuser would finish quickly.

Never again would she be too afraid to fight back.

"So, what's the plan?" Winter asked.

"Basically we're going to free Johanna and wreak havoc."

"*Nice.* Havoc is my specialty."

Deciding to sneak in and out of the enemy camp rather than charge full force, they'd come without backup. Gillian had even left her beloved and faithful war chimera, Peanut, at home. Guaranteed, he was pouting, eating her furniture and biting anyone who dared approach him.

She sighed and studied the camp. One hundred and fifty-four tents were set in rows, allowing neighbors to keep an eye on each other. Crackling fire pits were strategically placed as well, each one supplying light for four tents.

This was a mobile outpost. Meaning, the occupants could pack up and vanish in minutes.

Soldiers patrolled the outside perimeter, ready to ring a gong at the first sign of trouble. Other soldiers patrolled between the tents.

By attacking the site, the Shawazons declared war on the entire Walsh clan.

Actually, by imprisoning Johanna, a Shawazon general, the Walshes had *already* declared war. Sure, Johanna had invaded their territory while playing truth or dare with Winter, but she hadn't done it to make trouble. Only to steal a kiss from a handsome stranger.

For that, the Walshes thought to torture Johanna? Think again.

No woman left behind. Even if Gillian had to risk everything.

So other (former) Shawazons had betrayed her in the past, and set traps for her. So what? Johanna, she trusted. They shared a similar background and had talked about their experiences, helping to build each other up.

One of the first things Johanna had said to her, after Gillian had shared the worst of her abuse—*I believe you.*

Her own mother hadn't believed her.

Then Johanna had added, *What happened wasn't your fault. You know it. They* know it. *And now your body is a weapon. Never again can someone use your weapon against you.*

That day, something inside Gillian had changed, the truth had been snapping into place. The abuse had *never* been her fault. She'd been an innocent child placed in the care of an uncaring man. No look in her eyes had welcomed him. He alone carried the blame for his actions, now and always, and she would never accept such a terrible burden again.

When the heavy weight had lifted off her shoulders, she'd wanted to cry. So badly she'd wanted to cry in relief and fury and a thousand other emotions she'd been unable to name. But her tears had remained at bay. Maybe she'd shed too many over her mortal life and had no more to give. Even still, the lack hadn't stopped a tide of longing from springing to life. She'd wanted Puck's strong arms wrapped around her, holding her close. Wanted his warm breath to be a caress on her skin as he whispered words of comfort. Wanted the softness of his fur, so different from any contact she'd ever before known, to warm her.

Hoping to rid herself of such unwise desires, she'd gone searching for damning information about his past. Youthful misdeeds. Betrayals. Anything! Except, when she heard about the wars he'd won, the warriors he'd fought, the men who'd wanted to be him and the women who'd hoped to tame him, she'd *admired* him—and only missed him more.

Of course, she'd also found out he'd once had a crush on Winter, and she'd Hulked-out. Which made no sense! What did a past crush matter? Unless he still wanted the keeper of Selfishness?

Uh-oh. Familiar prickles on the back of her neck, heating skin. Inhale, exhale. Good, that was good. No reason to Hulk-out here, of all places. She'd run out of *cuisle mo chroidhe* syrup and hadn't had a chance to harvest more.

"Um, do I need to run for my life?" Winter asked.

"No. I'll be fine." Maybe. Hopefully.

As Indifference roared with more force, she moved her gaze up, up. Three moons glowed in the purple-red sky she'd come to adore, partially shielded by an array of storm clouds. Any moment, ice daggers would begin to fall.

"Almost time." What if she was too late? What if—

No! Unacceptable thought process. All would be well.

Winter kissed the handle of her favorite dagger. One she'd stolen from Puck's brother, when he'd dared to venture from his fortress of solitude. "Whoever kills the most soldiers wins. Loser has to admit the winner is superior."

"Deal," she said with a note of affection.

Her friendship with Winter hadn't formed overnight, or even over a decade, but it *had* formed. Now there was no one Gillian would rather have by her side.

She wondered, though. When—if—Puck ever returned, would Winter's allegiance change?

"Thinking about hubby dearest again?" her friend asked.

"Ex-hubby dearest. There's a statute of limitations on an un-contested unofficial divorce, right?" And yet, still she avoided dating other men. Though she wanted a boyfriend and roman-tic dinners, gift exchanges. Dancing and laughing. Long, lin-gering glances. Tender smiles. All the things girls dreamed of receiving from an admirer. All the things she'd been denied throughout her life. First, because of fear, then an unwanted marriage.

But, if she got cozy with someone else after hunting and kill-ing males who'd betrayed their wives, she would be a hypocrite.

She also killed hypocrites.

Winter bumped her shoulder. "You always tense like you're

about to be hit by my fists of fury. Don't worry. He'll come back. Indifference causes him to lose focus sometimes, or stop caring about his objective, but he always finds his way sooner or later."

"Shouldn't his kingdom be an exception?"

"*Nothing* is an exception with Indifference. Except maybe..." Winter's voice trailed off.

"What?"

Her friend shrugged and said, "Except maybe *you*. The way he looked at you before he left... I thought I would combust. I've never seen such intensity from him before."

A tendril of pleasure unfurled. Which was ridiculous!

Her body might burn for Puck some nights—most nights... fine, all nights nowadays—and he might beleaguer her dreams, but she wasn't going to mess around with him when he returned. She'd known him, what? All of five minutes? And too well did she recall the ease with which he'd moved from Ice Man to smoldering, back to Ice Man. No doubt he'd heat up if he got her into bed, only to freeze her out afterward. No, thanks. Gillian expected, and deserved, to feel respected afterward.

Maybe he'd surprise her?

Ugh. Wishful thinking would only lead to disappointment.

Would Puck even want her?

Of course! The bond made *her* crave *Puck*, despite everything that had happened between them, therefore the bond made *him* crave *her*. It was science.

Were they nothing but puppets on a string?

Did it really matter? Want was want.

Wait. Am I trying to talk myself into *a sexcapade with him, or* out *of it? I'm confused.*

He wasn't exactly boyfriend material. Romantic dinners, gift exchanges, dancing, laughing and long, lingering glances or tender smiles—not exactly in his wheelhouse.

Temptation said: *Why not use him, just for a little while? Satisfaction awaits...*

The idea wasn't repellent. She could experience the beauty of sex without fear. As many times as she'd fantasized about Puck, old memories had never surfaced. And it wasn't like she could get off all by her lonesome. *Whimper.* Any time she'd attempted it, her body had shut down, thanks to the bond. Or maybe Indifference. Or both! Deep down she suspected she needed Puck to finish the job, his presence somehow making her desire too strong to be denied.

And dang it, she was tired of writhing atop her sheets, desperate and aching, unable to satiate the need her husband had roused with a simple kiss. A need that hadn't abated in their time apart but grown. A need for Puck and Puck alone.

Part of her mind cried *Why not William?* She'd known him years longer and had hero-worshipped the crap out of him.

Yeah, body. Why? Though she thought of him every now and then, wondering if he could possibly be as gorgeous as she remembered—and though she always had fun taunting Puck about the other man in her letters—she'd never fantasized about him.

A crack of thunder returned her thoughts to the matter at hand. "If I get caught..." Gillian began.

"I know, I know. Slaughter everyone, risk my life *more*, and save you."

"No. Are you kidding? Retreat, steal more weapons, acquire more magic and return."

Another crack of thunder, followed by a blaze of lightning that spotlighted soldiers as they ran for cover; they knew no one in their right mind would attack during an ice storm.

They weren't wrong. Gillian hadn't had a right mind for centuries.

Shields were raised over the tents, offering protection for the people inside.

"After this," Winter said, as unconcerned with the coming

rain of death as Gillian, "the newly crowned Walsh king will probably stop courting you."

"That's just a bonus," she said.

Gillian had killed the last two sovereigns. The first had delighted in the pain he'd inflicted upon women, reminding her of her stephorrors. The next one had killed a beloved member of the Shawazons, not during battle but a shopping extravaganza. He'd stabbed her from behind.

After a third crack of thunder, the first ice dagger fell from the sky and speared the ground a few inches from Gillian's face. Indifference howled with surprise before vanishing from her mind.

Well, well. Near-death experiences weren't his thing. Good to know.

"Now," she said. Raising a shield of her own, she popped to her feet and raced down the sand dune.

18

MORE AND MORE ICE DAGGERS DESCENDED, DEL-
uging the land. Gillian had to jump, dodge and dive to avoid
slamming into each new obstacle, even as other ice daggers
slammed into her shield and shattered into a million little
pieces.

Thankfully, the same *thud, thud* and *clink, clink* echoed from
the shields that covered the roofs of the tents.

Winter remained a few steps behind her, guarding her back.

No wonder the Lords of the Underworld enjoyed their skir-
mishes. Protecting the people you loved was the greatest high.
The second greatest? Knowing the warrior at your side or on
your six would die for you, if necessary.

Family. Acceptance. Support. Everything Gillian had ever
wanted, delivered in a package she'd never expected.

Adrenaline surged through her veins, supercharging her.
Magic stirred, her runes glowing bright, soon becoming bea-
cons in the night. That wouldn't do. Unleashing a whip of
power, she caused grains of sand to rise and form a tornado
around her and Winter.

When she'd first learned about magic, she'd thought different types produced specific results. Like superspeed, or the

ability to flash. Superhuman strength. Unnatural endurance. Breathing under water. Night vision. Telepathy. Atmokinesis. Omnilinguilism. Echolocation. Mind control. Intangibility. Self-camouflage. Poison generation. Telekinesis. Pyrokinesis. Psychokinesis. The ability to fly. But it hadn't taken long to realize magic was simply power, and the more you had, the more you could do.

A certain amount of magic was needed to perform certain abilities. The more magic you used on those abilities, the less you could do, your power draining faster and faster. It was a vicious cycle.

Sin Connacht seemed to be the sole exception. According to word on the dunes, he'd possessed three abilities since birth: superspeed, shapeshifting and night vision. Puck had super-speed, too, and he'd shapeshifted the day he'd brought her into Amaranthia. Could he also see in the dark, like his brother? What else could he do?

She would have liked to—

Focus, girl!

She released a second whip of magic, increasing the speed of the tornado to create a type of force field. In the eye of the storm, she and Winter remained unaffected.

Unfortunately, her magic meter already teetered on empty. Finding the right targets had become increasingly difficult as men learned of her hatred for anyone willing to commit crimes against women and children. They were no longer so vocal about their crimes, no longer bragging or publicly punishing the people under their "care."

One day, Gillian hoped to find a way to self-power, so that her magic built and never drained, allowing her to tap into *every* supernatural ability.

It was good to have dreams.

As she raced onward, voices drifted from the tents.

"—telling you, I saw him with my own eyes." Panic in-fused his tone.

"What does he want?"

Who was *him/he?*

Rescue first. Gather info second.

Information could be as valuable as magic.

Because the tornado limited her vision, she had to use more magic to see past the wall of wind and sand and even tent flaps to peer inside the dwellings. Warriors cleaning weapons. Women cooking. Couples having sex. Arguing. Laughing.

When her gaze skidded over Johanna, Gillian stopped and backtracked. Heart thudding against her ribs, she used hand signals to send Winter racing to the other side of the most luxurious tent in the entire camp, where she would wait for exactly two minutes.

A countdown began in Gillian's head. Two minutes, or one hundred and twenty seconds. She took stock. A rusty cage occupied the center, and Johanna crouched inside. Mud caked her corkscrew curls and dirt streaked her dark skin. Her clothing—a leather top with thin metal links over her vital organs, and a pleated skirt—were tattered. She gripped the cage bars, her brown eyes narrowed, her lips compressed into a tight line.

One minute left.

Fury seethed in Gillian's chest. She remembered the day she'd met Johanna, hundreds of years ago. She'd heard rumors about a male who beat and abused his daughters, so she'd snuck into his home, intending to kill him and steal his magic.

He'd had sweet little Johanna by the throat, choking the life from her.

Gillian had erupted and choked the life out of *him*—like for like. At first, Johanna had feared her. Over time, as Gillian trained her to fight the same way she'd once been trained by Winter, they'd become friends. Family.

No one hurts my family.

Thirty seconds.

Johanna's captor—the commander of the outpost—lounged on a mound of pillows, sharpening a blade. "Looks like we're going to have another night together." He laughed. "Perhaps the Dune Raider will show up tomorrow. Or not. Perhaps she's afraid of me and washed her hands of you."

Fifteen.

The taunts of a cruel man, nothing more. *Deserves what's coming.*

Ten.

As quietly and quickly as possible, Gillian cut a slit in the side of the tent.

Five.

Before he noticed the sudden icy breeze, she slipped inside. Now! Mind locking on a single thought—*will do what I must, always*—she tossed her shield, nailing him in the temple, and palmed a second dagger.

With a bellow, he clamored to his feet, ready to punish her with his sword.

What he didn't know? Winter had entered the tent from the other side, a bow raised, arrow cocked. *Whoosh.* The arrow sliced through his wrist. His hand spasmed, and he dropped the weapon.

One step, two, then she was running. Winter tossed a shield in her direction. The second it hit the sand, directly in front of her, she dropped upon it, knees to metal. Her momentum sent her sliding across the sand—through the commander's legs.

She slicked her blades across his inner thighs. *Not enough damage.* The second she was behind him, she hopped off the shield, twisted and stabbed the backs of his knees.

He toppled, and released another bellow.

Winter had already freed Johanna and now needed to make the final kill. Or at least an attempt; she wouldn't want to, would want her friend to take the magic she needed to heal, but she would be punished by Selfishness if she didn't try.

Reflexes well-honed, Gillian tossed a blade at Johanna. The Shawazon general shouldered a grateful Winter out of the way,

caught the weapon and crouched in front of the commander—
who she then stabbed in the heart.

Dark mist rose from his body, quickly enveloping Johanna.
Savoring the influx of power, she closed her eyes and let her
head fall back. The runes in her hands glowed, almost brighter
than the sun.

"Thank you." Healthy color bloomed in Johanna's cheeks.
"Thank you so much."

"Anytime," Gillian replied, and meant it.

From her perch on the ground, Winter grumbled, "Just do
us a favor and *don't* get captured next time."

"I wish you'd given me such sage advice before I entered
the camp and tried to steal a kiss from a handsome stranger,"
Johanna said with a salute. "Would have saved me a little light
torture."

Impatience intensifying, Gillian tugged Winter to her feet
and grabbed the shield she'd discarded. "You guys ready to
fight our way out?"

Johanna claimed the dagger the commander had sharpened
and blew him a kiss. "Mind if I borrow this? No? Thanks
bunches."

"Hey. *I* wanted his dagger," Winter said with a pout.

"How about we take daggers and swords from his friends?"
Gillian suggested. The beauty of compromise. "And let's not
forget magic!"

Smiles abounded as they raced out of the tent and into the
still-raging storm. Soldiers were now rushing outside, shields
raised. Amid the chaos and confusion caused by the storm,
Gillian and company blended in with the growing crowd...
and performed the perfect sneak attack.

Girls against boys. Girls—killed—everyone.

By the time the last soldier died, ice daggers had ceased falling. The tang of old pennies and emptied bowels tainted the air.
Blood had turned the ground into a crimson sea of destruction.

Magic rose from the corpses and wafted to the rightful recipients.

Tendrils of strength flooded Gillian...but didn't heal her. Ugh. Despite her many kills, the men had been short on magic.

"How many Walshes did you kill?" Winter asked.

Breaths sawing in and out, Gillian cut a strip of cloth from a tent, wrapped her wound and replied, "Lost count. Sorry."

"Wouldn't matter anyway," Johanna said. "I bet I beat you both. How old are you grannies, anyway?"

"Ha-ha," Winter said.

"Come on. Let's go home."

Winter and Johanna trash-talked as they raced across the dunes. Gillian would have joined in, but she was too busy ignoring the aches and pains screaming for relief.

By the time they crossed the Shawazon border, the suns were in the process of rising, lovely golden rays glowing in the purple-red sky and highlighting...no, surely not. Gillian blinked rapidly, certain she wasn't looking at a tall, muscular form with bronzed skin, and silver razors in his dark hair.

Or maybe she...was? He was speaking to Rosaleen, his back to Gillian. His bare back. With a butterfly tattoo the color of shamrocks.

Tension stole through her body—but so did a familiar current of heat. Gillian came to an abrupt stop. Not yet getting the memo, her heart continued to race, faster and faster.

"Puck?"

19

A VOICE WITH THE POWER TO MAKE HIM GROW harder than steel. *Hers.* Puck spun so quickly he nearly gave himself whiplash. Frantic, he searched—there! Gillian Connacht stood at the crest of a sand dune, Winter and a woman he'd never met at her side. He noted the presence of the others absently, noted the dried blood and other things caked on all three females, as well. He knew he should wonder about the cause, and he would, just as soon as he stopped lusting like a lad with his first stable.

Gillian had undergone significant changes. Immortality hadn't frozen her at eighteen years old, but had allowed her to age into her perfect self. Her hair was longer, a shade darker, and wavy. Her cheeks were thinner, her breasts larger—luscious. Rounded hips were magnificently displayed in what must have become the Amaranthian woman's uniform: a black leather halter-top and short pleated skirt, bound together by metal links to shield vital organs. The rest of her was stunningly toned. Runes now branded her hands, the glittering swirls a stunning enhancement, like permanent flesh-jewelry.

He must have changed, as well, because what he'd felt for

her before paled in comparison to what he felt for her now. Desire *ruled* him.

Perhaps their bond *had* deepened over the centuries she'd lived. Perhaps her magic called to his. The urge to close the distance, yank her into his arms, to touch and taste, to brand, bombarded him, nearly irresistible.

I will have what's mine. Want her. Badly. Must protect. Must keep.

Ambition protested. *Must give her back to William.*

She winced and clutched her side as she shifted from one booted foot to the other. A crimson-soaked cloth was wrapped around her torso from rib to hipbone.

Someone had hurt her.

Someone would die.

Barely controlling his rage, he rushed across the distance. Gillian met him halfway. They stopped in unison, only a whisper separating their bodies—his thrummed with new tension, hers exuded feminine heat.

She kept her gaze steady on his, so unlike the girl he used to know. The one who had looked away at the first opportunity.

When he inhaled the sweet scent of poppiberries, he couldn't stop a moan. Nor could the men in her clan, men who'd halted what they were doing to watch her with palpable longing.

Puck bowed up, ready for battle. If they did not turn away, they would die just as surely as "someone."

They caught sight of him and turned away.

Better. As Puck returned his focus to his wife, fascination and awareness charged the air, and the rest of the world faded. Erratic and wild, his pulse points drummed against his heating skin. Each beat spoke: *Take. Her. Take. Her.*

Indifference erupted in a chorus of displeasure, but not even the fiend could distract Puck from the vision before him. "Gillian—"

She punched him, rattling his brain against his skull.

"Well. Hello to you, too," he said, rubbing his stinging cheek.

Up went her chin. "That's for lying to me."

"I'm—"

She punched him again, splitting his lip.

"—sorry," he finished, his ears ringing.

"That's for breaking my finger." Punch. "That's for abandoning me in a strange land." Punch. "That's for returning three hundred years later than promised."

He waited for the next blow, but she drew in a deep breath, exhaled and nodded, as if satisfied in a job well done.

Lifting a brow, he said, "Finished?"

"Yep. For now." She knit her brows. "Hey, why aren't I hurt, too?"

He tapped the gold cuff still anchored to his wrist. "Excellent form and flawless technique, by the way. Winter and Cameron trained you well. Until you began to train them, of course."

Pride brightening her features, she fluffed her hair. "Thank you." Then her cheeks bloomed a lovely shade of pink, making him want to reach out and touch. How hot did she burn? "You've already read my letters."

"I have." He'd used magic to absorb every word written by both Gillian and Cameron. But no amount of magic could have curbed his surprise as the details had been unveiled.

Gillian had built an orphanage for needy children and a shelter for abused females. She'd been courted by kings and princes—who would be executed when Puck united the clans. She'd learned to wield magic, had even killed for it.

With each new letter, Puck had actually *felt* her grow and toughen. And when she'd mentioned her happiness? His heart had fluttered, something it had never done.

She'd mentioned she had "Hulk-outs," and he'd almost smiled. Had his wee wife thrown a temper tantrum or two?

The urge to smile had faded when he'd come upon the Oracles' prophecy. *No happy ending.*

Even now, guilt welled. By bringing Gillian to Amaranthia, Puck had set her on a certain path. In essence, he'd doomed her, an innocent who'd experienced a tragic childhood. Because, even if he severed their bond right here, right now, he would do her no good. The prophecy had been spoken; it would come to pass, no matter how hard they tried to circumvent it.

Hadn't Sin proved this?

"So? Where's William?" Gillian asked.

That name on her lips! *Hate it!* Puck wanted to grab her by the shoulders and press her against the hard line of his body. He would kiss her so deeply, he would erase memories of the male from her mind.

Where's William, my sweet? He's dead, if you ask about him just one more time.

Ridiculous thought. Merely a pipe dream.

"The fool struck out on his own, hoping to track you down," he said, "even though he knows nothing about this realm or its inhabitants."

"And you just let him go?" Her chiding tone set his nerves on edge.

"Should I have tied him down?" Puck had searched the Shawazon camp instead, thinking Gillian might be hiding inside one of the homes. He'd found no sign of her but *had* found countless women sharpening swords, making repairs on different dwellings and practicing combat moves.

Some of the male residents had fetched and discarded debris as it blew into the camp. Others had cooked. Still others had sat on rocks and sewed. Everyone had looked...content.

Gillian hadn't created a clan; she'd created a miracle. Her people loved her. They followed her by choice rather than fear, so loyal they had refused to answer his questions about her.

Now, she took a step back and turned on her heel.

"Where are you going?" Puck demanded, latching on to her arm to hold her in place. He'd just found her. No way he'd let her out of his sight.

"Where else? To find William."

He ground his teeth until his gums ached. "Cameron is searching for him."

"You're one lucky bastard," Cameron had said before taking off. "Sure, Gillian has destroyed any chance of uniting the clans and achieving peace, but she's taken life by the balls and lived every second with passion. How many others can say the same?"

"They'll be back soon enough," Puck said.

Gillian wrenched free of his grip but didn't attempt to storm off a second time. He released a breath he hadn't known he'd been holding.

"I like our land," he said, hoping to distract her.

"*Our* land?" she choked out.

"Despite your talk of divorce, we are husband and wife. What is yours is also mine."

"By your reasoning, the shears are also mine. Give them to me."

Clever female. "How about I give you an apology instead? I'm sorry I lied to you, sorry I purposely harmed you. You have my word I will never do either again."

Shrug. A casual action, and yet she said, "You better mean those words. The prince of Fiáin lied to me a few months ago, and he's just now learning to walk again."

His wee little wife had immobilized a warrior who'd trained for battle for eons? Puck almost laughed. "Am I forgiven?"

"You were forgiven before the punches. Doesn't mean we're best friends or anything. Or that I trust you."

Good enough. For now. "I'm also sorry I took more time than anticipated...when you were so eager to start dating other men." Tone guttural, no longer masking the savagery that boiled inside him, he demanded, "Did you?"

She merely blinked at him as if he were a recalcitrant child.

Thought to deny him an answer? He'd killed people for less.

How many men would he have to murder for daring to covet what belonged to him—or worse, touching her? A warrior defended his territory. Always. No one had the right to look at Gillian without Puck's permission.

He would *never* grant permission.

Paying no heed to the demon's newest chorus, Puck snapped, "Tell me."

"What do you think? I mean, look at me." She waved a hand over her curvaceous little body he imagined lost in the throes of passion. "I'm a stunning five hundred and nineteen. Or is it eighteen? Twenty? I forget."

Her gaze clashed with his, so dark, so lovely, her whiskey-colored irises glowing as brightly as runes, daring him to naysay her. The soul-deep wounds he'd once noticed were no longer as prevalent, but the kindling hadn't yet been set aflame.

No one had made her burn.

His tension evaporated. "You are stunning, aye, no matter your current age."

She fluffed her hair again. "Despite my dotage, I don't need a cane unless I break or lose a leg, and I don't tremble when I'm using my sewing needles—to stitch up my friends."

"But you haven't started dating," he pointed out.

Bristling, she said, "How do you know? And why do you care?"

"Who said I care? You can do whatever you want, with whomever you want."

Her gaze roved over him and…heated? "You sure about that, Pucky? Your lips say *do whatever you want*, but the rest of you says *do me now*. And by *the rest of you*, I'm talking about the pocket rocket you're smuggling in your pants."

Noticed, had she? He straightened his spine, and squared his shoulders—with pride. *Look, wife. See what you do to me so easily.* "I said you could do what you wanted, with whomever you wanted. I didn't say I would allow the men to live."

His reasonable tone while discussing murder caused the corners of her mouth to curl upward, surprising him.

She schooled her expression, disappointing him, and crossed her arms over her chest. "You're the same as before, in looks and demeanor. Hot one moment, frigid the next. Your do-me vibe won't last."

"Then we had better hurry to our home, so I can do you while it lasts." *I'm kidding.*

I might not be kidding.

"There you go again. *Our* home? And no way, no how. There will be no doing." She sputtered a moment, then hurried to change the subject. "What do you think of *my* camp?"

Giving credit where credit was due, he said, "You've created something special here."

While the Shawazons he'd interviewed had flatly refused to answer personal questions about their leader, they'd been more than happy to brag about her conquests. She was known as the Dune Raider, a warrior without equal, and a bona fide weapon. She invaded rival camps, freed women from stables and abuse, cared for children, especially orphans, stole what she wanted, whenever she wanted, and punished soldiers for their crimes. She also trained former captives to do the same.

What was exaggerated, and what was true? Whatever the answer, he wished he'd gotten to witness her transformation from fearful to brave.

Earlier he'd said to Cameron, "What hardships did she face? Tell me everything."

"Well, let's see. Only *all* of them," his friend had replied. "But before you stare at me with your cold, hard eyes—yeah, just like that—she volunteered for many of them in order to be a better warrior and commander."

"Thank you," Gillian said now, preening.

"But," he added with a scowl. "Tensions are higher than ever. Brutal clan-on-clan battles are waged weekly. Savage ambushes and strategic raids are a daily occurrence. The only thing the citizens agree upon is their hatred for you."

"So? I regret nothing."

He should be angry with her. Instead, he was...even more pleased. *Such spirit.*

Puck reached out and traced his knuckles along her jaw-line. Just as she'd done on their wedding day, she leaned into his touch. Only this time, she uttered the sexiest sound he'd ever heard.

"Mmmm."

My wife is in desperate need of stroking. How could *he* regret anything now?

Though Gillian looked tougher than before, even harsh, she felt like warmed silk.

The longer he touched her, the thicker the air became, breathing more difficult. Tremors arced through him, desire sizzling deep in his marrow.

He longed to sweep her into his arms and carry her to the nearest bed. Which he absolutely wouldn't do.

Which he probably shouldn't do.

Which he just might do…

No, no. His next goal awaited him. He couldn't allow Gillian to distract him. Lust held no importance—or rather, it wouldn't.

Puck summoned more and more ice, until finally the heat of desire cooled, a layer of frost forming over his heart and mind, followed by another and another, until his frigid armor was in place, his thoughts and body calm.

20

"BETTER," PUCK SAID.

Gillian jolted, stepping away from him, swaying. "And he's back," she muttered, distaste dripping from the words.

Swaying? Her wound had weakened her, he realized. How could he have lost sight of it? "You're hurt," he said, the emotionless quality of his voice somehow obscene to him. "Who dared hurt my wife? Why weren't you protected?"

Scowling, she took another step back, increasing the distance between them.

"*Such* a dumb question," Winter said as she approached.

He zoomed his slitted gaze to his—former?—friend. "You had instructions to see to her well-being, and yet you allowed her to be harmed."

Winter waved the observation away and anchored her hands on her hips. "I waited on the sidelines *forever*, expecting an invitation to join the reunion. Since you guys were rude enough to ignore me, I'll be rude enough to butt in. By the way, this sucks."

"Agreed," Puck said. "You allowed her—"

"I had a plan," the keeper of Selfishness continued with a pout. "Puck would return, and I would introduce Gillian."

"I've met her," he snapped. "Now tell me why you allowed—"

"Go ahead," Gillian prompted, cutting him off. "Introduce me. He doesn't know my names have changed."

Names, plural?

Winter cleared her throat. "Puck Connacht, may I present to you Gillian Connacht, First of her Name, Queen of the Shawazons, the Dune Raider, Defender of the Weak, Stable Destroyer, Mother of the World's Worst Chimera, Scourge of the Sands, Sovereign of Every House, Friend of Winter."

A glowing Gillian gave her a thumbs-up, and Puck found himself powerless to do anything but stare, utterly entranced, as if he'd never put his emotions in a deep freeze. *What mad world have I entered?*

Winter kissed Gillian's cheek. "I'll give you a minute, maybe two, but probably only thirty seconds, before I return with supplies. Finish your business. Or pleasure. And don't forget to tell your ex how you divided up your joint assets when you divorced—by keeping everything yourself. It's a fascinating story, and I'm sure he'll be properly enthralled."

"Um, you're trying to take over the conversation, babe," Gillian said with an adoring smile.

Envy slashed what remained of his impassivity to ribbons. Her affection belonged to *Puck*, and only—

He popped his jaw and forced his thoughts to blank.

"Right. My bad." Winter mimed locking her lips and throwing away the key. Then she turned to Puck and said, "Don't try to blame me for your loss. You totally should have seen this coming. Everyone knows a love match versus an arranged one is like suicide versus murder. Besides, Gillian never believed me when I told her the secret to a successful immortal marriage is keeping your husband's armory full and his balls empty. You're probably better off because—"

"Only proving my point," Gillian muttered.

"Right again." With a wink and a finger-wave, Winter headed off to gather those supplies.

Not wasting a moment, Puck grated, "We are not divorced, and we are not getting divorced. Yet."

"I want my freedom from you and your demon."

"I know." He raised his brows. "You're ready for romance."

"And you sound real broken up about it." She pinched the bridge of her nose. "Look. Maybe you weren't aware, but marriage is the number one cause of divorce in every realm. These things happen. No one's at fault, blah, blah, blah. Except you. You're at fault. What did you think would happen when you stayed away three hundred years longer than planned? Did you forget how to count? By the way, I don't need Winter to protect me. I can protect myself."

"Obviously," he said with a sneer, and motioned to her wound.

"Like you've never been hurt in battle."

"Only very rarely. And I *didn't* think about what would happen during my absence." Not every second of every day.

"Let me guess. You just didn't care," she said. "Apathy in All Things might as well be our family motto."

Aye. Apathy in All Things. So why did he take a step toward her, *needing* contact? And why did the words "our family" on those red, red lips cause a shudder of longing?

Whiskey-colored eyes widened, and the pulse at the base of her neck raced. The beauty who put the suns of Amaranthia to shame began to pant as a rosy flush darkened her cheeks, and spread.

He remembered how badly he'd longed to investigate her blushes before his departure. How he'd wondered just how hot her skin felt, and just how far the heat spread. Now, his curiosity deepened.

"Do I look apathetic?" he rasped.

She gave him a once-over—and actually licked her lips,

shocking him. Then she flattened her palms over his pecs and
pushed.

Thought she needed space?

He stepped *closer*, so close his chest brushed against the
beaded crests of her breasts when he inhaled. A ragged groan
escaped him at the moment of contact. Not his fault. The *curves*
on this woman. She fit him perfectly, soft where he was hard.

He wanted to rub against her—wanted to rub against her
now.

Instead, he stepped back. *Careful. Proceed with caution.*

She flicked the tip of her tongue against an incisor as she
studied him more intently. What thoughts rolled through her
mind?

"Back to the *many* times you've gotten hurt throughout your
life, and not just in war but in romance," she finally said. "I
know you once wanted Winter."

She knew, and she was...jealous? Now *he* felt like smirking.
Keeping his tone bland, he said, "Once. Yes."

"What about now?"

"Why? Are you still willing to share me?" He hadn't forgotten how easily she'd given him permission to bed other women.

"Ha!" She patted his cheek. "Dream on, lover boy. You get
tit for tat. You plan to kill my lovers. It's only fair that I kill
yours, slowly. So," she prompted. "Are you or are you not still
attracted to Winter?"

Do not lean into her touch. "You would kill your friend?"

Her eyes narrowed. "Answer me."

"I am...not." He watched her face—there. A glimmer of
relief. She *had* been jealous. *My woman wants me, as she should.*
Tone a littler huskier, he said, "We'll discuss your jealousy later.
For now, let's get you patched up."

Her eyes *really* narrowed.

"You heard Winter," she said. "She's coming back with supplies. Besides, I'm immortal. A *non-jealous* immortal. I'll heal."

"Not all immortals heal from all wounds." And the color in

her cheeks was beginning to dull, beads of sweat popping up along her brow and upper lip. "Who did you battle?"

"The Walshes. If you want names, I can't oblige. I didn't stop to introduce myself to the guys dying under my sword."

"Now that I've returned, I can fight on your behalf."

She snorted. "No need. I can fight for myself."

"I'm strong." He liked the idea of protecting and defending her.

She rolled her eyes, unfazed. "So am I."

"You aren't stronger than me. Right now, you aren't stronger than the wind."

Shrug. "I can still take you down."

"Can you?" he asked with a rough tone. His height and width gave him an unfair advantage and highlighted her feminine delicateness.

"I can. And FYI, you can't intimidate me, big guy. Not anymore."

FYI? "Can I not?"

"No, but I bet I can intimidate you," she said. This time *she* stepped toward *him* and wrapped her arms around his neck.

Her gaze dared him to stay put as she slowly, languidly, lifted to her tiptoes to bring her lips closer to his...

She planned to kiss him? Here, in front of witnesses?

Want this—will have this. Will have her. *I'll stake my claim.*

The danger! Already lust threatened to overtake him, and ruin...everything.

Puck lurched backward.

She chuckled, taunting him, and said, "You lose."

Magnificent female. She'd already figured out his weaknesses, hadn't she?

"Why are you protesting a divorce, anyway?" she asked. "You planned to cut me loose from the start. Why put off the inevitable? And where are the shears?"

"The shears are somewhere safe," he said. "And you'll get your divorce after William dethrones my brother. No sooner."

"Well. Is that all that needs to happen before I can be rid of you? Okay, then. Let's find William and go dethrone your brother."

You will never be rid of me.

Enough! He scrambled to refortify his resolve. No one possessed a stronger will than him; he could do this, *would* do it…

"Hey, guys." As promised, Winter returned with a bag of supplies. "Are we getting right down to the baby making part of today's reunion, or do you two have a moment to play Dr. Love and Patient Zero?"

A flush spread over Gillian's cheeks.

"Supplies," he said. Barely.

Winter handed over the bag. "Now don't you go thinking I'm doing this out of the kindness of my heart or anything. If my girl dies of infection, I'll have to mourn. I suck at mourning, and no one likes to do the things they suck at."

She strutted off a second time, and Gillian snatched the bag from Puck's grip. Another woman rushed over to set a wooden chair in the sand. Gillian muttered her thanks, sat and cut away her bandage.

The moment he caught sight of her wound—gaping flesh, torn muscle, cracked bone—barbed wire seemed to sprout around his heart and squeeze.

She grimaced as she cleaned the injury. Then, with a shockingly steady hand, she ran a needle and thread through both sides of the laceration.

"I have an idea," she said, as calmly as if she were gardening. "How about you use the shears as a good faith gesture? I'll help you murder Sin without being bonded to you. Win-win for both of us."

Still can't wait to be rid of me. "How about…not."

She scowled at him, but let the subject drop as she wrapped a clean bandage around her torso and stood. "You were right about one thing. I did a lot of sewing while you were gone—on myself."

Who was this woman? And why was he *throbbing* with desire all over again?

"Poppet?" William's voice rang out, loud and clear, and dripped with astonishment.

"William! *You* found *us.*" Gillian laughed a magical sound, and Puck gnashed his teeth as she darted around him to throw herself into the other man's arms. Another laugh escaped her when William twirled her round and round.

Inside Puck, possessive instincts stretched and screamed. *Rip her from the bastard's embrace. Kill him with your bare hands. Claim your woman. Now.*

And feed William's vanity? Never!

In this, Puck's pride was too great.

As Indifference snarled and roared, banging against his skull, he offered no resistance. But he wondered. Was this the reason the Oracles suggested he temporarily wed Gillian? To hinder the demon, allowing Puck to feel while remaining strong?

He remembered how badly he'd once wanted to experience his emotions without suffering a consequence. Now he could, and yet... *Hate my emotions!*

"I can't believe you're really here," Gillian said, tears of joy streaming down her cheeks.

Where were her tears of joy for *Puck*?

"As if I could stay away. Look at you." William placed her on her feet and took her face in his trembling hands. "You've changed. A fact I hadn't expected to like. But immortality suits you well."

"And you..." She hugged him once, twice, then a third time, as if she couldn't stop. "You are as flawless as I remember."

"I missed you so much." Again, William swung her round and round.

"You did? Truly? I mean, when I bonded with Puck, you washed your hands of me." She knit her brows, which were a shade darker than her hair. "For that matter, why'd you agree to help Puck?"

William set her back on her feet. "Not Puck. You. And I

misspoke when I learned of your bonding. I was angry with myself, not you. *I* should have been the one to save you. Me. I should have manned up, but I didn't. Instead, I lashed out, blaming everyone else. Truth is, my choices brought us to that fateful day, not yours, and I want to make it up to you. I *will* make it up to you."

She listened, rapt and adoring.

Puck bristled with hostility.

"How are the Lords and Ladies?" she asked William.

"Alive and well."

A glint of happiness in her eyes…right alongside a glint of sadness. She missed her friends. Because of Puck.

Don't care—I don't! I did what I needed to do.

"Now, I want to hear every detail about *your* life," William said. "Start at the beginning, when we parted, and end with your gaze finding me in this hellhole. Leave nothing out."

Hellhole? "I'd rather hear about *your* adventures, William." Puck offered the pair a cold grin. "Why don't you tell us about your many bedroom conquests since Gillian's marriage to me."

If glares could kill an immortal, Puck would be bloody and dead.

William softened his expression and said, "All forgettable, my sweet. There's absolutely nothing to tell."

Gillian rested her head on his shoulder and clung to his arm, all while assessing Puck with a masked gaze. "How about I give you the highlights? I started my own clan, rescued women and children from bad homes, and became the most feared warrior in the land. Oh, and I recently decided to start dating. Because I'm divorced!"

"Enough!" The command spewed from Puck before he could bite his tongue. "You want a divorce so badly? Earn it."

"Ooh la la. Another show of heat." She exuded excitement, even as she braced for disappointment. "Return of the Ice Man in three, two…"

Bury emotions. Deep freeze. There. Better.

"And he's back," she said with a sigh.

William stuck out his lower lip, pretending to pout, and used his free hand to twist a fist under his eye. "Boohoo. Poor Pucky. Is our furbaby pouting about his lost kingdom?"

Puck rested his hand on the hilt of a dagger and contemplated removing the male's tongue. He needed his key alive— not able to speak.

"Be nice," Gillian said, her gaze on *Puck*. For some reason, his tension hemorrhaged the moment she released William. "I've spent a lot of time studying your brother. He's so paranoid he built a fortress the size of Texas, and conjured a maze around it. No one can get to him—because I've never tried. If I allow myself to be captured and carted inside, like a Trojan horse, I could kill the guards and sneak you two inside."

Puck said, "No," at the same time William gave an adamant shake of his head and shouted, "Not happening."

Her lips pursed with irritation. "Will I be hurt? Yes. I won't pretend otherwise. Am I afraid of pain? No. Will the little girl obey the big, strong men? Go screw yourselves!"

More spirit. More stubbornness. "Will I allow you to head straight to your unhappy ending?" Puck said. "No. You could be killed on sight. Or worse." Especially if Sin discovered what she meant to him. Not that she meant anything to him. Rephrase. Especially if Sin discovered Puck had bonded to her.

Better.

"Agreeing with Mr. Muppet grieves me, but in this, I must." William settled a fist over his heart, a position of faux dejection that in no way belied his immeasurable strength. "We go together or not at all. And what does he mean, unhappy ending?"

Gillian waved away the question as unimportant.

"We'll leave at first light." Puck pointed to her bandage. "Tonight, you'll heal."

"Sir, yes sir. We'll also feast." She saluted him, her expression unreadable. "Tomorrow, we'll head out to kick Sin the Demented off the Connacht throne and get me my divorce."

21

HE WAS BACK. PUCK HAD RETURNED, AS PROMISED, making Gillian feel as if unicorns were prancing through her chest, and fairies were dancing inside her stomach. He was even more beautiful than she remembered. *Otherworldly* beautiful, with his chiseled features carved from ice and stone. His long, dark hair. Those horns. His utterly divine scent, more potent than magic, more intoxicating than wine.

She shivered. Everything about the warrior appealed to her. His towering height and wide shoulders...all those cuts of glorious sinew and latent strength...his tattoos...his lean hips and muscular legs...

His massive hard-on.

Yeah, he'd gotten hard—for her? For someone else? And she'd noticed the moment it happened, despite wanting to stare at his face forever. His shaft was a magnet for her gaze. Apparently the Dune Raider wanted to go a-raiding—in Puck's pants.

Finally she had proof: old fears would *not* rise up and overtake her.

Dang him! The second she'd spotted him, a sizzling bolt of lust had slammed into her, igniting a wildfire in her veins and an aching need between her legs, making a mockery of everything she'd felt in the past. Even now, awareness tingled beneath the surface of her skin. Skin burned by a constant white-hot flush. Breathing was now a luxury, panting the norm. Her heart had yet to slow down.

Her body *craved* relief—and wanted it from him, only him. Her husband.

Already unofficially divorced? Who was she kidding?

Having been forced to bury her physical desires for centuries, she'd become a master at hiding her needs. Those skills served her well today, allowing her to fool both Puck and William. *Crave Puck's mouth and hands? What? When? Me?*

Once or twice, she'd feared Puck had figured her out, feared he could see underneath her calm facade, how her knees threatened to melt every time he revealed emotion, or heat. Once, she'd thought he'd gazed at her with palpable longing.

But, no matter how desperate she might be, or how much he might or might not desire her, the reasons for avoiding sex with him hadn't changed. He would freeze her out afterward, making her feel used and abused. She would kill him, and in turn, inadvertently kill herself. No, thanks.

Unless *she* iced *him* out afterward? Food for thought.

Or she could just wait for the divorce. As soon as the bond got axed, she would crave other men. Surely! Besides, what was a few more days or weeks of abstinence after half a millennium?

But oh, she was tired, so very tired of hearing about her friends' amazing sex lives. "Sex is beautiful," Rosaleen had once said. "A communion of bodies and souls. And the pleasure—" She'd smiled a cat-eating-the-canary grin. "I was so primed for an orgasm, I didn't care if the world around me ashed. Not until I was done with my man."

That. That was what Gillian craved.

"You guys want a tour of the camp?" she asked.

Puck nodded, his gaze never wavering from her face, as if he *couldn't* look away. As if he'd found a prize worth fighting for.

A coil of warmth unfurled in her belly, even as she chided herself for more wishful thinking.

"I would love a personal, private tour," William said.

William, sweet William. She'd been so excited to see him, more excited than she'd thought she'd be, considering he'd faded to a fond but distant memory in the back of her mind and heart.

His fairy-tale face and fantastical electric blues had grown harder in their time apart. And he had a sharper edge, too. If only her body responded to him. *He* was never cold with her.

As she led her guests through camp, Puck fell into step *between* her and William, his body heat razing her already sensitized nerve endings. Maintaining her casual facade jumped from possible to improbable.

Neither male noticed. At the moment, they were too busy glaring at each other.

William broke first, tossing a careless smile Gillian's way. "Tell me true, poppet. On a scale of one to ten—one meaning you nearly perished from heartbreak every minute of every day, and ten meaning you did, indeed, perish because you could no longer live without me, but hope of a reunion brought you back to life—how badly did you miss me?"

Snort. "We were parted?" she asked, feigning confusion.

"Oh, how you wound me." He bypassed Puck to stop in front of her and brush a lock of hair from her face. "You fared well here?"

"I did." She wouldn't trade her time in Amaranthia for anything.

Again, Puck stepped between them. Though he wore his favorite Ice Man expression, broadcasting zero emotion, he wrapped his hand around William's windpipe, squeezing while lifting her friend off his feet. "I will give you only one warning, Ever Randy. This is my land."

"Mine," Gillian corrected.

Still glaring at William, he said, "She is mine. Until we are unbonded, no one gets between me and her. Understand?"

Lightning crackled under William's skin as he slammed an elbow into Puck's forearm, gaining his release. "You have no right—"

"Don't I?" Puck jutted his chin. "Or do I need to remind you of our deal? You are to keep your hands to yourself."

Always so cold, yet so hostile, now intense and possessive. Why, why, *why* did she want to throw herself into her husband's muscular arms?

"What deal?" she asked.

"What deal do you think?" Puck replied. "The one where William helps me claim my crown—"

"Not that part," she said, and rolled her eyes. "The part about keeping his hands to himself."

He glared at William, but remained mute.

"Jealousy isn't a good look on you, Pucky," William snapped, though he did power down, the lightning under his skin fading. "But then, what is? Or is this an act to keep me in line?" He spread his arms wide. "Well, no need. Consider me lined."

"I protect my *investment*," Puck snapped back.

Ugh. She'd once referred to herself as an investment, hadn't she? *Silly little girl.*

"You'll lose her soon enough," William said.

The color in her husband's face heightened. He grabbed hanks of his hair, razors cutting his palms, blood welling. Eyes squeezed shut, he grated, "What's happening...instincts...kill threat...can't, can't."

Kill *William*? Because he'd threatened Puck's marriage?

Softening, Gillian reached for Puck, intending to distract him with touch. But she needn't have bothered. The Ice Man returned. Of course. He straightened, his arms falling to his sides, his expression devoid of any emotion.

Disappointment struck, but she ignored it. What had she expected?

"Gillian!" a familiar voice squealed.

The patter of footsteps echoed...a stampede of them, actually, growing closer by the second. Both Puck and William braced for attack a split second before a gaggle of children circled her, shoving the guys out of the way.

Her heart nearly burst with love as she received smiles, hugs and kisses. These rescued children adored her, and the feeling was mutual.

One of their teachers called out, "All right, children. Enough. You've got a paper to write, and our queen has duties to oversee."

Amid groans of disappointment, Gillian promised to visit the school later on. Just like that, the groans were replaced by cheers. The children raced away.

William gazed at her with a quizzical expression. "Queen?"

She shrugged. "Tradition is strong in Amaranthia, *aye*? Though I've created a democracy, most Shawazons prefer the old ways, with a ruling class."

"After your—I can't bring myself to say the B-word." He shuddered. "I researched Puck and learned a few things about his homeland. Females are often forced to become fillies in a stable with hundreds of others. They are banned from the battlefield and punished if they dare learn to read or write." He spat the words at Puck, as if her husband should carry all the blame.

"That is changing," she said, her chest puffing up. "A few of my women have stables of their own, where *men* are like kept stallions. We war, and we learn whatever we want without reservation."

Frowning now, William massaged the back of his neck. "I should have trained you to fight when we first met."

"I wasn't ready," she admitted. Back then, any hint of violence had panicked her.

With his arms crisscrossed over his chest, his biceps bigger than her hopes and dreams, Puck stared her down. "Do *you* have a stable of stallions?"

"Dude. If only!" She suspected having a stable wasn't the same as dating in his mind.

William gaped at her, as if she'd just admitted to being pregnant with triplet demons. "You desire a stable?"

"Like you have any room to judge," she said, and *humphed*. "You've been with ninety-nine percent of the female population. Boy, you get *around*."

He reached for her again, only to catch himself, fist his hand, and drop his arm to his side. A flare of irritation in his eyes before he said, his voice low and husky, "Merely practice for you."

Oh, please. "How many times have you used that particular line?"

"When compared to the size of my hit it and quit it number, practically zero," he replied, only slightly abashed.

How many did "practically" equal? She motioned the guys forward, not daring to look Puck's way. He'd gone silent, which wasn't a good sign. The best predators watched and waited...

"Come on," she said. "Let's finish the tour." The sooner she got to Peanut, the better.

In the ensuing half hour, every woman who spotted Puck and William had one of three reactions. A fit of giggles, a blush, or a seductive wave. William waved back, even winked a time or twelve, but Puck pretended not to notice—or maybe he *didn't* notice. He remained focused on Gillian as she talked about the homes she'd helped build. How, after paying an architectural engineer and finding out what she'd needed, she and her clanswomen had spent decades digging with tools and magic until reaching a layer of compacted soil beneath the sand. They'd also dragged, carried, magically hauled or manufactured different-sized stones and metals to the campsite to create screw piles, gravel for concrete, and everything else they'd required.

A lot of hard work, a lot of time and energy, and a lot of trial and error, but totally worth it. They'd created secure homes with all the essentials: stove, storage, arsenal and space for a bed.

Because the Shawazons lived near a gorgeous, pristine lake, other clans constantly attacked, hoping to take over.

Hat tip to anyone who managed to do the impossible.

"I'm amazed," William said. "My delicate girl has—"

"Delicate?" Oh, but he'd raised her hackles with that little gem. He refused to see her another way, despite everything she'd shown him? Well, she'd have to teach him better. "Hold my daggers," she said to Puck.

William hurried to reassure her. "I merely complimented you. You've changed, strengthened. Stories of your exploits will be told long after you've gone."

Her stomach flip-flopped as realization settled in. He expected her to leave Amaranthia. No doubt Puck did as well, after he'd won the Connacht crown. As archaic as he was, he might cut the Shawazons from an all-clan alliance.

Tingles on the back of her neck. Heat racing down her spine. She dug her nails into her palms, drawing blood. Inhale, exhale. *Hulking-out won't do anyone any good.* Searching for calm... there. A well of confidence.

No one cut the Shawazons from an alliance!

"Do you expect me to leave Amaranthia when you become king?" she demanded.

He frowned at her. "Of course."

Knew it! "Too bad. Unlike you, I finish what I start." She would be staying, and she would remain queen. Her people would be protected, always.

You will not have a happy ending...

She tuned out the Oracles' prediction, even as her stomach performed another flip-flop.

Frown deepening, Puck tilted his head, his study of her intensifying. "What are you trying to tell me?"

He needed clarity? Fine. She'd spell it out. "If you try to disband the Shawazons when you unite the clans, *I* will find a way to dethrone *you*." Gillian was tempted to use the last of her magic, just to prove her strength. Something she would have done without hesitation as a plucky two-hundred-year-old. But she was older now, wiser, and refused to waste the hard-won gift she'd acquired. She wielded magic for protection, defense and survival, not bragging rights.

She expected resistance. She'd threatened him, after all. But he softened. "Your clan will always have a place here, lass."

Really? "Okay. Yes. Thank you." Goodbye, indignation.

No, not goodbye. Not entirely. Like a parasite, indignation found a way inside William. He flicked the tip of his tongue against an incisor, as if he could taste the blood of his enemy—and liked it.

To divert him, she said, "I showed you mine, now you show me yours. What else did you do during my absence? And don't you dare tell me a gentleman never spills."

"Oh, I won't, poppet." His voice possessed a formal tone he'd never before used with her. "Even gentlemen spill with the proper incentive."

His meaning crystalized, and she blushed like a maiden of 216.

Puck sucked in a breath, as if he...what? *Liked* her blush? Or maybe he just wanted to murder William for flirting? Either way, meow. *Won't look.* Any heat would fade from his dark eyes with their glittering starbursts, and he would regard her with cold disinterest.

"Other than drinking myself into stupors and fighting beside my father in the underworld?" William sighed. "I threw man-tantrums, searched for you and considered all the ways to punish Puck."

Ha! Man-tantrums. The worst kind. And William's were even worse than most!

"So what's your favorite method?" Puck asked. He didn't sound curious or upset or even particularly intrigued.

"That's easy." William rubbed his hands together, all evil

overlord. "Skinning you alive to make a flesh coat, then wearing it as I hack you to bits. Slowly. You'll become a cautionary tale. The moral? When someone hopes to experience the horrors of hell on Earth, mess with my woman."

Puck stiffened, his body language saying more than words. Basically: *She's all mine, hands off, or get bent.*

At least, that was what *Gillian* heard. And dang it, the possessiveness kinda sorta delighted her. Not that it would last. "I'm not yours, or anyone's," she told William. "You're my friend, but…"

William took her rejection in stride, saying, "You aren't mine today…but you will be. I'll make sure of it."

She almost asked, *What about your curse?*

And, *Do you think I'm the one destined to slay you?*

Once, she'd been too feeble. Now? Threat to the max.

For some reason, *that* made her glance at Puck and—she gasped. He watched her, his stare penetrating and intense. Aggressive, even, as if he had already mentally stripped her.

Shivers danced down her spine. Her panties? Now soaked. "H-how can you be so sure?" she asked, forcing herself to focus on William. Stuttering? *Her?*

With a glare at Puck, he said, "I'm the total package, darling. Beauty, brains, brawn. And fated."

Fated. Aka "meant to be." Aka "everything happens for a reason." Aka her most reviled idioms.

Yes, she'd once been overjoyed by the idea of belonging to William. Now? "No such thing as fated." Over the centuries, she'd watched couples interact, fascinated by their nuances, how some crumbled at the first sign of trouble and others flourished. "There's attraction and then, if you want to sustain the relationship, there's hard work."

"But what causes the first draw, hmm?" William asked.

"If you're telling me the first draw is fated, then you'll have to tell me why the attraction sometimes fades."

He glowered. Because he had no response.

"Oracles can predict who will end up with whom," Puck said, his tone somewhat sharp.

"Prediction is different from fate," she pointed out.

"Fate is what drives us," William said.

Ugh. He was one of *those*. People who assigned a supernatural reason to every calamity, or blamed a higher power. And there *was* a higher power. Absolutely. Gillian's friend Olivia—former friend, she supposed, since they hadn't spoken in over five hundred years—was a Sent One married to Aeron, former keeper of Wrath. Olivia had often spoken about Most High's creation of humans and other beings. But the MH did not cause tragedies. He was the essence of Love. Bad things happened because people were in the wrong place at the wrong time. Bad things happened because evil existed. Because good people made bad choices. Because bad people did bad things.

The only reason an adult raped a child—his own sick desires. All that "I couldn't help myself" crap? A lie. Her stephorrors should have resisted temptation. Not that young Gillian should have been any kind of temptation. They made their choices. Them. No one else.

And, okay, say a female cheated on her male. *She* ruined the love match, not fate. Say a male ventured somewhere he wasn't supposed to go and died. His actions caused his death, not fate.

"Has Keeley or someone else foretold us?" she asked William.

He glowered again. "No. But I'm certain here." He tapped the center of his chest.

A rough sound sprang from Puck.

Continue walking. Tune out husband. "Trust me when I say you don't want to be mine," she said to William. "According to the Oracles, I'll kill my man's dreams, have to choose between what could be and what will be, and never experience a happy ending."

"The Oracles are wrong," he replied. "They probably aren't even certified as Foreknowledge Specialists."

Uh, there was no such thing. Right?

Puck believed the Oracles, no doubt about it. She did too—sometimes, at her lowest. But even still, she remained determined. Her life would be whatever *she* made it. She *would* have a happy ending, because she would accept nothing less. She would fight, and fight hard to achieve her goals. Nothing would stop her.

Look how far she'd come already.

"Gillian?" Warm, calloused fingers stroked her jaw. Drugging tingles followed. "You stopped. Why?"

She blinked rapidly, snapping to attention just in time to watch William knock Puck's hand away. Even when her mind had been unaware, her husband had made her body react.

The two men snarled at each other.

Mercy. Who was she supposed to vote for? Beauty or the Beast?

You know who...

Deciding retreat was her best option, she said, "I'll spread the word that you guys aren't to be harmed. Feel free to walk about, look around, whatever you want, but do *not* hurt anyone. Got it? And do not sleep with my soldiers." If Puck cheated on *her...*

Teeth clenched, she added, "I'll see you at the feast this evening." Head high, she marched off before anyone could protest.

Won't look back. Absolutely will not. She turned a corner, putting a house between her and the guys, voiding the temptation. *Out of sight, out of mind.*

Pasting a fake smile on her face, she made a beeline for Rosaleen, a petite beauty with gorgeous brown skin, dark hair and darker eyes. She would be considered flawless, if not for the X branded into her forehead. The mark of her former "master." The cruel brute had ensured his "fillies" could be identified with a single glance, if ever they managed to escape.

"Double the guard around the perimeter," Gillian said. The Walshes would know the Shawazons decimated the outpost, because she'd left her favorite calling card: no survivors. They would attack, and soon. "And ask our best cooks to whip up a feast fit for a queen. Tonight we celebrate the return of my husband and friend."

"Are we adding poison to expedite the end of your marriage? And if so, do you want him to die slow or fast?" Rosaleen asked, totally serious.

"Valid questions." She pretended to think over her response. "No poison. Tomorrow I'm escorting the men to the Connacht fortress. Winter and Cameron are coming with us, I'm sure, which means you and Johanna will be in charge."

Rosaleen nodded. "Be careful. I encountered Sin Connacht only once, but he spooked me for life. There's something seriously off about him."

"We'll defeat him." Failure was not an option.

Avoiding everyone else, Gillian made her way home. A small stone house she'd helped build. She'd never taken an interest in decorating, so the walls remained unpainted. The only personal touches—the weapons she'd hung here, there, everywhere, and the shelf holding jars she'd filled with trophies she'd taken from the most vicious of her victims.

What would Puck and William think of her living quarters?

Out of sight, out of mind, remember?

Through the door—absolute, utter chaos greeted her. Peanut *had* thrown a fit. He'd shredded her couch, dismantled her kitchen table, and removed a leg from a chair reserved for special guests.

The only thing her pet hadn't ruined was her bed, and only because she slept in a loft upstairs, and he couldn't climb the ladder.

No sign of him inside. With a sigh, she trekked to the backyard. A fence separated her boxed vegetable garden and potted fruit trees from Peanut's barn.

"Come out, come out, wherever you are," she called.

Though Gillian remained a vegetarian, Peanut required

meat. For his sake, she'd learned to hunt, skin and prepare meals that would keep him strong. In fact, she had a ritual. Once a week, she journeyed into the nearest forest on her own, hunted and mourned her kills—because yes, she always named the animals and envisioned a future as best friends.

Animals were awesome; killing them affected her in a way killing people did not. Maybe because most people sucked.

Peanut trotted out of the barn as if he hadn't a care and plopped in the shade offered by the apple tree—grown with magic—where he munched on a fallen fruit.

Well, not all animals were awesome.

He refused to meet her gaze, even turned his head away.

Worse than a toddler, she thought, and stretched out beside him.

He flicked her a glance that said, *I'll allow you to pet me.* Except, when she reached out to stroke the soft fur behind his ear, his glare said, *But only with your gaze.*

"I missed you, Nutty Buddy."

He *humphed* at her.

"I've got to go on another trip tomorrow, and I don't know how long I'll be gone," she admitted.

The apple fell from his mouth and rolled past her thigh.

"Good thing you get to go with me, huh," she added, before he could erupt into another fit. "You just have to be nice to—"

He was on his feet and licking her face before she could finish the sentence. Laughing, she nuzzled her cheek against his neck and wrapped her arms around him. "Tonight, I'll introduce you to my husband and friend. They'll be coming with us. I'm pretty sure you'll dislike them both."

Out of sight, but not *out of mind. Accept it, deal with it.*

"Puck is magnificent but terrible, sweet but cruel, kind but unconcerned, intelligent but clueless. He might want me, he might not. With him it's difficult to tell." Either way, her body continued to want his, and she wanted…

She just plain *wanted*.

Her plan to wait for an official divorce might have been a wee bit hasty. What harm could come from using Puck and taking her pleasure—her due?

After everything he'd put her through, he *owed* her.

And whether he'd admit it or not, he wanted her, too, and not just because of the bond. He must. The way he'd jumped between her and William…caressed her… The way he'd looked at her… She'd gotten her first lingering glance!

If she dared to encourage Puck—*truly* encourage him— would he dare to make a move on her?

Well. There was only one way to find out…

22

PUCK STAYED IN THE SHADOWS, OBSERVING GIL-
lian in her natural habitat, with her pet.

He might want me, he might not.

Wonder no more, wife. He wants you.

Once her pet fell asleep, she left to check on her people.
Puck tracked and studied her, unwilling to spend even a moment away from her.

*Left her for weeks without a problem, now I can't leave her for a
few minutes?*

Twice she stiffened, as if she knew someone watched her,
but she never called him out.

She had changed so much more than he'd realized. She
walked with confidence now, her head held high. Any room
she entered, she owned. Her people adored her, yes, but she
adored her people right back.

She had a big heart. Loved passionately and lived life by her
own rules.

The kitten had become a tigress.

When one of her soldiers stopped her to ask for relationship
advice, she said, "I don't have a lot of experience in this arena,
or any, but I'm pretty sure you're supposed to always leave him

wanting more. Unless he says something cruel. Or lies. Or hits. Then you leave him dead."

Though she clearly had a ton of work to do around the village, she always stopped to chat with anyone who approached her. She had hugs and praise for the children, and ensured livestock and chimeras were well taken care of.

Puck found himself oddly fascinated—and still hard. Too many times to count, he looked at her mouth and wondered how deep she could take his length.

He needed…he didn't know what he needed. His wife out of the picture? His wife underneath him? Over him? In front of him on her hands and knees? Yes, yes. All of that. He needed his wife to moan his name, and claw his back, and beg him for—

What are you doing? Resist her allure!

He hated all this wanting. Hated dreading the end of his marriage when he should be eager for it.

She was his, but not.

Without the bond to Puck, she would crave William once again. Unless Puck addicted her to his touch. Could he?

Yes. Absolutely. He could do anything, was known as the Undefeated for a reason. But he *wouldn't* addict her. He would be better served keeping his distance. There was no good reason to let his feelings intensify and complicate an already complicated situation. He could barely handle what he felt *now*.

An old adage he needed to remember: Why willingly walk into a sword when you could move around it?

Gillian popped a grape into her mouth and waited for Puck to grace the feast with his exalted presence. She sat before a crackling fire pit, William at her side. Shawazons formed a circle around them, sharing platters of food, jugs of ale and goblets of water. Laughter echoed through the night, blending with a thousand different conversations and the soft thrum of music as clanswomen played handmade drums, flutes and harps. In the center of the circle, a group of dancers rocked their hips while twirling scarves with wild abandon.

Cameron danced among them, teasing one woman in particular.

True to his nature, he often became obsessed with a single woman for weeks at a time, sometimes months, and did everything in his power to seduce and lure. The moment he won her heart, however, the chase ended, as did his obsession. He would move on to someone else.

This particular woman had held out longer than most, but she would cave. They *always* caved.

Gillian had bathed, changed into her best leathers and plaited her hair. Not that anyone could *see* her hair. She wore a bold, colorful headscarf. One of her favorites, though the material was too gossamer to protect against sand and wind. She simply liked the look of it. Crystal beads hung from the upper hem, giving her bejeweled bangs.

William had dropped to his knees the moment he'd spotted her, as if struck by a bolt of lightning. Even as she'd laughed, delighted by his antics, she'd shaken with anticipation to discover *Puck's* reaction.

Where was he?

Even Peanut had joined the feast. As predicted, he'd detested William on sight and had already peed on his boots, nipped his ass and spit in his face. To William's credit, he hadn't retaliated. Cursed up a storm, yes, but nothing more. Good thing. If he'd lashed out physically, he would have gotten the stinky boot out of camp, Puck's mission be damned.

Mess with what's mine, pay the price.

Dang it, why hadn't Puck shown up?

"You're doing it again," William grumbled.

"Doing what?" she asked, confused.

"Watching for Puck, missing all my best moves." Not just grumbled this time, but snarled. "You don't want him, poppet. Trust me. Please. The bond is screwing with your mind, nothing more."

"Those were your best moves? Wow. I feel sorry for you." And how had he known she desired Puck? How had he known to play on her fears about the bond? "Sorry, Liam, but you've lost your golden touch."

Eyes hooded, he leaned toward her, seduction incarnate. "You've never known my touch." His voice deepened, and developed a husky rasp. "I have a feeling you'll like it very much…"

Except, she remained unresponsive to him. "I remember a time you didn't want me. Not too long ago, in fact. Only a handful of weeks have passed for you. What's changed?"

"You," he said simply.

"I have changed, yes. And you were right, I do want Puck," she admitted.

Rigid as steel, he opened his mouth to say something, thought better of it, and ground his teeth. "He will never give you what you need."

"And what do I need, hmm?"

"Devotion."

"Actually, I need orgasms." A bald statement, and perfectly true. Except, a tide of longing rose inside her. Devotion sounded *amazing*. To trust her lover. To know he would never willingly hurt or betray her.

A commotion to the right. Out of habit, Gillian reached for a dagger, only to still. Puck had arrived at long last.

The rest of the world vanished as her gaze collided with his. In an instant, her blood turned molten, and her heart decided to do a hard-rock drum solo.

So badly she yearned to reach out and stroke him.

In the firelight, his horns appeared longer, thicker. He hadn't shaved, so a shadow of dark stubble covered his jaw. He had bathed, though. His damp hair dripped at the ends, sending water droplets careening down the ridges of his bare chest.

Those droplets disappeared under the waist of his sheepskin breeches.

He was a warrior, a man and an animal-like predator all at once, which only worsened her fascination with him.

What did he think of her?

He stared at her mouth as he rubbed his thumb over his bottom lip, as if he was imagining *kissing* her. *Yes, please.* Then his gaze traced over her body, lingering everywhere she ached, as if he knew how desperately she wanted his hands and lips to follow.

Did he know? Expression devoid of emotion, he closed the distance. His hands—she sucked in a breath. His hands were balled into fists. Well, well. He wasn't as stoic as he wanted her to believe.

I affect him.

Silent, he sat at her side. His bicep bulged as he plucked two fire-roasted squash medallions from a nearby platter, tossed one to Peanut and popped the other into his mouth. Her husband chewed, swallowed and concentrated on the dancers.

She liked the way his jaw moved, every motion carnal.

Shocker: Peanut sniffed him, then gently head-butted his hand, demanding to be petted. Her chimera had never accepted *anyone* so quickly.

"Your demon spawn scents you on Puck," William mumbled. "There's no more to it than that."

She tried, she tried so hard, but she couldn't remove her focus from Puck. "You do realize you ate a piece of squash, right?" Mimicking a caveman, she added, "Meat good. Vegetables bad. Remember?"

"I eat for strength, always, even if I'm offered trash food." *His* attention remained on the dancers, even as his deep, husky voice stole over Gillian's skin like a caress. Did he find one of her clanswomen attractive? "Besides, everything I eat is tasteless to me."

Though she hadn't inherited that particular disadvantage,

compassion trumped her urge to dismiss the dancers. "Courtesy of Indifference?"

He offered a single, curt nod.

"Are your lovers tasteless, as well?" William leaned over, grabbed the last medallion of squash and popped it into his mouth. His eyes closed and he moaned, as if he'd gotten caught up in the throes of a climax. When he finished, he licked his lips and smirked. "I bet you try your very best to give a woman a mediocre experience. Well, I wouldn't worry any longer. Go ahead and consider it missionary accomplished."

"I haven't taken a lover outside of my marriage. Perhaps I need more practice to reach your expert level of seduction," Puck said. "Tell me, Panty Melter. How many thousands of women does it take…after you've met the one you believe is your fated mate?"

Oh, baby, the claws were out tonight. Where was popcorn when she needed it?

And okay, excitement was probably the exact wrong reaction over another potential man-brawl. But come on! Puck just admitted he hadn't slept with anyone while they were parted.

Strung as tight as a bow, William said, "I have never wanted to kill a man more than I want to kill you, Pucky."

"The feeling is mutual, *Randy.*"

Wanting—needing—to know if sexual tension tormented Puck as fervently as it tormented her, if something she'd said or done had reached him on a primitive level, Gillian tracked her fingers along the rise of his knuckles. So soft, so warm. So perfect!

He whipped around to face her, his eyes narrowed and glittering, his breaths coming in great heaves—the bulge behind his fly was *massive.* "Touch me again, and I'll press you into the sand and slam inside you."

Her first thought: *Yes! Finally!*

Her second: *He wants me so bad.*

As her mind whirled and her body wept with relief, William's irises glowed red with menace. "I hope you like three-ways, Pucky, because I'll be throwing myself into the mix."

"You can *try*," Puck said, his jaw clenched.

"Uh, guys? I need you to…" What? *Kiss each other and make up?*

Mmm. Now, wouldn't *that* be nice?

To her surprise, Puck stood and stalked away without uttering another word. True to form, he never looked back.

Peanut, the traitor, leaped up to trail after him.

She wanted to do the same, but consoled herself with the silver-medal choice and glared at William.

"What?" he demanded. "What'd I do wrong?"

"Stop flirting with me in front of Puck. And stop antagonizing him. I'm not going to sleep with you, William. I'm not going to cheat on my husband." Her dreams of dating other guys had gone up in flames the moment she'd first entertained the idea, whether she'd known it or not.

"He's your temporary husband. There's a difference. And I'm not asking you to cheat on him."

"What are you asking me to do, then?"

"What else?" He spread his arms wide. "Give a suitor a proper kiss. What? What's that look? Kissing isn't cheating. It's one friend helping another friend refill her lungs. Kissing is *survival*."

"If you believe that, I feel sorry for your true ladylove." Just to be mean, because yes, Gillian had developed a wee bit of a cruel streak, she added, "Whoever she happens to be."

As he studied her face, perhaps searching for weaknesses in her resolve, he appeared flabbergasted, as if he'd never known rejection—of any kind—and had no idea what had just happened. He opened his mouth, closed it. Opened, closed.

Finally he settled on, "Your strong moral code turns me on."

"Please. A gentle wind turns you on."

"I want you," William said, and this time his tone had a little bite.

"Okay, say I wanted you back. How would we spend our life together?"

"I would war with Lucifer, you would tend my wounds. As before."

Ugh. "You think that would be enough for me?"

Crystalline eyes aglow, he said huskily, "Every moment in between, we would spend in bed."

Still. Not. Enough. "And if I wanted to fight at your side?"

"We'd…negotiate."

Meaning he would try to talk her into staying home. Old Gillian would have thrilled. New Gillian wanted to gag.

"Explain why you want me, specifically," she said. "Why you would come here for me. Why you would help Puck, just to free me from the bond. I have a vague memory of overhearing some of the Lords talking about how you were waiting for my eighteenth birthday to claim me. More vividly I remember you telling me that you would never fall in love or get married."

He tugged on the end of her thickest braid, a playful action that belied the growing strain in his expression. "From the beginning, I knew there was something different about you. I fought it. I told myself I wouldn't do anything with you, no matter how old you were, or weren't. But deep down I knew the moment you were ready, I would pounce. Then Puck took you away, and I felt as if I'd lost…"

"What? Your favorite toy?"

"Everything."

The single word hit her like a punch in the sternum. Her ribs seemed to crack, acid leaking out. For a moment, she said nothing. She couldn't. She hoped his intensity would lessen and he'd crack a joke. He didn't.

If he'd truly desired *her*, if he'd considered Gillian his fated mate, why hadn't he eschewed other women and waited for her?

He should have waited for her.

"William—"

"No. Don't say anything. Not until the bond is severed."

Was he right? Would her desire for Puck really fade? If so, would she want William in her bed—her body? Right now, she couldn't imagine wanting anyone but her husband.

A muscle jumped under his eye once, twice. "If you feel like you must be with him, go, be with him. Sow your wild oats. Get him out of your system." Staring up at the heavens, he said in a quieter tone, "I deserve this, I really do."

"I'm not doing this to punish you," she said, then frowned. She didn't owe him an explanation, or excuse. "I *will* sow my oats, and not because you permit it."

Had the circumstances reversed, Puck wouldn't tell her to get another man out of her system. No, he would keep his promise to kill anyone she even thought about dating. Because he wanted her passion all to himself. Clearly!

Touch me again, and I'll press you into the sand and slam inside you.

Decadent shivers, irresistible heat.

Get a grip!

"Just...take a cold shower tonight," she said. "Then kiss and make up with Puck, okay?" Oh, good gracious, that image again! Hubba hubba. "And make sure I'm there to serve as witness." She pressed her hands together to form a steeple. "Please, please, a thousand times please."

He *tsk-tsked*, his intensity lessening the slightest bit. "Cold showers are a myth. No man has ever taken one. We're more inclined to take *hot* showers, and exercise a bicep with a repeated up and down motion. *If* we can't find a suitable replacement for whoever left us swollen and needy."

"Then do that," she said, and waved her hand in a shooing motion.

"Which one? The shower or the replacement?"

"Either. Both."

"Harsh, woman. Harsh." He flattened his hand against his chest, right above his heart. "One day you'll want me to yourself, forever and always."

There went her amusement. "I'm sorry, William, but—"

"No, don't say anything you'll regret."

As the back of her neck prickled with awareness, perhaps anticipation, she scanned the crowd—and thrilled. Puck hadn't left the party, after all. Or if he had, he'd returned. He stood on the fringes, shrouded by shadows. Did he watch her?

Heart fluttering, she stood before she realized she'd moved. "Stay here and have fun, Liam. I might or might not be back."

"I might or might not be counting the seconds." William blew her a kiss before flipping off Puck.

Noticed him, too, had he?

Gillian hurried over. Just before she reached Puck, he turned on his heel and strode away. This time, she followed.

Rosaleen stepped into her path, stopping her. "Your friend. The one with baby blues. You didn't tell me he was the most beautiful man in creation. Is he single?"

"Very." Gillian looked around her. No sign of Puck. Dang it!

The general fanned her flushed cheeks. "Mind if I make a move?"

"Not even a little." If anything, Rosaleen would be doing her a favor, keeping William occupied.

Johanna came over and slung an arm around Rosaleen's shoulders. "Did you ask about the blue-eyed devil?"

"Single," the other woman replied with a wide grin.

The two high-fived.

"What about the horned one?" Johanna wiggled her brows. "You're done with him, right?"

Gillian stiffened, happy one moment, ready to commit murder the next. "He's still married. To me."

Both women paled as they held up their hands, palms out, all innocence, and backed away.

"Whoa, whoa," Rosaleen said. "No reason to Hulk-out."

"I'm not going to touch him, honest," Johanna said.

Deep breath in, out. "Sorry," Gillian muttered. "Look, I've got to go." She darted around her friends, searching, searching…

if she couldn't find Puck through natural means, she'd have to use magic.

With the coming journey, she would much rather *hoard* magic. Wait! There. Strange prints, the tread unequally distributed, as if a hoof-shaped weight had worn down the sole's center. Natural means for the win!

She trailed him to…her house. Excitement making her limbs weak, she shut and locked the door.

Puck occupied the living room, his back to her as he walked around, examining the many weapons that hung on the walls. Did he understand she'd taken them as trophies, or did he doubt her like William?

"Where is Peanut?" she asked.

"In the barn, resting."

A sudden thought struck her. How had Puck found her house? She hadn't shown him, and none of her soldiers would share her location without permission.

Tracked me, the way I tracked him, his desires too strong to be denied?

Shivers cascading down her spine, she said, "Why are you here?"

"We're married. I believe I've already informed you of our shared assets. What's yours is mine, and I wanted to see the inside of my new home." His tone was as emotionless as ever, but when he turned to face her—his gaze burned.

What's more? "You're still hard." The words rushed from her, as unstoppable as a freight train.

He raised his chin, as if proud. "Partway, at least."

"You mean it gets *bigger*?" she asked, suddenly breathless.

He might have smirked. "A lot bigger."

Definitely smirked. "Is it…for me?" *Please, please be for me.* "Or for all the beauties at the feast?"

"I don't want those other women…" He roved his gaze over her breasts—her *aching* breasts—and between her legs, where she now throbbed. Then he added, "To die when you throw another jealous fit."

Who? What? How? Me? "As if you have room to talk! You were ready to murder William, the man you need to win your crown."

His nostrils flared. "This is true."

Wait. He'd just copped to his jealousy?

"I told myself I'd stay away," he continued, "that I'd avoid the cut of the sword, yet here I am, only a few short hours later, willing to deal with the complications and fallout. What do you think that says about me, lass? No, stay silent. Do not answer. I'll tell you what it says."

As her entire world seemed to pivot on its axis, he cupped his groin and grated, "Yes, this is for you. I want *only* you."

23

PUCK'S WORDS ECHOED IN GILLIAN'S MIND. *AVOID the cut of a sword*—that's how he saw her? A sword? *Stay silent*—how dare he issue such a command! *Only you*—her knees wobbled.

Then he stiffened, and she wanted to screech, because she knew what would happen next. He'd go cold.

"If you turn into Ice Man right now, I'll poison your next meal," she said.

Looking like the very definition of detached, he winged up a brow. "Keep acting like a shrew, and I'll willingly eat it."

Shrew? How dare he?!

Gillian stalked closer, certain she was a bomb—with a rapid countdown clock. But, as their gazes remained intertwined, neither challenger willing to glance away, her inhalations became his exhalations, and she realized they were breathing each other's air. Anger morphed into arousal.

Tremors ruined her attempt to appear unaffected. Tremors, and her ever-hardening nipples. Probably the passion-fever flushing her skin, as well.

Have gone so long without his touch. Need it.

As if he'd read her mind—and was more than happy to

oblige—he jolted into action. Moving too quickly to track, he clasped her by the hips, backed her against the wall, and flattened his palms next to her temples. As his big body caged her in, the scent of masculine carnality enveloped her, and she felt her lids go heavy.

His muscular frame seemed to swell before her eyes. Suddenly he was bigger, stronger. Veins bulged as if he could barely hold himself in place—as if aggression filled him to the brim. The look he gave her...*ravenous.*

"What do you think you're doing?" she asked, and oh, she sounded eager. *Already too turned on to care.*

"I'm putting you where I want you."

Well, thank goodness for that. She liked where he wanted her. "So you do, in fact, desire me? You haven't reverted to the Ice Man?"

"I think the beast between my legs answers both questions, lass."

Her mouth curled up at the corners. "Did the king of apathy just crack a joke?"

"He merely spoke the truth." As he toyed with the ends of her hair, he tickled her scalp. "I used to summon ice to prevent punishment from the demon. Now I do it to protect us all. You should be grateful for it. If I did even half of the things I'm imagining..."

Summon the ice, he'd said. He truly froze his emotions? How? Magic?

"What kind of punishment?" The weakness he'd once mentioned? "And protect us all from what?" she asked, then the rest of his words registered and she shivered. What did he imagine doing to her?

His eyes narrowed, and he stiffened.

All right. He could keep his secrets. For now. "Sometimes you thaw, though. I've seen it."

A nod. "The ice doesn't melt on its own. I require an outside source to make me feel something hot. Like rage."

"Or desire." Desperate for contact with him, needing to gauge his degree of arousal, she placed her hand just over his heart. Hot skin, like molten gold poured over granite. Racing heartbeat.

His desperation matches mine. The knowledge sent feminine power rushing through her.

He took her by the wrist and lifted her hand—pinned her arm above her head. "Touching the bird tattoo is—"

"Off-limits." Yes, she remembered. "Why?"

"Because I said so."

Fair enough. Again, for now. Later... "What if, one day, you stop feeling entirely and remain the Ice Man?"

"I've often wondered the same, but right now I cannot imagine being in a deep freeze ever again." He brushed the tip of his nose against hers. "You are no longer afraid of intimacy."

"No."

"The strength you needed to overcome your past traumas. The strength you *need*. I'm in awe of you, lass."

Those words... Groaning, she undulated to rub her core against his massive erection. "So you've got me where you want me, warrior, and you're in total awe of me. Whatever are you going to do with me?" How she found the wits to speak, she wasn't sure. *Want more. Need it.*

He hissed, his grip flexing on her wrist. "I'm going to have you. I'm also going to let you go one day soon."

Were the words a promise or a warning? Did he hope to frighten or entice her? Like, *Hey baby, you don't have to worry about me becoming a clingy stalker because I'm going to bail ASAP.*

"Wrong. *I'm* going to have you," she said, "and let *you* go one day soon." *I won't be used and abused. I'll hump and dump.*

Something dark and primal flashed over his expression. "You are mine. Say it."

He could dish it, but not eat it? "I'm—" she hesitated, giving anticipation a chance to build inside him "—my own."

Was that thick, drugged tone really hers?

Well, why not? She'd wanted this man for centuries. And now, here he was, hers for the taking. They were so close they actually shared space. So close she could feel passion-currents rushing along his skin.

Any time she inhaled, her nipples brushed against his chest, sparking heat and friction. Any time she exhaled, her hips arched of their own accord, seeking more contact, more friction.

Puck took her face in his hand, his thumb on one side of her chin, his fingers on the other. An aggressive hold, and yet, still she wasn't afraid. "If you will not tell me you are mine, you'll show me."

He didn't wait for her response, but released the arm he'd pinned overhead to squeeze her ass with splayed fingers—covering as much ground as possible—at the same time swooping down to claim her mouth. This wasn't an easy exploration but a fierce demand. A stamp of ownership unlike anything she'd ever experienced. Between sensuous forays of his tongue, he massaged the pulse fluttering at the base of her throat.

Waited so long for this. The sweetness of his flavor maddened her. He was a drug. Her drug. All masculine heat and hardness, devastating her senses. Little mewling sounds escaped her as she wrapped her arms around him and rocked her core against him, again and again, unable to stop the motion. Every new collision with his erection made her hotter, wetter.

More. I need more. Five hundred years of frustration had turned her wanton. Or maybe Puck had done the honors? "Touch me. Touch me now," she demanded.

"Tell me where."

"Inside. Go for gold now, savor later."

"To me, *all* of you is gold."

"Inside," she insisted.

"What if I wish to play with your breasts first, hmm?" He reached under her leather halter to knead a breast and toy with a nipple.

"Please, Puck. Please."

"The warrioress pleads with me now. She is needful." With his free hand, he delved under the hem of her leather skirt. "Very well. You'll get what you're begging for."

As his fingers skimmed her inner thigh, she clawed at his back, probably drawing blood. So good!

"Between your legs...like this?" One of those exploring fingers edged closer to her core, only to dart away just before contact.

He teased her? Now? Different impulses hit her, one after the other. Free his erection, and grind. Walk away, leaving him aching for all the centuries he'd spent away from her. For this! Throw him down and ravish him.

"Do it," she commanded. "Feed me your fingers."

He obeyed, those naughty fingers shoving her panties aside, parting her and driving into her aching core.

With a voice like smoke dusted gravel, he said, "You are *soaked* for me."

Gillian's knees gave out entirely; if not for the hand pressed between her legs, the heel of Puck's palm rubbing against her little bundle of nerves while his fingers probed, she would have fallen and...and... "Don't stop! *Please,* don't stop."

He thrust a second finger deep inside her, and she went off like a rocket. Just like that. Just *boom,* finished. Finally! "Yes, yes, yes!" The most sublime pleasure exploded inside her, leaving no part of her unaffected. And he wasn't done! As she came apart, he continued thrusting those fingers, scissoring them to stretch her before feeding her a third, prolonging her climax—enriching it.

A scream fled past her lips, but he swallowed the sound and deepened the kiss. Good thing. He possessed the oxygen she needed.

William was right. Kisses were survival.

Inner walls clenched and unclenched. Her mind fogged, derailing her thoughts. Languid heat stole through her, a thief in the night, stealing all reason, leaving her limp and gloriously satisfied.

But the satisfaction didn't last long. Gillian only wanted more. More Puck. More passion. More contentment. Nothing compared. One orgasm wasn't enough. She desperately needed another. She needed sex. Now. Right now. No more waiting.

Except, when she reached for the waist of his pants, he lifted his head to meet her gaze, his irises bright and wild, set ablaze, and she stilled. With his tangled black hair, he looked as crazed as she felt. Crazed, and hauntingly beautiful. Flawless of form and face. Absolute male perfection—a man transfixed by a woman. Needful of her, and her alone. No others would do.

"Your eyes," he said, sounding awed. "They burn for me."

I'm not alone in this. Might not ever be alone again. A wave of vulnerability crashed into her.

Then the worst happened.

One moment she was horny, ready for another go, the next she was sobbing as if a treasured friend had just been murdered.

Tears poured down her cheeks, her entire body heaving.

Gillian hadn't shed a single teardrop in centuries. Now she could do nothing to halt the tide.

Puck wrapped his arms around her, held her through her sobs. He even combed his fingers through her hair, murmuring things like, "I understand. You once experienced betrayal, and this…this is freedom." And "I cannot stand to see my warrioress cry." Followed by "Tell me what to do and I'll do it."

He *did* understand. He'd suffered betrayal, too.

He'd called her warrioress.

He'd given her an orgasm. Her first. And she'd only had to wait five hundred and something years. The fear she'd suffered with so long…the nightmares…the pleasure her abusers had stolen from her… It was wrong! It was criminal! She'd been cheated, hurt, destroyed, ruined—

No! Not destroyed. Not ruined. Her body had been used by others, yes, and her self-worth had been kicked, punched, beaten and stabbed, but she'd picked herself up off the ground, she'd stood, she'd squared her shoulders and lifted her chin, and she'd lived. She'd learned to fight back. She'd helped others in need. And now she had *this*. A sexual experience born of mutual desire. A kiss worthy of going to war, if only to have another. A cherished memory to overshadow those she hoped to one day erase.

"I'm sorry I ruined the mood," she said when she caught her breath. The breakdown probably should have left her hollow and weak, but she felt invigorated, as if a broken bone had finally reset and healed stronger.

"Don't be sorry." With gentle swipes of his thumbs, he wiped the tears from her cheeks. So tender. So surprising.

"Do you think I'm weak now?" she asked with a sniffle.

"I think you *stronger*. The things you've had to overcome… you are an inspiration to me."

I inspired *a great warrior such as him?* She had to blink back a new round of tears.

"That was the first time you've ever climaxed?" he asked, still so tender.

There was no smugness in his voice, only curiosity, and perhaps a bit of pride. The only reason she responded. "Yes. That was my first time choosing my partner, too." Tenderness, gratitude and affection replaced her vulnerability—each directed at Puck. "Should we…take care of you now?"

A pause. Then, "No." He released her and backed away. "I should go."

Go? No! She didn't want distance from him right now—she wanted communion. "Stay." *Please.*

He gave a curt shake of his head. Then, before her eyes, he changed from a source of comfort to torment, from needful to removed.

The Ice Man had returned with a vengeance.

She told herself, *I'm too wrung out to be upset about this.* But she wasn't a fan of platitudes and wouldn't lie, even to herself. She *was* upset. Cutting disappointment nearly cleaved her in two.

Knew he would get off and run. Knew it! And it hurt just as badly as she'd suspected.

Although, he hadn't gotten off, had he? And yet he'd *still* found the strength to abandon her. Ouch.

What had caused the change in him? Why wouldn't he let her bring him to orgasm? Why would he deny her the privilege?

With this version of Puck, demanding answers would get her nowhere fast. "I wish you'd stop Dr. Jekyll and Mr. Hyde–ing into the Ice Man. He's a real bummer. And yes, I just turned names into a verb."

"We're going to talk," he said, ignoring her, his voice no longer filled with smoke and gravel, but frost.

Uh-oh. This couldn't be good.

Unease swamped her. Still, she pasted on a smile and crossed her arms over her chest to hide her puckered nipples, all *I've got nothing better to do.*

Mistake! She remembered how badly he'd wanted to attend to those aching nipples, but she'd protested, hoping to get off quickly. *Foolish girl!*

Next time she would…what? Would she welcome a next time? What they'd done had rocked her whole world, true, but this…this she couldn't tolerate. Acting as if nothing had happened, staring into uncaring eyes, unable to respond as she'd like without possible consequences.

Whoa! If there was a problem, Gillian fixed it. Consequences be damned. From now on, she would respond however she dang well pleased!

"You're right. We're going to talk." Though her legs were like jelly, she managed to walk to the couch Peanut had mauled and ease down. "You once told me Princess Alannah of Daingean is your female. Arranged marriage, blah, blah. Did you turn me down because you're saving yourself for her? News flash! I doubt she's saving herself for you. She's engaged to your brother. Has been for a while, though they've never actually pulled the trigger."

He offered no outward cues to his thoughts, the jerk.

Gillian had interacted with the princess only once, but had watched her, curious, anytime they'd visited the same village market at the same time.

Alannah was pretty in an understated way, soft-spoken and timid. *My opposite.*

Their conversation had been short and sweet.

Gillian: *I hear you were once engaged to Puck Connacht.*

Alannah: *Y-yes. But he has horns now and—*

Gillian: *I'm his wife, and I enjoy killing anyone who disrespects him.*

Alannah: *Please, excuse me.*

"Why does it matter?" Puck finally asked. He sat in the decimated chair across from her.

"Just making conversation, as you wanted. If you'd prefer, I can go back to the party...and William."

Still no reaction from him. Uh-oh. Maybe she shouldn't have gone there? Puck wasn't some schoolboy with his very first crush. He was a prince and future king, a warrior to the core and the keeper of Indifference. Though he desired Gillian—in his own way—he could walk away without hesitation, any time, any place. As he'd proven.

"I liked the idea of her," he replied, and relief careened through her. He moved a hand over one of his horns, as if self-conscious—impossible. "I ran into her after my possession, after my appearance had been altered. She fled."

Ouch. The rejection must have hurt, even if he hadn't felt the emotion at the time.

Wait. Did emotions build up inside him, and erupt later? If he needed ice to control his reactions...she'd guess *yes.*

Leaning toward him, she said in a stage whisper, "Want to know a secret?"

He shook his head. Then he scowled. *Then* he nodded. "Tell me. Tell me now."

Do I detect eagerness? Won't smile. "I've always considered you beautiful."

He gave her a look—one of hope and longing—only to hide it behind an indifferent mask a second later.

Her heart squeezed as she said, "What did you like about the princess?"

"The look of her, and that she was going to be mine. I didn't actually know her."

"You don't know me, either," Gillian pointed out. "Did you want to touch me only because of the way I look? Or because I'm already yours?" *A fact you insisted I say out loud.*

"I know plenty about you."

"Oh? Do tell."

"You…"

"What?" she insisted.

"You like helping people. You dislike liars."

"Facts I've told you. Hardly a news flash. I know you like the thought of hurting your brother, and you dislike William."

"Your favorite hobby is collecting trophies from the men you've defeated."

"Something you gleaned from said trophies hanging on my wall." The corner of her mouth lifted. "I think your favorite hobby just became collecting orgasms from your wife."

His chest rose and fell in quick succession, but still his expression remained blank. "You want to stay in Amaranthia, even after we divorce. Not just to keep your clan together, but to continue *ruling* your clan. You believe no one else can see to their well-being as completely as you."

All right. Maybe he *did* know her. "Correct again."

"But you can't stay here."

Instant fury. "You're going to try to kick me out of Amaranthia once you're king? And notice I said *try*."

"I won't try. I will do."

"So you lied to me. Again," she grated. "After you promised to always tell me the truth."

He didn't even flinch. "I didn't lie. I changed my mind."

"*Why* did you change your mind?" she demanded.

"Because I can." His gaze was as cold and detached as the day he'd broken her finger, just to prove a point. "This is *my* realm."

All right, she was a little too screwed in the head at the moment to deal with this. With him. "I'm done chatting with you. I don't like you when you get this way, so I'm going back to the party."

He said nothing as she stood and stomped off, soon entering the cool of the night. A second later, however, the door slammed. Footsteps echoed. Puck had followed her.

Her pulse points raced, her skin and blood heating, her body ready for round two.

Ignore him. As she approached the feast, a familiar buzz sped along her nerve endings. She stopped abruptly, breathing deeply to circumvent a Hulk-out.

"What's wrong with you?" Puck came up behind her, his warm breath caressing the back of her neck, adding kindling to her blood, sending shivers down her spine, and she gnashed her teeth. "You aren't going to argue with me?"

"Is that what you want?" She kicked into motion, and he kept pace. "Me to argue with you?"

"No. Yes. I don't know."

"Until you figure it out, back off."

Laughter boomed, now at a higher volume than the music. "Gillian!" Johanna called. "Come. Join us."

"She doesn't know you've already come," Puck remarked conversationally.

More shivers, more heat. But oh, he had no right to mention their dalliance after threatening to boot her from Amaranthia.

What was it that drew her to him? Besides the obvious, of course—his otherworldly beauty, wicked kisses and glorious touch. Why respond sexually only to Puck? Only the bond? Surely not. Her mind wanted him as much as her body.

Had to be the way he sometimes looked at her, as if she was a revelation. The way he sometimes focused all of his intensity on her, as if nothing else held any importance.

Addicted…

Johanna and Rosaleen sat beside a grinning William. Grinning, until he noticed Puck.

Puck must have noticed him, too, because he stiffened. "I want you to stay in my realm," he said, his voice soft, "but not with William. I'm tempted to gut him every time I see the two of you together."

What the ever-loving what! All this *you've gotta leave nonsense* over jealousy?

What am I going to do with this man?

Before she could think up a reply Puck stalked around her to rejoin the feast. Not knowing what else to do, she followed him.

When did I begin to love punishment and seek it out?

Puck tracked Gillian's every move as she chose a spot next to her generals, and William—*across from me.*

She wants me to watch her interact with the male?

Happy to oblige, wife. But she could blame no one but herself for his response, whatever it might be.

As one minute ticked into another, she avoided looking in Puck's direction, rousing a flame of anger. Her eyes were windows to her soul—*and she thinks to deny me a glimpse into her soul? After* she'd made him want her more than he'd ever wanted anything.

In his arms, she'd taken what she wanted, when she'd wanted it. She'd come alive, kissing and clawing and panting—for him, only him. And when she'd cried, she'd broken something inside him.

She'd revealed a potent wit and sass, as well as an earthy sensuality he'd found charming.

The keeper of Indifference? Charmed?

Hell, the keeper of Indifference *enchanted*.

Puck would love to blame the bond for his fascination—and growing obsession—but could he? He'd yearned for Gillian *before* the ceremony.

His gaze slid to William. The male laughed at something someone had said, though his body remained tense. He knew something had happened between husband and wife. He must. Gillian's eyes still burned, the kindling set aflame.

And I'm responsible. I lit the match.

Seeing those flames had done something to Puck. Had changed him. He'd never felt so on edge, or fevered. The demon had been loud—was loud—but then and now he'd easily ignored the fiend.

Passion had become a fire in his veins. Every inch of him had *needed*.

When would it end?

Earlier, when he'd first spied Gillian at the feast, he'd nearly hit the sand, as William had done. Only, Puck would not have been pretending. He'd been hit by a tsunami of blistering arousal, his knees going weak.

Then a desire to kill had risen. Had his wife dressed for the Ever Randy?

Puck slammed a fist into the dirt. A colorful scarf covered her hair, except for the tail ends of multiple braids. The material was too thin to be a deterrent for the wind, making it purely decorative. *Beautifully* decorative. Strings of crystals hung over her forehead. She'd replaced her tattered clothes with another formfitting leather halter-top to bind her breasts—breasts he'd had in his hands—leaving her midriff only partially covered by metal links. A kilt-like skirt stopped mid-thigh, her long legs on perfect display.

I've had my hand under that skirt. Want it there again.

She'd wanted it there, too. Had begged. She'd wanted *him*. *Will take what's mine!*

No, no. *Stop this!*

Could he stop? He wanted to howl at the night sky. Wanted to shake Gillian and kill William. Maybe he *would* kill William, once he had the crown.

But Puck also wanted to kiss Gillian breathless. Wanted to touch her until she moaned and writhed and begged some more...wanted to *claim* her, sinking deep inside her again and again, nothing held back.

Fool! He should have taken her while he'd had the chance. But he hadn't. Because, as her tight inner walls had squeezed his fingers, and her pleasure had drenched his hand, he'd nearly come. *Would* have come, if he hadn't forced himself from the brink. And when she'd cried, clinging to him, and he'd offered comfort for the first time, he'd experienced a measure of contentment, despite his crazed need for release.

He already felt possessive of Gillian. If they consummated their marriage, if he branded her, he would never let her go. His sense of possession wouldn't allow it—despite Indifference.

To keep her, he would have to send William away, before the terms of their blood oath could be met. That meant giving up the Connacht crown, damning his realm to Sin's destruction and his people to misery.

Puck had known Gillian only a few weeks, and had spent even less time in her presence. He could not, would not, forget his goals simply to experience momentary bliss.

Bliss he'd craved for centuries.

He peered at her now, this woman who both calmed and incited him. Ribbons of firelight shimmered over her golden skin, and he thought, *Maybe I can forget my goals.*

No! The madness had to stop. He would continue as planned.

Once he used the shears, Gillian's desire for Puck would wane, anyway, and her feelings for William would resurge.

She would choose the other man. *Leaving me with nothing more than an unwelcome memory.*

Therefore, he would not touch her again. Too risky. From now on, he would remain the Ice Man. He would resist his wife, no matter how potent her allure.

A shrill blast of a horn suddenly cut through the entire camp, and the dancers stopped. The music ceased. Everyone tensed.

"Go, go. Prepare for battle," Gillian called, jumping to her feet.

The crowd of females rushed off, gathering weapons along the way.

William palmed two daggers as he stood. "What's going on?"

"Retaliation," she replied, the single word dripping with relish. "We're about to get a magical refill."

Ears twitching as they detected a familiar march pattern, Puck closed in on his wife. "A Walsh army approaches."

"Yes." Still Gillian avoided looking in his direction, tempting him to force the issue. "We have traps set around the outside border. I tested them myself, and know it will take the soldiers roughly three minutes and twenty seconds—if they're good—to reach our walls. And my sword."

24

AS WILLIAM LAUNCHED INTO A DIATRIBE ABOUT keeping Gillian safely hidden, Puck noticed the fury pulsing from his wife and seized an opportunity to prove himself a better man. At least for her.

"I will fight by your side," he said. She didn't need skill for the coming battle, because he would protect her with his life. He would make sure nothing and no one got past him. The soldiers who focused on her would die first.

"Seriously?" Finally, she peered up at Puck.

He saw fire in those whiskey eyes—and gratitude. A strange clenching inside his chest sent Indifference into another tirade.

I get it, demon. You prefer the cold. Boohoo. Now shut your fool mouth.

"You trust me to win?" she asked.

As Puck held her gaze, he comprehended just how badly she wanted to be valued for her combat skills. To prove herself strong, brave and free—the characteristics she'd once longed to possess.

Puck trusted her to deliver. She'd been trained by Cameron and Winter. She'd started, ended and restarted wars. She'd survived five hundred years without his aid—she could survive another battle, another day.

"Can the staring contest end now?" William stepped between them, a now familiar transformation overcoming him. Eyes flickering red. Lightning flashes under his skin. Smoke and shadows rising from his shoulders.

His abilities continued to stump Puck.

What was he? What did he have that Puck did not? How would he overthrow Sin when Puck could not? How had he earned Gillian's adoration?

How can I?

Unimportant! Keep your head in the game.

"Pucker!" William snapped. "Are you even listening to me? If Gilly dies because of this attack, you die, and I leave your people to their demented king."

"No one is dying," Gillian said.

A woman flew by, accidentally bumping into her. Apologies were made as she stumbled forward. Puck reached for his wife, but William beat him to the punch, flashing to catch her and blocking Puck.

Fire blazed inside him. *Get between me and her?* "I warned you, Willy." Puck had decided to remain hands off with Gillian, yes, but that in no way meant the other male could swoop in.

"Calm down, both of you, or I'll use what remains of my magic to make you fall in love—with each other." Her runes glowed the most sublime shade of gold. "Now then. William, sweetie, you don't know this world or these clans. I do. *You* hide. I'll take care of business."

Puck's runes answered in kind, buzzing and sizzling.

"Gilly—" William began, trying again.

"I'm sorry, Liam, but I don't have time to humor you."

"Humor me?" the male sputtered as she rushed off.

Puck watched as she issued commands, her clanswomen obeying without protest. A true testament of her ability to lead.

"You, to the parapet," she called. "You, to the outer wall. You, get our first line in front of the gate."

The girl Puck left behind had lacked confidence. The woman he'd returned to had confidence in spades.

And I want her more for it.

"You did this to her," William snarled.

Ignoring him, Puck considered the defenses he'd seen upon his arrival at camp. A massive stone wall outlined the perimeter—a wall he would have had to scale, if not for Cameron's interference.

"Lower the gate and let him in," his friend had said. "Preferably without killing him."

Soldiers had lined the entire length. On each side—north, east, south and west—he'd noticed a lookout tower. Connecting those towers, a second parapet where archers waited at the ready.

"If she's hurt…" Literal steam wafted from William's nose.

"She's proven she can get hurt and recover." Tonight, Puck would do his part, prove *his* strength to *her.*

Done talking, he charged toward the northern tower. He confiscated a bow, a basket of arrows, three daggers and two short swords, either from tables loaded with weapons, or straight from a Shawazon. The vibrations in his horns intensified; the Walsh soldiers marched ever closer.

As Puck drew on centuries of unwavering focus—*will do what needs doing, no hesitation*—the demon quieted.

Up the stairs. Onto the parapet. On either side of him, archers formed a line, the women stood shoulder to shoulder, their bows nocked and ready.

"Try not to hit me," he said as he scanned the dunes. "My death heralds your queen's. Spread the word." Night shadows were thick, hiding trees, a nearby lake…but not soldiers. There.

He debated his options: stay here and kill the soldiers who scaled the wall, or plow into the army's midst and stop them from climbing altogether, but also put himself in the archers' sight lines?

At times like this, he missed his brother.

William materialized at his side, daggers replaced by curved swords. He scanned the masses. "Oh, goodie, another sausage fest."

Ignore. Option A or option B?

Logic raised a hand and said, *B, please.* Keep as many soldiers as possible away from the wall. The fewer Walshes able to invade camp, the safer Gillian's clan would remain. If Puck got pegged with arrows, he got pegged. Wounds healed.

Now, how to proceed with option B? The parapet was the width of a human road. On the far side, some sort of pulley-rope system. Bingo. Puck anchored one end of the rope to a pulley, tied the other end of the rope around his waist and barreled forward, nocking three arrows at once. As he fell, he released the arrows. Metal whistled through the air, blending with the howl of wind. Grunts and groans sounded.

Landing jarred him, bones juddering, perhaps even cracking. Refusing to slow, he nocked three more arrows, released. Nocked, released.

Magic floated from the bodies and flowed over him, absorbing into his runes. Power, such delicious power. *Missed this.*

A new chorus of whistles pierced the air as the archers atop the wall released *their* arrows. The soldiers kept running, merely lifting their shields. Arrows pinged off steel, and fell to the ground, useless.

Once again, William appeared beside Puck. "You're not getting all the glory. Try to keep up." He sprang into action, rushing forward to meet the cadre head-on.

Puck remained in place, continuing to slay from a distance, building his supply of magic. With every release of the bow, more bodies fell, more power absorbed into his runes. Filling him. Soon overflowing.

There. With a cold smile, he raised his arms and shoved a violent wave of magic through his fingertips. Mound after mound of sand gathered at his sides, creating a new wall, blocking the parapet.

He dropped the bow and withdrew his swords. Running forward. Engaging. Swinging, hacking. Heads and limbs detached. Blood sprayed. Every drop of magic he gained, he used to keep the wall of sand in place.

Felling one Walsh after another, William made his way back to Puck's side. To his shock, they worked together in harmony, taking out soldiers while dodging arrows, bodies piled up around them.

Runes glowed in William's hands, new symbols appearing. Symbols Puck had never seen before.

"All right. I've had enough of this." The Ever Randy kicked one opponent, punched another, then dropped a sword to slap his hand against Puck's.

Boom!

Absolute power detonated between them, crashing over the entire army, no one able to outrun it. Every man dropped, including Puck and William. Not even the sand wall was immune; it toppled.

Gillian, Winter, Cameron and a handful of others rushed over, their weapons at the ready.

"What happened?" Cameron asked.

Puck was panting, his limbs shaking. "Not sure."

William said, "I used you as a battery, unleashed my power. I guess that makes me the night's MVP."

Seeing the sea of crimson and motionless bodies, Gillian scowled. "You took our kills, and our magic. Magic we needed." Hostility blasted from her, charging the air. "You acted against my orders and stole from my people."

"Calm down, Gillian," Winter beseeched. "The boys didn't mean to take our kills, I'm sure of it. Or kind of sure. They'll probably apologize. Right, Puck?"

Confusion kept him quiet. Gillian's dark eyes gleamed like polished onyx, her pupils blown. Animal-like snarls were rumbling from her throat as she fisted her hands and braced her legs apart.

She'd just assumed a battle stance.

"No Hulking-out." Cameron gripped a pair of axes and shooed the rest of their audience away. "I don't want to hack off your hands again."

The Shawazons ran as if their lives depend on it.

A Hulk-out. Rage threatened to overwhelm her, then. But this was no little tantrum as he'd supposed. In the letters, she claimed she lost control of her actions and did things she later regretted.

Then the rest of Cameron's words registered. "*You* hacked off her hands?" he asked, his tone quiet but lethal.

"Gilly?" William said with a frown. "What—"

With a screech, she picked up two dead bodies as if they weighed nothing and tossed them at the male.

Puck jumped to his feet, intending to rush to his woman, but Winter moved in front of him, stopping him. "Don't. You'll lose an arm. Or more. You can't stop her. No one can. All we can do is let the rage burn out."

William failed to heed the warning and raced over, reaching for Gillian.

Annnd, yes, she ripped off his arm.

He bellowed in pain as blood spurted from the gaping wound.

All right. From this point forward, Puck wouldn't have to do any pretending about admiring her battle skill. The woman could hold her own, against anyone.

In only a few seconds, William regrew another arm. The fastest regeneration Puck had ever beheld. But the male didn't approach Gillian again. Eyes wide, he backed *away* from her.

What had reduced the little darling to such a state? The rage—as out of control as it was—could not originate inside her.

The day Puck and Gillian had bonded, he thought he'd felt

emotion flow between them. Had he somehow given her the rage he'd buried throughout the centuries?

Guilt slashed his insides to confetti, and Indifference feasted on the remains. No way Puck could stay away. He had to help.

As he approached, a body soared over his head, then another and another. "I'm not going to hurt you, wife."

As much as Puck enjoyed seeing the other man ripped to shreds, he would rather see his woman smile tomorrow. Violence wasn't her default setting, and she would most assuredly chastise herself for harming the bastard.

More bodies. One slammed into his chest, knocking him back a few steps. Okay, then. Slow and easy had failed. He'd have to go in hard and go in fast.

He picked up speed and dived, tossing her to the ground. Rather than twisting to take the bulk of impact himself, he forced her to hit first, and allowed his weight to crash down on her. Cruel but necessary. Air gushed from her lungs and her skull bounced off the sand, weakening her. Rendering her unconscious?

No such luck. Like a wildcat, she clawed at his back, and tore his shirt. She even sank her teeth into his throat in a clear attempt to remove his trachea. Pain seared him. Whatever. With magic, he caused thorny vines to grow from the sand, wrap around her neck, wrists and ankles, and hold her in place.

He lifted his head, grunted. Her teeth held on to his flesh as long as possible.

"Enough," he commanded.

She continued to struggle, one of the thorns cutting through her wrist and coming out the other side. As crimson rivers snaked down her forearm, his stomach twisted.

She would fight until she bled out, wouldn't she?

My brave, beautiful girl. "Gillian," he croaked. Warm blood poured from the wound in his neck and dripped onto her face.

The sight broke something in him. A heart he'd thought Sin had long since destroyed?

How could he help her? He didn't want to use ice, the way he'd often done with Cameron and Winter the times their demons had gotten the better of them. What if Gillian never melted?

Watch the fire in her eyes die? Never!

When she attempted to buck up, uncaring as the thorns sliced into her vulnerable neck, he flinched. Well. *No other choice. Must do something before she decapitates herself.*

Will be so careful. He straddled her waist, cradled her face with his big, bloody hands and focused inwardly, on the demon, then the bond—the site of her rage. Oh, yes. He was at fault.

With only the barest hint of magic, Puck summoned ice while thrumming mental fingers along the bond, as if he were playing a harp. Where he touched, fire died and ice spread.

Beneath him, Gillian's motions slowed, then ceased altogether. Half-fearful of what he'd find, he opened his eyes to peer down at her. She lay on the sand, panting, studying him right back. Her eyes were dull, no hint of flame.

He swallowed a shout of denial, one to rival Indifference.

"What did you do to me?" she asked, and the flatness of her tone made him cringe.

He dismissed the thorns, freeing her. She made no move to rise. "I summoned ice," he replied. "For you."

"I'm Ice Woman, then."

Aye. "You are well, lass?"

"This is what you feel when you go cold? This nothingness?" As if she didn't care enough to await his answer, she shut her eyelids and let herself drift off to sleep.

Chest a maze of land mines, Puck gathered his sleeping wife in his arms and stood. "I'm going to tend to her wounds. Anyone tries to stop me, they die."

Gillian floated in and out of consciousness. More than once she noted the heated blanket of fur pressed against her side and rubbed against it. So soft!

At different times, familiar voices penetrated her awareness.

Puck: *You were afraid of her.*

William: *I am all realms, all ages. I am darkness and light. I am power like you've never known. I fear nothing and no one.*

Puck: *Face it, Willy. You're still afraid.*

William: *I'm pissed! If you want your crown, you'll keep your hands off her from now on. Do you feel me? Oh, and one more thing. If she's indifferent when she awakens… She had better not be indifferent!*

Puck: *Keeping my hands to myself was never part of our bargain.*

The conversation dwindled from her awareness, another soon taking its place.

Winter: *Somehow you did what only the* cuisle mo chroidhe *syrup can do and calmed her. Nothing else has ever worked.*

Cameron: *Problem is, we've tapped all the trees.*

Puck: *There are plenty—in Connacht territory.*

William: *Perhaps, when the time comes, I'll wed her in Connacht territory. You can serve as a witness, Pucker.*

He'd gone from sleeping together to marriage? *Sigh.*

Gillian had no idea how much time passed before she opened her eyes, memories of the battle flooding her. Oh…crap. She'd harmed William, then Puck, then tangled with Puck's ice.

Her rage had vanished. *Every* emotion had vanished. She had cared for nothing and no one. Even the thought of dying was *meh*. So was the thought of living. Hurt the people she loved? Go for it.

The strength Puck wielded to persevere without causing widespread collateral damage…incredible! Her admiration of him skyrocketed. He was a warrior of warriors. And okay, yes, she wanted to hug him and kiss him and lick him all over, which meant the ice inside her had already melted.

Different emotions swamped her. At the forefront? Dismay. It bounced her heart against her ribs. What kind of collateral damage had *she* caused?

Sitting up, she took stock. She was in her loft, in her own

bed, alone and uninjured, wearing clean clothes. No head scarf. Muffled voices drifted from below...

She made her way to the first floor. Puck stood beside Peanut, feeding her pet an apple. *My family...*

Bounce, bounce. And not from dismay this time.

Puck had bathed, changed and anchored his damp hair into a warrior-chic ponytail, fewer razors than usual hanging from the ends. He looked flawless and otherworldly, so masculine he set her every feminine instinct on fire.

He looked like home.

Whoa! Home? She did *not* just think that. They'd fooled around once, and would hopefully go for round two soon. Because yes, she craved another orgasm and longed to witness— and cause—*his*. But she couldn't forget his tendency to freeze her out afterward. Or that he planned to let her go.

Would he ever think of her again? Maybe not. Until now, she hadn't fully comprehended the breadth of his apathy. To be hollowed out, completely devoid of emotion—she hadn't felt like a living being but lower than an animal.

There is no happy ending for you, Gillian Connacht.

She bit her tongue until she tasted the copper tang of blood. Stupid Oracles! Sure, happy endings weren't given away for free, but she would fight tooth and nail for hers. She would help Puck and William do their thing, even accept a divorce. As she learned what living without a bond felt like, she would rule the Shawazons and start dating, just like she'd hoped.

The idea wasn't repellent. Or exciting.

Why do I feel like I'm headed to my execution?

William stretched across the couch, a man of leisure. "I noticed Gillian doesn't wear your ring, Pucker. But then, you already gave her one, did you not? Five hundred years of suffering."

Puck went rigid. "Funny, when I held her in my arms, it wasn't *your* name she screamed."

Now *William* went rigid.

Dear Lord. "I thought you two were going to kiss and make up."

At once, all three males focused on her. William eased up, silent, watching her with something akin to suspicion. Peanut trotted over to nuzzle her, as if to say, *You can do no wrong, Momma.*

Puck... *Oh, my.* His dark eyes *devoured* her.

Do not react! "I Hulked-out," she said, shifting from one foot to the other to assuage the sudden ache between her legs. "I'm so sorry, William. And I know that's not good enough. But how am I supposed to atone for ripping off your arm? Fruit basket? Hug? Offer to pay for one hundred years of therapy? Say you forgive me. Please! Because, when I say I'm sorry, I'm one hundred percent sincere. I *mean* it."

"Poppet, I can't—"

"You can't forgive her?" Puck interrupted, and she thought she glimpsed a taunting gleam in his eyes. "You're being unreasonable, Randy Man. She said sorry *and* she was sincere."

William tensed with aggression, ready to strike. "Is this how it's going to be? If you want to play, Pucker, we'll *play.*"

"No!" Gillian pressed her hands together, forming a steeple. "No playing, no fighting. William, your gift to me—to pay me back for allowing you to forgive me—is to kiss and make up with Puck. No? Too soon? Okay, well, maybe you guys should stay away from me. What if I rip your head off next time? What if I *kill* you?"

Her friend offered a chiding smile. "I can't stay angry with you. You're forgiven—and I'll merely thank you for allowing it. But your worries are unfounded. I'm too strong, too fast."

Argh! Would he ever take her skills seriously? "Yeah, but what if you're not? You weren't strong or fast enough to stop your arm amputation."

He spread two perfect arms, all *I'm the last sane man in the universe.* "I was...surprised. Next time I'll be prepared."

"How about this," Puck said, as if her question was totally logical and she was smart for asking. "I'll rip off William's limbs at random times. That way, you aren't the only one causing him pain. We'll share responsibility equally."

"That is a really sweet offer," she replied, her hand fluttering over her heart. "Thank you."

"Sweet?" William bellowed.

"But," she added, "what if I rip off *your* arms? Maybe I should—"

"Stay behind? Excellent idea." William nodded.

"—do the mission by myself," she finished with a frown. He wanted to leave her behind?

"If you rip off my arms," Puck said, "you have to feed me by hand until they regrow."

Why, why, *why* did she have to like his response so much better than William's? "Deal."

"How often do Hulk-outs happen?"

"Once or twice a month."

"Then I'm the one who owes you an apology," he said, looking away. "I'm to blame for your rages. Emotions I bury are traveling through our bond, and you're the one forced to deal with them."

Dude! Really? The rage belonged to Puck? Well, that didn't not make sense.

The guy either felt too much or nothing at all. What a terrible existence.

"All right. Enough chatter." William swiped up a pile of folded T-shirts and stood. "We have a mission to start. You'll be pleased to know I took the liberty of making team uniforms." Smirking, he sauntered toward her.

Peanut hissed at him, a clear warning to stay away.

William rolled his eyes and tossed Gillian a shirt. On the front, he'd bedazzled Puck's face inside a circle. The caption read I Ain't Afraid of No Goats.

Next, he tossed a shirt at Puck. "No need to thank me. I know you love it."

Puck offered his patented cold smile. "My image nestled against Gillian's breasts? I *will* thank you, Willy."

Nostrils flared, William grated, "I. Will. Murder. You."

"You. Can. Try."

Gillian sighed. "We're heading out within the hour, and I've got things to do. Go, both of you. Prepare yourselves."

"Anything for you." William blew her a kiss and stalked outside.

Puck lingered. Eyes ablaze, he said, "Prepare *yourself*, because I *will* have you. I told myself I wouldn't touch you again because, no matter what, I will let you go. I made a vow to William, ensuring it."

His words shouldn't hurt. But...ouch.

"But," he continued, "I failed to stay away yesterday—and today. I have you for only a short while, and I'm going to enjoy you while I can. Congratulations, lass. You've defeated me."

25

YOU MUST PREPARE YOURSELF, BECAUSE I WILL
have you.

Going to enjoy you while I can.

Puck's words echoed inside Gillian's mind, sometimes on repeat, sometimes on shuffle as she rode Peanut across the sand.
His shorter legs made him slower than the other chimeras, his
gait choppier. To William's consternation, she used the goat
T-shirt as padding underneath her increasingly sore butt.

One moment she thrilled about Puck's announcement, so
hot and achy she thought she might die without his touch. The
next she floundered, so confused she thought she might sob.

Should she resist him? Or just give in?

Congratulations, lass. You've defeated me.

He had *not* sounded happy. But then, when had he ever
sounded happy? On the other hand—or maybe the same
hand?—he *had* sounded resentful.

Gillian had married him with a single task in mind: to make
him feel some kind of emotion. She hadn't known she would
come to crave his touch more than *anything*. Now, she wished
she could make him feel desire—desire laced with affection.

Grudging tolerance would not be, well, tolerated.

She stewed over a plan of action as their group of five traveled, playing mental tug-of-war. What to do, what to do. Let him go? Fight for him? Take what she could, while she could, as he hoped to do?

"I hate the beginning of a journey," Winter said, pulling her from her thoughts. "And the end. And everything that happens in between."

"But you love complaining about journeys," Cameron quipped, "so the rest of us have *that* to look forward to."

"That's true." Winter sighed, woebegone. "Great! There's an upside for everyone but me."

Like Winter, William also kept up a steady stream of complaints.

The suns hate me.

Poppet, can you do me a solid and put a little pep in your mangy mutt's step? And no, I'm not talking about Peanut.

I forgot to bring a deep conditioning treatment for my hair. If I develop split ends, someone is going to get neutered—not going to mention any names, but it starts with a P, or maybe an F, and ends with an uck.

Soon after, they came upon a small camp. The occupants caught sight of Gillian and squealed, "Not the Dune Raider!"

She recognized their faces in an instant. Two men on her Most Wanted list. Known abusers.

Before they had time to run, before anyone in the group had time to react, Gillian was on her feet, sword in hand, delivering justice.

Heads rolled, and magic filled her.

William frowned at her. "My baby doll needs to be more careful. What if they'd fought back?"

Baby doll? He would always see her that way, wouldn't he?

"Good kills." Puck nodded in acknowledgment but avoided meeting her gaze, as if he knew the tension between them would finally reach a boiling point.

In an effort to distract everyone with conversation, she remounted Peanut and trotted ahead, saying, "What'd you guys name your chimera?"

"Animals die before immortals," William said. "Best not make friends with them."

Winter frowned at her. "Why would I name a lowly chimera?"

Cameron stared up at the sky. "How many clouds? I must know!"

"Don't care," Puck said with a shrug.

Unacceptable! "*Don't care* is a horrible name. Puck, you'll call yours Walnut. William, yours is Pistachio. Cameron, yours is Almond. Winter, yours is Pecan." Gillian reached out to pet Peanut behind the ear. "They'll be our little nut jobs."

No response. Good. No response meant no objection.

Finally, just before nightfall, they reached their destination: the entrance to Sin's maze. A dark fog whisked where sand ended and a creepy forest began. Rather than enter, they made camp at a small river oasis nearby. They'd head in at first light.

"Think Sin has men waiting inside?" Winter asked. "They might exit and attempt to kill us before we can enter."

"Or warn Sin of our arrival," Cameron said. "We should— oh, look, another cloud!"

"He'll sense me the moment I reach Connacht land," Puck replied. "If he has men nearby..." He shrugged. "Let them come."

William dismounted, his gaze hot on Gillian. "How's your rage level?"

"Fine," she muttered. Shouldn't Puck ask about her *arousal* levels?

Ever the gentleman, William offered to set up camp for her while she took care of any personal needs.

She accepted, grateful, and led Peanut a good distance away, to the edge of the water, where she fed and brushed him. When he was resting comfortably on a bed of furs, she grabbed a bar of soap from her pack, headed behind a thicket of trees, stripped and entered the pond.

Once clean, she donned a comfy dress made of scarves. A gift from one of the women she'd saved. As she wrung water from her hair, a light patter of footsteps captured her attention.

Someone approached, and he carried a faint woodsy scent with him. In her veins, awareness fizzed like champagne.

"I brought dinner." Puck's husky baritone stroked her ears.

Not enough time had passed for any kind of hunt, which meant Puck had planned ahead. *Taking care of me, even though he claims he doesn't care for me?*

Though her heart raced, Gillian turned slowly...and came face-to-face with the object of her fascination. Moonlight accentuated the tragic beauty of a face cut by cruelty, with no hint of warmth or softness. Not tonight, at least. Like her, he'd taken a bath, leaving his hair wet. Where he'd bathed, she didn't know, since there was no other body of water nearby—to her knowledge. He was shirtless, his warrior's body a revelation of strength and sinew. Tonight, the butterfly tattoo ran from one side of his rib cage to the other, stretching over his navel and along his goodie trail, vanishing beneath the waist of his sheepskins. Her mouth watered for a taste.

Even the off-limits bird tattoo appealed to her. The one she wasn't allowed to touch.

Would he have any objections to *licking*?

Had she truly spent the day unsure whether or not to deny him? The answer was so clear now.

I will have him while I can.

But what could they do tonight? Soon, the others would make their way to the river, expecting to bathe. Wasn't like Gillian could hang a sock on a tree limb as a sign to stay away. How would William react to *that*? And what about any threats that might lurk nearby?

Wait. Puck still watched her, expectant. He'd made a comment about...oh, yeah. "Dinner. Thank you," she said.

He handed her a small satchel of berries and nuts. "Come on. We'll eat together." Like a date! She led him to the pallet she'd made for Peanut. Her pet was too exhausted to move, much less open his eyes.

Puck eased beside her, watching as she popped a plump red berry into her mouth. His pupils spilled over his irises like some kind of erotic solar eclipse as she moaned with delight and savored the sweet juice wetting her parched throat.

"You did well today," he croaked.

"Thank you." She arched a brow. "We are talking about the killings, right?"

The corners of his mouth twitched, causing her heart to flutter. "I'm talking about the way you rode your chimera without complaint."

She snorted. "Do I get a trophy?"

"Yes. You do. I have your trophy…in my pants."

Puck, making jokes and innuendos… *Do not fan your overheating cheeks.* She'd only encourage them both at a time she shouldn't encourage either one of them.

Although, she really wanted her trophy.

Not yet! "You do *not* win any prizes today. If you weren't sniping at William, you were stewing in disapproving silence."

"*Hate* him. He's as bad as Sin. What do you see in him?"

Easy. "Affection. Fun. Support." *To be fair, I'd rather see those things in* you.

"I have something for you." He dug into his pocket and pulled out…a ring.

Gift exchange! Only, she had nothing for him.

"This is your wedding ring."

Her heart fluttered as she accepted the glittering band. Or tried to. He brushed her hand away and slid the metal over her finger. Perfect fit.

"Pure Amaranthian gold," he told her.

Translation: priceless. Rainbow shards glinted inside pale amber hues. "Thank you." She knew William's comment about "suffering" had spurred the gift, but she cherished it anyway. A mark of Puck's possession, meant to warn other males away.

"But I have nothing for you," she said.

"Need nothing, want nothing."

How sad, but also inaccurate. "You want your brother's crown so badly you bonded to a stranger and bargained with a devil."

"*My* crown," he interjected. "Only mine."

"Right." She offered him a berry. After he declined, she said, "So what did he do, exactly, to earn his coming doom? I know he betrayed you, gave you the demon, blah, blah, blah, but there has to be more. And you *have* to tell me, since you've had your fingers inside me and all."

Gaze suddenly blazing, he rubbed a hand down his swollen length. She watched, fascinated. Then he realized he was practically masturbating before her eyes—*yes, yes, continue*—he stopped and fisted the pallet beneath him.

She swallowed a groan of disappointment.

"Do not worry. I'll have my fingers inside you again, lass. Soon. Along with other parts of me. But not here, not now. Your pleasure is mine to enjoy. Mine alone. Especially for our first time. Especially for *your* first time."

Feminine instincts sang. He was just so carnally *masculine*. "But I've been—"

"No, you haven't," he said with a shake of his head.

Darling man. Beautiful beast.

"As for the prophecy, the Oracles predicted one brother would kill the other and unite the clans with a loving queen at his side. Both Sin and I vowed we would never marry. Instead, we would rule side by side with equal control. I don't know when he began to plot against me, only know your friend Keeleycael gave him a trinket box that contained Indifference."

"But why?"

"According to Hades, she took steps to ensure William's survival."

Puzzle pieces clicked into place, one after the other, leaving Gillian dizzy with suspicions. If Puck hadn't become possessed, he never would have needed William. Or Gillian. Most likely Keeley never would have given Gillian a potion to make her immortal, and her marriage would have been a nonstarter. She never would have ventured into Amaranthia or learned to use magic. Or faced her fears and lived her dream.

I would have missed out on all the good things in life.

But, uh, Puck might not understand if she said, "I guess I owe your brother a debt of gratitude."

She ate another berry, using the time to think about her next words. "Before Sin's betrayal, you loved him?"

"More than I've ever loved anyone. Including myself," he said. And it was odd, hearing such heartfelt words spoken without a hint of emotion. "Now, as much as I want to protect my people and realm from him, I want to watch him suffer."

Thoughtful, she tapped a finger against her chin. "If marrying a loving woman is all Sin needs to do to kick-start the prophecy and ensure you're the brother who dies, why hasn't he married the princess yet? Unless she doesn't love him?" That was certainly the problem in Puck and Gillian's case, wasn't it? "You'd think he'd be extra motivated since *you've* already married."

"I have a wife, but not a loving one," he said, giving voice to her thought. "And we do not kick-start a prophecy. They kick-start *us.*"

"You sure about that? You never would have acted against Sin if he hadn't first acted against you."

"He never would have acted against me if he hadn't known the fate awaiting us."

Maybe, maybe not. "If you hadn't guessed, I'm not the biggest supporter of fated things."

"I don't believe fate plays a part in everything, only certain things."

"Certain things…like marriage and death?"

"No. Because relationship mistakes are made all the time. Some deaths are premature." He frowned. "Tell me. Which do you consider more powerful—love or hate?"

"Love, absolutely. But what does that have to do with anything?"

"I believe fate works us toward love, always, but people do not always cooperate. Free will. Hate. Evil. Whatever the reason. But I am willing to fight for the desired end, which is why I believe fate will ultimately have her way in Amaranthia. William *will* dethrone Sin at my behest, and free you. I *will* find my loving queen, murder my brother and unite the clans, saving everything I once loved."

Good point. Perhaps Gillian needed to *remain* married to Puck to save the Shawazons. "You could divorce me in order to meet the requirements of your vow to William...then re-marry me. I could help you with your goals."

"You do not meet the only requirement, remember?" He scowled, bared his straight white teeth and moved his grip to his knees, his claws digging in deep enough to draw blood. To stop himself from reaching for her? "You do not love me. You might even despise me once our bond is severed."

But what if she *did* fall in love with him? It wasn't impossible.

She twirled the band on her finger, not yet used to its weight. Could Puck ever love her back? Would *he* despise *her* the moment the bond was severed? Could she really help him unite the clans after she'd caused so much turmoil?

And what if the prophecy about his life came true, unfolding exactly as predicted? Gillian would be forced to take a much harder look at *her* prophecy. Kill her man's dreams...no happy ending...

Was that the fate she wanted for Puck?

"Do you *want* me to fall in love with you?" she finally asked, her tone soft, almost pleading.

"I want...no," he said. Growled, really. He shook his head, adamant. "I do not want you to love me."

He so totally meant those words. In his dark eyes, the pinpricks of light glowed with intractable resolve. And she wasn't
upset. Nope. Not even a little. Love would only complicate
their arrangement.

Get Off, and Get Out—Hump and Dump.

"Good," she said, all bravado. "Because this queen doesn't
want to be saddled with a bossy, unfeeling king."

No reaction from him.

Even better! She cleared her throat and returned to their
original subject. "So why didn't Sin kill you when he had the
chance? Why go to all the trouble of infecting you with Indifference and letting you walk away? Unless he loved you,
too, and hoped to find a way to beat the prophecy and keep
you both alive."

"He chose the wrong way."

True.

Leaning against the tree behind him, Puck crossed his arms
over his chest. "Yesterday you said you...find me attractive.
Beautiful, even. You do not mind the horns and hooves?"

If he didn't want her love—*why doesn't he want my love?*—
why did her opinion matter?

If she asked, he might walk away in a huff. So, she decided
to go a different route, and motioned to the horns with a tilt
of her chin. "May I?"

Eyes widening, he scrambled to his knees and bowed his
head.

Little quakes sped through her limbs as she drew nearer to
him, rose to her knees, as well, and traced a fingertip from tip
to base along one of the spikes. Warm, and as hard as titanium.
Layers of ivory overlapped, forming multiple rings. Ivory, or
whatever the protrusion happened to be made of.

At first contact, he stiffened. Then he moaned.

Gillian went statue-still. "Did I hurt you?"

"No! Don't stop. *Please.*"

In this, he begs? His desperation called to hers, and she wrapped a hand around the base of each horn and squeezed.

He sucked in a breath, as if she'd just squeezed a *different* appendage. "I've never liked these horns. Right now, I'm unsure I'll ever be able to part with them."

Blood, heating. "No one has ever touched them?"

"I'm unsure. I never cared to say yes or no, or to remember."

Simmering. Her belly quavered, and an ache ignited in her breasts, culminating in puckering nipples...nipples currently at eye level with Puck.

The ache quickly spread to the apex of her thighs.

Boiling now, about to reach a point of no return.

Gillian released him and returned to her perch. He lifted his head slowly, his midnight-sky eyes aglow with all those stars, almost as if runes ran through his irises as well as his hands. The air between them crackled with awareness, heat and aggression.

Can't have him. Not here, not now. Distraction! "What were you like before your possession?" she managed to rasp.

"Why does it matter?" He eased down. "I'm not that man anymore."

"Humor me, then."

He hiked his shoulders in a shrug but said, "I was known as the Undefeated. If I entered a war, I won it. Always." A tinge of pride layered his words. "Sin would plan the battles, and I would fight them."

Victory mattered to him, even now. The fact that Sin had betrayed him—defeated him—must make his hatred for the man so much worse.

Congratulations, lass. You've defeated me.

Would he come to resent Gillian, too?

"I was born with the ability to shapeshift into anyone at any time, no magic needed," he continued. "I didn't have a stable, but I ensured the woman in my bed was well-satisfied."

"Bragging now? No need. Baby, I have firsthand experience with your sensual prowess, remember?"

26

PUCK STAGGERED, NEARLY UNDONE. GILLIAN HAD
handled his horns. For the second time in two days, he'd nearly
come in his pants like a wee lad. Now she spoke of his "sensual
prowess" as if she would die without learning more.

Anticipation frothed through him, and he thought, *I will do
anything—even walk away from Amaranthia forever—to know the
feel of her soft hands on my horns again, to hear her pleasure-rich voice
cry my name as she comes.*

Fool! He wished he'd never learned the rapture of having
her hands on him. The kind he'd never thought possible. Passion had ruled him. A woman had *owned* him.

But Puck did not own *her.* He'd been so arrogant to think
he could addict Gillian to his touch, to make her crave him
forever. William's claws were embedded far too deeply in her
heart. William, who gave her affection and had fun with her,
who somehow made her feel supported.

At least, he used to. Perhaps her feelings for the male
stemmed from the past?

Either way, envy seethed inside Puck, a monster more powerful than Indifference. Every cell in his body screamed alongside the demon's constant wails: *win her from the other male.*

He hadn't given his rules a single consideration, had only thought about her. He was falling for her, hard and fast. And what happened when you fell? You crash-landed, and you hurt. You didn't walk away—you crawled.

Do you want me to love you? Her question still tormented him. He'd said no, and he'd meant it. The moment he used the shears, her feelings for William would return. Puck knew this beyond any doubt. If he had her heart, only to lose it...

He played her game: *what if.*

What if she gave her heart to Puck, then took it away? What if she gave her heart to Puck, but left it in his keeping? What would he do then?

What would he give up for this woman?

Should he walk into the sword, or continue to walk around it?

He bit back a curse. Why was he even contemplating this? The answer was simple. Walk around. Always around. He would settle for her body, as planned, and experience whatever satisfaction she had to offer. Nothing else.

"You told me about adult Puck," she said, oblivious to his turmoil, "but not about baby Puck."

Ruthlessly, he turned his thoughts from love, sex and different possible futures. "I was like anyone else, I suppose. I ate, wet myself and cried. Not sure what more you'd like to know."

"Only everything." She toyed with a blade of grass. "While you were off hunting William, I noticed a lot of child soldiers on the battlefield. How old were you when you began training?"

"Seven."

"Seven!" She sputtered for a moment. "So young."

"Not young enough, according to my father. But my mother agreed with you."

"Good for her," Gillian said with a nod. "No child of mine will *ever* go to battle."

How different his life would have been, if he'd had a champion like Gillian.

Then her words registered, and he stopped breathing. *No child of mine.* A child. Her child. *Their* child.

In his mind arose an image of Gillian, pregnant with his babe. An image he couldn't shake.

What kind of father would Puck be?

Daddy isn't proud of you, son. Daddy doesn't love you, or care if you live or die. Stop crying before I give you a reason to cry.

Besides, family made you vulnerable to betrayal, as Sin had proven.

Would Gillian one day marry William and birth his spawn?

As jealousy burned inside Puck, Indifference reacted as if his heart had been shocked with paddles, jolting into motion, prowling across his mind and howling with...pain?

Now you know how I have suffered, helpless to act, all at your behest, fiend. Cheers!

The butterfly tattoo on his chest slid over his skin, ending up on his back.

Gillian noticed and gasped. "Is the demon attempting to weaken you?"

"Probably, but he's failing." Back to the subject at hand. "Sin began training at five. Though he could have stayed with our mother, he chose to accompany me to the barracks."

"Sounds like a pretty cool brother."

A nod. "He was." Which had made his betrayal worse than...anything.

"What's your favorite memory of him?"

"There are too many to name."

"Pick one, anyway."

He thought for a moment, sighed. "A few days after we were taken to the barracks, I threw a fit about our treatment. No soft pillows on our beds. No platters of meats fed to us by adoring women. No clean clothes. I was beaten for my insubordination. Sin, too."

"Uh, this doesn't sound like a happy memory."

"I'm getting there," he said. "Patience, grasshopper."

"Grasshopper?" She grinned, and his gaze zeroed in on her mouth.

Hunger clawed at him, but he forced himself to go on as if nothing was amiss. "I expected him to complain, to hate himself for joining me. To hate me more for not insisting he stay behind. But he looked at me with wonder and said I was the strongest person in the entire world, that no matter how many times I was struck, no matter how many times I fell, I got back up."

Eyes luminous in the moonlight, she flattened a hand in the center of her chest. "You're right. A beautiful memory. You might hate your brother for what he did, but you love who he used to be."

He shrugged.

"How easily you dismiss what so many of us dream of finding," she said quietly. "I wish I could tell you vengeance is or isn't sweet, and you'll feel better when your brother is dead. But the evils of the past aren't washed away because the person responsible is gone."

"You feel no better suspecting your abusers are dead?"

A shake of her head, dark braids dancing over her breasts. "If they're dead, and I'm almost certain they are, my guilt and shame still have not eased."

"Guilt? Shame? Don't you dare blame yourself for what happened all those years ago. A man, any man, even a boy, knows better, always. They simply choose their pleasure over another's pain."

"What am I to feel, then? Hating them does no good. It certainly doesn't hurt them. Worse, it gives my abusers power over my emotions, my *life*."

"But look at you now. Thriving. A queen of strength and bravery. The past might have dragged you down *for a time*, but you fought your way up. And maybe you didn't always stay up, maybe you fell back down a time or two, but you kept fighting. Today you soar."

She seemed to bloom with every word, and it eased some of the tension inside him. "Thank you, Puck."

He nodded in acknowledgment.

"Tell me about your mother," she said.

A realization: he was speaking with a woman, sharing his past, learning more about hers—what he'd once dreamed. His secret desire, and it was better than he'd ever hoped.

"She was a gentle woman, kind to everyone she encountered." He reached out to sift Gillian's braids through his fingers. *Pure silk.* "She would sing me to sleep while caressing my face."

"You said *was*." She placed her hand over his and offered a comforting squeeze. "She died?"

Bad memory…seductive company. He should have kept his hands to himself. Now, he only wanted more.

Now?

"She killed herself after the stillbirth of my only sister," he said.

"Oh, Puck. I'm so sorry."

A pang in his chest, new howls in his head. "Tell me more about you. Any siblings?"

She shuddered but said, "I always wanted a sister."

"Now you have one in Winter."

"And William. Even Cameron."

She considered William a sister? *I call foul.* "I'm sure the two males would love hearing themselves likened to a female sibling."

"Please! They'd both welcome compliments to their feminine side."

Puck curled his hands into fists. "I don't want to talk about them." Especially William. How he hated hearing the man's name on Gillian's lips.

One day, the bastard would have what Puck wanted most.

★ ★ ★

"All right. Tell me more about Sin. Why can't *you* take his crown?" Gillian asked, sensing a dark change in Puck's mood. "You're certainly strong enough. And I've seen you in action. Despite the demon, you're amazingly fierce."

His chest puffed up with pride, and she almost laughed. In so many ways, he was a typical male. Proud to the max. In other ways, not so much. "I *am* fierce. There's no one fiercer. I should be able to take the crown without issue, but for some reason, I cannot. The man I no longer wish to discuss is the only one capable of the feat."

"The Oracles named William, specifically?"

"They did. Said he would live or die for you."

Live or die. For her. "Sorry, Pucky, but no one's dying for me." Although, if William died on her behalf, she'd get that not so happily-ever-after, wouldn't she? Her friend would have died for nothing!

Did one prophecy feed off the other?

Foreboding struck her. If someone had to die... *Put me in the game, coach.* Gillian would literally jump on a grenade for William. Her life for his. Puck's, Winter's and Cameron's, too. Even Peanut's. Johanna's and Rosaleen's. Any of her people, really.

"Has he-who-shall-not-be-named asked for more details about *your* prophecy?" Puck inquired.

She could have said, "I thought you didn't want to talk about him." Instead, she opened up, as Puck had done with her, and told the truth. "No. And I haven't offered, either."

"You prefer to discuss these matters with your husband, and no other." Moving at a speed she couldn't track, he took her by the waist, lifted her and reclined against the tree once more, ensuring she straddled his lap, her body pressed flush against his. "I'm an excellent multitasker. While I'm listening to you speak, I can show you affection."

"I think you're showing me lust," she said, grinding her core against his erection. "I think I'm showing it right back."

Hiss. "Affection *and* lust, then."

Electric currents raced from every point of contact, only to pool between her thighs. Aches ignited in her breasts, between her legs, stronger than ever before. The heat of his skin tantalized her while the calluses on his palms titillated her, a lethal combination for her resistance.

As if she had any type of resistance against him.

Their eyes met, held, Puck's indifferent mask falling away. He wasn't calm, or unaffected by their proximity. He was *agonized*.

"Please hear me when I say these next words," he intoned. "The Oracles have never been wrong."

"I do hear you. But there's a first time for everything. And what if we're looking at the prediction wrong, huh?"

He traced a fingertip along her jawline, as if he couldn't *not* touch her. "You ask *what if* often. Why do I find this trait adorable in you, and irritating in me?"

The Dune Raider, adorable? *Why do I want to preen?* "I'm gonna take a wild guess here. Maybe it's because I *am* adorable and you *are* irritating?"

His gaze lifted. She blinked innocently, and merriment flashed in his eyes. Just a flash, but there all the same.

"You're right," he said. "There's a chance we're looking at this one all wrong. Perhaps the Oracles meant you won't have a happy ending with…William." He wound his fist around a lock of her hair, not stopping until he reached her nape. The pressure…almost bruising. Okay, definitely bruising, but she liked it, choosing to believe he feared losing her, and held on tight. "Perhaps you're meant to have a happy ending with someone else."

Perhaps Puck, the keeper of Indifference, had gotten his hopes up? She thrilled. "You mean a happy ending with the man who doesn't want my love?"

"Perhaps he only meant to protect himself when he uttered those words."

She thrilled *more*. What if they could make this work?

Then other questions came. What if she made plans to stay with Puck, and she set her own prophecy into motion, the way Sin had? Would she one day destroy Puck's dreams?

"Look past the bond," Puck said—did she hear longing in his tone? "Tell me how you feel about me."

Can't destroy his dreams. Just can't.

Get off, get out. She brushed her fingers over the stubble on his jaw, and whispered, "Let's forget about feelings and futures and focus on pleasure right…this…moment." She punctuated every word with a sway of her hips.

Another hiss from him, as if he was pleased, then he scowled, as if he was ticked off. "William isn't worthy of you. You know this, yes?"

"I know I want you."

"Want me now…but not later?"

In lieu of an answer, she swayed her hips again. More pleasure. A flood of heat.

With another hiss and a curse, he set her aside and stood. "I'm returning to camp. You should, as well."

Wait. What?

Silent now, he marched away, leaving her panting, aching—mourning the loss of his touch.

What the heck had just happened?

27

GILLIAN WAITED FIVE...TEN...FIFTEEN MINUTES BEFORE
following Puck to camp, hoping her lust and anger would sub-
side. Outwardly, she appeared calm. Probably. Inwardly, she
lamented and questioned.

Puck had shut down when she'd...what? Refused to promise her future to him? Refused to disavow William?

Her husband wanted her, that much she knew. He'd been
hard as steel. Did he want more than her body, though? Did
he hope to protect himself from her prophecy, not wanting his
dream axed? Did Indifference still fight him?

The Lords of the Underworld had all suffered in some way
or another whenever they'd gone head-to-head with their demons. Puck used to weaken, but now...what happened? Could
he allow himself to feel, or did the demon provide the ice and
snuff out his emotions?

"Over here, poppet," William called from a sleeping bag
he'd set up while she'd bathed and chatted with Puck. He patted the empty bag beside him.

Before him, a small fire blazed, decorating his bronze skin
in shades of gold. He was a beautiful sex god...but she had no
desire to sample him.

A few yards away, Winter and Cameron had erected mini-tents. Easy to tell which tent belonged to which sibling. Winter had hung an immortal pelt over the door. A few years ago, she'd killed a man for offering a ride on his lap. Now the pelt served as a Keep Out sign for anyone who might have a similar request.

As she stretched out beside William, she saw no sign of Puck. "Why are Winter and Cameron in their tents?" Selfishness and Obsession *never* passed up an opportunity to interact with others. Aka entertain themselves.

William reached over, intending to take her hand, only to grunt with irritation when she didn't take his and drop his arm to his side. "I put them in a six-hour time-out for irritating me."

Uh, what now? "Did you hurt them?"

"Hardly at all. They're fine, promise. Or they *will* be fine, if you let them rest."

Very well. "Just…be nice to them, okay? They're my family."

"*I'm* your family," he said, his tone sharp.

She rotated to face him, sighed. "I still don't understand you. I mean, I get why you're here. You've mistakenly convinced yourself we're fated, blah, blah, blah. But why did you befriend me, all those years ago? I know you didn't take one look at me and think *she's the one*. You slept with, like, a thousand others. And let's face facts. I was clingy, needy and confused."

"I'm not hearing a problem," William said.

She huffed and puffed before he admitted, "It was your eyes. The first time they met mine, I felt as if I was staring into a raw, open wound that had festered for years. As a boy, I'd seen the same look in my own eyes every time I caught sight of my reflection. I wanted to help you."

Heart squeezing with sympathy, she softly asked, "You were abused as a child?" How had she not known?

"I was raised in the underworld, and I didn't always have Hades as a protector."

So yes. He was. She should have guessed, at the very least. "I'm so sorry, William."

He offered no reply, and in the silence, nocturnal insects serenaded them. In the distance, thunder boomed. A storm approached.

"Worry not," he said. "I've created a dome over our campsite. Ice daggers will never reach us."

Would they reach Puck, wherever he was? And what had Puck thought of her during their first meeting? Oh, wait. She could guess. *Finally, I've found my pawn.*

William sighed. "You're doing it again."

"Doing what?"

"Thinking of him. I promise you, the bond and only the bond is responsible. I would never lie to you. Once the bond is severed, Puke-in will be nothing but a nightmare you long to forget."

She couldn't even fathom it. "What if he's...not?"

"He will."

Desire for him had become an intricate part of her, a bodily function as necessary as breathing. A fire in her blood. A drug she craved. Though she was furious about his hot and cold attitude and confused about their future, she longed to curl up against him.

"Where is he?" she asked.

"Keeping guard." A muscle ticked under William's eye, but he smiled a charming smile. "Do you remember the time you asked me to teach you how to enjoy sex?"

"Um, you said you'd forget that night," she muttered. "So, forget it."

"I can't." He tapped his temple. "Blame her."

"Your brain is female?"

"All the best things are. And guess what? After your divorce, my answer will be yes. I'll start with—"

"No," she said, shaking her head.

"No?" he asked, and lifted a brow.

Whispering, speaking for his ears alone, she said, "I'm not interested in you romantically, Liam. Not anymore." Maybe not ever. As a teen, she'd wanted some type of normalcy. With his love of games, his familial affection and fierce protectiveness, he'd provided it. "I don't want to hurt you, but I don't want there to be any misunderstandings between us. I wish things were different. I wish I felt—"

"There's no need to apologize. You are perfect, and your feelings are understandable. I have to work to win you, that's all. My mission has been set, and I will emerge victorious."

Stubborn man. "I'm not perfect. Not even close."

"Name a single flaw," he challenged.

"Well, for starters, I've killed a lot of people."

"So have I. You know why? Because men are bastards, and bastards deserve to die. We did the world a favor. Doing the world a favor is good. Next."

A laugh burst from her, but she quickly sobered. "I don't consider this next one a flaw, but you do. William, I'm in major lust with another man."

He ran his tongue over his straight, white teeth. "What is it you like about him, exactly? Name something specific. Something he can do for you that no one else can."

As easily as she'd listed William's attributes to Puck, she listed Puck's attributes to William. "Life is a revelation to him. *I'm* a revelation. He lights up when he experiences new things with me. He appreciates how hard I've fought to get where I am now. Though he's possessed by Indifference, he does care for his people. He wants the best for them, and for this realm, and he's willing to—"

"All right. Enough," William said.

"I'm sorry." Hurting him wasn't her intention. "Go to sleep. Tomorrow is a big day. We enter the maze, face monsters and puzzles and whatever else Sin has cooked up."

"And we officially begin your divorce proceedings."

She almost protested. Almost.

I won't keep you, lass.

"Yes," she said, her tone hollow. "We do."

Puck stalked the camp's perimeter, the snippet of conversation he'd overhead between Gillian and William ringing in his ears, drowning out Indifference. *Life is a revelation to him. I'm a revelation. He lights up when he experiences new things with me. Though he is possessed by Indifference, he cares for his people. He wants the best for them.*

Then she'd agreed about beginning divorce proceedings.

I pine for her, and she secretly wants to be rid of me? Despite the things she likes about me.

Or she tries to protect herself, as I have?

Whatever her reason, she'd refused to answer his question about her feelings, which was an answer in itself. While they were together, she would use him for pleasure, nothing more.

As he stalked around the pond, Puck hoped against hope some predator would spring from the shadows and attack. A fight to the death might improve his mood.

Strange noises seeped from the maze—howls, moans, groans, screeches and screams. Each served as a warning: *stay out, or die.* Evil created a dark curtain over the maze's entrance, allowing only the barest glimpse into what appeared to be a tropical forest. Evil born from Sin, considering his younger brother had conjured every tree and trap.

Had Sin known Puck would come for him at some point, despite the demon? Probably. Sin was many things, but foolish wasn't one of them.

Tomorrow morning, nothing would stop Puck from entering the maze. The sooner he defeated Sin, the sooner he would be rid of William…and Gillian. Puck *needed* to be rid of her. Before he did something reckless, like abandon his people and realm for her, a woman who would abandon *him* when all was said and done.

Damn her! How had she put him in this state with a single

conversation? And why would she choose Puck over William after the divorce, anyway? Why give up affection, fun and familiarity?

Why did Puck even *want* to keep her, despite the obstacles? The woman twisted him up inside and out, and set him on edge.

She also turned him on, leaving him fevered. Fever meant sickness. Sickness meant he needed a cure.

He slammed his fist into the trunk of a tree, bark cutting his skin, the force fracturing his knuckles. Pain shot through his entire arm, but offered no relief from the pressure and strain inside him.

Thunder rumbled, rattling the trees. The third time in the last five minutes. The storm grew closer.

William had created some sort of magical cap over the campsite, but Puck had ventured outside the enclosure. *Would rather be plugged with ice daggers than accept any more help from that man.* Besides, the thick canopy of leaves overhead should keep him safe.

"Not exactly apathetic now, huh?"

He swung around, a dagger raised in reflex. As Gillian stepped into a stray beam of moonlight, a vision from his deepest fantasies, he sheathed the weapon with a trembling hand.

"Go to sleep," he said, his voice hoarse, his chest constricting and burning, as if he'd been scraped raw inside. "You need rest." *I need peace.* "You don't want to be around me right now. I'm neither affectionate nor fun."

"I'm sensing a theme," she said, staying put. "Are you able to feel emotion if you don't summon ice, without suffering some kind of punishment? Or does the demon snuff out everything?"

He turned his back on her. One more glance, and he would lose control. He would take her, obstacles and consequences be damned.

"Answer me," she demanded. "I'm not leaving until you do."

"The answer doesn't matter."

"It matters to me. *You* matter. So tell me true. Can you feel for extended periods if you allow yourself? Or were you pretending the times I thought you'd warmed?"

"Yes, I can feel for extended periods," he snapped in a quiet voice. More thunder. Louder, closer. The pitter-patter of rain sounded next, followed by the whoosh of falling ice daggers. A cool breeze blew in, damp with dew.

"What happens when you do? I know Indifference doesn't weaken you anymore. Does he punish you in other ways? You said you needed to protect yourself. Protect yourself from what?"

He needed her to go *now*. If she needed answers in order to leave, he would give her answers. "Yes, I'm punished, but not in the sense you think. I'm punished because I'm distracted. Because I forget what's important and endanger my goals. Because I hurt in ways I hadn't known were possible."

She flinched, as if he'd struck her. "What if I won't let you forget your goals? Would you be with me while we can? You said you would, and you never lie to me."

He wanted this. He wanted this so badly. Still he resisted.

"Without me, will Indifference regain power over you?" she asked.

He offered a single, curt nod. "For a time. But once we're parted, I'll rid myself of the demon the same way I rid myself of you." And he would pray the fiend took his emotions. All of this feeling… Puck *loathed* it more than ever and craved his icy, emotionless existence.

Again she flinched, but he refused to harbor any kind of guilt.

"Why are you here, asking these questions, Gillian?"

"I'm trying to understand how you can burn me up one minute but freeze me out the next."

"Well, wonder no more. I want to keep you but can't, so I war with the things you make me feel. They are my enemy, and I fight my enemies with every ounce of my strength," he snarled, and something inside him snapped. He spun, facing her, his chest expanding with raging desire and fury.

She took a step back, which only incited him further.

Blood rushed into each of his muscles, causing them to bulge. "Nothing more to say?" he chided.

She raised her chin. "You're clearly not done."

No, he wasn't. "To be with you, I must condemn my realm to destruction and my people to pain. But what kind of man abandons his people? On the other hand, what kind of man abandons his *wife*? A wife he craves with every fiber of his being. A wife who will not want him back once she's set free."

Her eyes smoldered. "I want you while we're together. Why isn't that enough?"

"Because—just because!"

"Stop thinking about tomorrow. What do you want right now, in this moment?"

In this moment? Her. He couldn't see past the want, couldn't think past the need. The two pulsed in his temples, his throat, and squeezed at his chest, vibrated throughout the rest of his body.

He wanted her—and he would have her. Right now. Walk around the sword? No longer. Some wounds you bore, because anything less was worse.

"If you want me while we're together, you'll have me," he vowed, "but you'll also have the fallout. I can barely deal with my emotions now. What do you think I'll feel after this?"

"I'll deal," she said, raising her chin another notch.

Then how could he do any less? "So be it."

Puck stalked toward his wife—his prey. As his long legs ate up the distance, tension lived and breathed inside him. Good thing. Because *he* couldn't breathe at all. But then, he didn't need to—soon, Gillian would do it for him.

When he reached her, he wrapped his arm around her waist, lifted her off her feet and kept walking until he pressed her back against a tree. Their bodies smashed together, chest to breasts, erection to cradle, as he lowered his head and took possession of her mouth.

His tongue tangled with hers in a mad frenzy. He poured himself into the kiss, feeding her every drop of his ferocity, nothing held back. He was too aggressive, and he knew it, but there was no slowing down. He'd been pushed too far, control beyond him.

And maybe she liked it. She combed her fingers through his hair and made a fist at his nape. Her other hand migrated to his chest—

"Not the bird," he grated.

Without a word of complaint, she moved her hand to his shoulder and sank her nails in deep. Both actions were a silent demand: Puck was *not* to walk away from her. As if he could.

"Off." He stopped kissing her only long enough to lift her arms and then her pretty dress over her head, freeing her breasts from confinement. Such perfect little handfuls, with dusky rose tips. His new favorite sight in all the realms.

The moment his mouth resealed over hers, her hands returned to his nape and shoulder. Puck's hands worshipped those luscious mounds, luxuriating in the pearl-hard nipples.

"Touch me," he rasped into her mouth.

"Yes, yes." The hand on his shoulder slid down his chest, delved under the waistband of his pants. Silken fingers wrapped around his length, stoking his need higher and higher.

Puck's roar blended with the next crack of thunder and the increasingly riotous patter of rain.

"You're so big," she said between panting breaths.

"More," he commanded. "Stroke more."

As his good, good lass stroked him up, down, up, he grew more frantic and set into her mouth with renewed vigor. Thrusting his tongue. Sucking on hers. Exacting a response. Nipping her lower lip before running the plump flesh between his teeth.

Only when she writhed against him did he tunnel a hand

between her legs, rip away her panties and slam two fingers inside her.

Her scream of pleasure…music to his ears. Her head fell back as she arched her hips, allowing him to drive his fingers deeper.

"So wet, lass. So hot. You like having a part of me inside you."

"Yes! I do, I do, I do. More!"

He thrust in a third, and her inner walls clamped down, gloving him as she came and came and came.

"Don't stop," she gasped out, her grip on his rigid length contracting. "Please, don't stop."

Not this time. "Would rather die." He took another nip at her lip before he pried her hand from his shaft. Sheer torture! Without the pressure she provided, pleasure-pain morphed into pain-pain.

Going to be worth it. Puck dropped to his knees.

Fingers continuing to glide in and out of her slick heat, he positioned his mouth between her legs…and licked. The sweetest honey on his tongue. He tasted her, he realized with awe. He hadn't tasted anything for thousands of years, but he tasted *her*, and he couldn't get enough.

The little mewling sounds she made—heaven! Pressure built in his shaft. So good, but so much worse. He desperately needed to come. Could he?

"This is…this… Puck!" With her fingers wrapped around his horns, steering him, she rolled her hips forward.

This was worth *anything*.

He pressed and rubbed and flicked his tongue against her little bundle of nerves, until her inner walls clamped down on his fingers, and Gillian unleashed another broken scream.

The newest climax turned her honey into wine, intoxicating him.

He stayed down there, licking at her, nuzzling, until she quieted…until her very last shudder waned. As he rose, their eyes met, and the inferno he saw in those whiskey-rich depths sent his butterfly tattoo moving over his chest.

Indifference hushed and hid, as if *he* couldn't handle the deluge of emotion.

Good boy. Puck wrapped an arm around Gillian's waist and yanked her closer. Pivoting, he dropped to his knees and spread her open on a bed of moss and wildflowers.

"Puck...my Puck."

Hers, always.

No, no. Now. Only now. As her legs parted, welcoming him, he tore at the waist of his pants to free his throbbing shaft. He wouldn't penetrate her tonight, would only teach her to handle his length. And he would come. He would. *So close already.*

They would have more nights like this, for he had a new goal: give her all the pleasure she had been missing.

As he lowered his body onto hers, Gillian slapped her foot against his chest to stop him. Though he wanted to snap and snarl in response—*nothing keeps me from what's mine*—he merely arched a brow in question.

She didn't notice, her hungry gaze remaining glued to his length. "Birth control?"

"No need." He stroked himself once, twice, before clasping her ankle to place a kiss on her calf.

"No need?"

He leaned down, hovering over her, and rasped, "Get your hand wet, lass."

A furrow of confusion between her eyes. Once again, she parroted him. "Wet?"

"Wet," he confirmed.

Only seconds ago, Gillian believed her body had been wrung out and incapable of experiencing another orgasm. The moment Puck had opened his pants, he'd taught her better. Pleasure had nearly burned her alive.

Pleasure still burned her.

Puck guided her hands between her legs and urged two of her fingers inside her core, along with one of his. For centuries, her own touch had brought her nothing but frustration and anger. Here, now, with Puck, the single stroke nearly sent her careening into another climax.

Moaning, arching her back, she opened her legs wider. Offering more. Offering everything.

"Now wrap your fingers around my shaft," he commanded.

Eager, she obeyed. Oh. *Oh!* The essence of her arousal provided an easy glide, allowing her to clasp him tighter. He rocked into her first stroke, then her second, his big body heaving over hers.

His expression…

Had any male ever been so beautiful? Caught up in the throes—*because of me!*—his eyes were closed and his lips parted. His skin was flushed and dewy with sweat.

"The things you make me feel," he said, now peering down at her. His inhalations sharpened and shallowed. The sounds he made…so carnal, so sexy. "Want this never to end. But need you to squeeze tighter, lass."

Once again, she obeyed. "Get inside me, Puck. Please." She *needed* him to. What had he meant, no need for birth control? Could he not get her pregnant? Perhaps he planned to use magic? Or did he not want to enter her because he feared she had some kind of disease? "I was tested after…just after. Haven't been with anyone since. I'm clean, I swear."

He stopped, just stopped, and she suspected the action—non-action—had to be killing him. Had the situation been reversed, she wouldn't have found the strength to pause. With his gaze steady on hers, he traced two fingertips along her jawline. A tender caress. A bead of sweat splashed onto her. No, not sweat. Cool raindrops were fighting their way through the treetops. Several caught in Puck's spiky black lashes.

"Never wanted anything more than I want you, inside of you," he intoned, "but I'm not going to take you. Not tonight."

She swallowed a wealth of disappointment. "Because the others are so close?"

"Because we're going to experience *everything*." He placed a gentle kiss on her lips, teasing her with his tongue, then lifted to his knees.

Going to leave her? No! "This is mine," she said, scrambling up to reclaim her grip on his shaft. As she stroked him harder, faster, his hips bucked. "I want your pleasure. Give it to me."

All the things she'd wanted to do with a man, Puck was giving her in a single night. He'd kinda sorta had her for dinner. What they were doing now, an erotic dance *and* a true gift exchange. He'd made her come; now she would do the same for him.

"Yes. Yours, all yours." He tangled a hand in her hair and cupped her ass with the other, yanking her closer, slanting his lips over hers and kissing the air from her lungs.

Then...*oh!* He used the hand on her ass to reach around and glide the tip of his fingers against the throbbing heart of her. Gillian began rocking back and forth, chasing those fingers while stroking Puck's massive erection. Soon, they were writhing against each other, mimicking the motions of sex.

Still chasing. Still stroking. Desperate.

"How are you...how can I..." She cried out as pleasure exploded inside her once more. Stronger than before, earth-crumbling—life-changing. For one blissful moment in time, absolute contentment filled her. She had everything she'd ever wanted, everything she would ever need.

"Lass. My lass. You're doing it. You're making me—I'm coming!" His head fell back and he roared up at the trees as his hips jerked again and again and hot seed spilled over her hand.

Once they calmed, they washed in the pond. He shed his pants along the way, presenting her with his naked form. *So beautiful. So perfect.* When they finished, they returned to their spot in the flowers, where Gillian cuddled up against him, and rested her head on his shoulder. The tension had drained from him, from them both.

"Puck?" she asked.

"Aye."

"That was fun." And amazing and wonderful.

"Aye," he repeated.

"Don't freeze me out," she whispered. "Not tonight."

He pressed another soft kiss into her temple. "Not tonight," he agreed.

28

GILLIAN SPENT THE NIGHT SNUGGLED INTO PUCK'S side, his heat and scent wrapped around her, just like his arms. His soft legs acted as the warmest blanket of all time.

What they'd done…better than her fantasies. And he hadn't even penetrated her!

How would he treat her tomorrow? Would the Ice Man return?

What would she do if ever the Ice Man returned for good?

She dozed lightly, on and off, too afraid to fall into a deep sleep. She doubted Puck slept at all. He remained tense and on alert, ready to slay anyone who neared their oasis.

Just before the suns rose, his body went lax. Gillian extracted herself from his embrace, pulled on her dress. A quick glance at her husband—anything more, and she might not be able to walk away. He maneuvered to his side, his eyes closed, his expression soft, almost boyish. Almost, because with his muscle mass, he could never pass for anything other than all man.

Regret pursued her relentlessly as she snuck back into camp, fed and watered Peanut, then slid into her sleeping bag.

"Everything you'd hoped and more?" William asked. For

the first time, *he* sounded possessed by Indifference, his voice devoid of emotion.

She heaved a full-body sigh and offered the truth, whole truth and nothing but the truth. "Yes." And she would not feel guilty. "I like him, Liam."

"I told you. The bond likes him. You don't know him."

He'd blamed the bond before. So had she. So had Puck. Didn't change how she felt.

Wasn't long before the suns appeared overhead, and Puck strode into camp, backlit by bright golden beams. Her heart fluttered, and her belly clenched as she remembered the things they'd done...the things she still wanted to do. He'd promised her *everything.*

He'd bathed, his hair damp once again, but he hadn't put on a shirt, his muscles and tattoos on spectacular display. He wore a clean pair of pants.

He never glanced her way. Did he regret what they'd done? She studied the blankness of his expression, hoping to catch some sort of micro-reaction the closer he came, but the Ice Man had returned with a vengeance.

Why? Why did he not want to feel while Indifference couldn't punish him?

Was this part of the fallout he'd mentioned?

"I took the liberty of conjuring new uniforms." Still refusing to glance in her direction, he tossed her a T-shirt.

Confused, she sat upright and studied the garment he must have used magic to create. Scripted across the bosom—I Like to Puck.

Gillian snort-laughed. How adorable. And surprising.

"Oh, goodie. A cleansing cloth for my groin." William flashed to Puck's side and commandeered a shirt. "I'll be back," he said before disappearing from view.

As Gillian changed into her new shirt and a pair of leather pants, Puck turned away. *Afraid of what he'll feel if he watches me, or uninterested?*

"Going to pretend last night never happened?" she asked when she finished brushing her hair and teeth.

"Would be best for both of us, but I can't pretend." He faced her, letting her glimpse the fire blazing in his eyes.

Already buzzing with anticipation and need, she took a step toward him. He took a step toward her—

Winter and Cameron emerged from their tents.

"Uniforms," Puck grumbled, and tossed both of the siblings a T-shirt. "Go team Puckillian."

Always grumpy in the mornings, Winter and Cameron mumbled nonsense as they made their way to the river. Gillian took another step toward Puck, only to stop when William reappeared. Argh! Time conspired against them.

William sported wet hair and a clean black T-shirt that hugged his biceps, as well as a pair of camo pants with multiple pockets. Silent, he packed up his gear.

Gillian hated hurting him. Hated seeing him so upset and distant. But she couldn't give him what he wanted.

When the siblings returned a short while later, William said, "Now that the band is back together, we should go. The sooner we start, the sooner we finish."

And the sooner Puck lets me go.

Stomach twisting, she approached Peanut. A waft of heat scented with peat smoke and lavender brushed against her nape as Puck came up behind her. He took her by the waist and hefted her atop the chimera. He said nothing, just kept walking over to—okay, she'd already forgotten which nut name she'd given his ride. Walnut? Pecan? Whatever. She'd call the guy Lil Nut Sack.

The others mounted up. With William in the lead, Cameron and Gillian in the middle, and Winter and Puck in the rear, they trotted to the entrance of the maze.

"Let the games begin…" William vanished inside the dark fog.

As sand dunes disappeared, evil prickled Gillian's skin, chilling her to the bone. A forest replaced the surrounding sands. A *creepy* forest, with twisted, gnarled trees, insects, and human bones scattered across the ground—remnants of those who had entered the maze and fallen prey to its horrors?

Gillian swatted a pesky fly the size of a grapefruit as she examined every tree, hoping to find a *cuisle mo chroidhe*…nope, no luck. What she did see? Cedars, pines and evergreens teeming with snakes and spiders. She shuddered and reached for a dagger, frowned. Empty sheath.

A glance over her shoulder revealed a glint of silver just outside the fog.

"Hang on." She hopped off Peanut and rushed over—denied! Her brain rattled against her skull as she slammed into an invisible wall and ricocheted backward.

Though dizzy, she marched forward—and crashed into the invisible wall once again.

Puck and William dismounted, too, and pushed at the wall.

"We're stuck," Puck said, and frowned. "Magic holds us here, without our weapons. Mine are missing, too."

"Mine, too," Winter and Cameron said in unison.

"I managed to keep mine." Lips pursed, William flashed—nowhere. He reappeared in the same spot and scowled. "I can't flash outside the maze."

Great! Wonderful! "All we can do is keep moving forward, then. And borrow your weapons, of course."

"By *borrow* she means *keep forever*," Winter announced. "A gift given to this gal is a gift never to be returned."

They stalked to their chimeras, where William passed out a surprising number of daggers and swords he pulled from nothing but air.

Mounted once more, they plodded onward, staying near the river, careful of every step. The scents of rot and decay seemed to marinate in the air as the temperature dropped.

"There are land mines," Puck said, easing Lil Nut Sack

around a flat plot of land. "There, there and there. We should proceed on foot. Slowly."

Agreed. But the deeper they trekked, the more traps they uncovered. Trip vines, falling nets and covered pits. Basically, the entire maze was designed to send trespassers fleeing in terror.

Too bad, so sad, Sin. Nothing scared Gillian anymore. Except maybe her growing feelings for Puck.

Focus had never been more important. Danger lurked around every corner, Indifference would not shut up, and yet, Puck couldn't stop thinking about Gillian.

He'd come in her hand while experiencing a deluge of pure pleasure. Afterward, he'd held her in his arms while she slept, protecting her from the world, and enjoyed just as much pleasure. Waking up to find her gone, however? Infuriating.

Needing her again, and knowing they had an expiration date—gut-wrenching.

But he had her now, and instinct demanded he remain at her side, guarding her. Which was why he trotted his chimera between Cameron and Gillian, no other reason.

Must ignore the sweetness of her scent. The hunger clawing at my gut.

After motioning for Cameron to hang back, Puck said, "Your turn, lass. I've told you about my past, now you must tell me about yours."

The look she cast him, one of amused affection, set him aflame. Or *more* aflame.

"What do you want to know?" she asked.

"Only everything." Every part of her intrigued every part of him.

"Well, I ate, peed myself and cried," she said, mocking him.

"All right. I admit I'm the second most annoying being in Amaranthia."

Now she laughed, the sound delighting and entrancing him. *I did that. I made her laugh—I made her have fun, like William.*

"For a while, I was a quintessential girly girl," Gillian said. "Loved fairy tales, unicorns and the color pink. At twelve, I decided I wanted to own a salon. My dad—my real dad—let me curl his hair and paint his nails." She grinned, aglow, only to frown and shudder. "He died soon after. Motorcycle accident. My mom remarried a year later and my stepfather...he..."

"He's the one who abused you." Puck shook with untapped rage, eager to commit murder. *Needing* to.

A nod. She drew in a deep breath, squared her shoulders. "He and his two sons. He'd raised them to be monsters, and they excelled."

Calm. Steady. "Your mother never helped you?"

"One day, I gathered my courage and told her what was going on." Voice harder with every word, Gillian said, "She was angry with me, told me I misunderstood perfectly acceptable displays of affection."

My poor, sweet darling. Desperate for help, finding none. "There is no misunderstanding rape." As a young solider, he'd had a front row seat as his father's armies pillaged enemy villages. The things grown men had done to helpless women and children...

When Puck and Sin had grown strong enough, they'd ensured the men paid for their crimes.

"No," Gillian said, her tone flat. "There's not."

"I'm sorry, lass. Sorry for every horror you endured. And I'm proud of the woman you've become. Brave, and bold. A champion for those in need. Always marching forward, never standing still. You don't just talk of what needs to change, you go out and *make* change." For Amaranthia...for *Puck*.

She blinked at him with surprise, gulped. "I...thank you."

"Once, you mentioned you believed William killed your abusers," Puck said.

"She was right. I did." William trotted his chimera to Gillian's other side and flashed a parody of a smile. "Even your mother, poppet. I hacked the gruesome foursome to bits, and enjoyed every second."

"Finally you admit it!" she exclaimed, frowning at him. "Why did you refuse to confirm or deny before today? And why kill my mother? I know she messed up. I disliked her, but I also loved her."

"That. That is why I kept quiet. You loved who she'd been to you years before, unwilling to admit you hated who she'd become. *I* knew you would ask me to spare her, and resent me for refusing." Wind blew, William's raven locks dancing around his face. "To be honest, I wasn't sure you were strong enough to cope with the truth. Until now."

Puck actually admired the male for his deeds, and envied the kills, wished mortals could die more than once. Though he doubted a thousand deaths would be enough for these particular mortals. But the prevailing emotion? Kinship. Gillian, too, had had her soul ripped to shreds by a loved one. She understood the anguish of a family's betrayal in a way so many others did not, could not.

She understood *Puck.*

"I don't resent you," she said to William. "I'm disappointed."

And there goes my admiration. Hate him!

"But," she added, "from now on, you do not commit cold-blooded murder on my behalf without chatting me up first."

Winter gasped. "Look, look, look. A *cuisle mo chroidhe* tree with no spiders or snakes!"

As if she welcomed the distraction, Gillian jumped from Peanut. "Winter, you are a lives-saver." She raced to the short, fat tree.

"Settle in, boys," Cameron announced. "We're gonna be here awhile."

Puck dismounted, calling, "Careful. Could be a trap."

Using magic like a pair of invisible glasses, he searched for any sign of trouble. No trip wires, or bombs. No magical weapons. But then, the tree protected itself, leaking poison whenever something pierced a layer of its bark—poison that could paralyze a person for days.

"All seems to be well," he said.

William flashed to Gillian's side, a saw in hand. "You want syrup, I'll get you syrup."

"That's so nice of you." She offered him a smile, and Puck gnashed his teeth. Really *hate him*. "But I'm not letting you risk—"

"*I* will retrieve the syrup for Gillian." Puck snagged the saw and, holding one end, positioned the blade in the center of the tree trunk. "This is my home-realm. I know the ins and outs. You do not."

"I know everything about everything." William latched on to the other end. "And I'm doing this."

They fought over the saw, one pulling left, the other pulling right—until they were actually working together.

"Well, all right, then." Gillian brushed her hands together. "I'll just stand back and enjoy the show."

Puck and William worked for hours. Every time they cut through one layer of bark, another formed, reproducing. Puck never stopped sawing, even when his hands blistered and bled.

When he began to overheat, he discarded his shirt. Or maybe he just wanted Gillian to see the way his muscles bulged from strain, and sinew pulsed.

She fanned her cheeks, as if *she* was overheated. Winter cheered.

When William removed *his* shirt, Cameron said, "I'm not gay, but you could change my mind, Willy. Just say the word."

"What about me?" Puck demanded.

Winter's arm shot into the air. "Me! Me! I'd go gay for you." He cast her a death-glare.

"What?" she said. "Horns aren't my thing."

Whiskey eyes glittering with mirth, Gillian covered her mouth in a failed effort to suppress a laugh.

His heart leaped, the butterfly tattoo moving over his body. He thought he felt the corners of his mouth lift…higher still…

His wife stared at him with something akin to awe—a look he thought he might like to see every day for the rest of his life.

The rest of his life…

For too long, Puck had been a dead man walking, fighting everything he felt, becoming more intimately acquainted with misery.

Want change? Do something different.

He should take a page from Gillian's book, and fight for *better*. To keep his wife, he didn't have to forget his goals, he realized. He just had to modify them.

29

TALIESIN ANWELL KUNSGNOS CONNACHT PACED the confines of his suite. He'd sent his trio of lovers and guards away. *Trust no one. Not even yourself!* He'd checked on his fiancée… aye? Or had he let her go?

Can't recall. Afterward he'd—

He sucked in a breath. Had he really done what he thought he'd done?

His mind whirled with suspicions, so many suspicions. He must have done it. He alone had the means.

For centuries, Sin had collected magic. He'd stored every power, potency and ability in boxes, the way the Red Queen had once stored Indifference. The boxes had become batteries—for him.

He'd only used the batteries twice. The first time, to create and power the maze around Connacht lands, protecting his people.

I'm a leader without equal. Why do they despise me?

The second…to create and power a bomb.

That was right! He'd used the bomb against the Sent Ones during one of their ceremonies, destroying their favorite temple, and killing many of their elite soldiers.

Why, why? Oh, yes. To save himself, and his people. Of course his people. This was their home, and the Sent Ones had planned to invade, to annihilate everyone and thing in Amaranthia. The Oracles had warned him.

Or maybe they'd told Sin the Sent Ones would annihilate Amaranthia if he set the bomb? The order of events confused him. But it didn't matter. What was done was done.

He needed to speak with the Oracles again, and decide his next move.

If the Sent Ones thought to retaliate...

He would ensure they couldn't enter Amaranthia.

Now, what to do about Puck? Sin's brother drew closer to the Connacht fortress every second that passed. He could *feel* the male's presence.

Love him...don't want to hurt him...

But Puck wanted to hurt Sin, to kill him. And now, Puck had a bonded wife. The Dune Raider. Did *she* love Puck? Maybe, maybe not. But probably. The prophecy...

Can't defeat it. Must *defeat it.*

Sin should have killed the girl as soon as he learned about her...however many centuries ago. But killing her meant killing Puck. He wasn't ready to end his brother's life. Might not ever be ready.

One or the other. Me or him.

Sin pounded his fists into his temples, then hurled vile curses to the ceiling. For too long he'd been the rope in a terrible game of tug-of-war. Do this. No, that. No, this. So far, nothing he'd done had helped him, his brother or their people. Sin had only caused destruction.

So why did he continue to war with himself? Why not give up and die?

Because! Can't give up. Puck needed him, would always need him. His brother had enemies, and Sin had to help him. Had to kill everyone. If he murdered the citizens of Amaranthia, there would be no one left to hurt Puck. Added bonus: there would be no one left to betray Sin.

And the citizens deserved his rancor. They did! Every day they attempted to steal from him, everything from money, to magic, to children. Nothing was safe anymore.

How many times had the women in his stable attempted to rob him of his seed? How many guards had plotted his downfall? How many enemies had hidden in the shadows, watching him, waiting for the perfect time to strike? Too many to count.

Sin had heard the whispers of his people. *Insane. Paranoid. Suspicious.*

Pacing, back and forth, back and forth. In this very room, he'd often tended Puck's wounds after battle. Puck the Undefeated, once determined to govern the entire realm with Sin at his side. But one day, Puck would have succumbed to temptation. He would have murdered Sin. Probably in his sleep. A brother's love could not trump a hunger to rule.

Better to betray than become the betrayed.

Was it?

He needed to speak with Puck. But first, the Oracle.

After loading himself down with swords, daggers and poisons, Sin used magic to bar others from his bedroom and traversed the secret passageways he'd created, going down, down, down to reach the dungeon below the fortress.

"You return at last." The familiar female voice echoed from the bloodstained walls.

Sin stopped in front of the speaker's cage and gripped the bars.

"Hello, Oracle."

She huddled in the far corner, caked in dirt, her cover of mist gone. With her flawless dark skin, hair as blue as a rushing river, and eyes as green as an oasis, she was a beauty unlike any other.

Beautiful, but not so all-knowing. *Never saw me coming…*

No one ever did. He'd captured the Oracle with ease.

Now a suspicion danced through his mind: What if she had *wanted* to be captured?

His blood ran cold. He should kill her. Before she could predict a worse fate for him.

No! He *needed* to know the future—so he could better protect himself against it.

"Has the original prophecy changed?" Sin asked. He'd heard Puck had visited the Oracles centuries ago, and offered his heart. What had been said? No matter how he'd tortured this girl thus far, she'd refused to tell him. "Will I be forced to kill my brother?"

"You know the price for my visions, King Sin."

Greedy wench. No matter. He'd come prepared.

"Of course." He palmed a dagger and shoved the tip into his eye socket. Ignoring the searing pain, he carved until his eyeball popped free.

The Oracle watched, as if dumbfounded.

"Perhaps you can use it to see the world through my eye," he said. Teeth clenched, warm blood pouring down his face, he tossed the macabre offering at the girl's feet.

Despite weeks of starvation, she possessed the grace of a snake as she glided over to heft the eye's slight weight in her palm. "This will make a nice earring. I can *see* it now—a statement piece for every woman of every realm. Never goes out of style." She laughed, as if she knew a secret he did not. "You'd think that was funny if you knew the terror headed your way."

"Enough! Tell me what I wish to know."

She smiled a white, toothy smile, perhaps the cruelest one he'd ever beheld. "Silly Sin. Perhaps our predictions always come true because perception is reality. Perhaps not. Did the Sent Ones plan to attack you before you struck at them? You'll never know. Would your brother have made a play against you, if you hadn't made a play against him? Again, you'll never know. But you want to learn whether or not the original prophecy has changed due to your actions. Very well. I'll tell you. No. One of you *will* die at the hand of the other. But now, there is an amendment."

He said nothing, simply glared.

Wind swept through the dungeon, whistling through the metal bars and rustling the length of her azure hair as she drew closer to him. "The day will come, the day will come soon, riding on the wings of fury. Vengeance against you will be meted. Finally you'll find your ladylove, but you will be unable to claim her, for you will be without your head."

Being one of nine kings of the underworld came with far too many responsibilities, but the health-care benefits package couldn't be beat. If Hades wanted you to live, you lived.

He stalked through the halls of the Great Temple, a backup meeting place for Sent Ones. His hand rested in his pants pocket, a casual pose, his fingers wrapped around a small sliver of glass. Nowadays, he never left home without it. A piece of *her.* An enemy, but also a coveted ally. One day, he would win her over. He had to, or all he'd fought for would be lost.

But he wasn't going to think about her.

Like any good chameleon, he changed his "look" depending on whomever he would be facing. Today he'd chosen a fitted black tee, black leather pants and mud-caked combat boots. Exactly what was expected of him. Let the Sent Ones assume they knew him.

Better to ambush them later.

He rarely visited the third level of the heavens, despite its reputation for carnal depravity, and *never* visited this second level, where Sent Ones tended to congregate.

Never—until today. Desperate times, desperate measures.

The winged demon assassins didn't like him, and the feeling was *very* mutual. He wouldn't be here if his son's life wasn't in peril.

William of the Dark had no idea of the danger headed his way.

At least Hades's view was nice. The temple had the largest

stained-glass windows ever made, shafts of colored light filtering into the building, illuminating his path.

Behind him marched an army. Eight other kings of the underworld, plus Hades's son and daughter, Baden the Terrible, and Pandora the Tasty Treat. A moniker she despised, which was why everyone used it liberally.

Among the eight: Rathbone the Only, Hades's right-hand man, and a shapeshifter unlike any other. Achilles the First, a terror most legends knew nothing about. Nero, who preferred no title, making him the Cher or Madonna of the underworld. Baron the Widow Maker. Gabriel the Maddened One. Falon the Forgotten. Hunter the Scourge and Bastian the Uninvited, who were brothers.

Each male bore Hades's brand: two daggers flanking a much longer sword in the center.

Together, they warred against another male who called himself King of All Kings: Lucifer the Destroyer. The Wily One. Sovereign of the Dead. The Great Deceiver. He had many names, none of them good. He used to be Hades's oldest son, adopted like William.

No longer recognize the connection.

Once broken, some ties could not be mended.

Hades came to a pair of double doors, shoved them open with a single kick and stalked inside a massive great room. Countless Sent Ones stood in rows, ready for battle. From the best of the best—Lysander and Zacharel—to newly elected Elite Seven with their golden wings, to the generals with their white and gold wings, to the warriors with their pure white wings. There were no Messengers or Healers in the bunch, not today. Also absent? Their leader, the Most High, aka The One True Deity—at least, Hades couldn't see him.

Raising his chin, Hades announced, "I have heard of your plan to attack the realm of Amaranthia."

One of the Elite Seven stepped forward, saying, "Do you know who I am?"

A nod. "Axel the something or other, recently promoted to Elite." Hades offered a cold smile. "I know all. Except the details too unimportant to remember." He even knew the reason Axel had the same dark hair, symmetrical features and crystalline eyes as William.

Axel was found as a baby, abandoned, and raised by a loving family of Sent Ones.

Hades had found William as a young boy—abandoned— and had taken him in.

The two were never to meet.

"I gotta say. You and your band of merry men are—" Axel took a moment to wink at Pandora "—hot. If we don't kill each other, I'd like the chance to get to know you better." She glared, and he blew her a kiss. "We've been watching Abracadabra or whatever for a long time. Serious evil mojo there. As proven by the bomb one of its kings set off in our temple." His tone hardened there at the end.

He had William's irreverence, as well.

A tall, muscular Sent One with white hair, scarred alabaster skin and neon red eyes stepped beside him. His name was Xerxes, and secrets seethed inside those eyes. Horrors he'd kept from his comrades.

"We have kept the bombing quiet, have told no one," Xerxes said, his voice deep and hoarse. At some point before he'd reached full-blown immortality, he'd damaged his vocal cords. "Half of our Elite were slain. Others were promoted, tasked with only one goal. The elimination of Taliesin Anwell Kunsgnos Connacht. He alone is responsible for our tragic loss. Perhaps he knew we watched his home and thought to deter us. There is much demon activity there. But whatever his reason, he must pay."

Taliesin. Puck's younger brother.

Through secret communications, William had kept Hades informed of everything that happened in Amaranthia, and how they were stuck inside a maze. If the Sent Ones struck now, William would be injured, or worse. Puck and the girl, too.

If something happened to the girl, William would blame Hades.

Also, Hades wanted Puck—and all of Amaranthia—on his side in the war against Lucifer. Soon the Great Deceiver would have no allies.

"You cannot destroy an entire realm based on one man's actions," Hades announced...despite the fact that he himself had, in fact, destroyed entire realms based on one man's actions. Twice.

For William's sake, he happily changed his tune. His son deserved happiness. Which meant Amaranthia had to thrive, Puck had to remain wed to Gillian, and William had to give the match his blessing. *Working on it.*

"We *can* do so," Xerxes said, his hands fisted. "We *will*. We have been unable to reach Taliesin any other way. He must be stopped before he bombs another temple, or even another species."

A blonde stepped forward. Thane of the Three. "There are impenetrable force fields surrounding Sin. If we destroy the realm, we destroy him. End of story."

"Yes. The end of one story," Hades said, "but the beginning of another. One of war, pain, death and loss, because I will stop at nothing to punish all those who chose to act against me in this manner. And let's not forget the innocents you will be killing. Hypocrite much?"

Hisses of disapproval sounded. Growls of aggression.

"You don't need to face Taliesin," Hades added. "William of the Dark has vowed to punish the warrior. He's inside the force field, making his way to Taliesin now, and his word is as good as gold. He just needs more time."

"Time is not something we are willing to grant." The grated comment came from another Elite named Bjorn, a male with dark hair, bronzed skin and rainbow-colored eyes. "Our revenge must be swift, and days have already passed as we've done our best to recover."

As other Sent Ones chanted "Kill him!" Rathbone shifted into a black panther, his favorite form.

The crowd went silent as the other kings of the underworld prepared for battle. Silver armor replaced Achilles's skin. A club with powers beyond imagining appeared in Nero's hand. Baron flashed his teeth—poison dripping from his incisors. A double-pronged ax appeared in each of Gabriel's fists—one strike could break every bone in a person's body. The tattoos on Falon's chest came *alive*, misting from his skin, surrounding him in shadows. Hunter and Bastian vanished, suddenly invisible to the naked eye.

Hades grinned. "You'll give my son two weeks, or we war now. Decide." He purposely omitted whether he meant mortal time or Amaranthian. After they agreed, he would inform them of the time zone.

"You already war with Lucifer," Xerxes said, his teeth clenched. "Do you truly wish to take us on, as well?"

"What I wish and what I will do are rarely the same." He did what he must, when he must, always. No matter how distasteful. There was no line he wouldn't cross.

The two sides faced off, taking each other's measure. The Sent Ones would find out the scrappers from the underworld backed down *never*. They would rather die for what they believed than live with regret.

Silence reigned...but only on the outside.

Like Sent Ones, his people had the ability to communicate inside their minds.

Nero: *The longer we wait, the weaker they believe we are. Let's prove our strength.*

Pandora: *Always so desperate to act, Nero. But then, you do like to overcompensate.*

Rathbone: *What do you have against action, Tasty Treat? Not getting enough lately?*

Pandora: *Screw you.*

Rathbone: *Here or when we return home? I'm game either way.*

Baden: *Children, please.*

Achilles: *Which one of you drank my latte this morning? Tell me before I start splitting open bellies to check.*

Bastian: *The Sent Ones have sixty seconds to make up their minds, or I'm killing everyone and going home. I left a woman tied to my bed—and her husband nailed to my wall.*

Hunter: *Isn't her husband our father and the woman our step-mother? And haven't you been doing this for nearly a hundred years?*

Bastian: *Some games are* always *fun.*

Gabriel: *Remind me to RSVP hell, no to your next family gathering.*

Falon: *Remind me to RSVP hell, yes to your next family gathering.*

Baron: *Anyone want to grab a burger after this?*

Baden: *My woman awaits me. If someone doesn't act soon—*

"Very well," Xerxes finally announced. "William has two weeks to kill Taliesin the Demented."

"Two weeks Amaranthian time," Thane added, and Hades expelled a breath—his omission had been noted. "If he succeeds, Amaranthia lives on. If he fails, we destroy the realm and all its citizens."

30

GILLIAN WATCHED AS A BONE-TIRED PUCK AND William tapped the syrup from the *cuisle mo chroidhe*. Finally, their hard work had paid off. And yet, she wasn't as excited about her favorite treat as before. Or rather, her *second* favorite treat. She'd found something sweeter and even more rare. Puck's smile.

And I thought orgasms were life-changing.

The award for Most Beautiful Man goes to…

His entire face had lit up. Eyes aglow, with little crinkles at the corners. Harsh features set in a soft expression. Mouth curved like a half-moon. Perfect white teeth on display.

When can I see it again?

Grinning, she bounded over. "You guys are my—"

A vicious bellow echoed in the distance, silencing her.

In unison, everyone reached for a weapon. With the next bellow, Puck cursed.

"Sandman," he spat.

Gillian groaned. She'd never encountered a Sandman, but she'd heard the horror stories parents told their children, cautionary tales to ensure innocent babes didn't go running around the dunes at night.

Unlike earthly legends, an Amaranthian Sandman did not go around encouraging good dreams. Made entirely of sand and magic, a Sandman buried you until you suffocated. And, because he had no organs to damage, you couldn't hurt him or even fight back.

"We'll dig a well." William pulled a shovel from thin air. "Water will weigh it down."

"No time." Puck rushed to Lil Nut Sack to unhook his pack. "Cameron and I will lead the creature away from the rest of you."

Wait. Hold up. "I have an idea," Gillian said. "We can—"

"You will protect Gillian, Panty Melter." Pointing a dagger in William's direction, Puck snarled, "Stay with her. Guard her with your life."

With a grunt of frustration, Winter tossed her arms up. "Does no one care about *my* safety anymore?"

"No way you get to be the hero," William said to Puck. "*You* stay here and guard Gillian. I'll kill the creature, and we'll move on. You can thank me later."

"Fool! You don't just kill a Sandman," Puck grated.

"You don't just let an enemy get away, either," William snapped.

"Guys," Gillian said, fighting past her annoyance. "All we need to do is blow him apart and—"

"He'll only re-form," Puck interjected.

"Don't you worry your pretty little head about this, poppet." William slammed his shovel into the ground. "We'll take care of it."

Another bellow, louder this time. As the guys continued to argue, Gillian kissed Peanut's snout. "Do not leave Puck's side, all right?" The two were friends, sort of. Puck would protect him.

No one noticed as she sprinted off. About a hundred yards ahead, insects, birds and reptiles hurried away as tree after tree fell...revealing a massive beast at least ten feet tall and five feet wide, and made entirely of sand.

Runes aglow, Gillian braced her legs apart and stretched out her arms. He paused to *sniff, sniff* the air before diving at her.

Boom! A blast of wind hit the Sandman directly in the chest, stopping any forward progress. Even as grains scattered and he thinned, he continued to fight, picking up dirt from the ground. And yes, Puck was right. The moment the wind ceased gusting, the Sandman could re-form. That was the reason for stage two.

Unleashing another burst of magic, Gillian caused the sky to dump a tidal wave over the beast. *Whoosh, splash!* Water and sand collided, dragging the Sandman down, down, until he was nothing but a pile of mud, his body too heavy to lift.

The wind died down. Gillian's arms felt as if they weighed a thousand pounds as her runes darkened. The loss of so much magic, so quickly, had drained her, and she dropped to her knees. She waited one second, two, not daring to breathe, but the Sandman remained immobile.

She'd done it, then. She'd defeated the Sandman, all on her own! Because she ruled!

As soon as she'd gathered enough strength to lumber to her feet, she fisted two handfuls of mud and returned to her friends—who were now arguing about who would make tastier bait.

"You're young, tender meat," William was saying to Puck as he continued to dig.

"I'm old and tough, chewy like leather." Puck stacked fallen limbs at an angle. To create cover for those who remained behind? "I bet you're aged to perfection. And seasoned."

Winter was building a shelter over the chimeras, muttering about how the animals better understand she planned to save them for her comfort and no other reason. Cameron was climbing a tree obsessively seeking a piece of fruit.

No one had noticed Gillian's absence.

"You guys are the worst!" She pelted Puck, then William, with the two handfuls of mud. "Not you," she told Winter. "You're wonderful. Keep being you."

Winter preened, and William sputtered. Puck blinked at her.

"The problem is taken care of." Gillian wiped her hands on her pants. "Now, if you guys are done acting like fools, we should finish collecting the syrup and get going."

Puck took the lead as their group navigated through treacherous twists and turns, clearings laden with more land mines, and a field of wildflowers with toxic spores. Somehow, they emerged successful every time despite his inability to pry his eyes from Gillian.

The few times he'd succeeded and looked away, he'd noticed William suffered from the same affliction, staring at her just as intently, as if trying to put together a difficult puzzle.

She'd impressed Puck today, boldly taking on the Sandman. Now...

She *still* impressed him.

As she rode Peanut, expertly guiding him with pressure from her knees, she lifted her chin to greet golden rays of sunlight filtering through the overhead canopy. Her spine remained ramrod straight, her shoulders pushed back, the position of a warrior ready to face any challenge.

My wife. Utterly magnificent.

Even with wrinkled clothes and her dark hair tangled, she was the most exquisite woman in all the realms. Strong. Capable. Wise.

Staring again.

Don't care.

After everything Puck had suffered in life, didn't he deserve to look his fill? To enjoy her?

To keep her?

Aye. His decision to change his goals was sound. William would remove Sin from power, saving the Connachts and even the realm itself, but Puck would not accept the crown. He would let it pass to another. A warrior deserving of its power. Puck and Gillian would rule the Shawazons together, and live forever as husband and wife.

As for the Oracles' prophecy about Gillian… Puck chose to believe she would have an unhappy ending with William.

Whatever obstacles he encountered along the way, he would destroy.

"On a scale from ten to ten, how delicious is the syrup I harvested for you?" William asked Gillian.

Little growls rumbled in Puck's chest, harmonizing with Indifference's whisper-soft snarls. "*We* harvested. But mostly *me*. I did the bulk of the work."

"You are both heroes," she said, her tone placating. "But you know what would be even more delicious than the syrup? If you two *finally* kissed and made up."

"Whoo-hoo. Yeah, baby." Winter shook a fist at the sky. "Kiss, kiss, kiss."

"Hard pass. Goat isn't my thing. I prefer warrior women." William reached out, as if to smooth a lock of hair from her cheek.

Puck tensed, ready to launch over the chimeras and tackle the male to the ground. Peanut beat him to the punch, swinging his head around to nip William's wrist.

"Ow!" William exclaimed.

That's my boy.

"Peanut." A grinning Gillian patted the top of the chimera's head. "Remember your manners. We ask Momma before we bite, don't we?"

The animal stuck out his tongue at William.

Rubbing the bleeding wound, the male said, "You need a bath, poppet. We'll spend the night next to the pond." He motioned to the left, and sounds of rushing water drifted to her ears. "When you're done, my magic fingers will be ready to soothe your aches and pains. A totally platonic massage, of course. Unless you beg. Or ask nicely. Or hint."

If he put his hands on Gillian, Puck would unleash hell.

"No, thanks," she said with a shake of her head. "We have a few hours until nightfall. The more ground we cover—"

"Let me stop you there, lass. We'll break here, set up camp and give the animals a rest." As much as Puck hated to admit it, he agreed with William. Gillian needed to rest. He'd caught her wincing a time or two. And really, he could use some rest, too, to solidify their bond and explain how things were going to be from now on. "If you push yourself to the point of exhaustion, I will push back."

She huffed and puffed but finally nodded and said, "All right, fine. We rest."

William dismounted without a word and flashed over to help Gillian to her feet. A shout of fury brewed in the back of Puck's throat—a shout Gillian gave voice to, bellowing to the sky.

He'd known they were connected, but this seemed...different, as if she was even more attuned to his every mood. As if they were becoming one being, with one heart.

No, I can never let her go.

"Go. Drink your syrup. Bathe." William gave her a gentle push toward a long row of trees shielding the pond. "I'll stand guard, and I promise not to peek...more than twice."

"You'll stay here," she told him. Then she turned to Puck. Her look of sheer unadulterated hunger said, *You'll join me.*

He offered a curt nod, instincts surging. *Going to take her this time. Gently, skillfully, masterfully. Slowly. Quickly, feverishly. Give her all the pleasure she's been denied throughout her life, and make up for every pain she's ever endured.*

If *she agrees to my terms.*

Peanut trailed her as she strode off. The moment she was out of range, William got in Puck's face, the air charging with challenge.

"Um, going to go set up my tent," Winter said. "Somewhere else."

"Here, let me help." Cameron joined his sister, and the two raced away.

"You will not join Gillian," William snapped.

"You will not stop me," Puck snapped back.

One second William had no weapons in hand; the next he plunged a dagger into Puck's gut. Sharp pain slicked through him, but other than a soft grunt, he gave no reaction.

No need to waste magic. Warp speed would serve him well. In a blink, he moved behind William, shoved a blade into his brain stem and held it there. A blow that would have killed a human only temporarily paralyzed the other man.

"You claim you want her to be happy," Puck said. "Do you lie? Because she hates liars."

William gurgled a sound of sheer hatred.

"I make her happy." Just in case Puck hadn't made his point, he shoved the blade deeper and added, "You had your chance. You didn't take it. Accept the consequences."

Though he knew the paralysis would wear off as soon as he removed the weapon, he yanked. Blood sprayed over his hand before William spun, facing him.

"Go, then." The command escaped through gritted teeth. "But know your time is limited, Pucker. Tick tock. Tick tock."

Puck had once heard the same countdown in his head. A countdown he refused to heed any longer. *I'm keeping her always. I'll never accept the Connacht crown and never fulfill the terms of our agreement.*

Say nothing! Remain mute! His competition would not learn the truth before he'd claimed his prize.

Possessed by ragged need, Puck maneuvered through a thicket of foliage and approached the pond. He spotted Gillian. His body hardened, readying to give this woman—*his* woman—pleasure. Starvation clawed at him. She swam, only her head and shoulders visible, a beautiful rose in the wilds of nature.

He searched the perimeter for any threat that might be lurking nearby, found none. On the other side of the pond stretched a wall of stone. A waterfall streamed from the top, pouring over the mouth of a cavern.

Wanting to surprise his wife, he shielded himself with magic before diving into the water and climbing the rocks, where he found a rare, ripe *spéir* growing from a vine.

He plucked the fruit free, stepped beneath the waterfall and waited...

Where is he?

Only minutes ago, Gillian thought she'd scented peat smoke and lavender. Anticipation had bubbled over, but Puck had never appeared.

Now, cool water soothed her sore muscles, but failed to dampen her raging lust. Her breasts ached, the crests like tiny little spears. Heat uncoiled in her belly to pool between her legs.

Wait. *Sniff, sniff.* Puck's scent had just gotten stronger. She swam closer to the waterfall—stronger still. Anticipation sparked anew. Was he hidden beyond the waterfall?

Tremors invaded her limbs as she ascended the rocky platform. She wore a bra and a pair of panties because they'd needed cleaning, too, and had a small vial of syrup dangling from a leather cord at her neck. Her hips swayed of their own accord—a mating call—as she made her way under the spray of water...

A jolt of pleasure shot through her as she ground to an abrupt stop. Puck *was* here.

He stood at the other side of a spacious cavern, leaning against the wall, his arms at his sides, his ankles crossed. A casual pose. Or so it seemed. Aggression and power radiated from him.

This man had no equal.

A shadow beard glimmered with water droplets. Wet hair hung over his broad shoulders, the ends dripping onto his bare chest, sliding down the ridges of his abs and catching in the waist of his pants. A newly scabbed wound decorated his torso, and she didn't have to wonder where he'd gotten it. William!

Irritation was no match for her arousal, however. Or Puck's. He remained as hard as a rock. As far from indifferent as possible.

Cool air kissed her overheating skin, and her eyelids turned heavy. Her heartbeat raced faster and faster. As she fought for breath, her nipples stiffened further, rubbing against the fabric of her bra. *Mmm. More.* Tingles spread through her, sensitizing every nerve ending.

Puck looked her up and down, slowly, as if savoring a bounty of riches, then offered her a small, violet...plum? "For you."

Had any temptation ever looked so sweet? "What is it?" Another gift?

"*Spéir.*"

Truly? She'd heard talk of the fruit found only on Connacht land, and only ever in the spring...sometimes.

Gillian sauntered closer, Puck's eyes tracking her every move. She accepted the treat, bit into the tender flesh and moaned with delight, tasting a blend of pineapple, coconut and spiced rum. Reminded her of a piña colada Cameron had once made her, using a secret stash of ingredients he'd brought from the mortal world.

Puck took the *spéir* and bit into the same spot, a kiss by proxy...and a carnal invitation. Shivers rained over her, and passion-fever ignited ever hotter.

In tension-drenched silence, they finished off the fruit, passing it back and forth, always watching each other. Awareness made the damp air electric.

"I'm still hungry," she whispered, need consuming her.

His pupils flared as, with measured steps, he circled her. "You want all of me? Want your first time to be with me?"

"Yes." Please. "Very much."

"Then you shall have me...after you agree to my terms."

She gulped. "Terms?" How ominiously he'd uttered the word.

"William will dethrone Sin. I will decline the Connacht crown. You and I will rule the Shawazons together, as husband and wife."

What! "But you long to rule the Connachts...long to rule all the clans."

"I want you more."

Realization dawned—and devastated. *I've killed his dream, just as predicted.* He could co-rule the Shawazons with her, no problem. If he put the work in, he could even unite all the clans with another man acting as Connacht king—but he could never actually rule the Connachts, which meant he could only ever rule five of the six. Five clans would never be enough.

Puck stopped in front of her, only a whisper away, so close her nipples brushed against his chest every time she inhaled. "Agree."

"No." No way, no how. "I told you I won't let you forget your goals, and I meant it. I won't kill your dream."

"I have new goals. A new dream. Agree, lass." He framed her face with his big, calloused hands. His thumbs brushed the rise of her cheekbones, soft, almost reverent. "Life is both endless and too short, and I don't want to go another minute without filling your beautiful body with all that I am."

Mercy! Thoughts muddled, heart like a speeding bullet in her chest, she leaned into him. "I..." She gulped. "I will *never* agree."

He narrowed his eyes, but nodded with slow, calculated assurance. "Very well. No agreement, no sex."

"You're *blackmailing* me?" she gasped out.

"I am." He lowered his head...only to let his lips hover over hers, one second ticking into another, the warmth of his breath fanning her lips. "I'd do much worse to win you."

For an endless eternity, he remained unwavering. At first, anticipation thrilled her. Her body ached...ached so badly. Heat melted her resistance, and her bones. She sagged against him, every point of contact setting off a new bomb of sensation, rousing primal needs. Eagerness *owned* Gillian.

She *had to have* more. But eagerness soon turned to torment. She was *dying.*

"Do something!" she demanded.

He brushed the tip of his nose against hers. She moaned. *He* groaned, as if he'd just gotten a hit of his favorite drug.

But it wasn't enough.

"Give me what I want." Warmth spilled through her once again. "What we both need."

"I'll kiss you," he rasped. "I'll touch you. But I won't take you until I have your agreement."

"Puck..."

"Gillian." Finally—blessedly—he kissed her. His lips pressed against hers, his tongue persuaded rather than demanded.

Soft. Tantalizing. She groaned and wondered where he would place his hands...

One combed through her hair to angle her head. The other slipped under her panties to cup her ass and draw her closer, putting them skin to heated skin. Her breasts smashed against his chest, and her nipples throbbed.

"More," she croaked. *Delicious...*

With a growl, Puck thrust his tongue past her lips, parting them. He jolted, lifted his head for a split second. "I love the taste of you." Another growl. His tongue dueled with hers.

The taste of *him* drugged her. He was molten honey chased by pineapple-infused champagne. Sweeter than the *spéir*, and the perfect contradiction to his wicked exploration.

He was more necessary than air.

To anchor her body against his, she wrapped her arms around

his waist. Pleasure bombarded her in waves, one after the other, but still she needed more. She needed…everything. Up, up, her fingers traveled over the ridges of his spine, his muscles jerking beneath her caress.

So much strength harnessed by one man. *My man.*

He kissed her deeper, as if ravenous for her. She kissed him back, just as deep, just as ravenous. Control? She had none. Desperate—a common occurrence in his presence—she chased every sensation he elicited, her nails digging into his shoulder blades, new moans escaping her.

Her world spun, the kiss never slowing. Then cold rocks chilled her back, and a hot man heated her front; she gasped. And he wasn't done. He kneaded one of her breasts. His other hand glided down her stomach, tunneled under her panties and played her until she writhed and screamed and begged.

"Agree," he grated. A bead of sweat trickled from his temple.

"N-no." His future meant more to her than pleasure. Barely. "Please, Puck. Please. If you refuse to give me an orgasm, I'm going to spontaneously combust."

"I'll simply combust with you. I doubt there's a better way to go." He stopped all movement, just stopped, and she screamed for an entirely different reason, frustration like her own personal demon.

She beat at his chest. "What are you doing?"

"The impossible. I'm…walking…away." He released her breast…lifted his hand from her panties—no! "Hardest thing I've never done. But going to do it. A future with you means too much."

"Puck." She clutched his wrists and stared up into his eyes. Strain tightened his features. He clearly needed to come as desperately as Gillian. "Stay."

"You know how to keep me here."

She opened her mouth, closed it. He fed her a swift, hard kiss and stood, severing contact.

But…but… "You said we could kiss and touch."

"And that's exactly what we did. I never said I'd let you'd come."

"You lowdown dirty rat!" Lungs heaving, she scrambled to her feet to face off with him. "You finish what you started or...or..." Nothing sounded violent enough. "Or I'll take care of myself."

"I don't think you will. Because of the bond, I don't think you can." Leaning down, putting them nose to nose, he said, "But either way, your orgasm belongs to me, and me alone. You will *not* make yourself come, Gillian. Do you understand?"

Always so possessive. "No!"

He crowded her against the rocky wall. With his hands on the rough surface beside her temples, caging her in, and his erection rubbing between her legs, he ran her bottom lip between his teeth. "The moment you agree to my terms, I'll be in you so deep you'll feel me for the rest of eternity."

Tremors. Wavering...

Again, she opened and closed her mouth. Then her defenses rallied. *This is for his own good.*

He must have sensed her momentary weakness, because he gave her a look so smug she wanted to smack him *and* throw herself into his arms. Smug looked good on him.

"Hear me. Heed me well. If you make yourself come now," he said, "I won't make you come later."

Her frustration spiked. By "later" did he mean "ever"?

"You're going to return to camp, aching for me," he continued with a silky tone.

"Yes," she said, staring into his eyes. Two could play this game. As he watched, she licked her lips. "But so are you."

31

AS THE OTHERS SLEPT SAFE AND SNUG IN THEIR
sleeping bags—everyone but Gillian, who tossed and turned—
Puck marched the perimeter of their campsite, weapons in
hand, a howling demon in his head.

The only reason he wasn't going insane right now, considering the awful racket in his head: *my woman needs me.*

Gillian hadn't made herself come. She'd waited for him.
Whether purposely or inadvertently, he didn't know, didn't
care. All that mattered? She ached for him. And she'd sought
to avenge him.

When she'd returned to camp, she'd gotten in William's face
and snapped, "I know you stabbed Puck. Don't do it again."

"What?" the warrior had replied. "He walked into my
knife."

"If you do it again, you'll walk into *my* knife—repeatedly."

A thousand times, Puck had almost given in and gone to her,
frantic to make her come, ready to follow her over the edge.

Too much at stake. Resist!

Take all or accept nothing.

Knowing he would be too amped to sleep, he'd requested the

first night watch. One hour bled into another and another until Cameron appeared, startling him. He reached for a weapon.

"My turn for guard duty," his friend said, grinning from ear to ear. "A bit agitated, are we? And distracted? Surprise! I've been your shadow for the last two laps. I considered stabbing you to prove a point, but I figured you were in enough pain." He motioned to the bulge between Puck's legs. "I'd put that thing away."

"That's the plan," Puck muttered. He sheathed his dagger and scrubbed a hand down his face. The fact that he hadn't heard the warrior's approach…he deserved a flogging.

He strode back to camp, letting his boots thump into the ground, not even trying to be quiet. As he slid into his sleeping bag—which he placed right next to Gillian's—she turned toward him with a low, needy moan.

My woman is agonized. Must give her—

No! Not until she caved.

Moonlight caressed her exquisite face as she blinked open her eyes and peered over at him. "Puck," she whispered.

"Agree," he grated softly. William and Winter slept only a few feet away, but he didn't have the strength to end the conversation.

"Agree to my terms—sex without commitment," Gillian said, her tone just as soft, "and I'll do anything you've ever fantasized about. I'll do *everything*."

Yes. Harder than I've ever been. Need her. "Do you want me, lass?"

"So much." A ragged admission that only made him harder.

"Prove it, then. Agree to my terms. Give us both a happily-ever-after."

She sucked in a breath, as if he'd just scraped a raw wound with his claw. "You don't fight fair, husband."

"Never have, never will." Not with a prize of prizes awaiting him. "Agree."

"I...can't."

"You can, but you won't. So we wait, and discover who can outlast whom..."

Puck never managed to fall asleep, the demon too loud, and his need for Gillian too great. He waited, hoping against hope that she would be the first to cave. But, as morning light dawned on the horizon, she remained still and quiet.

Resting peacefully? He—

The ground beneath him began to rattle, and he frowned.

Threat? Ready for battle, daggers in hand, Puck got up in a hurry. William, Gillian and Cameron joined him. A wide-eyed Winter stood at the camp's perimeter, holding on to a tree branch for balance.

Between them, small circles of ground *crumbled*, imploding from deep in the realm's core.

"Get over here. Now," Cameron demanded, motioning to his sister. "What the hell is happening?"

"I don't know." Winter bounded over, twisting and leaping to avoid falling into one of the pits. "The shaking doesn't reach the chimeras. Let's gather our gear and haul ass."

Good plan.

"I'll take care of the gear," William said. The bags and weapons vanished.

But getting to the chimeras? Impossible. Wind blustered through the camp. Magical wind. *Sin's* magic. In an instant, everyone was flashed to a new location, yards apart from the others, each standing directly in front of a pit.

Some of the pits were bottomless, some weren't. In the yawning hole before Puck's feet, spears were anchored into the ground and angled up. A fall inside guaranteed impalement.

Winter teetered, and Cameron lunged to catch her. At the same time, William snatched up a fallen branch to extend toward Gillian, but Puck had already followed Cameron's lead and lunged toward her. He stood behind her, one arm wrapped around her waist to hold her steady.

"This is Sin's doing," he said.

"You know him best." Gillian gazed around, her mind clearly whirling. "Would he create a way to stop this?"

More rumbling.

"Do we move? Do we stay put?" Winter asked.

Too late. New pits formed.

"Need to think." Puck's scattered thoughts began to align. Sin had always liked to toy with his enemies, so yes, he would create a way out, ensuring the game continued.

The first pits had formed when Winter stood at the perimeter, and the rest of them were close to the fire. The second set of pits formed after the wind had blown in, and magic had flashed everyone to new locations.

Sin's magic had purposely separated them, then. Proximity mattered…which reminded Puck of a game Amaranthian children often played, where two teams lined up in front of each other, a single goal in mind—to stay together while forcing the other team apart.

That was it. Hopefully. "Come to us," he commanded the others. "Line up side by side. Now."

William and the siblings skittered over without protest, and the tremors ceased. No new pits.

Puck expelled a heavy sigh of relief. "All right. We move forward together, remaining side by side, and—"

Another gust of wind, another flash. One second Puck was in line, the next he was a good distance away. The shaking intensified, new sections of land crumbling.

"Move to the right side of the fire," William shouted.

Everyone obeyed, doing whatever had to be done. In a game of survival, there wasn't time for a pissing contest. As they pressed shoulder to shoulder, the shaking decreased, annnd yes, the land ceased crumbling.

"Grab hands," Gillian said.

Too late. Just like before, wind blew. They were scattered once again, the line broken. Shaking. The creation of more pits. Soon, there would be no land left.

"What do we do?" Cameron shouted.

The foundation at William's feet just…dissolved. In a blink, the warrior vanished. With a scream of denial, Gillian scrambled after him.

Magic! Puck forced a thorny vine to spring from the ground and wrap around her ankle, catching her before she careened to her death. He rushed over, careful not to fall, and tugged her up, hating the pain the thorns must be inflicting upon her.

"Let me go!" She fought his hold, determined to reach the other male.

"Stop. Now." Indifference upped the volume as realization dawned. *My wife kissed me one day, and nearly sacrificed herself— and me!—for another man the next.*

William materialized at Puck's side, comprehended Gillian's attempt to save him and helped get her back on her feet.

Cameron and Winter jumped from their tiny plots of land. Another line. Without pause, everyone leaned, contorted and rotated to join hands. Still Puck braced, expecting another flash. But one second passed. Two, three. Nothing happened.

Ignoring a prick of resentment, he focused on William. "Flash Gillian to the chimeras on my count." Puck didn't have enough magic to whisk her or anyone else to safety. Only enough for his vines, his ice, perhaps a handful of other tricks.

Fury darkened the male's electric blues, all self-directed. "I can only flash solo."

Right. In the chaos, Puck had forgotten.

"Flash yourself to safety, idiot," Gillian screeched. "We'll find a way out of this without you."

"Or the entire area will collapse as soon as I'm gone," William responded.

He wasn't wrong. Sin would punish anyone who tried to save

himself—by killing everyone else. Guilt could be a weapon sharper than any sword.

"Uh, guys. I've got a wee bit of a problem," Winter said.

Puck groaned, knowing what she was going to say. "How long do you have?"

Hatred darkened her silver-rimmed eyes. "Not long. Self-ishness is *screaming*. If I don't abandon ship, madness will creep in. Can already feel it…have no idea what I'll do."

"You're not the only one with a difficult demon." Cameron rubbed his chin against his shoulder, wiping away a fresh bead of blood. "Obsession has questions about those bottomless pits, and wants answers."

"Just hold on, guys." Gillian's gaze darted over the forest. "We can do this. We *will* do this. We just have to stay together and move toward the chimeras."

Puck used the barest hint of magic to study the land, searching, searching. There! A glittery outline marked the perimeter of the "game." Roughly five hundred square feet away.

"We don't have to go as far as the chimeras," he said.

If they could cross the threshold together, they could—hopefully—escape unscathed. So how could they cross the threshold together?

Think! He tried, he did, but his mind had become far too jumbled with emotion. Fear for Gillian's safety. Regret that he hadn't claimed her while he'd had the chance. Anger that he would die, his time with his wife cut short, his realm and people doomed. Sorrow that he'd brought good people into a hopeless situation. Well, good people and William. Fury and jealousy over Gillian's devotion to the male. On top of all that, the demon was simply too loud.

"I'm sorry, Gillian, but I must…need to think clearly…" he began.

"No!" she said. "We'll figure this out. Don't—"

"Too late." Puck summoned ice. Now wasn't the time for hesitation.

A frigid storm brutally and savagely slaughtered each and every emotion. Indifference quieted, Puck's thoughts settling and aligning once more. There was no way the group could walk forward while holding hands. Too many pits bled into others, widening the gaps. If two people fell at any given time, they would drag down a third, then the fourth and fifth.

So. Moving on.

If they couldn't go across, beside, or under, they'd have to go over. The only way over? Magic. Of course. Magic was the problem, magic was the solution. He scanned the trees surrounding the clearing, found one with a thick trunk and limbs. Sturdy. Strong enough to hold one of his vines, plus the weight of the entire group? They'd find out.

Bugs crawled all over the bark, and those bugs would try to chew through the vine. Time would not be on their side.

Any other way?

Logic said: *no.*

The vine it is.

"I need a free hand, which means we must rearrange our positions." At present, Gillian and William hemmed him in. Amid protests, he added, "Once my hand is free, I'll use the tree to produce another thorn vine, and we will swing over the pits. In theory."

Cameron and Winter radiated dread. William donned a mask as cold as the ice. Puck met Gillian's gaze, noted she was ashen, knew he should be bothered but felt nothing.

"On my count," he said. "One. Two. Three."

Hands untangled. New pits formed. Puck switched places with William, dragging Gillian with him when she refused to let go of his hand. Cameron tottered over a ledge.

Winter grabbed his hand, saving him. A selfless act. Her head tilted back, a scream of pain bursting from her. The siblings tottered *together.*

William proved his strength, knocking Cameron back with a kick and holding Winter up with one hand, Gillian with the other. At the same time, Puck extended an arm. A vine shot from the tree and wrapped around his wrist, thorns puncturing his skin and muscle. Blood trickled.

As Winter's deadweight threatened to drag them all down, he leaped, taking everyone with him. Swinging. The added weight caused the thorns to dig deeper, hitting bone, but still he held on.

As soon as the vine leveled out, he shouted, "Release!"

Together they soared through the air, slammed into the line of trees and tumbled to the ground.

32

GILLIAN WAS ON THE CUSP OF A MAJOR FREAK-OUT. Hours had passed since the group had survived a game of hide-and-seek with chunks of land. Cameron was now catatonic, barely even breathing. He hadn't investigated the bottomless pits, and was being punished. Winter was in the throes of a punishment, as well, rocking back and forth, mumbling non-sensical things.

"Clock rewinds to hell," she said. "Crimson rain, beautiful destruction. The bell demands a toll. The darkest light. He comes. Help me die."

Gillian sat between the siblings, combing her fingers through Winter's hair one minute, caressing Cameron's face the next. Nothing she'd done had helped.

Nothing Puck had done had helped, either. She'd asked him to share his ice with the pair, but he'd said, "I do, and I'll make everything worse. Right now, they care about the havoc they'll cause if they stop fighting. If they stop caring..."

Claiming he needed to erect a wall of thorny vines along the (new) camp's perimeter, he'd taken off soon after. William had stalked after him, radiating menace.

Would EP—Emotional Puck—be the one to return? Or would she have to deal with Ice Man?

Finally—answers! Puck strode through the trees, approaching. He had a black eye, his clothes dirt-stained, bloodstained and torn.

What she didn't see? Warmth. He looked more terrifying than any foe she'd ever faced.

Her hopes plummeted.

He and William must have fought, despite Puck's cold state. But then, Puck had rules. He'd never listed them all to Gillian, but she figured one had to be: Always strike back.

"We can't stay here, and we can't take the siblings with us," he said, his voice cold and hard. "They'll only slow us down."

She would think of something to help her friends. She must! But first, she had to help her husband. He'd once told her an outside source had to make him feel something strongly enough to break the ice. Very well.

She stood, closed the distance. Peering up at him, she demanded, "Kiss me."

Ignoring her, he said, "Get your bag. We head out."

"No," she said with a shake of her head. "We aren't leaving yet."

"We are," he insisted. "If you resist, I'll hurt you."

"Do it, then. Hurt me."

He…didn't. Didn't even make an attempt. Because he couldn't!

She placed her hands on his shoulders. "If you were *my* Puck, you'd want to kiss me, and you'd want to stay here."

"I'm not your Puck."

"I know! That's the problem."

He stepped back, so strong and competent, so wonderfully masculine as she crumbled inside. "Get your bag," he repeated.

"No." In the years Gillian had spent with the Lords of the Underworld, she'd watched one alpha male after another fall in love and change, wanting to be better for his Lady.

Puck doesn't want my love, remember? No, no. He did. He must. His terms...

Did she love him?

She wasn't sure. So, moving on. The Lords' mates always had a potent effect. Battle-hardened warriors became putty in the right hands.

Powerful Sienna, current queen of the Greek gods, fascinated Paris simply by strutting into a room, despite the fact that he'd lived for multiple millennia and had already experienced every vice, trick and treat.

The delicate Ashlyn calmed Maddox with only a glance, touch, or spoken word.

The feisty Kaia aroused Strider with the wicked things she said.

What would others say about Gillian and Puck one day? The hot mess Gillian melted Puck with...what?

"For once, I agree with Pucker," William said, materializing beside her husband. *His* tone was just as emotionless as Puck's, just as cold, hard and uncaring. He, too, had a black eye and bloodstained clothing. "We shouldn't stay here."

"In this condition," Gillian said, "Winter and Cameron are defenseless."

"Not my problem," Puck replied.

Just how deep did his coldness run, that he would voice such a callous remark?

William went stiff, anger glinting in his eyes. "There's business I must attend to. I'll be back." He flashed away.

Relieved to have a private moment with Puck, Gillian said, "We can't leave while he's gone. You need him, remember? So for now, you're stuck here. We can use the time to melt your ice." *Please.*

"The ice is not the problem," Puck said. "You are."

What? "Me?" She pointed to herself, just in case he needed clarification.

"You would have died for William. You would have killed me to save him."

Was that the problem? Jutting her chin, she said, "I'd do it again, if necessary." Know the truth, deal with it, because there was no changing it.

He took a step back, as if she'd kicked him.

Then she added, "But I would have gone after you, too. Probably faster. Okay, definitely faster. And, if necessary, I would have mowed William down to do it."

His gaze bored into hers, searching, his pupils dilating. His breathing became uneven, and his hands balled into fists.

The ice was melting at last!

Triumph blended with feminine power—the kind of power only he could rouse—and it was more heady than magic. One day, people would say the wily Gillian melted Puck with *truth*.

"Come, lass. We are going to chat." He stalked toward her and, without a pause in his stride, hefted her over his shoulder and carried her to the blanket Peanut rested upon. "And do not worry about the others. The thorny vine I set will keep predators at bay."

He sat, then tugged her into his lap, her body sideways with her shoulder pressed against his chest.

"You like me better than him," he said, and smirked with satisfaction. "You want to stay married to me forever."

One thing was certain. Smirk still looked good on him. "I'm not sure how you went from I like you better than William to I want to stay married to you forever." Whispering now, she said, "But I think you're right."

His grip on her tightened. "I will make your happiness my mission, lass."

"Even though I refuse to agree to your terms? Because I won't destroy your dream, Puck. I won't. If we're going to be together, you're going to become king of the Connachts. Maybe we can convince William to *release* you from your vow?"

Would her friend be willing?

No. No, she didn't think he would. So, there had to be *an-other* another way.

No happy ending...what could be versus what would be...Foreboding settled on her shoulders.

"Be warned now," Puck said. "Let there be no misunderstandings between us. I won't let you go. I will do whatever proves necessary to keep you, and I will choose you over anything. Life will no longer be about what is best for others or me. Life will be about what is best for Gillian and Puck. We are a team. A family. I will trust you, and you will trust me."

Never, in all her days, had she heard a more beautiful or heartfelt pledge. Tears stung her eyes, the urge to wrap her arms around him and cling nearly too strong to deny. But even now, she couldn't agree to his terms. The past few days, he'd given her more than she'd ever imagined possible. So, from now on, she would give to him; she would do *anything* to ensure he lived his dream.

Needing a distraction...another dinner date...Gillian dug into her bag, withdrew the satchel of berries and nuts she'd brought from home, and placed the ripest piece of fruit at his lips. "We missed breakfast and lunch, and I know how my warrior likes to keep up his strength. Open."

"I *am* hungry." His eyes smoldered, all darkness and light. "But not for food."

"Too bad." He usually ate on a schedule, but he'd been forgetting lately. "You need sustenance if you're going to keep up with me, old man. I'm young and I've got *stamina*."

The corners of his mouth twitched before he accepted the berry. As he chewed, his brows drew together with surprise. "I can taste the richness of the flavors." He swiped the satchel and popped multiple berries into his mouth, chewed and frowned. "Tasteless now."

She took two berries, placed one on his tongue and one on her own.

Pleasure washed over his expression. "I can taste the flavors again, just as I once tasted *you*. So sweet. Delicious."

He tasted...because she'd fed him? And because he'd feasted on her? How exquisitely tantalizing.

"Give me more." With his hand wrapped around her wrist, he guided her fingertips to his open mouth to nip another berry. "Astonishing. When you feed me, I taste. When I feed myself, I don't."

Astonishing indeed. And there was a very good chance she was the one smirking with satisfaction now. "I might make a vegetarian out of you yet," she teased.

"Yes." Like a kid at Christmas, he motioned to the satchel. "Feed me more. Do not stop until we run out."

His eagerness was contagious. Smiling, she placed a pecan-like nut inside his mouth, transfixed as he chewed. His eyes closed, a ragged moan leaving him. His throat moved sensuously as he swallowed, sending a spear of bliss straight to her core.

"Just as delicious." Sultry tone, hooded gaze. He peered at Gillian as if she were a miracle. "Salty."

She squirmed in his lap, her need for him only intensifying. When her hip brushed his erection, she stilled. He stilled. Neither of them dared to breathe. Then, with a grunt, Puck lifted and turned her, so that she straddled him.

A whimper spilled from her mouth. "William could return at any moment." Even as she spoke, she twined her fingers through his hair and rocked against him. Another spear of bliss. A gasp. "We can't." *But I want to...* "And we must remain on alert for a magical attack from Sin."

"We can do this while remaining alert." His hands flexed on her hips. "My woman needs to come, so I'm going to ensure she comes. I left her needy and aching."

Come...yes. With him, only ever him. Here and now. Tomorrow and always. Her inhalations turned ragged, scraping her throat. Arousal throbbed between her legs. "Yes, we'll re-main alert."

Impossible.

Shut up.

When she pressed her forehead against Puck's, her hair created a curtain around their faces. In that moment, they were the only two people alive—and staying still wasn't an option.

Helpless, Gillian rocked against him, taking, giving. Yes! With her breasts flush against his chest, her nipples rubbed, rubbed. More bliss. Rapture, rippling through her. "I can never get enough of you."

"Never," he agreed. "Want you always."

"Need you."

"Lost without you."

Don't lose track of—Oh! That felt good. He anchored his hands on her ass, fingers splayed, and ground against her with more force.

A twig snapped. Leaves swished together. Incoming.

Noooo! Not now. Puck stiffened and stood, his body shaking with rage. Gillian choked back a whimper and rose, a dagger palmed.

William entered the clearing, took one look at them and scowled. "I spoke with Hades. We have two weeks to over-throw Sin, or the Sent Ones will destroy this entire realm."

The *entire* realm? "But why?"

William glared at Puck. "Apparently your asshole brother bombed a sacred temple, killing hundreds of Sent Ones, and the entire race is out for his blood. But no worries. Hades is sending reinforcements."

Two weeks to figure out a way to be with Puck *and* keep his dream alive. Two weeks at most. If they found Sin sooner...

Gillian's stomach churned, arousal and good humor gone. A countdown had been placed on her happiness, and she could think of no way to stop it.

33

WITH GILLIAN NO LONGER WRAPPED IN HIS ARMS, Puck struggled to remain calm. His emotions had gotten caught up in some sort of crisis, causing the demon to protest louder than ever. Think, think. Help from Hades? Sent Ones determined to attack? The coming destruction of Amaranthia? Sin marked for death by an entire species?

All part of the prophecy?

Fury besieged him, battering at his skull. Urgency joined the fray. Raw lust and a soul-crushing frustration, too. Unending hopelessness. Loneliness and betrayal. Hatred. Love. Pride. Sorrow. Grief.

He'd hated Sin for what he'd done. Mourned the loss of his brother. Needed to help…who? Who did he need to help?

To figure this out, he had to find peace and quiet. And yet he couldn't bring himself to summon any more ice and disappoint Gillian.

He ripped at his hair, his breaths churning with mounting aggression. Somehow he'd been stripped bare of his defenses, everything he'd felt before a mere blip compared to *this*.

Gillian would—

Her name spurred a new deluge of raw lust. Blistering waves

of it. He was hard and throbbing. If William hadn't returned, Puck would be inside her.

Rage, so much rage.

Indifference scrabbled across the bond, leaving Puck's head eerily silent.

Gillian noticed the intrusion and gasped.

He wanted to go to her, offer comfort, but felt tethered in place by his emotional chains. How was he supposed to deal with this?

Deep down, he'd known this day would come. Had known the things he'd buried would resurface; though Gillian had filtered out a good portion of it, what remained made mincemeat of his legendary control.

How was he supposed to *survive* this?

Arms spread, Puck threw back his head and roared at the sky. No relief.

He wanted his woman, and he would have her. If necessary, he would move mountains to reach her. He would kill anyone who dared step between them.

He needed to ensure her unhappy ending with William— and establish her happy ending with Puck. He wanted his friends safe and sound. Wanted Sin defeated and dying under his hand, the Connacht crown on another's head. But Puck also wanted Sin...alive. How could he harm the man who used to be his beloved little brother? More rage. *Can't contain it...*

Helplessness. Puck was going to have to leave Cameron and Winter behind. His friends, abandoned when they needed him most. In the coming hours, the two would worsen. Winter would cease her ramblings and attack anyone nearby. Cameron would come out of his comatose state and attack *himself*. Blood would pour. Lives could be lost.

Still Puck couldn't stay behind. If he failed to kill Sin within the next fourteen days—a mere three hundred and thirty six hours—*everyone* in Amaranthia would die.

Too much, too much. With a roar, Puck charged forward

and rammed into a tree trunk, horns first. Impact jarred him, bits of bark and insects flying. Once he'd wrenched the horns free, he backed up and rammed again. And again, until the tree toppled.

Short, choppy breaths razed his sternum. Red dotted his line of sight as he rammed another tree, then another. He would fell the entire forest! Nothing would stop him.

"Enough." Gillian's voice cut through his thoughts. Her *trembling* voice.

My woman fears me?

Puck spun, facing her. Her eyes were wide, her arms criss-crossed over her torso, creating an X—a shield—her fingers anchored on her hips.

William stood at her side, a pillar of protection.

He thinks to take her from me.

Chin down, horns forward, Puck sprinted closer. Faster and faster. William stepped in front of Gillian. *A mistake. His last.* Faster still. The bastard braced for a brutal collision, only to fly out of the way when Gillian shoved him from behind. She stood at the ready, intending to meet Puck head-on.

He skidded to a stop just in front of her, panting, unable to catch his breath. She didn't hesitate to reach up and cup his face, then brush her thumbs over the rise of his cheeks.

"Never thought I'd have to say this to you, Pucky, but I need you to calm down."

Inside, the sharp edge of his emotions blunted, her touch, her very nearness, soothing him as nothing else could. "Do not...fear me." The words emerged broken, ragged.

"Never."

"You are mine," he said.

"I am yours."

Calmer still...

Her gaze slipped over his shoulder, and she frowned. "Some-one's coming."

He whipped around, noticed tree limbs slapping together in the distance as a massive shadow moved over the land.

Must protect. Puck decided to deal with the threat in the sky first. A blond male with enormous white wings flew into the camp and landed only a handful of yards away.

The newcomer's identity clicked. Galen, keeper of Jealousy and False Hope, as well as Hades's helper. He was the world's most despised immortal. For centuries, he led a human army with the sole purpose of slaughtering his own kind. He'd betrayed friends and enemies alike and couldn't be trusted.

Puck had learned about him while researching William. Galen lusted for a woman named Legion—or Honey, or whatever she called herself nowadays. Her past was as fraught with pain and violence as Gillian's. Currently, Legion was being kept from him. Galen spent his time searching for her, warring in the underworld and attempting to regain lost friendships with the Lords of the Underworld—males he once tortured.

Two others stepped from the line of trees, arriving on foot. Pandora, Hades's only daughter, had shoulder-length black hair that framed an arresting face with dramatic hazel eyes.

Beside her stood a shirtless, muscular man with skin the color of blood, and eyes tattooed from neck to toe. "Red," the one who'd flashed Puck to the alley in Oklahoma City. His true identity crystalized: Rathbone the Only, another of Hades's allies, and a king of the underworld himself. Multiple piercings glinted in the sunlight and—

Had one of those tattooed eyes *blinked*?

"Reinforcements have arrived," William said.

Puck should have rejoiced. The Ever Randy's motivation had just shifted; no longer was he invested in Puck's success in the name of Gillian's freedom. Now he fought for her life.

If Amaranthia died, Puck would die. His magic—his very life force—was tied to the majestic realm. With Gillian's life force tied to *him*, she would perish with him.

Indifference swooped back into Puck's mind and cackled

with glee, as if he savored the thought of all those deaths. Especially Gillian's. *And why not?* She was the source of the demon's weakness and Puck's greatest strength.

She is the source of my everything. Only moments ago, he'd thought their life together would be about Puck and Gillian. Now he saw the truth. It was all about her—his life revolved around Gillian. He would do what was best for *her*, always.

If Puck hadn't defeated Sin in thirteen days, he would use the shears to release Gillian from their marriage. She would no longer have a bond to Puck, which meant she would no longer have a bond to Amaranthia. Of course, she would refuse to leave her clan behind, so he would have to force the issue.

Let her go? A roar of denial beat at his lips, but he held it back. To save Gillian's life, he *would* let her go. No matter how terribly he suffered afterward.

Defeat Sin in time, and all would be as Puck hoped. William would dethrone the Demented One. Puck would then kill Sin, despite their past. Puck would ensure the right Connacht soldier wore the crown, and keep Gillian at his side.

He had his goals—*Kill. Select.* He had his time frame. Thirteen days. He would not fail.

Kill Sin, not just dethrone him? Truly?

Do not sweat the details now. In the meantime, he would show Gillian how good it could be between them. No more waiting. No more terms. No more interruptions. From now on, he took what he wanted, when he wanted it.

"How did you find us?" he demanded.

"Finding you was the least of our problems." Rathbone shapeshifted into Sin's form, then returned to his own. "There's a shield around the entire realm, preventing anyone other than Sin or those in his company from leaving or returning. I had to become your brother to gain entry."

Sin must have erected the shield soon after Puck arrived with William. Or else Puck and company were an exception.

"Looking good, Gillian." Galen gave her an enthusiastic thumbs-up. "All grown up now. I approve."

"Well, thank goodness for *that*," she replied, her tone dry. "Life is finally worth living."

Boom! Peanut head-butted Galen in the stomach with zero warning, knocking the winged male off his feet. Then the chimera chomped on Rathbone's hand, earning a pained yelp.

A laugh bubbled at the back of Puck's throat as Rathbone cursed, the stoic Pandora scrambled out of reach and a grumbling Galen lumbered to a stand.

Amusement? At a time like this?

The fact that Indifference could do nothing but skitter across his mind in a huff made the moment so much sweeter.

"How do we know you are who you say you are?" Gillian stepped forward, intending to approach the newcomers, but Puck held out his hand, blocking her. "Could be a trick," she muttered. "Another challenge, even."

"Who would you like me to be, lovely?" Rathbone's image changed from a cute little puppy, to Puck, to William, to a jaguar, to Rick from *The Walking Dead* and finally back to his own. "Spoiler—it really doesn't matter. I'm a cold-blooded killer no matter what I look like."

"I vouch for them," William said.

Puck curled a finger under Gillian's chin and gently lifted her face, ready to handle the situation however she preferred. "We need to hunt Sin, which means we need to leave Cameron and Winter behind. But," he added before she could protest, "one of Hades's people will stay here and stand guard." An order he expected to be obeyed. "Do you approve?"

She closed her eyes for a moment, drew in a deep breath and nodded.

"Then it's settled," William said. "Rathbone, you'll stay with the siblings from hell. Galen, you'll fly overhead and warn of us any impending danger. Pandora, you'll ride alongside us, your only task to protect the girl, and die in her place if you must."

"Oh, that's all?" Pandora offered him a double-birded salute.

"I agree with the Randy Man," Puck told her. "Die if you must."

"No one dies for me," Gillian snapped.

William waved to the chimeras. "Did no one hear me? Everything is settled, my word is law. Let's go."

Puck, a born prince and once a future king, longed to attack this usurper who thought to take charge. No one ordered his troops but him!

Jealous? Now? Over *this*?

"Pandora is really attractive," Gillian said, her tone sharp enough to cut through steel. "Do you want her?"

She battled jealousy, too?

Clarity. Puck jabbed a finger in Galen's direction. "Control your demon."

The male hiked a shoulder, unconcerned. "Counter offer. I do me. You do you. We both do the girls."

Puck was in his face a second later, punching, breaking his nose. Gillian and Pandora cheered.

Galen grinned as blood poured down his face. "What? Was it something I said?"

William delivered the next punch, merely earning a laugh from Galen as he popped his jaw back into place.

Crazy male! Puck ushered Gillian to the chimeras, helped her mount, then mounted Walnut.

As William trotted past Puck to take the lead, he muttered, "Remember what I told you."

Their group trekked through the forest, leaving Rathbone, Winter and Cameron behind. To circumvent a surge of guilt, Puck replayed the conversation he and William had earlier, as Puck set a thorny border around camp.

"Fun fact," William had said. "I collect skulls. Pretty ones, ugly ones. Male, female. Young, old. Immortal, human. Those of my enemies and friends alike, and even a person I met in an elevator."

"Is it story time?" Puck had been in a deep freeze at the time, and antagonizing the male had seemed like a wonderful idea. "Gee whiz, Willy. I wish you'd warned me. I would have dressed in my pj's and snuggled under my favorite blanket."

The beloved son of Hades had continued on, unperturbed. "I have thousands of skulls. The only thing they have in common? I murdered the person they once belonged to."

"Yawn. You're big and bad, and you do creepy things. Noted. Your point?" He'd spread his arms wide. "Wait. Let me guess. If I'm not careful, I'll end up as exhibit A in your collection."

William had run his tongue over his teeth. "I hate those skulls. Every...single...one. They remind me of the worst deeds I've ever committed. Once, I considered getting rid of them. Before I'd made a decision, however, a friend stole my least favorite of the bunch. Do you know what I did?"

"Bored him to death with this story?"

"Tracked him down, cut off his head and turned his skull into a urinal. My point, as you so eloquently requested, is this— *you do not steal from me.*"

A fetid stench permeated the air, cutting into Puck's reprieve. He grimaced as he picked up notes of death, decay and sulfur.

"Galen," Pandora bellowed. "I *told* you not to eat those burritos."

"You're blaming me for this?" White-feathered wings gliding in a measured back and forth motion to keep pace with the chimeras, he said, "I thought you were to blame. I was going to be a gentleman for once, and not comment on your raging flatulence. My mistake."

Puck scanned the area, and discovered four rotting bodies partly hidden by piles of leaves about a hundred yards away. Using magic for an up-close inspection, he realized the victims had been ripped to pieces.

He slowed his pace, coming up beside Gillian. "See the

bodies? They died badly. Whatever killed them could still be out here."

"Don't worry," she said. "I'll protect you."

He glanced at her, and she curved her lush red lips in a smile, setting Puck aflame with lust.

Must have her. Soon.

Pandora, who rode at Gillian's other side, withdrew a sword from a crisscross sheath on her back. "What kind of beast could we be dealing with here, Indifference?"

"You may call me Your Majesty." He wasn't the demon. Would never be the demon again.

He forced the devastation to reclaim center stage in his mind. Limbs had not been cut from the bodies but ripped. There were bite marks on every visible patch of skin, but not fang marks. Scratches made by dull nails rather than claws.

Considering each hand had blood and tissue caked under every nail bed…almost seemed like the people had attacked each other.

Surely not. "The beast… I don't know."

"I'm more concerned about the maze." Gillian pointed to the right. "I feel like I've seen that tree three times already."

Maze…maze. The word poked and prodded at Puck's mind. Gillian had called Sin's creation a maze more than once, but he'd never treated the forest as anything more than, well, a forest.

Had he erred? "Fly up, Galen, and tell us what you see."

Galen obeyed, and the higher he went, the wider his eyes became. "You guys should see—"

He smashed into an invisible ceiling, impact snapping one of his wings. Like a falling star, he streaked down, down, before crash landing a few feet from William, skidding across the ground and slamming into a tree.

Both of his wings were now crimped and twisted at an odd angle. His shoulder was clearly out of its socket, and his ankle broken; bone cut through flesh. What had to be thousands of bugs swarmed from the tree trunk to glom on to him.

In unison, everyone dismounted and rushed over to help. With a yell, Galen rolled away, knocking into Gillian, who fell.

Cackle, cackle. Indifference enjoyed the show.

Tensing, Puck hustled to his wife's side—but William flashed, reaching her first. He expected rage. *The bastard touches what's mine.* Instead, he experienced…gratitude. The bastard helped her when she needed him.

"I'm fine," she said, and smiled. "Truly."

All right, *now* he experienced rage. *That is* my *smile.*

Galen jammed his fist into his dislocated shoulder, popping the joint back into place. Even though his ankle flopped uselessly, he stood and limped toward Puck. "Prick! Did you know I would—"

Peanut head-butted his midsection. Once again, Galen slammed into a tree.

"Well?" Puck prompted. "What did you see?"

Galen stayed down. Glaring, he said, "I saw our doom."

Gillian listened, sick to her stomach as Galen described a nightmare of biblical proportions. Sections of the maze were trading places. Meaning, no matter how far the group traveled, or how new the landscape appeared, they might never reach Sin's fortress.

"Do you know how I know we're going to escape this maze?" Pandora announced. "Because *I'm* here."

Hey! That's my line.

Gillian rubbed the back of her neck, only then noting the drop in temperature. From *somewhat cool* to *welcome to the Arctic*, so cold her teeth started chattering.

The others noticed, too, frowning as snowflakes twirled from the sky, landed on exposed skin and were absorbed through pores.

Inside her, blooming heat chased away the cold. Blooming…

blistering. Her runes flickered on and off as her blood became lava, and her organs became ash.

Magic?

"Puck." She tried to say more, but searing agony suddenly and unequivocally *consumed* her. She whimpered—and then she screamed.

"Help..." The bones in her face, chest and limbs elongated, thickened and rotated. Dark fur sprouted, overlaying every inch of her skin. Her gums developed a heartbeat of their own as tusks extended upward, past her upper lip. Claws grew from her fingers and toes.

With the horrid change, she lost her center of gravity and toppled.

Peanut swung around, screeched and backed away from her.

Where was Puck? She needed him. *Vision hazing.* Where, where? Her gaze landed on—no! Her teammates were gone. In their place? Horned, fanged monsters.

Thoughts devolving, almost indistinct, savage instincts taking over. *Not my friends, but my enemies. Food. So hungry.*

Gillian reared back, readying herself...and then attacked.

34

MIND A WAR ZONE, INDIFFERENCE'S PROTESTS CLAT-
tering, Puck struggled to make sense of what was happening
around him. Gillian, William, Galen and Pandora had dropped
to all fours and now prowled around each other, snipping and
snarling.

Foreboding deluged him. *This will not end well.*

Appropriate. William launched at Galen, teeth bared. Locked
in a battle to the death, the two males bowled over twigs and
rocks.

Gillian released a war cry and hurtled her body at Pandora,
who met her midway. Biting, slashing. Blood spraying.

This was no ordinary Hulk-out. A strange madness had
overcome everyone but Puck. Why not him, too? Indifference?
But Gillian had a connection to the demon, as well.

Puck's magic, perhaps? Still a flaw in his logic. Gillian and
William had magic of their own.

Puck's inborn magic, then? *Connacht* magic? Something the
other two *didn't* have.

Exactly. There was only one way to stop this, then.

The solution unsettled him. So drastic. Maybe he could reason with Gillian and the others instead.

Worth a shot. Puck leaped at the females, knocking the two apart. They pounced on him, nails slicing into his flesh, teeth biting into his neck. Despite the influx of pain, he did little to defend himself.

Careful. Must protect Gillian at all cost. But not Pandora. He grabbed the other woman by the hair and flung her into a bank of trees before trapping his wife beneath him.

She bucked, a wild thing, and tried to rip out his throat. In her eyes, he saw no hint of recognition.

"Calm down, lass. Breathe for me. In, out. Just—"

Nails scraped his face, his neck, and pain seared him anew.

A heavy weight slammed into his back, but failed to budge him. Pandora had returned. She scratched, punched and kicked the most vulnerable parts of him. Rage beneath him, fury atop him. Fun times. He reached overhead, grabbed Hades's daughter by the hair and flung her a second time—at William.

A distraction. Mistake. Gillian jammed the heel of her palm into his nose, and cartilage snapped. He grunted, battling a brief bout of dizziness. Warm blood poured down his face.

After kicking and dislodging him, she leaped into a crouch. Her sights zoomed to William, who was shaking his head and howling at the sky, daring her to close the distance; he would not go easy on her.

"You're staying right here." Puck clasped her ankles and yanked, sending her crashing into the ground face-first. She winced. *He* winced, hating that he'd caused this precious woman pain.

When he had her pinned, he said, "Gillian. I know you're in there." She had to be. "Concentrate on me. Think about—"

She slammed her forehead into his chin, dislocating his jaw. More pain, stars winking before his eyes. And she wasn't done! Arms free, she whaled at his face while bucking and kicking with more force, desperate for freedom.

Despite his injuries, he rasped, "Gillian, I'm your husband. Remember my kiss, my touch. We are—"

Lifting her head, she pressed her mouth against his, sucked his tongue into her mouth—and bit off the tip. In seconds, blood filled his mouth, nearly choking him.

Spit. He used magic to expedite the healing process, his jaw realigning, gashes weaving back together, tongue regenerating.

"Enough, lass!"

Again she kicked him, managing to free herself. A mindless state might hold her prisoner, but it *hadn't* wiped away centuries of training. Then she drew back her leg, broadcasting her intention. She wouldn't. Surely she wouldn't—

She punted his face.

All right, then. There'd be no reasoning with her.

Using superspeed, Puck grabbed her ankle when she made another play for his face, and yanked her off her feet. He pinned her beneath him, wrapped his fingers around her throat and squeezed just hard enough to immobilize her. As he'd done during her Hulk-out, he turned his attention inward, to their bond. This time, he gifted her with a tendril of Connacht magic.

You didn't have to die to cede magic to others. Not even inborn magic. You could offer it willingly. Though he'd never met anyone keen to do so.

What would Puck lose, in doing this? His ability to shapeshift? Run at the speed of light? Either way, he'd never get the magic back, unless he killed the ones he shared it with, or they willingly returned it. But Galen and Pandora, whom he would have to brand with runes, wouldn't know how to return it for centuries, and William wouldn't out of spite. *Hardly matters. Must help Gillian.*

Her motions slowed, stopped. She peered up at him, wide eyes darkening with horror as her mind cleared. "I attacked you. Oh, Puck. I'm so sorry."

Relief. Pride. He'd succeeded. "Do you not yet realize I would endure *anything* to get you into this position?"

"How did this happen?"

"Magical illusion. A trap set by Sin, programmed to start whenever we breached a certain point. You believed you were an animal, aye?" At her nod, he said, "The others still do." He stood, helped her to her feet. "If we can pin them, I can feed them Connacht magic." A bond wasn't needed for a gift of magic, only made it easier to give.

Her eyes widened with horror when she spotted William, Galen and Pandora tangled together, each covered in wounds and soaked in blood.

Anyone else might have run screaming, but not Gillian. She kept pace at Puck's side and approached the combatants.

"I'll take William," she said. "You take the other two."

"He won't recognize you. Might harm you." *Then I'll be forced to retaliate.*

She tossed him a quick smile, causing his heart to careen out of sync. "Have more faith in your wife." After withdrawing four daggers—two in each hand—she punted Pandora in the face and elbowed Galen in the jaw.

As the combatants fell away, Puck struck, pinning Galen to the ground with daggers.

Movement at the corner of his eye. He paused to watch as Gillian masterfully maneuvered William to his back, and staked his wrists and ankles into the ground. Just *boom, boom, boom, boom,* and the guy was pinned.

My woman is skilled.

Considering William's strength, Puck wasn't sure how long the hold would last. Puck abandoned Galen—for now—placed a hand over William's brow and unleashed the barest tendril of Connacht magic. Just enough. The male ceased fighting, frowned. No time to explain.

Puck vaulted into Pandora. With her, he had no qualms about using necessary force. After he'd staked her, he reached for a dagger, realized he'd dropped his somewhere along the way. Very well. He palmed hers, quickly carved a rune in her hand and fed *her* the barest hint of Connacht magic.

Finally, he turned his sights to Galen. Rune. Connacht magic.

Done.

"I thought I'd transformed into a beast," Pandora said, between panting breaths. "Why?"

Gillian explained the situation while ripping the daggers from William's wrists. Silent, he sat up, freed his ankles, then rubbed wounds already in the process of healing.

"What if this is only the beginning?" she said. "What comes next might be worse. Which sucks, because we're running low on *everything*."

Her fears were not misplaced. Each challenge had proven more difficult than the last.

"We'll deal," Puck said. They must. They had no other choice.

They traveled the rest of the day.

Gillian couldn't keep her eyes off Puck. He'd saved her, saved them all, by sharing his magic. He could have turned into the Ice Man at any point, but he'd chosen to stay with her and, judging by the heated looks he'd been casting her, feel *everything*. Never had a man appeared more tempestuous. A storm brewed in his eyes and darkened each of his features.

Time is running out. Don't know what the future holds.

Need him. Need him now.

Never had she been more ready for a man's possession. Even now, her heart assaulted her ribs, racing faster and faster. Her nipples ached more than ever before, her belly quivered and the apex of her thighs *throbbed*.

Can't have him. Yet. Soon...

They came upon a pond about an hour before sunset. After setting up camp, everyone took turns bathing to wash away battle blood. Puck first—she wanted to join him, but there was no time—then William, then Pandora and Galen. Finally

Gillian stripped and waded into cold water that failed to cool her heated skin.

She waited…but Puck never showed up. Disappointed, she dried off and dressed in a shirt and short leather skirt for easy access and Puck's torment.

On edge, on alert and sexually frustrated, she returned to camp. William sat in front of a fire, sharpening his daggers with an almost obsessive concentration. Pandora and Galen lounged beside Puck, peppering him with a million questions about Sin, Amaranthia and magic, but he wasn't in the mood to chat, or even be sociable. His answers were "yes," "no" and "shut up before I cut out your tongue."

When he spotted Gillian, he gave her a look of such blatant hunger, such palpable desire, she grew dizzy with lust and missed a step, nearly falling flat on her face. Ecstasy beckoned, her body already overly sensitized from hours, days, of anticipation.

William popped to his feet and muttered, "Father calls." With no more explanation than that, he flashed away.

Galen and Pandora shared a moment of aggravation before standing.

"Where he goes, one of us must go," the dark-haired female said.

"Thankfully, Hades equipped us with a WNS." Galen tapped his temple. "William Navigation System."

"William will be gone for hours," Pandora said, and wiggled her brows. "I'll make sure of it."

"Good to know," Puck said. "Make sure you *all* stay away from the pond, then."

A blush burned Gillian's cheeks.

"Aren't desirous of a little light spying, eh?" Galen asked. "Fine. *I'll* go after William, and *I'll* make sure he stays away. Pandy cakes, you guard the perimeter. I have a feeling our little lovebirds are about to lose track of everything."

Pandora snapped her teeth at *Pandy cakes*. "Come on. Before you lose your favorite appendage." She dragged the winged male away.

Finally!

Puck stood, his kohl-rimmed gaze tracing over the curves of Gillian's body. As if he could stand their separation no longer, he advanced on her, all dark and lovely and hot and aggressive. He hefted her over his shoulder in a fireman carry, and carted her away from the campsite.

Her pulse quickened as his scent enveloped and intoxicated her. "Puck?"

"This is happening, woman. Best get used to the idea."

"Um, did you hear a protest from me?"

"No, but I *will* hear your agreement."

"You mean I get all of you, no matter what?" she asked, breathless.

"Every inch." At the edge of the pond, he set her on her feet.

Arousal blistered her as she peered up at him. He was pure wicked indulgence, a buffet of sensual delights. Shirtless, his bird tattoo on spectacular display. The one he wouldn't let her touch—yet. *Soon I'll touch every inch of him...*

"You want me," he said, framing her face with his hands. "Say it."

"I want you." Desperately. Madly. Moonlight fought its way through the canopy of trees, stroking him with loving fingers. "We'll have to be quick. The danger..."

"Quick?" Warm breath caressed her brow as he chuckled. "Impossible, wife. This is our first time. Your first time, period. We will savor every second. If Sin tries anything, I'll sense his magic. I'm prepared now."

"All right. Okay." How could she resist? "My answer is yes." A thousand times yes.

Groaning, he fisted a handful of hair at her nape and urged her face to his. "Give me what I've been missing."

"Always." Their lips met in a heated clash, their tongues

twining, dueling. A deep kiss. Reverent. Wild and yet still sweet.

He kissed her as if his survival depended on it, demanding total surrender. Surrender she happily ceded. Scorching desire swept her up, down, in, out and everywhere in between. Ravenous, they devoured each other. This wasn't an appetizer, but a full-blown meal.

Never had Gillian known hunger like this. Every cell, every organ, every inch of her craved his possession.

Puck lowered her onto a bed of moss and maneuvered to his side. With one hand, he cupped her ass—a favorite position? With the other, he palmed her breast and brushed his thumb against the distended crest. Paradise!

"You been missing *me*, lass?" The huskiness of his tone—audible porn.

"Every inch of you." Shivers and heat invaded her bones and when he kneaded her flesh, she would swear he considered her body a temple—would swear he worshipped every inch of her.

At eighteen, she hadn't been ready for him. At one hundred... two hundred...maybe even four hundred, her issues might have gotten the better of her. After multiple wars and countless trials, battles, friendships and betrayals, hurts and pains, creating a clan and a home, she finally knew what she wanted, and what she needed. For her, everything revolved around Puck Connacht. Warrior prince. Future king. Adored husband. The man who felt everything—for her.

He deepened the kiss, and she spread her legs, letting his thigh rest between hers. Instant rush! Liquid heat drenched her panties. Unable to remain still, she arched her back, grinding her core against him.

A whimper escaped. The rush *and* the pleasure!

"Puck," she cried.

"Stop?" he asked, his tone ragged.

"Don't stop. Ever."

35

GILLIAN SLID A HAND OVER PUCK'S CHEST...OVER
the bird tattoo. Magic pricked her, rushing up her arm, making her shiver. Well, well. No wonder he hadn't wanted her to
touch it. The tattoo meant something. But what?

Mind too fogged to unravel a mystery.

"Want *me* to stop?" she asked, tracing her fingertips over the
beautifully detailed wings.

"*Never* stop."

His heartbeat thundered against her palm, racing in sync to
hers. The silk and heat of his skin...the glorious cut of solid
muscle...the musk of his scent combined with the sweetness
of his taste...*making me* crazed.

Since his return, she'd felt as if she were burning up, sometimes at a low simmer, most times at a full boil. Ravaged by
this newest passion-fever—or rather, this extension of the last
one—she arched her back to gyrate against his thigh.

"That's a good lass," he praised. He kneaded her ass harder,
helping her gyrate with more force. "Let's get you nice and
primed."

Already primed, warrior. She'd never been so drenched.

When he shifted his leg, his thigh grazed her where she

ached most. She groaned. He moaned. Every point of contact became electrified, the currents supercharging her arousal.

How long had this beautiful man been deprived of affection and adoration? Since before his possession? Taken from his mother's arms as a child, forced to fight in his father's armies, punished for anything perceived as a "woman's softness."

As much as Gillian wanted to take, she wanted to give.

"Puck," she gasped out, growing more desperate by the second. "I need to touch you, too."

"Touch me, then. *Please.*"

Brimming with eagerness, she lifted her head to watch his face as she delved her hand beneath the waist of his pants. Though she had little experience, she faked confidence and wrapped her fingers around his erection.

"Tell me if I do something wrong," she said.

"You do…everything right." Strain tightened his features, his breaths turning ragged. Lust glittered in his dark eyes, the starry pinpricks so beautiful. He had an entire solar system in those irises, and she felt like she was the sun.

Up and down, she stroked him. Up, down. His hips arched with each upward motion.

"The things you do to me, lass." With a hand draped over her nape, he drew her down for another kiss. A frenzied one, with teeth and tongue and an exchange of air. Of life.

He slipped his free hand under her panties, pressed the heel of his palm against her core. Pressure grew, made worse by lance after lance of incomparable sensation.

"Puck…please." So ready!

He plunged two fingers deep. Yes! She cried out, releasing his length to clutch his shoulders, her nails sinking into his skin. *Her* skin pulled taut over muscle, her mind reduced to its most animal state. *Take my pleasure, ensure his.*

She rocked her hips, forcing his fingers deeper. Hotter heat. More pressure. Little mewling sounds rose from her as his thumb pressed against her clitoris.

"I'm so close," she said, her voice ragged.

"That's the way, wife. I'm going to make you come hard and fast. A swift, brutal climax, but it won't be enough. Not nearly enough."

No, no, never enough. She couldn't catch her breath. She... she...

"You're going to need more...and more..." His voice drugged her, luring her to obey...

Gillian *erupted*! A scream burst from her, pleasure overwhelming her. Muscles contracted. Bones liquefied. Her heart either stopped, or it raced so quickly she could no longer discern a single beat. Her mind soared with the stars, wonderment leaving her in a daze.

But just as "hard and fast" as she'd come, she crashed. Empty, her body was so empty, his fingers gone. She needed to be filled.

Panting, she said, "Diabolical man. You were right. It wasn't enough. I only want *more*."

His eyelids hooded, his breathing choppy. "Then take it from me."

Oh, she would, happily. But not until she returned the favor...

"Let's get you primed first," she whispered. Trembling, knowing she played with fire, Gillian traced her fingers over his lips, his cheekbone, around his eyes, through his hair... and over his horns. Every touch was a revelation of his innate power...and agonized *her*.

The danger of arousing him? She aroused herself, too.

When he tore open the waist of his pants, just enough to free his length—so long and thick and hard—her inner walls squeezed, as if desperate to glove him.

He ran his hand up and down, utterly magnificent. "This is what you do to me. This is how much I crave you."

He craved her *greatly*.

"Want to taste it." Tremors intensifying, she crawled

down his body and fit her lips around his erection, took him down...down.

The ferocity of his reaction delighted her. He gripped hanks of moss, dug the heels of his feet in the dirt, and hissed up at the sky. "Yes!"

She moved up, down. Repeat, again and again. He trembled with every upward glide, and groaned each time she descended. His strength...heat...silkiness...incredible!

He was desire made flesh, carnal and deliciously wicked.

She sucked him, faster and faster, until he tensed, gripped her under her arms and lifted her. His mouth claimed hers, and he fed her a fierce, frenzied, savage kiss. With a deft twist of his wrist, he removed her shirt, cupped and kneaded her bare breasts. He pinched her nipples, and she gasped. Every cell in her body hummed with rapture.

"More." She had to have more.

He ripped off her panties. "Straddle me. Will use magic... birth control."

Finally take him inside? Yes! "Running low on magic."

"Worthy sacrifice."

So true! As fast as immortally possible, she climbed onto his lap. The pleats in her skirt offered no resistance as she spread her legs, welcoming his erection against her core.

"Not yet," he croaked. Hands on her hips now, he forced her to her feet, and positioned his mouth over her aching femininity. "Need a taste of you first."

He flicked out his tongue, wrenching an agonized groan from her. The pleasure...she let her head fall back. He licked and devoured while he prepared her with his fingers, moving one in and out of her. Then two. He scissored them, stretching her. And it was good, so good. All she could do was hold on to his horns and enjoy the ride, rocking, rocking, back and forth. Back and forth. Soon, incoherent words left her. Her muscles were tensing, readying for climax—

But he didn't let her have it. He stopped before the moment

of no return, wringing a frustrated shout from her. Then he drew her to her knees once more, positioning the tip of his erection where she needed it most and feeding her another kiss, letting her taste the very pleasure he'd roused in her.

Gillian pressed down…slowly…slower, giving her body time to adjust. His fingers had prepared her, but his shaft…it was so big even the tip seemed to fill her up.

Sweat glistened on his brow. "Taking me so perfectly, wife."

The roughened tone caused a tide of arousal to drench his length, allowing her body to slide farther down. When Gillian perceived a white-hot burn, she stopped. Centuries had passed since she'd had—no! She'd never had a man inside her. What happened in her childhood did not count. Puck was right. *This* was her first time.

His grip on her flexed, as if he wanted to yank her down but resisted the urge. "Killing me, lass. Never felt…so good. But I need… I need…"

When he needed, she would give, always.

Gillian pressed down once again…the burn intensified… down. Finally, she had taken all of him. Puck expelled a breath.

One minute passed and—yes! The pain faded, and her muscles went lax.

Roaring, Puck thrust his hips up, and…*oh! Oh!* She'd had another inch to go, and it felt *incredible.* A stream of ecstasy sluiced through her.

Now he impaled her. Sweat slicked their chests, friction sparking every time she inhaled.

"You good, lass? Tell me you're good."

"Mmm. Very good." She moved. She *had* to move. Balanced on her knees, she rose up, up, then slid back down. *Amazing.* So she did it again, and again, tentatively at first but soon gaining confidence and speed.

"That's the way." He tightened his grip, guiding her up and down with more force, even forward and back. Missing his hands on her breasts, she cupped them and pinched her nipples. "The sight of you… The *feel* of you."

Nerve endings crackled, pressure built deep inside her… deeper still. "Puck," she cried. "Please."

My woman needs me to finish her.

Desire consumed Puck, so intense he had no perception of Indifference, had lost sight of the world around him. He could only focus on Gillian, his wife, a live wire of pure energy and raw passion, so hot and tight and wet as she rode him.

Moonlight bathed her, golden skin flushed, the runes in her hands glowing. Those whiskey eyes were *alive*, the kindling an unstoppable inferno.

Pride puffed his chest. *I did this. Me.*

With her head thrown back, her hair a dark stream framing her face, she was a vision. A goddess without equal. The incarnation of carnality.

"Let me," he said. With his cheek, he nudged her hands away and flicked his tongue over one nipple, then the other.

Breaths heaving, she rode his shaft faster, faster. Tension stole over him, collecting in each of his muscles, threatening to explode, or kill him. He'd be happy either way, would die with a smile.

"You are mine." His voice was thick and low, as much a growl as anything. "Say it."

"I'm yours. Yours. All yours."

That's my female. "Gonna make you come so hard, lass." He thrust up even as he drove her down, down, at the same time giving her nipple a little bite.

"Puck!"

Must taste my name on those lips. Mouth on her mouth. Tongues dancing together. He reached between their bodies and strummed where she ached most.

"Yes, yes!" Her entire being shook, her inner walls clenching around his shaft as she climaxed.

Puck became frenzied, pounding in and out of her…pounding…she felt so good, so right. Nothing had ever felt better, or more perfect. The pleasure was irresistible. Would he blow?

Heat at the base of his spine, radiating around his hips, collecting in his testicles. His body readied. Soon he would…he would…

Puck roared until his throat cracked, his voice going hoarse. He came and came and came inside her, his entire body bucking under the onslaught of bliss. And still he did not stop thrusting, did not stop jetting into his wife as she milked him, as if greedy for more—for all of him.

He'd waited so long for a woman to be his and his alone, had craved having the same female in his bed again and again. And yet, when he'd experienced multiple nights with another, he'd found the whole thing lacking. This? With Gillian? Not nearly enough. He wanted every night. Every morning. Every moment in between.

He hadn't known it at the time, but he'd waited for *her*, had craved *her*. Only her. A woman strong enough to feel when he could not. A woman unwilling to let him shut down his own emotions, who knew the rarity of joy, who would settle for nothing less.

Finally, when she'd wrung him dry, he collapsed, Gillian remaining draped over his chest.

That was…so…so…amazing! A revelation.

Gillian marveled. She'd just had sex. Wicked, mind-blowing, delicious sex. The kind in novels and movies. The kind she'd always wanted, but feared she'd never have, and she'd loved every second of it.

The right man had made all the difference, just as she'd suspected.

With Puck, pleasure had possessed her, driving her to new heights. And it—this—had forged a bond as strong as their vows. It must have. Gillian had never felt closer to her husband.

She lifted her head and caught Puck grinning. The sexiest grin she'd *ever* beheld. Also the most beautiful. His entire face lit up, warming her inside and out. And…and…and…

A tear suddenly slipped from the corner of her eye, surprising her. Ugh. Was she going to cry *every* time she had an orgasm?

It was just, this was another first. This beautiful act had once been a living nightmare because of bad, bad men. Finally, she was free!

Puck had owned her. Not her memories. Not her past. Puck. He'd owned *all* of her.

As a teenager, she remembered thinking she needed to have normal sex with a normal guy in order to feel normal herself. Puck was anything but normal. He was *extraordinary* and exactly what she'd needed.

And he's mine. For now.

How can I ever let him go?

Gentle, so gentle, he wiped her tears away. "What is this, my sweet wife?"

Pretending she wasn't feeling all kinds of vulnerable, she said, "I'm just… I'm happy. Not bad for my first time, eh?"

He combed his fingers through her hair, his need to touch her as strong as her need to touch him. "Woman, you have remade me." A pause, then, "I will hear *your* praise now. Tell me you'll replay this encounter. Tell me you'll remember your soft feelings for me, no matter what happens between us."

Remember…because he'd ditched his terms and planned to divorce her, after all?

Has to be this way. You know it.

Just…don't go there. Not yet. Chest constricting, she lifted her head, cupped his stubbled cheeks in her hand. "As if I could ever forget my soft feelings, or you. You are my…" What? Husband, yes. Life? Maybe. Family? *Love?*

I think… I think I do want his love. I think I want to love him back.

A war cry cut through the night—*William's* war cry.

In a blink, Puck had pulled out of her and maneuvered to

his feet. She groaned, regretting the abrupt loss of him. Actually, regretting the loss of him period.

No time to waste. As she stood to unsteady legs and righted her skirt, then pulled on the rest of her clothes, Puck tied his pants and weaponed-up. Perfect timing.

A blur of darkness slammed into him, propelling him into a tree.

Puck and William tumbled over the ground in a violent clash, one over the other. Somehow they managed to both injure and disarm each other.

Not that the fight was any less brutal without weapons. They began to use claws and teeth to inflict maximum damage.

"Stop," she commanded. "Now!"

"I thought I could deal with this." With his eyes glowing red, William looked like the incarnation of wrath. "For the first time in my life, I was wrong."

"She's my wife." Puck might not have red eyes, but savagery etched every inch of his face.

"Not for long."

Puck charged, head-butting William and reminding her of Peanut; only, Peanut had no horns. The protrusions gouged William's torso. Merciless, her friend grabbed her husband by the base of the neck and twisted, breaking his spine.

For one terrible minute, Puck was motionless. Just enough time for William to work himself free, and punt the other man in the face.

Her stomach protested. "I said enough!"

They ignored her, too busy rolling across the ground once again, striking at each other. Their growls blended together. Blood sprayed.

Gillian's heart rate accelerated, her breaths growing hectic. "I mean it. Stop!"

Ignored again.

William grabbed a dagger by the blade, the metal slicing

his hand as he hammered Puck's temple to punctuate his next words. "You took advantage of her."

Puck deflected the next blow and delivered a brutal upper-cut to the underside of William's chin.

"He didn't take advantage of me. I begged him for it." She vaulted between them and held out her arms. "Please, stop this."

If something happened to one of these two men...

William darted around her to swing at Puck. Her husband blocked before delivering a punch of his own—one loaded with magic he couldn't afford to waste. William flew back-ward, crashing into a tree, splitting the trunk in half.

As William came barreling back, ready to slam into Puck once again, Gillian jumped between them a second time. But William couldn't stop, his speed too great. Noticing her, how-ever, he flashed past her, successfully avoiding her and smack-ing into Puck. Another violent clash ensued.

Argh! If she inserted herself into the fray, one of them could injure her, and both men would blame the other. The fight would definitely end in death, then.

Having heard the commotion, Galen and Pandora burst past the line of trees. When they caught sight of the in-progress battle, they stopped—and grinned.

Amusement? Really? Gillian's anger sparked.

"Twenty bucks says William takes home the gold," Galen said. "And Puck's family jewels."

"You're on," Pandora replied. "Puck's not letting Willy win his girl. I've seen the way he watches her."

Twenty dollars. No offers of help. Anger turned to rage. Tingles along her nape. Thoughts derailing. Oh, no, no, no.

She reached for the vial of syrup hanging around her neck. Too late. *Must...kill...everyone!*

Gillian grabbed hold of Galen, lifted him over her head and slammed him into Pandora. Red suffused her vision as she followed the pair to the ground. Punch, punch, punch. Kick, kick. The abuse she inflicted on one, she then inflicted on the other.

They tried to fight back, to escape, but they were no match for her superior strength or speed. Blood sprayed her face, and she grinned. The *pop, pop* of breaking bones rang in her ears, and she laughed with maniacal glee.

"Gillian. Lass." Puck's voice seemed to call to her from a long, dark tunnel.

He was near. Her husband. Did she want to kill him? No, no. The thought repelled her.

"That's my sweet lass." Soft fingers stroked the ridges of her spine. "Calm down, *a chuisle*. For me."

A chuisle. Or "pulse." But...the endearment made no sense. Why would Puck call her a pulse? Unless he meant...*she* was *his* pulse, the very reason his heart beat.

He already loves me?

Maybe, maybe not. She definitely loved him, she realized. No longer did two different Gillians battle for supremacy inside her—all of her wanted Puck.

She'd fallen for him, all right. Head over heels, nothing held back. She loved his strength, and ferocity. Loved his calm, and his cunning. Loved who they were together.

But he was more than the love of her life. He *was* her life. When he smiled, she melted. When he looked at her, she desired. When he neared, she lost focus of anything else.

So, he could rest easy. Puck Connacht remained undefeated. He'd won her loyalty as well as her heart.

And now that he had himself a loving queen, she could help him unite the clans!

Problem: she wasn't supposed to receive a happy ending, unless the Oracles were wrong for the first time in Amaranthian history.

She'd told herself she could overcome anything, even the prophecy, that she would fight for what she wanted. Too, she'd told herself she couldn't risk dragging Puck down with her.

He was a born king, and he might grow to resent the woman who kept him from his dreams.

She couldn't do both. Had to pick one or the other.

His happiness mattered to her—far more than her own! And his leadership mattered to *everyone*. The maze was a creation of Sin's and a peek inside his mind. He was diabolical, crazy and straight up evil. He had to be stopped. According to the Oracles, only one Connacht would govern Amaranthia. So, that Connacht had to be Puck.

Also according to the Oracles, only William could win the Connacht crown on Puck's behalf. But…what if *Gillian* found a way? What if she killed Sin? Would Puck grow to resent her for that, too? After hearing affection in his voice when he'd spoken about young Sin, she thought he might not be too eager to shack up with his brother's killer.

Damned if I do, damned if I don't.

The chance of one prophecy being hogwash, and the other golden—not great. So. She had to proceed as if both were true or both were false.

Okay. If William dethroned Sin and presented Puck with the crown, Puck would have to divorce Gillian. No matter what, he had to deliver his brother to the Sent Ones.

He might marry a (different) loving queen, and unite the realms. If that happened, Gillian would…what? Stick around in Amaranthia to watch? Never! She'd rather pack her belongings, say goodbye to her clan, Peanut, her home and go. Because, if she stayed, she'd end up killing Puck's new wife.

Take what's mine and suffer.

William expected Puck and Gillian's desire for each other to vanish as soon as the bond got cut. Would it? Would Puck ever want her again? *Should* he?

The clans hated her and would never accept her as queen. And okay, okay. She was one hundred percent willing to put in the work to win everyone over. Safer villages, havens for widows, orphans and former stable members, as well as interclan schools. No more sending preteen boys to war or training preteen girls how to please a master.

That's my campaign promise. Unlike most politicians, Gillian would actually follow through.

Would other clans forgive her for mistakes she'd made in the past?

No happy ending…

Dang it, her mind kept getting stuck on that one thought.

"Lass, come back to me." Puck's gentle voice called to her, wrapping her mind in peace. "That's my darkling."

Darkling? *I'm racking up the nicknames tonight.*

Light filtered through the storm clouds in her mind. Blinking rapidly to focus…focusing…she groaned. Galen and Pandora lay on the ground, their eyes closed, blood splattered over their skin and clothes.

"Did I kill them?" she asked in a soft tone.

"They live." Puck stood at her side, petting her, offering comfort.

When her gaze found him, she nearly lost her last meal. One of his horns hung at an odd angle. One of his eyes was swollen shut, his nose broken and his lower lip split, the lower half of his face covered in dripping crimson. He had gashes in his neck and chest, and his pants were tattered.

"Did I do this to you?" she asked, her chin trembling. Gently she traced her fingertips around one of the worst gashes.

"This? This is nothing."

"I'm fine as well, thanks," William snapped.

Gillian turned and found him standing at her other side. He was in as bad of shape as everyone else, a cut arching from forehead to chin. Bits of his throat were exposed, and one of his ribs poked out of his chest.

"I'm sorry," she rasped. More than he could possibly know, in a thousand different ways.

He said nothing to her, just moved his narrowed gaze to Puck. "You don't have to worry, Pucker. I said I'd help you regain your crown and I will. And *you* will keep your end of the bargain. You will cut her loose as soon as the crown rests upon your head."

Next he concentrated on her, and she wished the ground would open up and swallow her. "Whether you want me or not, you need to be free of the bond. You won't know your own mind—or heart—until it's broken." Then he did something she would have sworn he'd never do again. He stalked away from her, and just like Puck, he never looked back.

36

MUMBLING CURSES UNDER HIS BREATH, SIN PACED inside his suite. A common occurrence nowadays. The Oracle had escaped. Not that her location mattered. He'd marked her with a magical tracker her first night in the dungeon—after drugging her, of course. She had no idea he could find her in an instant.

He believed she planned to find and help Puck. To retrieve her, Sin would have to face his brother.

Not ready.

The Oracle's final taunt clanged inside his head.

The day will come, the day will come soon, riding on the wings of fury. Vengeance against you will be meted.

Puck might mete vengeance, but he wouldn't prevail. How could he?

If the newest prediction was true, Puck would fail to kill him. Because Sin would find his "ladylove" afterward. And then, only then, would he lose his head.

Don't want to kill my brother, but I can't let him kill me.

Sin slammed a fist into the wall, cracking stone. His knuckles throbbed as dust coated the air. Blood dripped from torn skin, staining the fur rug his mother had picked out…however long ago.

Every crimson drop reminded him of the night he'd cursed Puck. His brother had entered the war tent, soaked in the blood of their enemies, proudly clasping the Walsh king's sword.

What Sin had done—"gifting" his brother with Indifference—he'd considered a necessary evil. But there was no such thing as a necessary evil, was there? Only evil pretending to be good. *Excuses, excuses.*

Had he let the prophecy dictate his actions? Yes. Had he turned a supposition into a self-fulfilling prophecy? Perhaps.

Would he do it again? Unequivocally.

No other way to save us both.

Except, what if there *had* been another way? What if he could have spent these centuries with Puck, working together as planned?

No, no. Impossible. Puck's greatest weakness was also his greatest strength: his possessiveness. Despite what he'd claimed—that he would co-rule with Sin—he'd considered the Connacht clan his. The other clans, too. The entire realm, in fact. His, his, his.

Puck had tried to circumvent the prophecy by never sleeping with the same woman twice, never staking a claim, never risking falling in love, never stoking the desire to marry a loving queen. But one day, he would have caved.

The moment their father announced Puck's betrothal to the princess, Sin had seen his brother jolt, and he'd known the truth. Puck had just thought: *she's mine.*

I helped him let go of such foolish proclivities. I gave him peace. He knows no fear, impatience, guilt or failure.

And how had Puck thanked him? By bringing a group of immortals into Amaranthia to usurp him.

Did the wife love him?

As Sin passed a mirror, he caught sight of an image he hated above all others—the butterfly tattooed on his chest.

The mark of his demon. The mark of Paranoia.

Puck had no idea Sin was possessed. Sin hadn't known, either. Not at first. Not until the Red Queen had appeared to him a second time and explained what had happened to him.

In the neighboring realm, Sin's peace talks had been unfruitful. The other realm had not feared him, had laughed in his face, whatever suggestion he made. He'd hated the thought of returning to Puck a failure. Oh, the humiliation!

The night before he was to return home, the Red Queen had appeared to him for the first time and offered a solution: a bejeweled box containing the power necessary to make *any* realm fear him. All he had to do in return? Present his brother with a box of his own, on a night of her choosing.

Hoping to impress Puck with his skills—wanting Puck to have the same power—Sin accepted and opened the box. Moments later a black mist with red eyes had risen and jumped into his body.

The demon of Paranoia had possessed him, *dominated* him, and Sin had erupted into a maddened rage, slaughtering his own men.

Everything Puck had experienced during his possession, Sin had experienced weeks before. Horrifying darkness. Unending gloom. The total loss of control. But so worth it. The power! The fear he'd inspired in others! The Red Queen had not lied.

Now Sin gave a bitter laugh. He'd never meant to hurt Puck. Had only wanted to live in Amaranthia together, forever. If Puck no longer considered the Connacht crown his, and no longer yearned to unite the clans, then the prophecy would be voided and all would be well.

But after his possession, Puck hadn't cared about Sin.

Must kill him before he kills me.

No! Sin banged his fists into his temples. Never! "Be silent!"

What thoughts originated in his mind, and what thoughts came from the demon? He couldn't tell the difference anymore. Had he ever?

Kill Puck. Killpuck. KILLPUCK.

Spittle spraying from the corners of his mouth, Sin unleashed a stream of magic, causing a wall of sand to form in front of the mirror. In the center, an image of Puck and his entourage appeared. The group of five trekked through Sin's maze, so close to the end. Only one more challenge, and a door would open, leading to a Connacht outpost—a safety measure in case Sin himself ever got trapped.

A king had to plan for every eventuality.

Besides, a part of Sin—the boy he used to be, perhaps—had hoped Puck would find a way through.

There had to be a way to live together in harmony. *Think!* Sin had worked far more complicated puzzles in the past, and succeeded.

The problem was the prophecy. Which meant the solution was the prophecy, as well. Keep something from happening, and nothing could happen. Change one variable, change all variables.

The variable on which the entire prophecy hinged? The loving wife.

If Sin removed the Dune Raider from the picture…

Could he truly hurt his brother's female?

No other way, the voice inside his head whispered. A dark voice. Beguiling. *Otherwise he'll kill you, or you'll kill him. Is that what you want?*

No, no. Of course not.

Very well, then. It was decided. The girl had to die.

First problem: Puck and Gillian were bonded. If she died, Puck would die. Maybe Sin would capture her instead and lock her in the dungeon, where she could spend the rest of eternity.

Would Puck be willing to bargain for her safety?

Sin would have only two demands. (1) Puck forgave him. (2) Puck loved him again.

Option two. Sin killed the wife—and Puck. He could marry

his princess at last; she would love him, then. She would have to. The Oracles had said so. Sin would unite the clans on his own.

Thought I wanted to avoid this?

Fool! Once he fulfilled the prophecy, all of his problems would go away.

So. It was decided. He would kill the wife—and his brother.

Though a pang ripped through his chest, Sin exited his room and called for his guards. Determination directed his steps. It was time. Past time to end the war with Puck. One way or another.

The guards would accompany him and serve as a shield as Sin tracked the Oracle. Hopefully she hadn't found and warned Puck of Sin's intentions—yet. If she had, well, he would deal.

Two of his men marched around the corner, but neither would meet his gaze.

"King Sin," one said, shifting nervously. "How may we help you, O Great One?"

Nervous? They've betrayed me in some way. Will probably try to kill me on our journey, while I least expect it.

Change of plan. Sin would go alone.

As he came upon the soldiers, he withdrew his short swords. Without a pause in his step, he removed their heads. "Betray me now."

Hades lounged atop his throne, his arms rested on his middle, his legs extended in front of him, his ankles crossed. A deceptively casual pose. His men were gone, dismissed for the day. The other kings had returned to their kingdoms, protecting their subjects from Lucifer's wrath and the increasingly violent war taking place in the underworld. But Hades wasn't alone.

His gaze bored into his favorite mirror. Siobhan, the goddess of Many Futures, was trapped inside, her hatred for him emanating from the glass. She had the ability to look into forthcoming days, weeks, years and see the different paths a person could take. She then had a choice: to show the outcomes, or not to show them. So far, she'd shown Hades nothing of importance.

Had she lived in Amaranthia, she would have been touted as an Oracle.

Once, as a teenager, she'd asked Hades to marry her. Told him they were fated. Of course, Hades had rejected her. Wed? Him? Laughable! Wed a child? Never! He might be a man without a moral compass, but even he had a line.

Although, this particular teenager had then proceeded to coldheartedly murder all of Hades's lovers. Past, present and—apparently—future. So, like any rational male, he'd arranged for her to be cursed in the mirror until she learned her lesson: do not mess with Hades.

"You're still learning, obviously," he said.

So badly he wanted to know what was coming for him. Would William save Amaranthia—and himself?

Hades had sent Rathbone and Pandora to help, only to add Galen as a last-minute tagalong. If an air evac was needed, wings would come in handy. Besides, the keeper of Jealousy and False Hope would do anything for the woman he desired... and Hades had her tucked away where the warrior couldn't reach her without permission.

Do as I say, and visits are encouraged. Betray me, and watch as I seduce the one you desire.

For the right to see Legion, Galen would do anything to keep William safe. Even kill the girl, Gillian, if such an action proved necessary.

Even still, Hades should have gone himself. Instead, he'd returned home to quell another rebellion spurred by Lucifer.

Now Hades *couldn't* enter Amaranthia. The shield stopped his every single attempt. He needed Rathbone, but couldn't communicate with the warrior, only William, and William had no idea where Rathbone was. William had even flashed back to the last location he'd seen the male, but Rathbone, Cameron and Winter had already moved on.

"You must know I'm the type of man who will gather your family and loved ones and murder them right in front of you," he said. "If this is what you want, continue showing me nothing. I'm happy to oblige. Or, perhaps you still consider me your fated male? Perhaps you'd object to watching me plow through a battalion of females."

Nothing. No reaction.

Very well. He would do as promised. Because he never made idle threats, only promises.

The back of Hades's neck suddenly prickled. Someone approached.

Cloaking the mirror with invisibility, he glided to his feet. Just in time. The Red Queen appeared in the center of his throne room, a vision of cray-cray loveliness with her pale hair in rollers and her body clad in only a lacy pink bra and panty set. One leg had shaving cream slathered from thigh to ankle.

He smiled a genuine smile. "To what do I owe the pleasure of your company, my sweet?"

She *humphed*. "First, I'm not your sweet. I never was, or you wouldn't have sold me for a barrel of whiskey and happily continued on with your life while I was tortured and imprisoned."

"Trifling offenses. I've done much worse to others."

"You aren't wrong. But. I'm Torin's sweet, and he's quite mad for me." Puffed with pride, she fluffed her rollers. "Second, I came to warn you."

His shoulders squared with a single, jerky movement. "Tell me." Keeley, too, would have been known as an Oracle in Amaranthia. Once, she'd had quick glimpses into the future. Lately she'd had long stares.

"Someone we love is going to die," she said. "I sense it."

Hades tensed. There was only person they both loved. William.

37

PUCK KNEW HE'D REACHED A SERIOUS CROSSROADS.

Only hours before, he'd experienced utter and complete satisfaction. His first climax inside a female in centuries. His first climax inside *his* female, ever. Need had governed him. A need to possess Gillian, to claim and brand her. To *fill* her, two bodies made one.

He'd been crazed with lust for her. Still was. He'd longed to enjoy the afterglow. Deserved it. *One day, I will* murder *William for interrupting the best moment of my life.*

The son of Hades stayed away from camp most of the night, Galen with him. Pandora patrolled the perimeter, and despite the demon's loud bellows inside Puck's head, he remained on alert for any sign of Sin's magic.

He felt a looming sense of doom, which only made him want to gather Gillian in his arms and never let go. But when he'd tried to embrace her a few minutes ago, she'd pulled free in order to pace around the campfire.

She agonizes—over him. Over the man she loved; the man she would always love.

Gutted, Puck could only watch her and long for his ice. With every minute that passed, he was scraped raw inside—rawer—wounded in ways he'd never thought possible.

He'd once thought himself done with all familial ties. No ties, no betrayal. Gillian had changed his mind.

Having a tie to another person, the *right* person, didn't make you vulnerable to attack; it made you stronger. Look at what had happened with Indifference. Gillian had helped reduce the fiend to a whiny toddler. Family gave you a solid foundation on which to stand. When storms came, you had someone there to prop you up if you fell.

And perhaps Puck's emotions were not so bad, after all. The satisfaction in his chest every time he gazed at his wife...the completion he found in her arms...*worth any hardship.*

But William remained a problem. Gillian's feelings for the other male weren't romantic, or so she believed. But romantic or not, that love bonded the two together. And, at the end of the day, her bond to William was greater than her bond to Puck. Because she'd chosen William with her heart; she'd made a choice without duress.

No matter. Puck had decided to fight for her, and he would. Nothing, not even this, would stop him. He would *make* her love him, even without the bond. Would ensure she chose him, now and forever.

Always follow through.

But how? How did he reach her?

Gillian paced before the campfire, her head a maze as dangerous as Sin's. Her tasks were set. Acquire everything Puck wanted, appease William, fulfill or override both prophecies with satisfactory endings for everyone involved, make other clans like her, and help everyone live happily-ever-after for the rest of eternity.

Each one alone was impossible, but all?

First, she would have to stop William from winning the Connacht crown. If she failed, if Puck refused to accept it, she would have to find a way to force him. Also, she had to operate under the assumption that he would want her after he used the shears—no other outcome was acceptable. Which meant she still had to find a way around her predicted unhappy ending.

Forget about making the clans like her. They could hate her all they wanted. They just had to do whatever she commanded.

Okay. One task crossed off her list.

Now to figure out how to keep Puck without jeopardizing his future. And she *had* to keep him. He was her man—*her* pulse.

He *must* love her as deeply as she loved him. More than once he'd put himself at risk just to be with her. In so many ways, they balanced each other. Sometimes he felt too little, and she felt too much. He got her and all her silly "what ifs." He respected her battle skill and never attempted to leave her behind.

A presence behind her, heat, her husband's unique fragrance. Gillian whirled and came face-to-face with a savage-looking Puck. His chest rose and fell in quick succession, every breath labored and shallow.

For a man who'd felt nothing but hollow and empty for centuries, he projected a lot of emotions right now. Utter starvation. Desire. Adoration. Affection.

He definitely *loves me.*

"You. Are. Mine." His voice was so rough, it scraped her ears. "You said so, and you do not lie. I will be yours, all you want, all you need. Forever." He pulled at her clothes. Top, gone. Skirt, shed. Panties, ripped. "Naked this time."

Forget the turmoil, the uncertainty. *Seize the moment!* "Naked," she agreed, and tugged at his clothing as desire scorched her.

When he was bare, he slipped his palms to the backs of her thighs, picked her up and walked her to the sleeping bags, where he sank to his knees. Never relinquishing his hold, he pressed his lips against hers, and thrust his tongue into her mouth, stroking.

She met him stroke for tantalizing stroke, pouring herself into the kiss, giving him everything but taking it, too. Surrendering, but also demanding surrender. Ceding her heart while doing her best to conquer his. And she thought…she thought he was doing the same to her.

Tension radiated from him, his every action aggressive. *More.* Lost in pleasure, Gillian clawed at his back, rubbed her breasts against his chest, and grinded upon his erection.

With a growl, he pushed her to her back. He remained on his knees, drinking in every inch of her, and even that was aggressive. His gaze *devoured*. He traced a fingertip around each of her nipples, along the plane of her stomach…between the wet, tender flesh at the apex of her thighs.

Eyelids hooded, he ran his tongue over his teeth. "My wife is more exquisite every time I look at her. I want to see more." He set her feet outside his hips and pushed her knees farther apart, opening her, leaving her vulnerable.

Tremors spilled through her. She gasped his name. "Your wife *needs*." As his gaze devoured her, her gaze devoured him. He was all hard muscle and delectable sinew. Flawless brown skin, and gorgeous tattoos. Between his legs, the tip of his mouthwatering shaft glistened.

"Needs more pleasure? Or me?"

"You *are* pleasure. You, only you."

He leaned forward, his weight braced on his hands, his expression fierce. Sweat glistened on his skin as firelight flickered over him. His eyes—she gasped. How had she ever thought them like frosted coal? Those eyes *burned*.

Those eyes made promises. *I will love you always. I will cherish you. I will fight to give you the world.*

Pucky is soooo going to get lucky.

He crawled backward, pausing to tongue and suck her nipples into hard little points. As she writhed, lifting her hips in an attempt to grind on him, he kissed the center of her stomach. He moved lower, his beard stubble leaving pink scratches behind—marking her.

He let his mouth hover just over her pubic bone, and anticipation nearly killed her. Her temperature rose, fever setting in, turning the air in her lungs to vapor.

"Must have another taste." He lowered his head, warm breath caressing her most intimate place. Then he settled in, getting comfortable, as if he planned to be there awhile. *Then* he licked.

He made little growling noises in response. "*My* honey. *My* wine."

Mercy! Tremors rocked her, stroking already electrified nerve endings.

He licked some more, sucked. He pressed his tongue on the throbbing heart of her and thrust two fingers all the way in, staking an undeniable claim; she bucked against his mouth.

Still he licked. Still he sucked. "Will never get enough," he said, punctuating every word with another thrust of those fingers, another press of his tongue. With every motion, he became even more aggressive.

She couldn't...she was going to... "Puck!" His name burst past her lips as she climaxed, as pleasure filled her, shattered, killed and remade her. She was overcome, overwhelmed.

He surged to his knees. Leaning over, he used his hips to wedge himself between her thighs. "Can't wait." After positioning himself at her entrance, he slammed inside her.

He grunted in approval. She cried out in bliss, shocked into a second orgasm. She was no longer Gillian Shaw, Gilly Bradshaw or any other name she'd used in the past. She was Puck's woman. She belonged to him, and he belonged to her. *My man. My home.*

"So wet. So tight." He paused, peering down at her with concentration, as if memorizing her features. He was panting, every breath ragged. A bead of sweat trickled from his hair, down his cheek, and fell from his jawline, splashing onto her shoulder. Even that acted as a stimulant, the droplet sizzling before evaporating.

"Move in me," she pleaded, her voice ragged.

He did. In and out. Slowly. He filled and consumed her. Sliding in, sliding out. Gaining in speed. Agony and ecstasy.

"You glove me so perfectly, lass. Yours... I'm yours. Always." He thrust again, and again. Harder. The more he thrust, the more frantic he became, driving her need higher.

Gillian clawed at his back, bit the cord of his neck and locked her ankles against his lower back. Pressure continued to build inside her. In an attempt to draw him back, she arched her hips every time he withdrew. For too long, she'd been empty and alone. Now she belonged.

She'd been claimed—possessed.

Puck took her by the nape, fisting her hair. "Give me your pleasure. Take mine." As he stared into her eyes, satisfaction beckoned...

Helpless to resist.

Gillian screamed his name, her inner walls clenching and unclenching on his length.

"You're making me come, lass. Making me—" Quick as a blink, he shifted to his knees and pulled her up without slipping out of her. The new position sent him surging deeper. To ensure she sat upon him, he wrapped his arms around her, holding her flush against him. Chest to chest. Male to female. Her hair tumbled around them, a curtain of dark silk shielding them from the rest of the world.

"My Gillian. All mine."

"My Puck. All mine."

Ragged noises left them both as he jackhammered inside her. When she ran his lower lip between her teeth, he lost all control, going wild. Slam, slam, slam. One of his hands gripped her hair, tugging. The other gripped her bottom, bruising, and it was beautiful, every second, every motion.

"Gillian!" He bellowed to the sky and held his hips steady as he jetted inside her, giving her everything...*just as he's* my *everything...*

38

EXHAUSTION SET IN, JOINING HER CONTENTMENT, leaving Gillian boneless as she cuddled into Puck's side. Her head rested in the hollow of his neck, a sleeping bag draped haphazardly over them both. Lazily he combed his fingers through her hair, a mesmerizing, drugging delight, but she couldn't sleep. Or rather, wouldn't sleep. She remained on alert for any potential attack.

As the suns rose, light filtered through the treetops, high-lighting Puck's gloriously naked chest. Knowing there was no snooze button while out on a mission, she figured she had five or ten more minutes before she had to get up and dress. Besides, the others would return soon. Actually, she figured William had stayed away on purpose, not wanting to deal with what he'd find—again.

Won't feel guilty.

As she drew a heart over Puck's pec, he said, "Do you have affection for me, lass?"

"Have I not proven it?"

"I need words."

Her chest clenched. "Yes, Pucky. I have affection for you."

"Do you have fun with me?"

"Yes," she replied readily this time, only then realizing where he was headed. "I also feel accepted and supported when I'm with you. More than I ever have with anyone else."

He nodded as if satisfied. "Your birthday is coming up."

"Is it?" She'd lost track.

"Only two hundred and twelve days away."

"So just around the corner, then," she said with a laugh. "When is *your* birthday?"

At the sound of her laughter, he radiated satisfaction. "Don't know," he finally replied. "I stopped celebrating once I was taken from my mother."

Clench. "Well, then, we'll celebrate your birthday when we celebrate mine."

He tensed, which caused her to tense. Did he not think they'd be together that long?

"If we fail to find Sin in the allotted time, I'm going to use the shears and ensure you leave the realm," he admitted, his voice heavy with…dread? "I won't let you die with Amaranthia."

No! "I won't let you die, either. There's got to be a way to get everything. The crown. Vengeance for the Sent Ones. Our marriage." *So why is my stomach twisting with dread, as if I know he's right?* "I love you, Puck. I don't want to give you up, but I also don't want you to give up your clan."

"You love *me*?" He sat up, staring down at her, and thumped his chest.

"Yes, silly man. I love you. And you love me."

The prompt—*agree with me*—flew right over his head. "You love me. My Gillian loves me." Awe lit his face. Then he narrowed his eyes. "Do you still love *him*?"

"Yes," she admitted, and he tensed all over again. "I'll always love him. As a friend. Only ever as a friend. Please believe me."

Quiet fury—that's what he was just then. It filled his eyes, pulsed from his body and held him rigid as stone.

"Honey, we're home," a voice called, and she jolted upright, her breasts bouncing. "But don't hurry on our account. I'm enjoying the show."

A short distance away, Galen hovered in the air. He wiggled his sandy brows, unabashed by his voyeurism.

Moving fast—though not as fast as usual—Puck grabbed one of the rocks circling the fire pit and threw it. "No one looks at her but me."

The missile pelted Galen's wing, sending him crashing to the ground. As he lumbered to his feet, Peanut galloped over and performed a perfect head-butt.

Gillian rushed to dress alongside her husband, saying, "Good boy."

"You're welcome for the warning, by the way," Galen grumbled.

Footsteps sounded as Puck fastened his pants. She looked up just as William and Pandora stepped from the line of trees.

Unwilling to meet her gaze, William sidestepped her, grabbed his go-bag and mounted his chimera. Ouch.

Pandora cast her an apologetic glance. "Let's save any arguments for later and move out."

Gillian hurried to gather her belongs. By the time she sat atop Peanut, the others were well ahead of her. Everyone but Puck, who waited for her.

"I'm sorry," she said, "but I have to speak with him."

A muscle flexed in his jaw, but he nodded. Thunder cracked, jolting her as she trotted forward to sidle up to William. A cold wind blew, causing her hair to slap her cheeks. A storm brewed, the sky now darkening.

"Talk to me," she beseeched. "Please."

Annnd still he ignored her, never relaxing his stance.

"Okay, *I'll* talk and you'll listen. I never made promises to you, Liam. In fact, I did just the opposite. I told you I wasn't interested in you romantically. I told you I wanted Puck."

Now he growled, shifting to glare at her, his eyes blue one moment, red the next. "You're not even sorry, are you?"

Sorry for being with Puck? Never! "I'm only sorry I hurt you. But, if you think about it, you're *glad* I turned to another man."

His nostrils flared as he inhaled sharply.

William wasn't grieving over her loss, wasn't devastated or even jealous. In those extraordinary eyes she saw anger, hurt and injured pride.

A rumble in his chest, almost a match to the thunder in the heavens. "We'll be back." He dismounted, saying to the others, "Do *not* come looking for us." He forced Gillian to dismount, not that she put up any kind of fight, then took her hand and dragged her away from the group, toward a thicket of trees.

"There isn't time for this," Puck called.

Do not look back. Do not—

She looked back. *Stay. Please*, she mouthed. She needed to hash things out with William once and for all.

Puck stared at her until the last possible second, his expression unreadable, his chest rising and falling with quick, labored breaths. Then tree limbs whisked together, hiding him from view.

She gulped, torn. Feminine instincts screamed, *Return to him. Now.*

No, no. She had to finish this.

William stopped abruptly and whirled to face her. "You are mine, and yet you turned to that...that...*goat man.*"

She anchored her hands on her hips. "He might be a goat man, but he's *my* goat man."

"*I told you* the bond would affect you. *I told you* to wait until you were free."

"You also told me to sow my wild oats."

"A moment of insanity."

"Maybe, maybe not, but here's the truth, plain and simple. I was intrigued with Puck *before* we bonded."

"No." He glared daggers at her. "You're mistaken. Too many years have passed for you. *Centuries.* Your memories are skewed, which is understandable in more ways than one. You were sick at the time. If he was your fated mate, you wouldn't enjoy spending time with me, wouldn't laugh with me, or miss me when I'm gone."

Stubborn male! "You might want to rethink your argument, Ever Randy. According to your logic, you would have kept your joystick in your pants if I were *your* fated mate. You wouldn't have bedded every woman in creation. You would have considered celibacy a privilege as you waited for me."

A flash of outrage, quickly tamped down. "You were a child."

"And you are an immortal. Time is nothing to you. Would waiting two years have been such a hardship? Truly?"

Another clap of thunder. Lightning lit the sky, highlighting the beautiful face she loved...as a friend. A brother. The father she wished she'd had.

"I did wait, just not the way you preferred," he grated. "Or have you forgotten the night I found you in my apartment?"

A flush of shame heated her cheeks. "You know what I mean."

He spread his arms, all *look at me now.* "I haven't been with anyone since I got here."

"You've gone an entire week? What strength! What will-power! You must be *so* proud."

Silence stretched between them as he stared at her, hard, studying her. Then he scrubbed a hand down his face. "Why are we even arguing about this? Or are you afraid I'll walk away from your precious Puck before he's made king? Well, worry no more. I'll kill his brother and gift Puck with the Connacht crown. In return, he'll sever his bond to you, as agreed, and you'll realize I was right all along. You'll beg for my forgiveness. One day, I might even grant it."

Was he freaking kidding? "*You'll* forgive *me*?" With every word, her volume rose. "I don't want your forgiveness, William. I haven't done anything wrong."

"You've done *everything* wrong!"

She blinked, and William changed. Gone was the gentle teaser she knew and loved. In his place was the vengeful warrior who'd found her seconds after she'd married Puck. Wings of black smoke sprang from his back. The same smoke seemed to branch around his eyes, as if he'd somehow donned a mask. Those branches extended over his cheekbones, the perfect contrast to the lightning strikes that appeared under the surface of his skin.

She expected him to shout, to rant and rail. Eyes like wounds, he said, "You broke my heart, Gillian."

"No. No." *I can't have hurt him.* "I never wanted to cause you pain."

He was lethally quiet as he flashed to a tree a few feet away and slammed his fist into the trunk. Again and again, until half of the trunk split from the other.

Tears blurred her line of sight and streaked down her cheeks. "I'm sorry. I'm sorry," she babbled.

"You never even gave me a chance." Steps eating up the distance at an alarming rate, he approached her. "I told him I wouldn't touch you, and I always sometimes keep my word. But I never said I wouldn't kiss you."

Finally he was there, standing directly in front of her, swooping down to press his mouth against hers. His tongue thrust past her lips and teeth to stroke inside.

The kiss devastated her, but not the way he hoped. The kiss broke *her* heart. All she tasted was salt water from her tears.

She adored this man, but she could not bring herself to return the kiss. Not to give him closure, not even to say goodbye. Gillian could not, would not betray her husband in such a way.

With her palms flat against William's chest, she pushed him away. "Stop, Liam. Stop."

Her mind noted the slow pace of his heart—it wasn't racing with a passion too great to be denied.

Her tears continued to fall, a sob bubbling from her. His

electric blues were not dazed as they studied her a second time—they were confused, and sad. So incredibly sad.

"Shh, shh," he said. He reached out to collect her tears with his thumbs. "It's going to be all right. Everything will be all right."

Would it? So much was unknown. So much was unfinished.

"I love you," he said.

"I know. I love you, too. That will never change." But what she felt…it had *never* been romantic love. Deep down, a part of her had always known it, but other parts of her had mistaken protectiveness and security with teenage infatuation, and desperation with lust.

Another sob escaped her. "I'm sorry," she whispered.

"No, poppet. No. Don't be sorry. I lied before. You did nothing wrong."

A moment ago he wasn't sure he could forgive her. Now he was comforting her. "What changed?"

"I cannot do it. I cannot hurt you. You mean too much to me. And I…"

She waited for him to say more. He didn't. "Tell me," she pleaded.

He sighed, his warm breath fanning the crown of her head. "You are a terrible kisser. Like, seriously bad."

She barked out an unexpected laugh. "Right back at you, Ever Randy."

"I love you so much," he said, squeezing her. "More than I've ever loved another."

Hello, new tears.

He gently chucked her under the chin to guide her gaze back to his. What she saw? Tenderness. Understanding. Disappointment. "I've lived a long time. I've heard thousands of people—immortals and mortals alike—talk about the power of a single kiss. How one kiss can change you forever, ruining you for another lover. One kiss can teach you, calm you or incite you. Your kiss… I felt your love for him. I found it strangely…beautiful."

"William," she whispered, anguished. "I never wanted to hurt you."

"I know, poppet. I know." Still so gentle with her. "I'll recover. I always do," he said. "And don't go thinking I'm Puckillian's number one fan. I haven't changed my mind. I believe the bond is responsible for this, but I'm not going to—" He stiffened, frowned. "Hades is screaming at me. Danger. Death. Near."

Magic? she thought as a breeze blew past. Last time, Sin's magic had hit with wind.

The ground shook with so much force, Gillian stumbled to the side. She gasped, struggling to remain upright. Dread turned her blood to sludge as cracks formed in the dirt. More pits?

Puck! Peanut!

Gillian ran, pumping her arms and legs as quickly as possible. *Must reach them!* As she cleared the trees, her gaze found Puck. He was doing everything in his power to calm a frightened, bucking Peanut while also watching for Gillian's return. The moment he spotted her, relief brightened his expression… until his gaze dropped to her lips. He scowled.

Not what you think, hubby. Okay, it was. But she hadn't participated.

Halfway there…so close, but not close enough.

When they reached a safe place, she would explain what had happened. Except, between one step and the next, the ground—just—vanished. Unlike before, there were no pieces left to stand upon, and Gillian tumbled through the air.

39

"GILLIAN," PUCK SHOUTED, ALREADY USING MAGIC to cast a vine from somewhere above in a desperate attempt to catch her. The ground had dematerialized, there one moment, gone the next, taking Gillian with it.

Indifference howled, incensed by Puck's panic. How could a day that began so beautifully end up like *this*?

He also cast vines to the others—Peanut, Pandora and William—using up what remained of his magic. Galen's wings had saved him. The other chimeras had sensed something wrong and scattered just before the land loss.

Had Puck caught Gillian and William? He couldn't see the pair; thick gray clouds had replaced the forest.

He *must* have caught her. He hadn't died, so he knew she hadn't died.

"'Go on a mission for Daddy,' Hades said." Scowling, Pandora planted her booted feet on thorns, allowing her to stand rather than dangle. "'It'll be fun,' he said."

"If Gillian and William are down there, I'll find them." Galen angled his body and dipped beneath the clouds.

Only moments ago, Puck had been furious with Gillian. Her

lips had been red and appeared bee-stung, just as they looked after he kissed her. Only, he hadn't been with her.

Betrayed by my own wife!

Indifference had beckoned at him like a siren's song. *Want nothing, need nothing.* If he summoned ice, the jealousy and rage would dissipate. His feelings of betrayal would vanish. But Puck had resisted. He wasn't a coward, and he wouldn't run from his emotions any longer.

He would feel, and he would deal. But oh, he'd wanted to shake Gillian, had wanted to kiss her so hotly he would be forever branded on her lips. Him, not some other male. And he would. Soon. Then he'd wanted to remove William's head with a single strike.

He'd thought, *Consider the kiss a goodbye, lass. You'll kiss me, and no other.*

Then he'd realized there was no one more honest than Gillian. She wouldn't cheat on her husband, ever. William might have kissed her, but guaranteed she hadn't kissed him back.

"I'm here, I'm safe." Her beautiful face appeared above the clouds, the thorns providing the perfect hand and foot rails as she climbed to a position level with Puck's.

Relief tore through him. But, when he noticed the blood dripping down her arms, he worried all over again. "You're injured?"

"Got stabbed by a few thorns, but I'm fine. William, too. He has a lot more vine to climb." The color drained from her cheeks when she spotted a flailing Peanut. The vine wrapped around the animal's middle, the thorns buried deep in his belly. "You used magic to save him. Thank you, Puck."

"For you, I will do anything."

"It's okay, baby," she called. "You need to calm down."

Peanut panicked further. The more he thrashed, the more he bled. He had to be in great pain, with no idea why. But, if he didn't stop, he might cause the vine to snap.

"You're only hurting yourself worse." Desperation threaded Gillian's voice. "Calm down. Please."

"The vines are anchored to a piece of land above us," Puck said. "I'm not sure how far we'll have to climb, but there *is* a destination to reach. Once we're at the top, we can hoist Peanut to safety."

"Why not go down?" Pandora asked.

"There's no way we can safely lower Peanut to the ground." The strained words came from William as he broke through the clouds.

Though the chimera had never liked the male, he settled when William traced a fingertip between his eyes. No, Peanut didn't just settle; he slept, his body going lax.

"He'll remember none of this," William said. "I would flash to the top and hoist him up myself, but I can only appear in locations I've previously visited. Or can see. With the cloud cover..."

"It's going to be okay. We're going to get through this." Ever the warrior, Gillian drew in a deep breath and squared her shoulders. "Let's start climbing."

That's my woman.

On cue—because *nothing* could go right today—thunder boomed and a zip of lightning raced across the sky, directly above their heads.

Galen returned, the smooth glide of his wings allowing him to hover. "I flew down pretty low but found no trace of land. However, I did find a doorway to another realm. Which one? I have no idea."

"We can't risk it," Puck said. They could end up inside a volcano, or a prison. Or worse. "Up we go."

"I'll do a little scoping, find out what we're dealing with." Wings flapping, blowing the vines, Galen ascended.

He'd been gone only a few seconds when another clap of thunder heralded the fall of rain. *Acid* rain. Every drop seared Puck's skin, the catalyst to great waves of agony. Flesh and muscle sizzled, and he caught the scent of cooked meat.

Everyone bellowed with shock and pain, creating a horrifying chorus usually only heard in nightmares.

Galen returned, his entire body jerking each time a droplet
of rain pelted him. "Never mind the solo trip." He clasped a
vine and snapped his wings closed, becoming a smaller target.

If this persisted, everyone in the group would wither to ash.
Would the vines? Without magic, Puck couldn't even create
a shield over Gillian.

Indifference turned up the volume—he specialized in making everything worse.

Hate *that fiend.*

When Peanut's vine juddered without provocation, Puck
cursed. The chimera's massive weight had caused the center
of his harness to fray.

Gillian noticed and gasped with horror. "We have to help
him!"

"His vine is going to break. There's no stopping it." Gaze
on Puck, William said, "I'll take care of the chimera, you take
care of the girl."

No time to ponder the ramifications of the plan, or why his
nemesis would willingly part from Gillian. The rest of Peanut's
vine gave way, and the chimera dropped.

"Peanut!" Gillian reached for him, freefalling to chase after
her pet.

William followed the chimera, and Puck followed Gillian.

Heart thudding against his ribs, arms smashed to his sides,
he angled his body headfirst. The second he came upon Gillian, he grabbed her by the waist with one hand while clasping
onto a vine with his other. His claws dug into the stalk, slowing their momentum. Finally they stopped, Gillian in front,
Puck hanging on behind her.

William reached Peanut and wrapped his arms around the
animal's neck. The two vanished through the portal.

"Let me go!" Tears streamed down Gillian's cheeks as she
craned her neck to glare at Puck. Raindrops burned sores all
over her face. "Don't make me hurt you."

He glared right back, no longer caring about the raindrops splashing his skin. "Don't you dare act so foolishly again. William has Peanut. He'll ensure they both survive. You know this. Now haul ass." Merciless, he nudged her with his knee. "Up, up."

"My orders were to stick with William, no matter what. Sorry, guys, but you're on your own." After giving them a farewell salute, Pandora dropped, tumbling toward the portal.

"Ditto what she said." Galen shrugged, all *what are you gonna do?* "See ya, wouldn't wanna be ya." Then he, too, dropped.

"You're right, Puck." Gillian wiped away her tears with a trembling hand. Then she did what only a warrior could do and once again pushed her feelings aside. "William and Peanut are going to be okay," she said as she climbed.

Something he noticed: as long as she cried and wiped at her tears, her cheeks and hands remained free of burns.

Comprehension dawned. "Keep crying," he commanded. "Your tears neutralize the acid."

"You're right," she repeated, pausing to wipe away her newest tears—and smear a droplet over his burns. The generous action nearly undid him. "And it makes sense, in a terrible kind of way. Your brother probably believed you were the only one strong enough to make it this far, and since you are the keeper of Indifference, he would expect zero emotion."

"Save *your* skin, wife. Not mine."

Pause. "I'll do what I want." She wouldn't quite meet his gaze as she bathed another one of his wounds. "Suck it up and deal."

Very well. He sucked it up and remained on Gillian's heels as they climbed. She never slackened or lagged, even as one hour...two...ticked by. More rain. More sores.

He imagined his brother waited somewhere up top, and persevered. He wondered if he would be the one to fight Sin, now that William was gone, and hurried.

Had Puck been the one all along?

Only the male who will live or die for Gillian can defeat Sin the Demented.

I *will live or die for Gillian. I am* him. *I am that male.*

She was right. He loved her. The lass had brought his deadened heart back to life.

Just have to complete my two goals. Kill. Select.

"What are we going to do without William?" Gillian asked between panting breaths, her thoughts obviously similar to his.

"He has served his purpose. *I* love you. *I* will live or die for you. *I* will dethrone and kill Sin."

Her jaw dropped as she glanced at him over her shoulder. "Will you forgive yourself for killing him? And don't you dare die for me, Puck Connacht. I mean it."

"I want to keep you, Gillian. Do you think there is anything I *won't* do to ensure I can?"

"N-no. I think you'll do anything to keep me." The words held a twinge of sadness he thought he understood. The whole dream-killer thing.

How could he make her understand?

Their vine shook, as Peanut's had done, and Puck cursed. Just above them, the stalk had begun to fray.

Gillian went rigid. "Puck!"

Acting quickly, he swung them toward a second vine. "Grab it."

As she obeyed, transferring her weight to the other vine, he hoisted himself above the fraying piece. Just in time. The end of the vine dropped with a *whoosh*.

They continued climbing, climbing, finally breaching the clouds. Only then did the rain stop, but by then flesh hung from muscle and bone in large chunks. However, it was hard to lament about aches and pains, when he spotted salvation—a cliff—only a few hundred yards above.

Climbing, climbing. At long last, he and Gillian reached the top and collapsed on land.

40

EXHAUSTION SETTLED INTO GILLIAN'S BONES LIKE an old friend, all *I'm here to stay, what's on TV?*

What had happened to William and Peanut? Part of her longed to curl into a ball and sob, but she resisted. The two were alive. And she wasn't deluding herself about that. She knew William. His will to live pervaded every aspect of his life, and despite their differences, he would have found a way to save Peanut. He'd promised.

I'll get the chimera, you get the girl.

His love for her hadn't dwindled, even though he'd felt her adoration for another man during their (non) kiss. They would finish their talk when he returned. And he *would* return. So she would not mourn his loss. Ugh, wrong phrasing. She'd lost nothing. She would *celebrate*. Her friends lived—and so did Puck.

For now, she would concentrate her efforts on resting and re-covering, then saving Amaranthia. They had only ten days left.

She crawled to Puck, the sight of him making her stomach flip-flop. He looked like death.

Gillian uncorked the vial of *cuisle mo chroidhe* syrup, her most valued possession, and dumped the contents down his throat.

"You're going to get better," she assured him.

Giving the healing properties time to work, she studied their new terrain. A rushing, rocky river to the left. To the right, sand dunes peppered with tents. Had they reached the Connacht clan at last? Or at least an outpost?

Men wandered about, each one clad in a white tunic and sheepskin pants. By the prime cuts of strength she spotted, she'd guess they were warriors. Eighteen to be exact.

Someone spotted her and shouted, "Female!"

Other cries rang out.

"Stay back. She's mine."

"I'll fight to the death to claim her."

"Secure her, *then* fight over her."

"Thanks for the offer," she called, "but I'm taken."

An alarm sounded.

"But you don't care, obviously," she muttered, and sighed.

Puck staggered to his feet, braced for a fight. He'd healed some, but not fully. He wasn't in any condition to engage in combat, but she knew nothing would stop him.

The males grabbed weapons and stalked toward them, intent on cornering their prey. Every set of eyes leered at her, reminding her of her stephorrors—and sparking fury.

"Do you know these people?" she asked as she withdrew the only two weapons she hadn't lost in the maze. Mismatched daggers, one bejeweled, one made of solid gold.

Puck's claws and fangs extended, the tips of each a deadly point. "This is a criminal outpost. They covet what's mine, they die."

Almost upon them...

"Your jealousy is cute, and I'm super into it," she told him. "I just want to make sure you won't be mad if I murder, like, everyone here? They're Connachts, after all."

"I've seen you fight, know how good you are. Kill as many as you can and acquire their magic. Then, you'll prove just how super into my jealousy you really are."

Her chest puffed up with pride—in him. He trusted her skill, as she'd hoped, and wasn't going to insist she wait on the sidelines while the big bad boy took care of business. "You take the ones in front, and I'll work my way to the back, making sure no one leaves to warn other outposts."

"Done and done," he said.

"Happy fighting." Gillian pressed a swift kiss into his lips before launching into a mad dash to meet her would-be stable masters.

Puck ran with her, passed her. She noted he moved swiftly, but not as swiftly as usual.

Impact! She reached the fray, stabbed a brute in one eye then the other, while kicking another brute in the stomach. As he hunched over, gasping for breath, she turned the daggers on him.

In her periphery, she saw Puck ram someone with his glorious horns. A dirty move. Even dirtier when he tore the guy off the appendages—in pieces. Pieces he used as clubs on other criminals, until he decided to use his claws to render a few decapitations. Grunts and groans. Spurting blood.

When others attacked, he feinted. Attacked. Dodged. No one landed a blow. He was a hazard to everyone but Gillian.

Perhaps waiting on the sidelines and watching wasn't such a bad idea. *So sexy...*

No! Must do my part.

Moving on, Gillian stabbed a man in the gut. Removed another's trachea. Six others fell as she worked her way past the tents.

Magic rose from the bodies, absorbing into her runes. Almost there...

Running, never slowing, she bent to pick up a sword someone had dropped. A sword she used to hack an opponent in two before tossing the weapon a good distance ahead. Metal skidded over sand. As soon as she reached the sword, she jumped atop the blade, using it as a snowboard, propelled by magic.

Reaching her next target, she ducked between his legs and raked a dagger over his femoral artery. Putting her weight on her heels, she turned the sword so that her body blocked the last man in her sights.

With a backward hop, her boot slammed into the hilt, sending the weapon whirling in the air. The man swung a sword of his own. Gillian leaned back, the blade soaring over her. As she straightened, she caught *her* sword, twirled it, and slicked the blade through his neck.

Steal his sword. Go. His magic tracked her as she zigzagged through the tents, granting a fresh infusion of strength. She came out the other side—just in time to see two men galloping away on chimeras.

Though she hated to relinquish her blades, she tossed one, then the other, nailing one male in the nape, and the other between his shoulder blades.

The two fell from their rides as Gillian sprinted forward. She would finish off her targets, and spend the rest of the day—

A bolt of magic hit her from behind, buckling her knees. Air emptied from her lungs, and stars winked before her vision. When she landed, dirt filled her mouth.

Dang it! Rookie mistake. *Never let anticipation give you tunnel vision. Always check for a third man.*

Whoosh.

Another bolt of magic headed her way? *Shields up!* Her own magic surrounded her, stopping a second hit. Ignoring little aches and pains, she jumped up and faced off with a male who looked to be in his early twenties.

She geared up to attack, ready, but Puck appeared behind him. In a flash! He'd acquired enough magic to move from one location to another with only a thought. Lucky Pucky.

In a beautiful show of strength and hostility, he grabbed the man by the nape and forced him face-first into the ground. "You hurt her." Fury pulsed from him, a palpable current in the air. "You do not hurt her, ever."

The guy who'd once broken her finger looked murderous that someone else had given her an owie, and it was probably the cutest thing she'd ever seen. "Yeah," she said, and kicked the guy in the mouth, satisfied when several teeth popped out. "You don't hurt me, ever."

Puck looked ready to grin now. "You want to do the honors, wife?"

Toothless squirmed and gasped out, "Prince Neale? Is that you?"

Ignoring him, Gillian said, "You take his magic. I'll take theirs." She pointed to the two males she'd knocked from their chimeras, who were still in the process of crawling away.

"Deal." Puck finished him off without hesitation.

Just as eager, Gillian ended the others. Magic rose from both of her victims, filling her coffers. She'd gone from empty to overflowing in mere minutes.

Now, satisfaction carried her back to her husband's side. Blood smeared his skin, and bits of other people's flesh hung from his hair, but he'd never looked more beautiful to her.

"Your battle skill amazes me," he said.

She fluffed her hair, trying to act cool. A little difficult to do when you were peering at someone with absolute adoration. "What's with your speed? Why didn't you kick things into high gear?"

A hike of one shoulder. "Can't."

Whoa. "What do you mean, you can't?"

"Don't have the ability anymore."

"I don't under—" She gasped, puzzle pieces clicking. "You gave it up. You were low on magic when the rest of us thought we'd turned into beasts, empty even, and yet you freed us with magic."

Another shrug.

He'd given up so much! Too much. And now she wanted to give back.

"Hey," she said. "I have an idea. What if we spend the day—"

At the same time, he said, "We are going to stay here and—"

In unison, they both stopped and laughed. And oh, Puck's laugh! Rusty, but musical and magical—magnificent. A sound she wanted to hear every day for the rest of her life.

"Did you notice I asked and you ordered?" she said.

"I did." Puck hefted her over his shoulder fireman-style. "That's how I know my way is better."

She had to swallow another laugh. "This is getting to be a habit." She tried for a stern tone, failed. So, why not admit the truth? In a stage whisper, she added, "But I like it."

He caressed her bottom. "We are on a clock, I know, but we're not going to defeat Sin if we're weak. We need to rest today, so we are stronger tomorrow. And since we're out of the maze, standing on Connacht land, I doubt we have any more challenges to face. I feel no charge in the air, as I did in the maze."

"I agree. But I get the feeling we're not going to be resting..."

"With good reason. We won't win if we're distracted by all this pent-up sexual desire you have for me." He swatted her bottom now, adding, "I used magic to check the tents. There are no other occupants. We're alone, and no one will be showing up unannounced. I've used my new magic to create a shield around the camp."

The wickedness in his voice sent full-body shivers coursing through her. "What are you planning to do with me and all my pent-up desire, then?"

He remained silent until they reached the edge of the river. "It's not what I'm planning. It's what I'm going to do."

More shivers. "And what are you going to do?" she asked, breathless.

"Enjoy what's mine."

★ ★ ★

Puck tossed Gillian into the water. As she came up sputtering, he stripped out of his blood-soaked clothing. She watched him, her pupils expanding.

Naked, he stood in place, his arms at his side, his legs braced apart, allowing her to look her fill. He was hard, his erection at full attention, ready for her.

She licked her lips.

My woman wants me.

Indifference hadn't shut up, but Puck hardly cared. He was too passion-drunk to be bothered. Too…happy.

Me? Happy?

Almost drunk with desire, he entered the water. Cold liquid lapped at him but failed to cool the fervor in his veins. Actually, he was pretty sure he'd turned the pond into a hot spring.

Gillian trod water, waiting as he dunked a few times to clean the blood from his hair. The closer he came to her, the more anticipation churned in his gut. Only a whisper away, he planted his feet and straightened, the waterline reaching the middle of his torso.

Gaze hot on him, Gillian raised her arms to offer herself like a war prize. He removed her top, tossed it to shore, triumph consuming him. Such beautiful breasts. A heavenly bounty, pert and plump, tipped with berry-pink buds he would soon be sucking.

"I want you," he rasped. "All of you." Always.

"We'll trade. All of me for all of you."

"Accepted."

He let his mouth crash down on hers. She moaned and opened for him, entrancing him with her sweetness.

Her hands moved up his chest, her nails scraping lightly. When she stepped closer, she pressed her body flush against his, heated skin against heated skin. She rubbed her core against his erection once, twice, using him for her pleasure, and he wouldn't have it any other way.

GENA SHOWALTER

He cupped her ass, helping guide her into a faster rhythm, increasing pressure. Little cries of desperation left her, making him pant.

Then he spun her around, placing her back at his chest. Motions deft, he removed her skirt and panties, cupped her breasts, squeezed, then slid his hands down her stomach and thrust a finger into her hot feminine sheath. Her inner walls gripped him, burning him so perfectly.

With another moan, she rested the back of her head against his shoulder. The urge to slam inside her and come now, now, now made his testicles heavier, but he resisted. He would last, and he would make this good for her. Better than ever before. He would brand his essence inside her.

Puck walked forward and lifted her onto a rock. "Hands and knees," he said, and she eagerly obeyed, placing her core at eye level.

"Let me see my beautiful wife." He pushed her knees farther apart, revealing the most mouthwatering sight in all the realms.

She was wet, swollen with need and the prettiest pink.

"Going to feast on you." He traced a finger along her silken heat, dragging a groan from them both.

"Like this?" she asked, clearly scandalized—and intrigued. "At this angle?"

"This angle," he agreed. *Liiick.* The taste of this woman!

She cried out, and undulated her hips. High on her essence, he reached out to knead her breasts, pluck and play with her nipples. Only when she begged did he thrust two fingers inside her, offering a modicum of relief.

His wife, always a powder keg ready to blow, came on those fingers, her screams of bliss an erotic song.

He was a powder keg ready to blow. The climax made her even sweeter.

More... To wring a second from her, he used his tongue as he used his shaft, thrusting into her. He massaged his thumb over her clitoris again and again, increasing pressure. Little whimpers filled the air.

More! He crawled up the rock and loomed behind her, on his knees. Though every fiber of his being demanded he sink inside her, he merely teased her wetness with the tip of his erection.

"How badly do you want me?" he said between kisses he placed along her spine.

She met his gaze over her shoulder, her red, red lips swollen from his kisses. A slow grin bloomed, sending his heart into a wild gallop.

Was any woman more perfect than this one?

"I want you—" she stretched her arm between her legs to stroke his length from base to tip "—*this* bad."

Too good! *Careful, careful. Must not blow.*

"Then you've never wanted anything more," he said, and drove his shaft all the way home.

41

SUBLIME PLEASURE RIPPLED THROUGH GILLIAN. PUCK filled her up, stretched and consumed her. She'd already come twice, but like the addict she was—the addict this amazing man had made her—she only wanted more.

He was as hot as fire, as hard as stone, and he branded her inside and out. Male and female. Husband and wife.

As he thrust and thrust, harder and faster, his motions became rougher. She could feel his desperation and hunger.

"Kiss," she said.

"My wife wants to be kissed?" He pulled out long enough to flip her to her back. But he didn't kiss her. He thrust back inside her, twined his fingers with hers and raised her arms over her head. The new position forced her back to arch, lifting her breasts for his attention.

He stared down at her, and she stared up at him, watching as the pinpricks of light in his irises *moved*, like falling stars streaking across a midnight sky. Beautiful man. *Brilliant* man.

"There are different kinds of kisses," he said, and began to move again. The tempo of their mating changed. "Is this the kind you want?" Moving in and out of her so slowly, torturously, deliciously, he leaned down to flick his tongue over one of her nipples.

"Yes, yes, that kind. All kinds." Electric currents rushed straight to her core, and she rocked her hips, taking him deeper, harder. This was what sex was meant to be, a communion between two consenting adults. A perfect give and take. Balm for a wounded heart. Pleasure without guilt or disgust. Even...fun.

The bond alone couldn't be responsible for this...this...miracle.

"You've possessed me," she rasped.

"*A chuisle*, I am the one possessed...by you." With his next plunge, he rocked her entire body.

Pulse again. He might as well have cast a spell over her.

"Kiss. This kind now," she said, clasping the sides of his face to bring his lips to her mouth.

His tongue dominated hers as he fed her a passion as wild as the beat of her heart. Still plunging. Harder. Again. And again. Harder and harder. Faster. Her sensitized nipples created irresistible friction with Puck's chest, desire spearing her anew.

More pleasure. A bomb set to detonate. She tangled her fingers in his hair, dug her nails into his scalp. Her nerve endings hummed and vibrated, fire blazing inside her bones. The flames grew and flickered over every inch of her.

The rest of the world had long since vanished from her awareness.

She arched her hips to meet his next thrust, sending him even deeper. Yes, yes, *yes*. A breathless cry, needy and plaintive— had the sound really left *her*? "Puck!" She arched her hips again, gasped. Yes, yes! "More of *that*."

"You feel so good, wife. Nothing better." Slam, slam. *Slam*. Three...two...one. Detonation!

Her mind shut down, bliss ripping through her, another plaintive cry leaving her. This was more powerful than any other climax, strong enough to shatter her piece by piece, but sweet enough to put her back together again.

"Can't last...going to... Lass!" Puck shouted. He thrust once more, deep, so wonderfully deep, his entire body shuddering against hers as his orgasm overtook him.

As soon as he collapsed on top of her, he shifted his weight. His arms remained wrapped around her in a hold that said *my wife goes nowhere without me.*

Content but still breathless, Gillian cuddled against him. When her thoughts cleared, she said, "Have you ever been in love? Romantic love, I mean. With a woman besides me."

"No. I never allowed myself to get to know one."

Besides William, and then Puck, she'd never taken the time to get to know a guy, either. Puck wasn't perfect, but he was perfect *for her.* And he would make an amazing king. In the maze, she'd gotten a front row seat to his strength, ingenuity, determination, honor and resilience. Amaranthia needed him. The *clans* needed him.

I *need him.*

"You said the Oracles have never been wrong," she said.

Rubbing the bird tattooed on his chest, he said, "That is correct."

"What if we can do the impossible and prove them wrong— about everything? What if I can help you achieve your dream, without killing it? What if I can have a happy ending with you?"

"I want this," he said, his tone fierce. "I will have this."

On the other end of the spectrum... "What if I *can't* prove the Oracles wrong?" Fears deluged her, a scourge she couldn't beat back. "What if I destroy your dream? What if I can't have a happy ending with you?"

Prepare for the worst, hope for the best.

"In this, we cannot live by 'what if.' And I did warn you. I won't let you go unless I must do so to save your life. Haven't changed my mind. Won't. Know that I will do *everything* in my power to ensure you remain mine. I *will* kill my brother, and I *will* fight for your happy ending."

Such ferocity...she shivered. "Do you want children? One day, I mean."

His pupils flared over his irises. "I do. And you?"

"Yes." Little boys with midnight-sky eyes. Little girls with long black lashes.

Silent, thoughtful, Puck peered up at the sky for a moment. "Come," he said, and swooped her up against his chest before standing. As he waded across the river, cool water caressed her overheated skin.

Once they reached the other side, he continued holding her, and carried her to the camp.

"Time for our rest," he said.

"We should find clean clothes and weapons first," she said, and yawned.

He shouldered his way into the biggest tent and gently placed her on her feet. With a grin, he gave her butt another playful smack. "You're part of my stable now, woman. You'll do what you're told if you expect mercy from your master."

That grin...he looked so young and boyish, so silly, beautiful beyond imagining. His eyes glowed like runes; the stars had completely taken over.

This was the man he was born to be. The sweetheart his father had tried to beat out of him. The party-on-legs his brother had nearly destroyed.

This was Puck Connacht, Gillian's husband.

Then his words computed, and she sputtered. Part of his stable? "Ha! In this relationship, I'm the master, and you are a stallion in *my* stable. You've already got the legs for it, big boy."

He gave a mock growl. "You like my legs."

"Do I?" She studied her cuticles.

"The day I returned to Amaranthia, you Hulked-out. I carried you to bed, and for the longest time, you refused to let me leave it. You clung to me, rubbing against my legs at every opportunity."

Had she? Well, why not? She was a smart girl. "FYI, if you

try to form a stable, I'll cut off your precious and make you eat it. Mean that from the bottom of my heart, baby."

Her words must have pleased him. His shoulders squared, and his spine went ramrod straight with pride. "You can't get enough of my precious. Perhaps I should take my desires elsewhere, however. I remember a time when you told me I had permission to—"

"Consider your free pass revoked. You are mine," she told him, adamant. "Only mine."

Again, he grinned down at her, causing her heart to skip a beat. "My wife is so possessive."

"Your wife is dangerous when crossed." She scanned the tent. Well, well. The former owner had collected weapons, everything from axes to swords to bows. A mound of furs provided a soft, warm bed and a pot of stew simmered above a fire. Smoke curled to an opening in the tent's roof.

Every need met.

"You want the truth? No other fillies compare to you." He smoothed tendrils of hair from her cheeks before tracing his thumb over her lips. "Why would I ever attempt to ride another?"

She stepped closer to him, so close her breasts flattened against his chest. They were skin to skin, male to female. Desire to sizzling desire.

Shivers slipped down her spine as she gripped the base of his shaft. He was hard again. Just the way she liked him. "I'm going to make you so glad you said that."

42

WITHOUT A DOUBT, THIS IS HAPPINESS.

Yesterday, Puck had done all of his new favorite things. He'd skinny-dipped with Gillian. He'd made love with her on the rocks, and come so hard his brains had rattled against his skull. Later he'd made love to her in the tent. He'd fed her by hand and enjoyed being fed *by* her before going to sleep with her body cradled close to his.

Gillian before war.

Gillian before everything.

This morning, he'd left before she'd woken, writing her a note in the sand.

STAY PUT. PLEASE. I'LL BE BACK.

Then he'd gone hunting. Hours had passed before he'd found what he needed. More hours had passed as he'd worked to acquire what he wanted. Upon his return, he'd expected protests from Gillian. Or a demand for answers, at the very least. Instead, she'd brightened and run into his arms. Her splendid laughter had filled the camp, and his soul, as he'd swung her around.

"I won't destroy your dream. I won't," she'd said, as if she'd worried about nothing else all day. Though he'd soon come to learn his wee wife had spent her time gathering every weapon in camp and studying a map of Connacht land. "One Connacht murder and crown, coming up. We're forging ahead, all systems go. Right?"

"Right," he'd said, and relief had wafted from her.

Without William here, Puck had no worries. He *would* defeat Sin, *would* save Amaranthia and *would* have everything he wanted.

He'd planned to abandon the camp today, but his time in the forest had cost too much daylight. They had to stay one more night. Such a travesty.

Now, moonlight streamed through a crack in the tent flap, bathing Gillian with a soft amber glow. She was splayed naked atop a mound of furs, purring as Puck traced a slice of *spéir* around her nipple. The little bud puckered when he licked away the droplets of red juice.

Her breathy moan delighted his ears. Who was he kidding? Every part of this woman delighted every part of him. Indifference was nothing more than a buzz in the back of his mind.

Puck switched direction, tracing the fruit over Gillian's lips. As she opened, ready to bite, he popped the slice into his mouth.

"Brute." She laughed, so sensual, so erotic. "That was mine."

"No, this is." He reached under the pillow beside her and withdrew a large jar of *cuisle mo chroidhe* syrup he'd managed to harvest.

With a squeal of joy, she jolted upright and clutched the jar between her breasts. "This is why you were gone so long?"

He nodded.

"Oh, Puck." She leaned over to nip at his lips. "Thank you. I mean, I haven't had any more Hulk-outs since, you know, the last one and everything, and right now I'm almost positive I'll never have one again, because I'm just so happy, but thank you!"

I did this. I made her happy. "For you, I'll do anything, at any time, anywhere."

"Then you'll stay right where I put you, right now, and let me have my wicked way with you." After pushing him to his back, she opened the jar and dribbled syrup over his chest... and lower.

Then she used him as an all-you-can-eat buffet.

When she collapsed on his chest, he marveled at the feel of her body draped over his like a blanket. For a long while, they lay together, hearts calming as they breathed each other's air. This was heaven, a satisfaction he'd once only dreamed of achieving.

"I was going to ask if you liked what I did," she said, "but my ears are still ringing."

"You amaze me." He lifted his head to rub the tip of his nose against hers, a playful gesture from the boy he used to be.

"You sate me."

"Good. Remember that. Because I think I'm about to anger you." His grip on her tightened, lest she try to run. "I figure part of you wants to stay here as long as possible in case William and Peanut show up. Is this correct?"

She nibbled her lip, nodded.

"We must move on tomorrow, whether they've arrived or not. You know this, aye?"

She surprised him by nodding again. "I do, and I agree. For all we know, they're outside the realm, unable to return. But that's okay. You've got me, and I won't rest until you're king. So what will be your first act?"

Easy. "Women will be granted the same rights as men. Equal citizenship. I will erect more shelters and orphanages. Will enforce steep punishments for those who harm others."

She smiled and petted his chest, clearly pleased with his answer, and so beautiful he was instantly snared, unable to look away. He'd already memorized the stunning purity of her irises, light brown ringed by darker brown. The beauty of her cheekbones. The delicacy of her nose. How her lips were ruby red and tantalizingly plump.

But a horrifying thought arose, one he couldn't shake. If he truly loved this woman, could he keep her bound to him when her feelings for him might not be true without the bond? When, if unbonded, she might want another man?

Puck…cared about this. He cared deeply. So deeply the plans he'd made began to go up in flames, one by one. His certainty, gone.

He *would* do anything for this girl, he realized. Even let her go.

There was only one way to learn the truth. And they *had* to learn the truth. Otherwise Puck could cheat her of the life she wanted and deserved. "I think… I think I should sever our bond, as planned. No matter what."

"What? No." She sputtered for a moment. "We decided. Without William, you get the crown and the girl. We stay together and ensure I get my happy ending."

"I hope so." Once, he'd lied to her to get what he wanted. Never again. He trusted and respected her, and would always do right by her. "I hope you still want me afterward."

She jolted upright, her cheeks pale, waxen. "You believe the Oracles. You think I'll destroy your dreams."

"You've already destroyed my dream, lass." Truth was truth.

She flinched, as if he'd struck her.

Puck reached for her, but she scrambled to her feet to dress in the clothes they'd found last night. A small white tunic, sheepskin pants and a pair of combat boots.

Covering her nakedness should be a crime.

He hurried in front of her and gripped her forearms to hold her in place. When she tried to break free, he gave her a gentle shake. "Let me finish."

"Why? Is there another part of my heart you'd like to trample?"

Ignore her words or crumble, my only choices. "My dream of ruling Amaranthia has been replaced by a dream of making you happy, always. I do not mourn the change."

Her features softened but her gaze pleaded. "The thought of ruling the entire realm at your side makes me happy."

"I would love nothing more than to spend the rest of eternity with you at my side. We'd have babies, make a family and govern the clans together. When I sever the bond, all you must do...is want me." Their future was that simple, and that complicated.

"I want you now," she said, lifting her chin.

His heart broke, but he refused to change his mind. "I will set you free. I will not bend on this."

"Well, excuse me if I don't believe you. Only minutes ago you said you'd keep me no matter what!" Rather than slap him, like he expected, she clung to him. "You're being foolish, listening to fear rather than your wife. I'm telling you, I know I want you, and the bond is not responsible."

"Gillian—"

"Are you the Ice Man right now?" she demanded. "Is that how you are able to say and do this?"

"I am not the Ice Man," he said. "I'll never be that man with you again. I *can't*. I feel too much. I feel *everything*."

She flinched a second time but said, "If you let me go—" For a moment, she looked as if she was going to hurl the contents of her stomach. "If you let me go, I won't get my happy ending. *That* is the reason it was prophesized. I *feel* it."

No. No! This was the only way to ensure she *got* her happy ending. "How can you know what you want? The bond speaks for you."

"I speak for myself." Ashen, she pressed her hands against her chest. "Does the bond speak for *you*?"

Did it? How could he know? As soon as he lost his connection to Gillian, Indifference would have power over him again. Only for a bit, sure. Puck would use the shears. If he could. Could he use the artifact more than once?

So many unanswered questions.

"If you want me afterward," he said, doing his best to sound reasonable, as if his mind wasn't a war zone, "we will bond again."

She stumbled backward as though he'd pushed her. How could she not understand? He did this *for* her. "You hesitated," she said. "You don't think you'll want me."

His hands fisted at his sides, mighty weapons rendered useless in the greatest battle of his life. "I can't imagine *not* wanting you, lass."

Tears spilled over her cheeks, and she wheezed for breath. Those tears—little droplets of water—affected him like a dagger through the heart; they were *killing* him.

She used the back of her wrist to wipe the moisture away. Narrowed her eyes. Lifted her chin. Squared her shoulders. A transition he'd witnessed many times before.

Gillian had just gone full-blown warrior.

"I understand now," she said, her tone almost deadened.

Bit by bit, the emotion on her face simply vanished, until she peered up at him with cold, hard eyes devoid of affection, adoration and tenderness. All the things he'd grown to love and crave. Things he couldn't imagine living without ever again.

He hadn't been dying before, he realized. No. Oh, no. He was dying *now*, watching this. Watching Gillian use magic to summon ice. This slayed him. Her tears had been difficult to witness, even more difficult to witness than the ones she'd shed after sex, because she hadn't been broken, then. She'd been free.

She was broken now. *Because of me.*

Too much!

"I truly don't get a happy ending," she said in that horrid, deadened tone. "You'll break our bond. Our precious, holy bond that gifts us both the family we've always wanted. I'll yearn for you still, but you'll no longer yearn for me. Or maybe we'll yearn for each other, but won't be able to do anything about it. Maybe the shears will prevent us from ever bonding again." She laughed without humor. "Perhaps I'm an Oracle. I can see the demise of our relationship so clearly. But I don't care. Not anymore."

"No one has ever broken a bond and survived, but we will beat the odds." He rubbed the bird tattooed on his chest before he tugged on a pair of pants, a pair of boots. "If we cannot bond again, but still yearn for each other, we can marry as humans do."

"Won't be the same. Our bond allows you to control the demon and feel without consequence. Our bond makes me immortal. What will happen when he overtakes you again, huh? What will happen when I'm mortal—if I even survive the transition?"

"You will live, will remain immortal. You took the potion, and you made the transition. That won't ever change. You are strong enough now."

"But I won't matter to you," she said, and turned away.

"You will matter to me, always," he hissed. "What you won't do is turn me into a villain over this. I'm willing to give up what I want most, so that you can have what you *need* most. Because you deserve free choice. I won't be like your stepfather. I won't take what you don't wish to give. If your heart belongs to William, you deserve to know it."

If the male touches her, I will—

Nothing. Because nothing mattered more than her freedom of choice. He forced his mind to blank—as blank as Gillian's features.

"I told you I loved you and I meant it," she said. "I loved you. Then. Now?" She shrugged.

His heart sped into a gallop, and sweat beaded over his brow. He felt as if he'd run hundreds of miles in an instant, adrenaline flooding his veins. "The ice will melt. I'll make sure of it. You'll love me again."

"You fear," she continued as if he hadn't spoken. "You fear

I'll betray you the way Sin betrayed you. That is the only reason you plan to do this."

Perhaps it was a reason, but not *the* reason. "What if you only *think* you love me?" he croaked.

"In this, we can't live by *what if*."

Words he'd spoken, now used against him. Still, he hardened his resolve. For her. "In this, I can't live any other way."

A moment passed in silence before she lifted her chin another notch, as if she'd just made a world-altering decision. "You convinced yourself that you're doing the right thing, but all you've done is tear me apart." She loaded up with different weapons and a canteen of water. "There's no power great enough to make me desire someone I don't actually want. If I thought there was the slightest chance I belonged with William, I would have resisted you. But you...some part of you suspected I wanted someone else, but you took me anyway. So congratulations. You don't have to wait to sever the bond to find out if we can be together. I'm done with you. *We're* done."

"We are *never* done," he roared, ruining everything he'd previously said. He took her by the shoulders, spun her and yanked her against his body. Then he kissed her. Kissed her until she softened against him and kissed him back.

Relief flooded him. Her ice was melting.

"Show me you love me," she croaked. "Show me now."

And he did.

"Time to go," Puck said.

Gillian strapped on her weapons and marched behind her husband, glaring daggers into his back as they abandoned the camp and trekked through the sand dunes.

After they'd made love, after he'd told her they would never be done, after he'd shown her just how much he loved her by worshipping her body with his hands and mouth, he'd acted as if nothing had happened and dressed.

She would have liked to return to her cold, emotionless state, detached from the pain still festering inside her, but she didn't. If she was going to make him understand her side of this, she needed every emotion in her arsenal.

Two suns glowered overhead, and only heated with each new mile they traipsed. When the sand dunes gave way to a forest-like oasis, Puck glanced back at her for the thousandth time, silently beseeching her to understand *his* point of view.

She gave him the finger.

Although, she couldn't help but remember how—when he'd first brought her to Amaranthia—he'd walked away without looking back once. Today? He couldn't stop casting her longing gazes.

The realization shouldn't soften her, but dang it! She was easy as pie where Puck was concerned.

He didn't trust his feelings for her, or her feelings for him. And okay, okay. She hadn't trusted their feelings for each other, either, but only for a little while. Or off and on sporadically. Whatever! Then she'd gotten over it and decided to fight for him. To fight for *them*. And yes, okay, earlier she'd let fear about the prophecies scare her again. Or more. But he wanted to cut her loose, just in case some secret part of her wanted William.

Unacceptable!

And yes, it seemed honorable on the surface. But truth was, he didn't trust her, and a bond without trust wasn't a bond at all.

Or maybe she didn't trust him, and believed he wouldn't want *her* without the bond? Maybe she feared he would revert to his old ways, become the Ice Man again, and decide to wed Princess Alannah of Daingean and open a stable.

No, no. This was his crime. His! He might destroy their family. The risk was too great, with no real reward. Why couldn't he see that?

I want my happily-ever-after! But even now, she sensed the end of all she held dear.

A distant moan of pain drew her out of the chaos in her

head. She frowned when she realized they'd left the forest and entered another stretch of sand. "What was that noise?"

"Came from there," Puck said, pointing. "Up ahead."

She scanned the dunes...and found a woman in tattered clothing, slouched on a dune, wind blowing the scarf she wore, causing the material to wave like a flag. Skin the color of the sands, hair the color of the sky and eyes like emeralds.

As she detected a telltale essence, recognition dawned in her heart, then her mind. "One of the Oracles!"

The woman held out her arm, but she wasn't strong enough to keep it in the air. How long had she been without food or water? Her cheeks were hollow, her eyes sunken. She was dirty and probably cold.

"Help. Please..."

"What are you waiting for?" She gave Puck a little push forward. "Let's help her."

He planted his heels, keeping her in place. "What is she doing in Connacht territory?"

Oh...crap. "You think she's a trap?" *Help, please*— Everyone in Amaranthia knew a woman's plea was basically Gillian's bat signal.

"Possibly."

She scanned the dunes again, searching for any hint of foul play this time. No creeping shadows. No odd scents in the air. No glint of metal peeking from the sand. No disturbances in the sand whatsoever. No hum of magic.

"Help," the girl called again.

"We can't stand here, doing nothing." Gillian remembered her first few years in the realm. She'd been lonely, hurting and desperate. Could she truly turn her back on a woman in the same condition?

"Stay here," Puck said. "I'll approach her."

Stand idle, watching, as he put himself in danger? No. "What happened to being impressed with my skill? *You* stay here. *I'll* test the waters."

Weapons at the ready, Gillian rushed around him. Half-way there, however, she slowed to better gauge her surroundings. Too late. Between one step and the next, a glittery patch of air—a doorway, or portal—opened up. Inside her, magic pinged, as if it had just brushed up against an electric current.

She stopped, spun. She hadn't changed locations, or entered another realm. The sand dunes still encircled her, the Oracle a few feet away.

"Stay where you are, Puck." Just in case. "There's some sort of magic shield around me. Maybe. I'm not sure what it is, exactly."

No response. She glanced over his shoulder and found him standing in the same spot. He hadn't moved an inch, and yet strain contorted his expression, a vein bulging in the center of his forehead. He acted as if he wanted to move, and fought with every muscle in his body to do so, but couldn't. His mouth was the only thing in motion, opening and closing. She thought she read her name on his lips, but no sound reached her ears.

She frowned as her stomach churned with unease. This *had* been a trap. Set by the Oracle? But why?

Perhaps Sin had learned of Puck's return and had used the unwitting Oracle to snag him?

But when was an Oracle ever unwitting?

Gillian backtracked, only to bump up against an invisible wall. Yep. She'd been enclosed by a magical shield. Trapped. But better her than Puck. Although, if he continued to strain, he might break every bone in his body.

She banged on the invisible wall, ripples sweeping over the air, hazing her view of him.

"Don't worry about me. Take care of yourself," she called.

Maybe the Oracle could help? Even if Gillian had to use force. Very well. With a dagger in one hand and a canteen of water in the other, she crouched beside the Oracle, ready for anything. She hoped.

"Here. Drink."

The Oracle reached for the canteen, her hand shaking so badly it affected her aim. Their fingers brushed, and the other woman inhaled sharply, horror filling her eyes.

"Do not trust your husband. You cannot trust him."

What had she seen? Determination mounting, Gillian grated, "I will always trust Puck. And you're going to help me get back to him. So drink up, and strengthen." To assist the Oracle, she tilted the canteen to her lips.

The weaker woman drank greedily, water dribbling down her chin. When she finished, she cried, "Thank you." Tears left streaks on her dirt-smeared cheeks. "Thank you."

"Look, I know this is a trap," Gillian said. "What I don't know is whether you're knowingly involved. Yes or no, you're going to help me get past the shield."

"I didn't know... I'm so sorry... Should have seen... He used me, plans to—" Her eyelids closed, her head slumping forward, as if a switch had just been flipped inside her mind. Her body followed, tipping over.

Gillian lightly tapped her cheek. Nothing. No response. The Oracle slept—because of magic?

Frustration and anger pricked the back of her neck, and she rose, palming a second dagger. Puck—

Was gone, she realized, no longer standing by the tree.

Panic beckoned. Where had he gone? What had happened to him?

A split second later, he reappeared, *past* the invisible wall. He must have flashed, using his newest surge of magic. Relief and dread went head-to-head, both overshadowing the frustration and anger. "I told you to stay back. We're trapped by magic, unable to leave the immediate area."

"No worries, lass. We'll find a way. We always do."

His easy tone held hints of relish, and it jarred her. Especially when it was followed by another gust of wind that carried the scent of wildflowers and maple. Her brow furrowed with confusion. What had happened to the heady mix of peat smoke and lavender, her favorite fragrance ever?

One made her blood burn with passion while the other left a chill of dismay in her veins.

"Puck," she said, taking a step toward him. Then she stopped, her heart pounding against her ribs. Her head tilted to the side as she studied her husband more closely.

He wasn't looking at her with hope, lust, adoration, anger, or even total emotionlessness. He looked at her with hate and suspicion, despite the slight smile curving the corners of his sensual mouth. In each hand, he clutched the hilt of a short sword. His knuckles were white, completely leached of color; he appeared to be posed on the brink of attack.

Do not trust your husband.

Puck would never hurt her. She knew it soul-deep. But this man...

"Come to me, wife," he said.

"Of course." The only conclusion she could draw: this wasn't powerful Puck, her beloved.

This was Sin, the shapeshifter.

43

PUCK COULDN'T MOVE. THE MOMENT GILLIAN
had raced ahead of him, a bolt of magic had disintegrated his
weapons and cemented his feet in place. Powerful magic…
chaotic, evil. Demonic?

No. Couldn't be. At the moment, Puck was the only demon-
possessed male in town. But the crux of the matter? Sin had
come for him.

Why his brother hadn't attacked him outright, he didn't
know. Didn't care. Only one thing concerned him right now:
saving Gillian.

Sin appeared at the glittering shield that separated Puck
from his wife. He cast Puck a look of abject longing—one
Puck mirrored?

First view in centuries. Should have expected a punch of affection. A reaction ingrained in him since his younger brother's
birth.

The years had certainly changed Sin, and not exactly for the
better. He looked older, harder. His dark hair had turned white,
despite his immorality. His muscle mass rivaled Puck's, but he
carried it awkwardly, as if he'd never gotten use to the bulk.

A circle of gold glowed just over his head. Mortals would

call it a halo, but it was actually a king's crown. Taken only through death, or a king's willing relinquishment.

A confusing mix of love and hate crashed through Puck. A terrible awareness of betrayal followed. Longing for what could have been. More adoration. An urge to kill, violently, savagely, ruthlessly—blood would flow in rivers. Regret strong enough to send him to his knees. *If* he could move.

In Sin's eyes, he saw the same emotions reflected back at him.

How could he kill the man who had once been an extension of himself?

How could he not? Sin was an obstacle between husband and wife. Obstacles between Puck and Gillian got crushed.

As he watched, Sin shapeshifted into a monstrous form with horns, claws and hooves. *Puck's* monstrous form, with no hint of the halo.

"Do not hurt her." Puck strained for freedom with every fiber of his being.

"I will do what I must," Sin replied, and he sounded sad.

"Gillian! Gillian, run!" If she saw or heard him, she gave no notice, continuing to minister to the Oracle. "Sin, please. I beg of you." What was pride without Gillian? "If you bear me any love, you will not harm her."

Sin closed his eyes, let his head drop, and Puck thought maybe he'd reached the little boy he'd once loved. Then the male he'd become faced Puck, determined and crazed, and turned away. He approached Gillian.

She had no idea an enemy drew near, would have no defenses against him. Puck fought harder, frantic.

"Come to me, wife," Sin said to Gillian, and motioned her over.

"Of course."

"Give your husband a kiss."

She smiled with all kinds of sweetness—though none of the affection Puck had come to know ever reached her eyes. He paused, certain he was reading her wrong.

"I'd love to kiss my husband," she said, her tone as sweet as her expression. She closed the distance, her steps clipped.

"No. Gillian!" *Fight, fight!* Puck was willing to break bones, tear muscles and lose limbs to reach her. Anything!

"Put the weapons away," Sin-Puck said. "They aren't necessary."

A curse left Puck as Gillian obeyed.

She reached her "husband" and dragged her hands from the waist of his pants up his stomach, chest, and let her fingers linger over the bird tattooed on his heart. But Sin's tattoo was a mirage while Puck's had unimaginable power...

Metal glinted against Gillian's forearm as she slowly rose on her tiptoes. Puck dared to hope. She hadn't sheathed her weapons, after all?

Sin slowly lifted his arms, as if to embrace her. At the last second, he angled his wrists, preparing to strike.

"No! Gillian!" Panic choked him, but Puck kept fighting.

Indifference cranked up the volume, screaming inside his head. The butterfly tattoo slithered all over his body, sizzling against his skin.

Just before Gillian's lips met Sin's, *she* struck, angling *her* wrist to reveal the dagger. A dagger she shoved into Sin's neck without hesitation. Blood gushed, a crimson river. His brother howled with shock and pain as he stumbled backward.

"I know who you are," Gillian said, her tone hard and sharp. Kick, kick. She easily disarmed him. "What have you done with my Puck?"

She had realized the truth. But...how was that possible? Not even their parents had known when Puck and Sin had shape-shifted to switch places.

Whatever the reason, pride struck Puck. *My woman knows me.*

Sin's wound must have weakened his magic. Suddenly Puck could move his arm. Muscles strained and bones threatened to break, but he managed to work his hand to his chest and press two fingers against the rounded claws of his bird tattoo.

Long ago, he'd used magic to hide the shears of Ananke inside his flesh. Today he would use the shears to break Sin's hold and aid Gillian.

Except, he hesitated. What if the shears could only be used once? He'd wondered before, but feared now. He wouldn't be able to divorce Gillian—bonus—but he also wouldn't be able to part with Indifference. And if they could only be used twice? He could divorce Gillian, as planned—because yes, he would always give her what she needed, and she needed her freedom long enough to learn the true emotions in her heart—and Puck would be stuck with Indifference, *without* a filter.

His gaze on his wife, he decided, *I'm willing to chance it.*

By unleashing a tendril of magic and lifting his hand, he extracted the shears. The moment the artifact encountered air, it solidified. He opened and closed the shears. Once. Twice. How was he supposed to—

The magic that held him in place ripped apart, as if cut. Just. Like. That.

Satisfaction had no time to sprout. Rage overtook him. *Attack!*

Sprinting forward, boots flinging sand, Puck returned the shears to his chest. They melted into his skin, searing him, annnd he breached Sin's wall of magic, as easily as he'd done in the past.

Puck had a split second to take stock. Sin had already begun to heal. Gillian stood a few feet away, gearing for another clash.

Unleashing a battle cry, Puck tackled his brother. They skidded across the sand in a tangle of limbs, even mowing over the Oracle. She never roused.

They bit at each other. Punched, kicked and stabbed. Two predators, with one purpose: victory at all cost.

Adrenaline added kindling to Puck's rage, the emotion so hot no amount of ice would ever cool it; Indifference would never be able to hide it. With expert maneuvering, he pinned his brother beneath him, knees to shoulders.

"You do not hurt Gillian." This time, he was the only one to attack. Punch, punch, punched. Bits of flesh and muscle tore with each impact. "You do not *look* at Gillian."

"I will do that and more." Blood wet Sin's teeth as he grinned. "She's your greatest weakness." His brother shuffled his legs between them, planted his feet against Puck's chest and kicked with enough vigor to break his sternum.

Breathing hurt, but it didn't slow him down. He launched at his brother a second time. He didn't just punch; he clawed. He didn't just bite; he ripped and tore. He didn't just kick; he punted specific organs.

Sin…let him?

"How could you do this to me?" Between each tide of rage, he caught a glimpse of hurt. "I loved you, only wanted to protect you."

"Yes, but for how long? One day, you would have betrayed me." Sin hit him with a blast of magic, flinging him backward. "You're only upset I struck first."

Sin speed-raced, grabbing a sword and moving beside him. Their gazes met—and he paused. He might wear Puck's face, but he couldn't mask his emotions. In his eyes blazed hatred, uncertainty…and the barest threads of affection and hope.

The same emotions continued to bubble inside Puck. Affection wouldn't be tolerated. Sin had taken everything from him, and Puck had wasted away…and found Gillian.

The hope only intensified.

Gillian, at Sin's side, a sword in *her* grip. She swung. Whoosh! The blade sliced through Sin's wrist. His hand fell to the ground, still clutching his weapon.

He roared in fury and anguish, blood spurting from an open artery. Gillian prepared to swing again. Her next target? Sin's neck.

"I'm sorry, Pucky," she said, tears in her eyes.

Old instincts surged. *Must protect Sin.*

No! Must destroy Sin.

Puck needed a second to think, only a second. He hurled his body at Sin, knocking him to the sand.

Gillian missed his throat by a mere half an inch.

Lying beneath Puck, a panting Sin morphed into his true form. Gashes littered his cheeks, neck, and stretched all the way to his—

Puck did a double take. Sin had a butterfly tattoo on his chest. The mark of a demon.

His brother was possessed?

No time to process the revelation. Sin kicked him, sending him flying. As his brother stood, he grew a new hand. A regeneration as fast as William's.

"How do you want this to play out, Puck? Tell me, and I'll respect your wishes." Gillian remained in place, sword held steady. "I'm happy to give him a little internal body bling. Or, if you want him alive and unharmed, I'll back off—as long as he stops attacking you."

Sin looked between Puck and Gillian, his pupils dilated to the size of teacups. Envy, sadness, relief and anger played over his features. "She loves you."

"Yes. As I love her." A love that burned hotter than his rage, hotter than anything he'd ever known. It had no beginning and no end. It just…was.

"The prophecy," Sin whispered. "You have your loving queen at your side."

Yes. One brother would unite the clans with a loving woman at his side. The other would die.

Sin swallowed. "One of us will die today. I suppose it must be me. There's no changing fate, is there?"

"Puck," Gillian insisted. "Dead or alive? And by the way, there *is* a way to change the outcome of a prophecy, there must be, and we're going to prove it."

Puck stood slowly. He had no idea what he would say, until the word left his mouth. "Alive." He had too many unanswered questions. How had Sin become possessed? When had it happened? Which demon did he host? Did the demon lead him now? Had the demon led him all those centuries ago?

A blur of motion before something—a chimera—charged past the shield and slammed into Sin.

"That never gets old," a familiar voice announced.

Stunned, Puck met William's ice-blue gaze. The warrior loomed inside the wall of magic, along with a few others. Winter and Cameron, who appeared sane, Keeley and Torin, Rathbone, Galen and Pandora. Even Hades had come to watch the final showdown. Everyone who'd played an active role in Puck's life since his possession.

"Hey, guys," Keeley said with a wave. "I remembered there was going to be a party today and insisted the hubs and I join the fun."

Gillian gasped, her features brightening. "William! Peanut! How...what..." She stepped forward, halted, keeping her weapon trained on Sin. "I knew you were alive."

"Nice to see you, too," Winter said, her pique clear. "I'm well, thanks for asking."

"Winter." Grinning, Gillian offered her a thumbs-up. "You're only half-cray now. That's awesome."

Winter flipped her off but also returned her grin.

Peanut trotted to William, who scratched him behind the ear and said, "That's my good boy."

Gillian's grin widened as she exchanged excited greetings with Keeley and Torin.

Meanwhile, Cameron spat curses at Torin. He still blamed the keeper of Disease for leaving them trapped inside a prison realm, and longed to attack. Understandable, but not allowed, either.

Keeley and Torin had helped Puck win Gillian. In Amaranthia, they fell under his protection.

"Cameron," he snapped. "You will do nothing."

Careful. Distraction can kill. Puck fixed his attention on his younger brother, bent down and withdrew a pair of daggers from the sheaths on his ankles.

"William, can you ensure Sin remains here until I decide my next move?" he asked. "Trapped inside his own magic walls?"

"I can," Hades said, sounding offended that he hadn't been asked first.

Very well, then. Determined, Puck closed in. Sin scowled at him—and flashed. A new ability, and a testament to the level of magic now charging his runes.

Puck tensed, knowing his brother would have to reappear... any second now...

Sin reappeared next to Gillian. Only, he no longer looked like Sin or Puck. He'd shifted into Gillian—an exact replica.

The real Gillian's jaw slackened. "What the—"

Sin plowed into her, taking her to the ground. A clear attempt at misdirection. *Which card is the queen?*

When one of them finally broke free, both stood to unsteady legs.

William cursed. "Who is who?"

"I...have no idea," Winter said.

Hades scratched his head. "I have an idea. We kill them both."

Puck tossed a dagger, end over end, nailing the vaunted king of the underworld in the heart. No one threatened his wife.

"Fool." With a frown, Hades plucked the weapon from his breastbone. "I'd need a heart for that to work."

"How about we just *stab* them both?" Galen suggested, and Pandora nodded her agreement. "Just until the impostor fesses up."

Puck tossed another dagger, the tip embedding in Galen's shoulder.

"Ow!" Scowling, the winged male yanked the weapon free. "What was that for? I didn't threaten her life."

"Suggestions to harm Gillian will be met with swift and severe retribution." Puck's gaze returned to his two possible wives, and in an instant of startling clarity, he understood how Gillian had guessed Sin's true identity. He recognized the sweetness of her scent, and the emotions glittering inside her eyes—anger, dismay and indignation.

"Suggestions can be ignored without bloodshed," Galen grumbled, rubbing his wound. "Just sayin'."

Now that Puck knew which was which, how should he proceed?

"I'm Gillian," one of them snapped.

"No, I'm Gillian," the other one said, her voice an exact match.

"You're dead," Cameron said to Torin, and finally attacked.

Puck grew a vine of thorns between the two males.

The distraction, slight though it was, came with a steep price. Sin-Gillian took an offensive position, throwing himself into real Gillian a second time, slashing and stabbing.

Real Gillian—now wounded—had to take a defensive position, and do everything in her power to save herself without hurting her opponent. Because she knew Puck wanted Sin alive.

Or *had* wanted his brother alive?

No one hurt Puck's wife.

44

PUCK ENTERED THE FRAY, WRAPPING HIS ARMS around the real Gillian and kicking Sin in William's direction, shouting, "Subdue him!"

"How do you know—" William began.

"Just do it," Puck commanded, applying pressure to a gash in Gillian's side. Warm blood soaked his hand.

"I'm fine, I'm fine," she rushed to assure him. "But how did you know I was the right girl? Same way I knew you?"

"As if I couldn't pick you out of a crowd of thousands, lass."

"If you're wrong about who is who…" William grabbed hold of Sin, anyway. Then the pair vanished together—Sin attempting to flash them both away?

He failed. The two reappeared in front of Puck.

"Oh, yes, our Pucker was right," William said. "Give me the shears. Now!"

Puck didn't have time to protest or question. Acting on instinct, he lifted the shears from his chest.

"I knew it," Gillian mumbled.

William punched his fist, and the shears, *into* Puck's chest—and withdrew Indifference.

Withdrew the demon?

Black smoke writhed in William's grip, red eyes glowing from within.

The shears had done as promised?

Waiting...waiting...

Puck remained standing, his limbs strong. No residual pain. His mind was quiet, the dark presence gone.

He drew in a deep breath, savoring. Finally he was free of the demon! His horns began to recede. The fur sloughed off his legs, blowing in the wind. The hooves fell away, revealing his feet.

A heavy weight lifted from his shoulders, all of his emotions sparking with new life. A thousand watts of love, relief, adoration, affection, amusement...hate, resentment, grief, remorse, anguish. Joy like he'd never known. Sorrow.

With the good came the bad—and Puck wouldn't have it any other way.

"The shears," he began.

"Back on your chest. And don't worry about your brother. Class isn't over yet." William shoved the demon into *Sin*.

The male's entire body jolted before his knees gave out. He collapsed on the sand, thrashing in pain. No longer did he resemble Gillian. No, he was himself...but not. Horns sprouted atop his head, fur grew over his legs and hooves materialized over his feet.

Puck felt sorry for his brother, and longed to use the shears on him. One day. Maybe. But first...

His gaze moved to Gillian, and his chest clenched. Tears streamed from her eyes, raining down her cheeks.

"You are hurt?" he asked softly, willing to murder anyone who'd dared.

She threw herself into his arms, trembling against him. "Are you okay?"

Not hurt—she worried for him. "I am, lass. I swear it."

"Your brother..."

Puck peered down at Sin, who'd gone motionless. When

he looked up at Puck, his eyes emptied of all emotion. Indifference had a new host—and a new victim. *Pang.*

"You're going to leave him alive?" Gillian asked, then chewed on her bottom lip.

"I...am. I'll lock him away for now," Puck said.

Gillian smiled, her face beaming. "Then you're doing it. You're changing the prophecy. We can be together!"

He wanted to be together. He'd earned a happy ending with this woman. After everything he'd suffered, she was his prize. And yet, he was still going to break their bond.

Her happiness comes first, always.

"Not sorry to be the bearer of bad news, but you won't be locking Sin away. Sent Ones are pissed, remember?" Hades marched to Sin and lifted him by the nape. "Sin is to be a gift to their Elite. He killed hundreds of their race, and he will answer for his crime. This is the only way to save your hide and your realm, Pucker."

"No. I'll find another way." Puck shook his head, razor blades clinking together. "I will oversee his punishment. *Me.*"

"My words weren't part of a debate," Hades said, his tone casual and yet laced with menace. "They were an FYI. But don't worry. The Sent Ones aren't planning to murder him for centuries to come."

Puck stepped toward the underworld king with every intention of lashing out, but a delicate hand wrapped around his ankle, surprising him. He looked down to find the Oracle had awoken. Her otherworldly gaze stared up at him, glimmering with remorse.

"You saved my life," she croaked, "so I owe you, and I always repay my debts. The brother you once knew and loved is dead. If you want him back, let him go. One day, he'll lose his head. He'll return and what once was will be again."

Lose his head? Literally? Then how could he return?

Couldn't be literally if what once was—the love and fellowship he'd had with Sin—was to be again.

Another pang assailed Puck, but he forced himself to nod. Very well. He would leave Sin to the Sent Ones. For now.

Oh, how quickly a life could change.

"What other demon possesses him?" Puck asked.

"Paranoia," Keeley replied. "He acquired the fiend during those peace talks with your neighbor. Someone gave him a box...who could it have been? Oh, yes. Me! And oh, wow. Think about it! He's got Paranoia and Indifference now. The two totally do not mesh. I have a feeling he's going to vacillate between total batcrap crazy and ice-cold apathy." She turned to Torin. "Can we spy on him? Please!"

Paranoia. The reason for the change in Sin, all those centuries ago, and the total assurance that Puck would betray and kill him.

A miracle Sin hadn't murdered him outright.

"Why would you do this?" Puck rubbed the center of his aching chest. "I heard what you said in the cave. You love us. Or you will love me, one day. Which I still don't understand. Why would you hurt the people you claim to love?"

She offered him a sad smile. "Puck, do you have any idea how many lives are touched by a single person? Especially an immortal person? The ripple effect is enormous. I saw you so long ago. In here." She tapped her temple. "You were my friend, though we had never met. I helped you survive centuries you would have otherwise missed. I helped you find a way to keep Sin alive. I helped you find Gillian. I helped you spank William. I helped you... I helped all of you. Moral of the story? I'm *amazing*."

Hades coughed into his hand, saying, "William."

"Right." The dark one closed in on his father. But it wasn't Hades he focused on. He reached for the crown still glowing above Sin's head. "And so the reign of Sin the Demented ends."

The crown!

Gillian raced forward—too late. William already had the

crown clasped in his hand. Sin offered no protests, just blinked with a total lack of emotion.

"*Now* I make my goodbyes." With a salute, Hades flashed away with Sin.

"Which means we do, as well," Keeley said, then stopped. "Oh! Before I go. William, sweetheart, I found the only woman—or man—in the history of all histories with the power to break the code. You know, for your book. The one you think has a solution to your greatest problem...your death at the hand of your lover. Stop me if you've heard this."

William went rigid. "Who is he?"

"Or she."

"Tell me!"

"Okay, okay. Geez. You kids and your impatience these days."

"Keeley!"

She held up her hands, all innocence. "Next week, there will be an adorable cryptanalyst convention in Manhattan. At last count, there were fifty-three nerds planning to attend. Like, seriously geeked-out mortals. Maybe a handful of geeked-out immortals, too. You have only to find her—or him—among the crowd. Toodles."

"Next week?" William roared. "Manhattan?"

Rathbone winked. "Make that fifty-four in attendance. This is something I don't want to miss."

"Oh, and Galen," Keeley said. "If you want a chance to win Legion, come find me. Hades will have a thousand other tasks for you before he lets you near her. I only have seven...teen." With that, she flashed away with Torin.

Galen roared now, and tried to catch her before she vanished, but failed. He whipped to Rathbone. "Take me to her."

Rathbone revealed a catlike smile. "Of course. I'll explain about payment when we reach her."

The winged one nodded without hesitation. As Rathbone

wound one arm around Galen, Pandora stepped up to his other side to clutch his bicep. The trio vanished.

"Please, don't do this, William," Gillian beseeched. "Don't make Puck fulfill his vow. Please."

Puck lifted his chin. He'd decided to use the shears—or try to—no matter what happened. There was no reason not to accept the crown, even though he would rather be with Gillian. The Connachts needed a king. *Amaranthia* needed a king. And, to be honest, Puck had no reason to doubt Gillian's love. Not anymore. She'd proven herself time and time again. When the bond broke, her love for Puck would endure. He was certain of it. Just as his love for her would endure, always and forever.

Deep in his heart, he knew she was both right and wrong about the prophecy. She thought they had changed Puck's future by allowing Sin to live, but as the Oracle had said, the brother Puck had once known was dead, a new man living in his place. The prophecy *had* been fulfilled.

Gillian's prophecy claimed she wouldn't have a happy ending.

For a while, Puck had convinced himself she wouldn't have a happy ending with William. Then he'd let fears cloud his thinking and latched on to the idea that she couldn't have a happy ending with Puck. But she could. She would. She would rule at Puck's side, joyous. He knew it. They simply didn't understand the prophecy.

William zeroed in on Puck, but spoke to Gillian. "This must be done, poppet."

"No," she said, and stomped her foot. "Please, no."

She was frightened. Frightened the end of the bond would mean the end of their relationship, which meant a part of her did, in fact, believe her love for Puck would be diminished. But love wasn't just a feeling, he realized. Feelings fluctuated, changing because of circumstances and a million other factors. Love was a choice. A commitment to put someone else first, to give rather than take, to protect and never harm.

By keeping the bond in place, he would be choosing Gillian's future for her. To have that happy ending, she had to choose her own path.

So, Puck planted his heels in the sand, ready to face the future. "Do it, William."

"No!" Gillian tried to stop the male, but he flashed beyond her.

When he reappeared in front of Puck, he paused only a moment before placing the crown where it belonged. Gillian whimpered, nearly undoing Puck. In the next instant, however, he lost sight of everything but the power flowing through him. A cache of Sin's magic. Magic from every Connacht king ever to live.

Each of his abilities returned, and then some. The things he could do...the power he could wield...

Amazing. Magnificent.

Heart-wrenching.

"It's done," William said. "I've given you the Connacht crown."

"Yes." Puck opened his eyes and nodded.

"Now you will free Gillian."

"William, please," she said, dropping to her knees. "Free him from his vow." Looking panicked, she said, "I can't have a happy ending without him."

"You can. You will. I insist on it." The Ever Randy reached out, ghosted his fingertips along her jawline. For once, Puck didn't begrudge the man such a touch—for it was his last.

"No! You know there's a catch with the shears," she said. "Over the centuries I've learned there's *always* a catch with ancient artifacts."

Puck had once had the same thought himself.

"The shears can be used only once every hundred years. Mortal years," William said. "Unless the shears *aren't* used for a hundred years. Then they can be used twice in a hundred years. Think roll-over minutes for cell phones. If the shears aren't used in three hundred years, they can then be used three times. So on and so forth."

"I've had them three hundred mortal years." Thousands of Amaranthian years. "Which means I have one more use." For Gillian. In a hundred mortal years, he could help Winter. Another hundred years, and he could help Cameron. Then, finally, a hundred years after that, he could help Sin.

He wouldn't reverse the order, either, even if Sin returned tomorrow. His friends had helped him for centuries, so he would help them first.

"Are you doing this to hurt me?" Gillian asked William. "Because I hurt you?"

William, usually the roughest, toughest male on the block, softened. "No. Believe it or not, I'm doing this to *aid* you."

Looking defeated, she sat back on her haunches. "Too much has changed already. Just…give us fifty mortal years. Or better yet, a hundred. Then we can revisit this."

So badly Puck wanted to gather her close and assure her all would be well. He hated seeing her afraid. Hated wounding her. He would rather die. But he would rather suffer for eternity than deny her a right to choose.

William gave her a chiding tsk-tsk. "This isn't like you, poppet. You should want this."

"Want it?" she screeched. "My life is finally perfect! Do you know how long I've been waiting for this? Why would I want to change anything?"

"I'm going to guess you've been waiting, oh…five hundred and nineteen years?" William said. "But sweetling, you are wrong. This isn't perfect. But it will be when we're done."

"No!" she repeated. "I want to keep Puck. And I want his horns returned. And his fur. I'm negotiable on the hooves. I just… I need more time with him before we take any risks, okay? I sense that breaking the bond is what causes my unhappy ending. Let's prove this prophecy wrong."

Puck's heart shattered, his resolve weakening. But he sensed the truth, too. This was the right thing to do. "Without the demon, I have the ability to shapeshift. And I will, anytime you desire." To demonstrate, he shifted into his beastly form. "I love you, Gillian. I love you, and there's nothing you or anyone else can do about it. This, I vow to you. Now let *me* prove it." He reached out, smoothed a strand of hair from her cheek. "Let me do this for you. And us."

"No." She radiated all kinds of violence. "I told you, there's too much at risk."

William expelled a heavy breath. "Enough. This has to be done. The effects should be immediate, but we'll give it the rest of the day, just in case. If you still want him by the time the sun sets, your new marriage will have my blessing. But one way or another, you will know your true heart—and his. This is a gift I'm giving you."

She leaped to her feet and slapped him. Hard. The *crack* probably echoed for miles. "Why are you doing this? To win me? Even without the bond, I'm not going to—"

Puck flashed in front of her, just in case William decided to attack.

I can flash now? Apparently.

The other man rubbed his cheek and rolled his eyes at Puck. "Perhaps this is a gift to *you*, Pucker. If you don't want her, you won't have to deal with her temper."

Puck realized the truth then: William had fully bowed out. Had no claim, and wanted none.

With a grin, Puck stepped aside to let the two friends speak.

Tone gentle, William said to Gillian, "I allowed a need to protect a scared, abused creature to confuse me. And while I love the warrior woman you've become, your feelings for another man are a deal breaker, and your strength a hard no. I cannot be with a woman who might or might not have the power to defeat me. Unless, of course, I find that code breaker." His eyes narrowed. "And I will."

Puck kept his attention on Gillian, looking away impossible.

She *was* strong, had faced so much with her head high. And yet, here and now she dropped to her knees a second time, willingly placing herself in a position of vulnerability and supplication. But this time, she didn't beg. She bowed her head and sobbed.

The sight of her broke what remained of Puck's resolve, and if he'd loved her any less, even just a fraction, *he* would have begged William to end this. But just as much as she needed to know she'd chosen Puck freely, she needed to know *he'd* chosen *her* freely.

"Trust me, lass. Please." He dropped to his knees in front of her, took her hands, kissed her knuckles. "Let me prove my love for you is real and lasting, bond or no bond."

Tears streamed down her cheeks, but finally she nodded.

Not wanting to hesitate and risk changing his mind, Puck lifted the shears from his chest...and cut.

45

GILLIAN KNEW THE EXACT MOMENT HER BOND
with Puck broke, because what remained of her heart broke
with it. Wave after wave of sorrow eroded the contentment
she'd managed to obtain. Grief replaced exhilaration.

Every cell in her body mourned the connection with her
husband.

Once, she'd gone five hundred years without him, and she'd
(mostly) thrived. Now, she couldn't go five seconds?

The metal band around Puck's wrist unclicked and fell to
the ground. Like the final gong meant to call warriors home
from battle.

She gazed at her husband—her ex—who watched her with
a blank expression, and she wanted to vomit. Had he reverted
to the Ice Man? No, no. He no longer hosted Indifference, so
he had no need of the ice. Unless he just didn't want to deal
with his emotions?

No! He wouldn't summon the ice, not around her. He'd
promised.

Had he fallen out of love with her, then? Had her unhappy
ending arrived?

Had *she* fallen out of love with *him*?

She looked from Puck to William, who watched her expectantly. As she peered into his ice-blue eyes, love overshadowed mourning but...that love was still seeded in friendship. She had zero romantic interest in William.

Her attention zoomed back to Puck, and her heart began to race, spurred into action by love and lust, an unfathomable amount of each, and *fully* romantic.

Her gaze searched Puck's unreadable face. "Have your feelings for me changed?" If they had, she would...what?

You are a warrior. You will fight for what you want, that's what.

That was right. Gillian raised her chin. If necessary, she would woo him. She would fight for him and win him back. This wasn't the end.

Why had she feared this, anyway? When she didn't like something, she changed it.

"I don't want what I feel for you to influence your decision, but..." The mask fell away from his features, revealing adoration, affection, tenderness—love. "You aren't just the love of my life, lass. You *are* my life. I've told this, have I not?"

Throwing her arms around him, Gillian cried, "I love you, too." So much. All that worry—for nothing. Absolutely nothing! She could have saved herself, and Puck, a ton of angst if she'd just trusted their connection.

Love never failed.

"This is boring." Winter winced, all *I'm embarrassed for you both.* "And kind of gross. Love sucks."

"For once, I agree with you, Winnie." As Winter sputtered about her hatred for the new nickname, William pulled Gillian to her feet. He couldn't force her to let go of Puck, however. Perhaps he understood he'd lose a hand if he tried. "You two aren't going to spend the bulk of your single hours in a staring contest. If you do, in fact, decide to get together again—"

"We do," Gillian and Puck said in unison.

"—you need to secure the Connacht fortress so I can make sure my Gillian has a forever home."

"*My* Gillian." In a blur of motion, Puck was on his feet and punting William in the stomach. His grip on her never slipped. "Only ever mine. Never yours."

William held up his hands, palms out, in a show of innocence. "Your Gillian. Fine. Whatever. Consider your claim staked. Anyway. Let's go tell your people there's a new douchebag in charge."

Very well. Puck gave Gillian's knuckles another kiss before heading for the tree where they'd last made love, where William and company had tethered different chimeras. He glanced back once, twice, thrice to ensure Gillian hadn't ran off, and her heart soared.

He still loves me. I still love him.

This was going to work!

Hopeful, she mounted Peanut. William rode at her left, and Puck rode at her right, making her the meat in a beefcake sandwich. Winter led the charge, and Cameron remained in the rear.

One hour bled into another, conversation on hold. Was everyone else watching the suns as diligently as Gillian, waiting for them to set?

Winter kept up a steady conversation—with herself. Cameron counted trees. His new obsession, apparently. Gillian felt sorry for whatever woman he ended up falling for. His pursuit would be relentless. Until it wasn't.

Could the keeper of Obsession have a happily-ever-after?

Could *Gillian*? No happy ending meant a life without Puck. *He still loves me. I still love him.*

She would never tire of those words.

When they reached a dense thicket of trees, Puck dismounted, and everyone else followed suit. One after the other, they led their chimeras through the foliage.

"All right," William said, his voice drenched with exasperation. "I've been waiting *forever* for someone to question me about how I managed to pull off the greatest victory of all time. Since every member of my team is determined to be rude and freeze me out, I'll have to take my story to the grave. Not that I'll ever die."

Gillian arched a brow, purposely remaining mute. He'd crack in five, four, three, two—

"Fine. I'll tell you. Stop begging me with your eyes," he said. "The Red Queen had a premonition and, because she's a Curator, bound to the Earth, its seasons and even its other-realms, she was able to link with Amaranthia to create the portal below the clouds. Peanut and I fell through, along with Pandora and Galen, and we ended up in the underworld. Hades caught us with a stream of power and eased us down."

"How did you return to Amaranthia?" Puck asked. "And with so little time passing for us."

The timbre of his voice sent shivers of desire rushing through Gillian.

"No one keeps me from my best friend," William said. "As soon as Sin used magic to trap Gillian with the Oracle and pin you in place, the barrier he'd placed around Amaranthia weakened. I busted through, contacted Rathbone, and ta-da. Here I am. As for defying time itself." Shrug. "Let's just say my magic is better than your magic."

Friend. He'd called her friend. She reached over and patted his hand.

They led their chimeras over a dune, and the Connacht fortress came into view. Breath snagged in her throat. The structure reminded her of a giant sandcastle. The most beautiful thing she'd ever seen. Except for Puck, of course. The highest point disappeared in the clouds, and a tower loomed on each side, connected by a parapet where armed soldiers patrolled.

The suns had lowered just enough to create a golden aura around—

Wait. The suns were in the process of setting! William said he wouldn't protest if Gillian and Puck waited until sunset to bond a second time.

Should she ask for a ceremony now? Or wait until Puck had settled in? Or wait until *Puck* asked *her*?

"This is your home?" she asked Puck.

"*Our* home," he replied, his tone fierce.

She grinned. "Will the citizens put up a fight when you reveal your new, exalted status?"

"No. The one who wears the crown rules. No questions asked. Though they might complain behind our backs."

So. Her ex-husband was officially the Connacht king, and Gillian was going to be the Shawazon *and* Connacht queen, and help him unite all the clans.

Their group marched onward. One of the guards spotted them, and a battle cry rang out. Next, a bell clanged.

Someone shouted, "Wait! I think that is... Prince Neale?"

Neale? Gillian's brow furrowed. Then she remembered. Neale was the name his people used.

More shouts. "Prince Neale is prince no longer. He is king!" The shouters didn't sound overjoyed.

The soldiers sank to their knees. "All hail King Púkinn!" Nope, definitely not overjoyed. The words were grumbled.

"They expect me to be like Sin," Puck said, voice tight.

The front gate opened, revealing more kneeling people.

"You'll win them over," Gillian said. "We both will." *Hint, hint. Ask me to marry you again, Pucky!*

"All right. Before we part ways, I need to do a little disclosing." William pushed out a heavy sigh. "I kissed your wife, Puck. Now, now. Don't go getting that vengeful look in your eyes—yes, that one. She didn't kiss me back. And I'm glad. I felt like I was kissing my great-aunt Trudy. If I had a great-aunt Trudy." He shuddered.

"I know you kissed her," Puck replied through gritted teeth. "If you ever do it again, I'll kill you without a qualm."

William laughed—until a thorn vine shot from the ground, and tripped him. He hacked at the vine, then stood and spit out a mouthful of dirt.

Now *Gillian* laughed, a well of happiness springing up. Happiness...

Realization struck with the force of a baseball bat. The prophecy was right! She wasn't getting a happy ending. Nope. Not her. She was getting a happy *beginning*. A bond forged because she and Puck had willingly chosen each other. And once they had their beginning, they would have their happily-ever-after.

They would have an eternity together!

"Don't worry, Lucky Pucky," she found herself teasing. "I won't let William kiss me again. I have better taste. I mean, I expected masterful skill from someone who spends the bulk of his time screwing anyone who breathes. Alas, William was..." In a stage whisper, she said, "Inept."

William gave a mock growl. "How dare you, poppet? I'm amazing." One second he was on her left, the next he stood in front of Puck, cupping the back of his neck and jerking him forward to plant a wet one on his lips.

Whooping and clapping, Winter danced around. Cameron hid a snicker behind his hand while Gillian didn't even try to mask hers.

"Better than I imagined," Gillian called, fist pumping the sky.

When William lifted his head, the corner of Puck's mouth twitched. Her ex-husband-soon-to-be-husband-again looked to her and said, "You were right, love. Inept."

William brushed an invisible piece of lint from his shirt. "I'll be sure to tell everyone Puck kisses—never mind. I won't say anything. I don't kiss and tell. I only shag and brag."

Gillian shoved William out of the way and launched herself against Puck. Forget waiting. "I love you, and I want to marry you in all ways."

"I love you, too. But I want you to be sure, because I'll never let you go again."

"I'm sure. I know I didn't get a happy ending because—"

"I don't care what the Oracles say," he interjected. "I will—"

"No, you didn't let me finish. I didn't get a happy ending because I got a happy beginning. We will bond again. *Now*. In front of everyone. We will be together forever. I thought about waiting for you to ask, but..."

His smile was slow, but wicked and oh so bright. "You choose me of your own free will."

"I choose you," she confirmed. "I will always choose you. And our people. And I agree to marry you in all ways, if I didn't make that clear. One day soon, I'd like to have a ceremony with the Connachts and the Shawazons together." Winter, Cameron, Johanna and Rosaleen would be bridesmaids. William would be her maid of honor. And yes, she would call him by the title for the rest of his life.

Their entourage cheered.

"I give you my heart, soul and body," Gillian said, remembering the vows they'd once spoken. "I tie my life to yours, and when you die, I die with you. This I say, this I do."

After he repeated the words, she added, "I will help you unite the clans. I will be a help, not a hindrance. I will love you, and support you, and build you up, never tear you down."

His grip on her tightened, an action she interpreted to mean *I wasn't kidding; I will never let you go.* "I will cherish you, all the days of my life. I will put your safety before my own and always welcome your wise counsel. I will love you forevermore and nothing—no one—will ever have the strength to rip me from your side."

Her heart overflowed with love and joy. She rose to her tiptoes as he lowered his head, and they met in the middle, sealing their promises with a kiss.

Long minutes passed before he lifted his head. Panting, he withdrew a dagger and made an incision in the center of his palm. Blood pooled. She accepted the dagger and made an incision of her own. Then they drank of each other.

"Blood of my blood, breath of my breath." He took her hand in his. "Until the end of time."

"Blood of my blood, breath of my breath. Until the end of time."

A new bond clicked into place—a stronger bond. Freely chosen, nothing but truth between them. Connection! She reveled.

"You are my wife," he said, tracing his thumbs over her cheeks.

"And you are my husband."

Pride glittered in his dark eyes. Dark, but so bright. The stars were aglow. "We are going to have a beautiful life together."

"Always and forever." Gillian would fight for him, and make his happiness a priority.

And she would succeed. She could do anything! After all, the frightened mouse had blossomed into a warrior. The teenager afraid of men had grown into a woman who'd fallen in love with the most savage immortal ever to live. An ordinary girl had risen from the ashes of her own destruction to become queen of an entire realm.

Well, she would be queen of the entire realm soon enough.

Best of all? A beast with a frozen heart had melted, becoming the sexiest incarnation of Prince Charming ever to live.

My *Prince Charming, anyway.*

Smiling, Gillian said, "Introduce me to our people. I'm ready to begin our happily-ever-after."

Epilogue

PUCK AND GILLIAN HAD BEEN BONDED—AGAIN—
for a little over a month. Not long in the scheme of things,
but blissful nonetheless. They had introduced the Shawazons
to the Connachts, and only fifty-three fights had broken out,
with only eighteen near-deaths.

Puck considered it a raging success.

Cameron and Winter had returned to the mortal world
to help Galen for reasons they hadn't shared with Puck. The
girl Galen desired—Legion—had disappeared for the third—
fourth?—time, and Galen was frantic to find her.

Rumors also suggested William was on a rampage about his
book of prophecies and codes, and the "geek" he might or might
not have found. A friend of the Lords of the Underworld—a
demon-possessed woman named Viola—was now missing, and
so was the fallen Sent One who'd been chasing her for whatever reason.

But, while things outside of Amaranthia were chaotic, things
inside could not have been better.

Today Puck and Gillian had been officially crowned as king
and queen of the Connachts and Shawazons. Soon to be High
King and Queen of Amaranthia. He'd watched his wife daz-

zle their people with her beauty, wit, charm and strength, and nearly burst with pride.

She'd worn a fitted black dress with an open back, silver beads hanging from a high neck collar, draping over her shoulders in varying lengths, with blades tied to the ends. He'd wanted to rip each layer away with his teeth…and had, only hours ago.

Now she was curled up in his arms, drawing little hearts over his chest.

There would be resistance when they united the other clans, but they would overcome. They always did.

As for Sin, Puck had scheduled a meeting with the Sent Ones to negotiate his brother's punishment and return.

Could life be any more perfect?

He and Gillian had made the decision to start their family. One day soon, little dark-haired princes and princesses with whiskey-colored eyes would be running around their fortress.

Puck would be forever grateful that Gillian had trusted him with her new beginning, and honored to ensure she remained happy for the rest of eternity.

"I'm cold," she said as she shivered against him. "I need your fur."

He shifted into his beastly form, and she uttered a sigh of contentment. "Better?" he asked.

"Much."

He kissed her temple and combed his fingers through her hair, content, satisfied and, because of this woman, anticipatory. Every day with Gillian was sweeter than the last. Had he known what awaited him, he would have borne his sufferings with a smile.

Some fairy tales do not have a happily-ever-after…but this one did.

★ ★ ★ ★ ★

Dear Readers,

IF YOU ARE INTERESTED IN READING THE FIRST handful of chapters (in *The Darkest Warrior*) from Gillian's point of view, check out *The Darkest Torment* (Baden's story). For those who have already read it, you might have noticed a few differences. I did my best to tighten everything for better flow and impact.

Wishing you all the best!

Gena Showalter

Glossary of Terms and Players

Aeron—Lord of the Underworld; former keeper of Wrath; husband to Olivia.

All-seeing Eye—Godly artifact with the power to see into heaven and hell; aka Danika Ford.

Amaranthia—Desert realm, home to Puck the Undefeated.

Amun—Lord of the Underworld; keeper of Secrets; husband to Haidee.

Anya—(Minor) goddess of Anarchy, eternally engaged to Lucien.

Ashlyn Darrow—Has supernatural ability to listen to past conversations; wife to Maddox; mother of Urban and Ever.

Axel—Sent One with a secret. Resembles William the Ever Randy.

Baden—Lord of the Underworld; former keeper of Distrust; husband to Katarina.

Bianka Skyhawk—Harpy; sister of Gwen, Kaia and Taliyah; married to Lysander.

Bjorn—Sent One.

Cage of Compulsion—Godly artifact with the power to enslave anyone trapped inside.

Cameo—Lord of the Underworld; keeper of the demon Misery.

Cameron—Keeper of Obsession, brother to Winter.

Cloak of Invisibility—Godly artifact with the power to shield its wearer from prying eyes.

Cronus—Former king of the Titans; former keeper of Greed; husband to Rhea.

Danika Ford—Human female; wife to Reyes; known as the All-seeing Eye.

dimOuniak—Pandora's box.

Downfall—Nightclub for immortals; owned by Thane, Bjorn and Xerxes.

Elin—Phoenix/human hybrid; mate to Thane.

Ever—Daughter to Maddox and Ashlyn, sister to Urban.

Fae—Race of immortals descended from Titans.

Flashing—Transporting oneself with just a thought.

Galen—Lord of the Underworld; keeper of Jealousy and False Hope.

Gideon—Lord of the Underworld; keeper of Lies.

Gillian Shaw—Also known as Gilly Bradshaw; human female recently made immortal. Wife to Puck.

Greeks—Former rulers of Olympus.

Gwen Skyhawk—Harpy; consort of Sabin; daughter of Galen; sister to Kaia, Bianka and Taliyah.

Hades—One of the nine kings of the underworld.

Haidee Alexander—Former Hunter; keeper of Love; mated to Amun.

Hera—Queen of the Greeks; wife to Zeus.

Hunters—Mortal enemies of the Lords of the Underworld; disbanded.

Josephina Aisling—Queen of the Fae; wife to Kane.

Juliette Eagleshield—Also known as the Eradicator; Harpy; self-appointed consort of Lazarus.

Kadence—Goddess of Oppression; deceased yet in spirit form.

Kaia Skyhawk—Part Harpy, part Phoenix; sister of Gwen, Taliyah and Bianka; consort of Strider.

Kane—Lord of the Underworld; keeper of Disaster; husband to Josephina.

Katarina Joelle—Formerly human; Alpha of the Hellhounds; consort of Baden.

Keeleycael—A Curator; the Red Queen; engaged to Torin.

Kings of the Underworld—Nine rulers at war with Lucifer.

Lazarus (the Cruel and Unusual)—An immortal warrior; only son of Typhon and Echidna.

Legion—Demon minion in a human body; adopted daughter of Aeron and Olivia; aka Honey.

Lords of the Underworld—Exiled immortal warriors now hosting the demons once locked inside Pandora's box.

Lucien—Coleader of the Lords of the Underworld; keeper of Death; engaged to Anya.

Lucifer—One of the nine kings of the underworld; son to Hades; brother to William.

Lysander—Elite Sent One; consort to Bianka.

Maddox—Lord of the Underworld; keeper of Violence; father to Urban and Ever; husband to Ashlyn.

Morning Star—Thought to be hidden in Pandora's box; with it anything is possible.

Most High—Also known as One True Deity; leader of the Sent Ones.

Olivia—Sent One; mated to Aeron.

Pandora—Immortal warrior; once guardian of dimOuniak (newly resurrected).

Pandora's box—Also known as dimOuniak; made of bones from the goddess of Oppression; now shaped as a small apple charm; once housed demon high lords.

Paring Rod—Godly artifact with ability to rend soul from body.

Paris—Lord of the Underworld; keeper of Promiscuity; husband to Sienna.

Phoenix—Fire-thriving immortals descended from Greeks.

Puck the Undefeated—Full name Púkinn Neale Brion Connacht IV. Keeper of Indifference; prince of the Connacht clan in the desert realm of Amaranthia. Husband to Gillian Shaw.

Rathbone—One of the kings of the underworld.

Reyes—Lord of the Underworld; keeper of Pain; husband to Danika.

Sabin—Coleader of the Lords of the Underworld; keeper of Doubt; consort of Gwen.

Scarlet—Keeper of Nightmares; wife of Gideon.

Sent Ones—Winged warriors; demon assassins.

Sienna Blackstone—Former Hunter; current keeper of Wrath; current ruler of Olympus; beloved of Paris.

Sin Connacht—Full name Taliesin Anwell Kunsgnos Connacht. Brother to Puck the Undefeated.

Siobhan—Goddess of Many Futures, cursed to live inside a magic mirror.

Strider—Lord of the Underworld; keeper of Defeat.

Taliyah Skyhawk—Harpy; sister of Gwen, Bianka and Kaia.

Tartarus—Greek god of Confinement; also the immortal prison on Mount Olympus.

Thane—Sent One; mate to Elin.

Titans—Rulers of Titania; children of fallen angels and humans.

Torin—Lord of the Underworld; keeper of Disease; engaged to Keeleycael.

Typhon—Father of Lazarus.

Urban—Son of Maddox and Ashlyn; brother of Ever.

Viola—Goddess of the Afterlife; keeper of Narcissism.

William of the Dark—Immortal warrior of questionable origins; adopted son of Hades; aka the Panty Melter and William the Ever Randy.

Winter—Keeper of Selfishness, sister to Cameron.

Xerxes—Sent One.

Zeus—King of the Greeks; husband to Hera.

If you enjoy Gena Showalter's bestselling
LORDS OF THE UNDERWORLD *books,*
don't miss her all-new, sizzling paranormal romance series,
GODS OF WAR…

After being trapped in an ice prison for centuries, a group of otherworldly immortals have finally broken free. In a bid to rule the Earth, their fight to the death resumes, and the whole world becomes a gladiator arena. But this time these savage warriors will risk more than their lives and the survival of their realms—they'll also risk their hearts.

The epic saga begins with book one, SHADOW AND ICE, coming soon from Gena Showalter and HQN Books…

*Turn the page for artist Jennifer Munswami's incredible rendering
of reader-favorite character William of the Dark!
Our gift to you.*

Love, Gena